"What am I doing here?" she remembers asking herself as she numbly sat in her small truck at the end of Camino Real. "What's gotten into me? Who's looking after my children?" Her watch read 8:30 P.M.

Barbara, now shivering, pulled her light coat around her, wiping her nose with the back of her hand. It was now freezing inside her truck. She looked at her hand. It was streaked with blood. "Oh my God!" Her nosebleed could only mean one thing. Her watch revealed it was 10:30 P.M. She shuddered. "They" had taken her again.

THE
MYSTERIOUS VALLEY

CHRISTOPHER O'BRIEN

St. Martin's Paperbacks

THE MYSTERIOUS VALLEY

ISBN: 0-312-95883-8

Printed in the United States of America

St. Martin's Paperbacks edition/September 1996

10 9 8 7 6 5 4 3 2 1

ACKNOWLEDGMENTS

A controversial book of this type could not be written without the help and guidance of many people. I'd like to thank and acknowledge the following individuals: Isadora and Brisa Storey, for lovingly supporting the process; Daniel S. Johnson for editing and honing my writing skills and literary humor; Jim Pinkston at Sherry Robb Literary Properties for his faith and representation; Jennifer Enderlin at St. Martin's Press for seeing the potential; and Amy Kolenik at SMP for her editorial expertise.

Also, David Perkins, Tom Adams, and Gary Massey for their guidance, knowledge, and humor; Jacques Vallée, John Keel, and Brendan O'Brien, for their pointed insight; "Rocky" and Chip K. for their incredible support; Linda Howe and Dr. John Altshuler for setting the investigative standard; Kizzen Dennett, Mark Hunter, Brian Norton, Berle Lewis, Emilio Lobato, Jr., Ernest Sandoval, and Pete Espinoza for their courage and honesty; BG and Al Purvis for use of their camera.

Finally, the members of Laffing Buddha—Chris Medina, George Oringdulph, Lyman Bushkovski, and Jeremy Wegner—for their infinite patience and talent; the crews and researchers from *Sightings*; and Varied Directions. A big thank you to everyone who has supported the process, and all the many witnesses who have courageously come forward on the record, making the writing of *The Mysterious Valley* possible.

Suggested Rules of Investigation

RULE #1
Controversial subjects generate polarized responses.

RULE #2
Record or write down everything as soon as possible, no matter how inconsequential or insignificant it might seem at the time.

RULE #3
Always credit your sources and respect requests for anonymity.

RULE #4
Always be ready for anything, anytime. Look for coincidences when investigating claims of the unusual. Often, there may be a synchronistic element at work.

RULE #5
It is impossible to be too objective when scientifically investigating claims of the unusual.

RULE #6
Always assume there is a mundane explanation until proven extraordinary.

RULE #7
Appearances can be deceiving. There may be more happening than meets the eye.

RULE #8
If you publicize claims of the unusual, choose your words wisely, for your "spin" may have tremendous influence.

RULE #9
Media coverage of the unusual, because of its sensational nature, is often inaccurate and cannot be accepted as totally accurate by the investigator.

RULE #10
The human mind, when faced with the unknown, reverts to basic primal symbols to rationalize its experience.

RULE #11
When investigating claims of the unusual, one cannot reach conclusions based on intuition alone.

RULE #12
There is a possibility that the (sub)culture itself may cocreate manifestations of unexplained, individually perceived phenomena.

RULE #13
We must be extremely careful not to perpetrate our own beliefs, suspicions, or actual experiences into the minds of those who desperately want to have a "special" event happen in their lives.

Contents

FOREWORD

What do the following have in common? UFOs, extra-terrestrials, Bigfoot, covert military operations, Native American medicine men, cowboys in white hats, cowboys in black hats, stand-tall lawmen, cultists, hungry thought-forms, and hitchhiking, shape-shifting she-devils. No, they are not the characters in a new Tony Hillerman novel. They are the real-life denizens of Christopher O'Brien's myste-rious valley—the isolated and awesome San Luis Valley of southern Colorado and northern New Mexico.

Proving once again that the truth is *far* stranger than fiction, Chris spins a compelling tale of amazing weirdness that even the harshest critics of so-called paranormal phe-nomena will find hard to dismiss.

My own interest in this subject matter dates back to 1975. As a writer/journalist living in the region, I became aware of the wave of mysterious cattle "mutilations" plaguing cattlemen in Colorado and throughout the West. Indeed, it was hard to miss. In that year, the mutilations were voted "story of the year" by the Associated Press of Colorado and Governor Richard Lamm was calling the sit-uation among "the greatest outrages in the history of the western cattle industry."

Hundreds of reports poured in to western law enforce-ment officials in 1975. In a typical "classic" case, the cow was found dead and drained of blood with no signs of struggle. The sex organs were neatly removed and the rec-tums were "cored out." Other missing parts included eyes, ears, tongues, portions of the lips or snouts, teeth, patches of skin, or the hearts. To make matters more complicated, ranchers were reporting strange "helicopters" and even UFOs flying around their pastures in the middle of the night. Citizens were up in arms and lawmen, despite their best efforts, were totally baffled.

At first pranksters and cultists were believed to be the culprits. Then, with the advent of the mystery helicopters, suspicions were cast on the military. Finally, facing the sheer scope and "impossibility" of what they were confronting, a growing number of people (including lawmen) began to ask the question: "Is it possible that the mutilations are the work of extraterrestrial beings?"

As preposterous as it seemed, it was a question that had been raised as early as 1967 when the owner of a "mutilated" horse told the press "flying saucers killed my horse."

What began for me as a challenging piece of investigative journalism has turned into a twenty-year odyssey through the farthest reaches of the Twilight Zone. After personally examining scores of mutilated carcasses, conducting hundreds of interviews and reviewing thousands of cases worldwide, I admit to being more puzzled than when I started. As O'Brien succinctly puts it, "If I had known then what I *don't know* now, I'm not sure I would have knowingly embarked on this journey into the unknown." A long, strange trip indeed!

With his refreshing "everyman" approach, Chris poses the same questions that any rational person would ask when confronted with such imponderable conundrums. He is not here to beat a drum or promote an agenda. He is not a Chicken Little running out to tell us that "the sky is falling and aliens are taking over the Earth!"

Chris *is* a man with a very healthy sense of curiosity: "When I sensed something unusual was going on in this area, I took it upon myself as an 'interested resident' to document it the best I could. I just intuitively felt that it was important."

Using the San Luis Valley as "a laboratory of paranormal events," Chris has diligently and objectively recorded his "quixotic" journey of discovery. Instead of tackling the Big Picture head-on, he has wisely chosen to take the "microcosmic" approach. Take one defined geographic area and study it exceedingly well. Document everything, no matter how ridiculous, irrelevant, or frightening it may seem at the time. Study the local folklore, the Native American traditions, the history, the geology. Leave no stone unturned.

In his search for the truth, Chris rightfully casts much scrutiny on the circuitous process by which unusual events are originally perceived by the "experiencers" and eventually find their way to mass consciousness. He finds that "the true nature of many strange events become lost in the inevitable process of dissemination." He understands his role in this process and the responsibility that goes with it. In peeling away the layers of this onion of illusion, O'Brien arrives at the very birthplace of myth, "the fodder of new legend."

Whether or not "the greatest unsolved mysteries of our times" are *unknowable* is another question. Only a handful of researchers have persevered through the frustration and ridicule that go with the territory.

First among equals of this tenacious few are the Texas investigators Tom Adams and Gary Massey. The intrepid duo first visited the San Luis Valley in 1970 to study the aftermath of the world famous "Snippy" the Horse case. They admit to being drawn back year after year "like moths to a flame." Says Adams, "We passed the point of no return years ago. Once you get into this business it's difficult, if not impossible, to get out." Chris calls it "embracing the Tar Baby."

Adams and Massey consistently caution newcomers to the field to resist the tendency to jump to unwarranted conclusions. As Adams puts it, "We bear the onus of ontological concerns. Consider everything and believe nothing." Will the identity of the mutilators ever be revealed? As Massey has stated, "If we didn't catch 'em in 1975, when all hell was breaking loose, we're never gonna catch 'em.'"

Tom Adams shares Chris O'Brien's implied conclusion, "When we first started coming to the San Luis Valley, we were exposed to a wide range of unusual phenomena. It has led me to see the intrinsic interrelatedness of all paranormal phenomena."

Linda Moulton Howe, another colleague and veteran researcher, is more definitive in her conclusions. In her books, documentary films, and lectures during the last fifteen years, she has consistently promoted the view that: "We are dealing with an off-world intelligence." According to Linda, mutilations, UFOs, and human abductions are the harbinger of a scientific revolution; "We may be getting closer to a new definition of the universe."

While Chris O'Brien stops far short of saying that extraterrestrials are intervening in human affairs, he does come to suspect "a shadowy presence" at work: "Could this 'presence' have existed alongside humankind for thousands of years, mocking our attempts at proving its very existence and agenda by hiding its true nature and purpose behind a veil of religion, magic, and superstition?"

As for myself, I'm still trying to figure out what psychologist Carl Jung had in mind when he speculated in 1958 that UFOs could be "materialized psychisms" emanating from the human collective unconscious.

As Chris observes: "This subject matter has stretched my rational world view to the breaking point. These are mysteries wound around a riddle, locked inside a puzzle that's effectively obscured by haze, behind a veil . . ." Linda Moulton Howe compares her research to entering "a hall of mirrors with a quicksand floor." Are you starting to get the picture?

What I've learned in my own "journey of transformation" is that these are highly complex and challenging questions. Absolute truth may well be unobtainable at our present level of development. What is important is the *search* for the truth. If, as I suspect, the answer is within us, we are going to have to dig deep. I agree with Chris that "data alone may not be able to solve these mysteries."

Hopefully, this wild *Star Wars* western thriller, *The Mysterious Valley*, will bring these issues to the attention of larger segments of the scientific community, the government, and the public at large. Or perhaps it will at least shed a little light on some very dark corners of the human psyche. As "paranormal" writer John Keel says: "To hell with the answer, what's the question?"

Happy Trails.

—David Perkins

PROLOGUE

The newly arrived ranching family was excited. The early February day was crisp and cloudless, and the Cases (not their real name) had just closed on their picturesque San Luis Valley ranch and were in the process of cleaning up the previous owner's garbage strewn around the weather-worn outbuildings. Dana Case started up her four-wheel all-terrain vehicle (ATV) and prepared to check the fence line of their new spread for the first time. Her horses were due to arrive, and she and her husband Bernie were concerned that a break in the fence would allow their animals to stray.

Dana sat warming up her ATV, soaking in the breathtaking view of the towering Sangre de Cristo Mountains shimmering fifteen miles to the east. She kicked the machine into gear and started out across the pasture with the former caretaker of the ranch, a young man who also was mounted on an ATV. As they approached the eastern corner of the ranch's fence line, the former caretaker stopped and bent down near a clump of sagebrush and called out matter-of-factly, "Dana! Look at this."

She stopped and turned around, thinking he was referring to a cow skull lying on the ground, bleached by the incessant sun that baked the almost eight-thousand-foot-high mountain valley floor. Something caught the reflection of the sun and blazed like a burning torch in his hand.

"What in the world is that?" she asked as she turned

the ATV around and headed toward him. She could not believe her eyes. "Oh, my God!" she whispered as the grinning young man carefully handed her the enigmatic artifact. . . .

As a result of my extensive investigative efforts in the San Luis Valley, many locals now know who to call when something strange occurs. I received a call from the Saguache County appraiser who, as fate would have it, happens to be an ex–Air Force member. The appraiser had just returned home after visiting the Cases' new ranch and immediately called me. "Give her a call, and go out and see what she found. I won't tell you what it is; I want you to see it without any preconceptions, but I guarantee you won't be disappointed."

Intrigued, I gave the Cases a call. Over the phone Dana seemed like a pleasant, engaging person. She invited me to come out to her ranch and have a look at the artifact. I honored the appraiser's request and didn't ask specifically what it was. Dana was certain it was important, and she couldn't help but give me a clue: "It looks like an ant person." I immediately remembered that there were Native American legends of ant people living underground in the San Luis Valley. I obtained directions to the ranch, and as I hung up, I wondered if she knew about the Indian legends.

That afternoon, with video camera in hand, I headed out the door to begin the journey down into the mysterious valley. My gut was telling me that this alleged mystery object could be an archeological find of historic significance, but I wondered if this report was simply a ruse by the rural family to get publicity, or worse, an outright setup. But of whom?

Cattle stood peacefully as the dust cloud from my speeding pickup truck obscured their quiet numbers in a thin gritty veil. I shook my head. Here was another of those wonderful but perplexing developments I had to contend with in my quest for understanding in this place I now call home, the San Luis Valley. . . .

INTRODUCTION

"Perhaps if we go forward in the search we may stumble upon the thing which we are looking for; but if we stay where we are, nothing will come to light."

—Plato, *Theaetetus*

THE SETTING

The San Luis Valley (SLV) is the largest alpine valley in the world. Zebulon Pike was the first white American to cross the Sangre de Cristo Mountains into this 120-mile-long-by-forty-five-mile-wide territory. The four-thousand-square-mile, semiarid desert valley floor sits at an average elevation of 7,600 feet, over a mile and a half above sea level, and averages less than five inches of rainfall per year.

Its entire wishbone shape is ringed by majestic forested mountains on all sides. Along the eastern side of the valley stands a solid wall of rock soaring to heights of over fourteen thousand feet—the imposing Sangres. The second youngest mountain range in the continental United States, the peaks owe their jagged appearance to their relatively young age.

One cluster of promontories I call the Blanca Massif (for convenience) contains the valley's highest mountains. Situated midpoint in the Sangres, this twenty-five-square-mile jumble of peaks stands like a host of brooding sentinels. For thousands of years, Blanca Peak and its neighbors have been the focus of Native American myth and tradition. The valley itself was known as the "Bloodless Valley" because many tribes considered it sacred and refrained from warfare while visiting.

On the surface, SLV visitors simply note a large mountain valley with a proud, conservative, rural population. A place to raise your "young'uns" in clean mountain air. A place where everyone knows each other. A place with few secrets. But appearances are deceiving. There are secrets, secrets hidden for thousands of years among the craggy spires of the mountains. Secrets buried in the forty-square-mile, seven-hundred-foot-high Great Sand Dunes Monument.

Twelve miles south of Monte Vista, on the western side of the valley, a ridge named Greenie Mountain juts out into the valley, casting a foreboding shadow in more ways than one. Dozens of reports of conventional and unconventional aerial craft, starting in 1993, have made this area figure prominently as another key location in our journey.

The southern end of the SLV is dominated on its eastern Sangre de Cristo side by Wheeler Peak, the highest mountain in New Mexico.

The western valley is bordered by the older San Juan Mountains rising above a labyrinth of deep hidden valleys and roaring rivers. The famous Rio Grande River originates in the San Juans before snaking its way from the valley's midpoint southward to the Gulf of Mexico.

Both the San Juan and Sangre mountains merge at the extreme northern end of the valley in Saguache County after emptying over one hundred creeks into the largest freshwater aquifer in the country.

Aside from the southern end of the valley that opens from Colorado into New Mexico, there are only four main entry points. These Colorado mountain passes, Poncha in the north, Cochetopa in the northwest, Wolf Creek to the west, and La Veta to the east all cross above nine thousand feet and are often temporarily closed during the long winter months due to snowfall amounts of over one hundred fifty inches. Wolf Creek Pass, astride the Continental Divide, can receive as much as three hundred fifty inches of snow in a single season.

Three main highways bisect the SLV. Running east and west, State Highway 160 crosses the valley at the center, entering and exiting over La Veta and Wolf Creek passes, serving as "Main Street" of the valley's largest towns,

Alamosa and Monte Vista. Alamosa, with a population of just over ten thousand, sits in the valley's center. State Highways 285 and 17 travel the length of the valley north and south like twin shotgun barrels meeting to exit over Poncha Pass to the north. The incredible view of the surrounding mountains from Highway 17 prompted a group of visiting Tibetan monks to call the area "America's Tibet."

The southern and middle portions of the valley were the first settled regions of Colorado, and over the border in New Mexico are some of the oldest settlements in the country. San Luis, founded in 1720, is the oldest Colorado town. As a result of the sixteenth- and seventeenth-century influx of settlers from New Mexico, the valley has a rich cultural tradition, with Spanish speaking residents making up one half of the total population.

Physically and metaphorically isolated from the outside world, this Spanish-American culture has developed its own unique character, combining elements of indigenous Native American beliefs with an old world style of fundamentalist Catholic piety. This close-knit Hispanic subculture is very superstitious and generally wary of outsiders, creating an effective roadblock for researchers and investigators who've come here attempting to uncover the many secrets this valley holds so tightly.

According to the Department of Labor, farming is the largest employer in the San Luis Valley. Potatoes, hay, alfalfa, barley, and other high-altitude crops are the mainstay of the local economy. Although crop values fluctuate from year to year, potatoes consistently lead the way with over fifty percent of the total crop value. In 1993 potatoes generated $142,800,000 with alfalfa second at $37,100,000.

The 5,542,800-acre Colorado portion of the San Luis Valley is divided as follows: national forest 40%; range 23%; public domain 12%; irrigated crop land 8%; woodland 7%; state land 4%; irrigated hay and pasture 4%; local government .5% (US Department of the Interior).

Large cattle ranches, some over one hundred years old,

utilize the native hay and grasses for vast herds of beef cattle. The most famous of these ranches is the Luis Maria Baca Land Grant #4, which was chosen by the Luis Baca family in 1860 as partial reparation for land appropriated by the United States government in New Mexico. This hundred-thirty-thousand-acre ranch sits in the northern part of the valley in Saguache County.

Bordering the Baca Ranch sit the curious community of Crestone and the Baca Grande development. With a population of around seven hundred, this mountain town and the neighboring subdivision represent the only residential communities situated at the base of the Sangres in the Colorado portion of the SLV. It is also the fastest growing community in the entire valley.

The town of Crestone is a hundred-year-old former mining town whose population, until recently, mainly consisted of lifelong residents descended from the original miners and settlers. Then came the tide of artisans, New Agers, and "back to the earthers." All sorts of unique structures began to pop up on "hippie hill" and a new post office had to be built.

Adjacent to Crestone is the Baca Grande development. The "Baca," as it's known locally, is divided into two sections: the Chalets, which extend up the foothills of the Sangres, and the Grants, spread out on the valley floor below. Temples and shrines representing most of the world's great spiritual traditions dot the foothills, attracting a potpourri of spiritual seekers, urban refugees, and individualists.

Both the Baca and Crestone are "no shooting zones," and local deer populations show up in droves during hunting season. Bears drop by when sparse summer rains fail to make enough berries and someone saw a mountain lion walk down the main street one evening in 1993.

It is said that the famous mystic scientist, Wilhelm Reich, visited the valley before the government threw him in prison for discovering "orgone energy." These same rumors say that Reich declared the valley to be a "chakra," or energy center, on the earth. Shirley MacLaine must have tuned into the same energies as she bought one hundred and eighty acres here, intending to build a therapy center. Her plans didn't jive with the other property owners and her land remains undeveloped at the time of this writing.

Every school (and its curriculum) has rules. I entered into the secrets of the mysterious valley out of naive curiosity and instantly found myself immersed in a complicated process of education. As I mentioned, the locals rarely speak about unexplainable happenings, especially to possibly judgmental outsiders.

My journey has uncovered the many incidents, stories, legends, and personal experiences that follow. Until now, most of these experiences have been hidden from public view and are, at times, ominous, ecstatic, terrifying, and even, in some cases, downright unbelievable.

So please join me on this quest into the dim reaches of myth and legend, culled from both the historic record and my own experiences in the present. I am grateful for the opportunity to document so many examples of the unexplained, to produce a testament to some of the greatest unsolved mysteries of humankind. At first glance, many of these anomalies appear to defy explanation. However, when examined in a geological context, certain clues emerge as to who or what caused these events.

At various times during my investigation, I experienced what I can only describe as moments of Gnosis, or realizations. I emphasize these axioms as "Rules of Investigation" in this book in the order they were realized. I can only hope that my personal insights will provide clues that will enable the reader to further his or her understanding and processes of growth.

These rules have helped my objective process immeasurably. When grappling with paradox, absurdity, contradiction, and uncertainty, one tends to find out a lot about one's true motivations and beliefs. At first, the more I investigated the puzzling events and unexplained phenomena I heard about, the more intellectually confused I became. Fear ebbed and flowed and lack of clarity created intellectual confusion. Like a mirror image to my confusion, I became aware of a heart-centered intuition, or clarity, slowly emerging within me. The more confused I became, the more I found myself constantly having to trust this intuitive clarity.

If I had known then what I know I don't know now, I'm not sure I would have knowingly embarked on this journey into the unknown. I am now convinced that answers to many of life's mysteries are found in the very questions we ask ourselves. And the answers may be as individual as the questioners.

I conclude that we are all on our own individual paths, processing our experiences and gaining personal insight into the very nature of ourselves and the reality we all share. In your process, you hold a part of my process in your hands.

THE DUNES

Ten miles north of the Blanca Massif lies one of the San Luis Valley's most spectacular sites: the Great Sand Dunes National Monument. Soaring to heights of over seven hundred feet above the valley floor, the Dunes are the tallest and most mysterious dune fields on earth. This forty-square-mile dune field at the base of Medano Pass, on Pike's route, is cradled in an indentation in the Sangres.

The Dunes area, especially "the cattle-guard site," offer some of the earliest traces of humans in North America. Early paleolithic hunters are believed to have arrived in the area around eleven thousand years ago, hunting a profusion of game animals and birds. Mastodon tusks have been found in conjunction with the breathtaking spear points that primitive man hurled to bring down these huge beasts.

Publicly, the experts who work at the monument offer a reasonable-sounding explanation for the dunes' creation, that of prevailing westerly winds piling Rio Grande River sand into a mountain indentation. Privately, however, some scratch their heads in puzzlement, not positive if this is factual. The official age of the dunes is only a surprisingly young ten to twelve thousand years, although many believe it is older, and the actual formation of this wonder of nature may be much more complicated than the official version. If the age of the Dunes is correct, mankind may have visited the San Luis Valley before this seven-hundred-foot-high, forty-plus-square-mile pile of sand was deposited here!

Early pioneers were charged a five-dollar toll as they crested Mosca Pass before descending into the SLV, with the dune fields glistening less than a mile away. Intriguing stories of a mysterious herd of web-footed horses living in the dunes and tales of vanishing herds of sheep were passed around the campfires.

SUBJECTS OF MYSTERY

The subject of UFOs (Unidentified Flying Objects) and cattle "mutilations" are two of Western culture's most controversial subjects. The word *mutilation* is a subjective word assigned by the media and early investigators in the early 1970s for unexplained animal deaths and may not always be accurate. I have elected to use the more general term UAD (Unusual Animal Death) instead.

Our modern era of UFO phenomenon began on June 24, 1947, near Mount Rainier in Washington State with the Kenneth Arnold incident. Arnold described nine crescent-shaped objects he observed while flying his plane as resembling saucers skimming across the surface of a pond. Reporters promptly dubbed the objects "flying saucers."

The first publicized and still unexplained UAD of the modern era occurred some twenty years later on September 7, 1967, in the San Luis Valley, thirteen miles from where I presently reside. "Lady," a beautiful three-year-old Appaloosa filly, was found completely stripped of tissue from her shoulders to the tip of her nose. Her rear end appeared to be surgically removed and the carcass seemed to be completely drained of blood and fluids. The press promptly misnamed the horse "Snippy," after her sire who escaped the ghoulish surgeons that fateful night.

UFOs and UADs have figured prominently in my personal sojourn through one of America's most anomalous regions but they are by no means the only unexplained phenomenon that we will examine. Appearances of a "devil" have been reported in the southern end of the valley for generations. Reports of Bigfoot recently have been investigated and documented. Indian myths are intertwined with numerous New Age channelers' emphasis on this area as an important world spiritual center in the not-so-distant future. According to many New Age devotees, vortexes of as-yet-undefined energy are said to ebb and flow at various sacred sites in the valley, and around the world.

Recently, in Sedona, Arizona, investigator Tom Dongo has amassed an impressive body of data attesting to unexplained occurrences in the Sedona area. Dongo observed a curious twist in his 1988 book, *The Mysteries of Sedona:*

> Sedona has become the recent home to many adventurous residents who were irresistibly "drawn" here. Drawn by a magnetic force few understood, but a force few could resist. Each story is surprisingly the same. Typically it is told like this, "I felt such a strong pull to Sedona that after a period of time, Sedona became an obsession. One day the decision was made; I quit my secure job, sold my house, said good-bye to my astonished friends and relatives, and moved two thousand miles to a place I had never seen. When I arrived, I felt I had come home!"
>
> Ask a hundred New Age immigrants to Sedona and you will hear the same story. Perhaps with slight variations, but the theme is always the same. Some arrivals find fulfillment and accomplishments beyond their wildest dreams. While others drift away after a

time frustrated and disillusioned, never really discovering what they sought. . . . The type(s) of energies that exist in the Sedona area tend to quickly bring out the best in people, or the worst.

Replace the name Sedona with "the Baca" and you have an uncanny parallel. Many who are drawn to the Crestone-Baca area describe an identical attraction or compulsion. I myself can personally attest to this. This perception of a mysterious attraction to both locales may be an important clue to better understanding the magical nature of sacred sites in general, and the locales of Crestone-Baca and Sedona in particular.

Local populations and some UFOlogical circles whisper about other more mundane but equally mysterious presences. Anywhere from one to four secret underground bases are rumored to be located in the San Luis Valley area. Sedona has long been rumored to have some kind of secret facility just west of town. These facilities are variously described as belonging to extraterrestrial groups, i.e. "Aliens," or terrestrial groups, "the Government." A few advocates of the government theory maintain that the alleged facilities may be connected with underground complexes in Cheyenne Mountain (CO), Dulce (NM), and Los Alamos (NM).

Dimensional portals are said to open and close in the San Luis Valley, allowing access by nonhuman entities to our three-dimensional space/time reality. Although no hard proof exists, the stories persist, and, as you will see, they are worthy of our inspection.

I have taken great care in documenting the facts and events in this book. When dealing with such sensational and controversial subject matter, one must temper one's enthusiasm with as much research and corroboration as possible. Aside from my own personal experiences and investigation, all these reports of unexplained phenomenal occurrences in this book have verified, and in most cases, corroborated sources.

Due to the sensitive nature of some of the following events, a few names, where noted, have been changed at the individual's request.

This is not a work of fiction. As you will see, in Colorado and New Mexico's San Luis Valley, reality can be far stranger than any fiction.

PART ONE

"We all go on the same search, looking to solve the same old Mystery. We will not, of course, ever solve it. We will finally inhabit the Mystery."

—Ray Bradbury

WEIRD AMERICA

Before moving here, I had heard of the many unexplained phenomena alleged to have occurred in the area in the past.

In 1979, while reading a book called *Weird America* by Jim Brandon, I was reminded of the strange death of "Snippy" the horse and the many UFO sightings in the SLV. This book, a county-by-county, state-by-state listing of anomalous areas in the United States, led me on an extended expedition around North America. Armed with our copy of *Weird America*, photographer Fritz Kleiner and I were en route to the valley when a renegade snowstorm turned our journey back just fifty miles south. We headed to Canyon de Chelly, Arizona, instead. Although this was a smart move, I vowed that someday I would make it to the book's mysterious valley. Images of UFO sightings, "Snippy," and sacred Indian legends were hard to forget.

I had taken piano lessons as a kid but gave up playing music all through the early to mid-1970s. With the onslaught of the Punk Music wave of the late seventies, I started playing keyboards again, in 1978. I thought, "I can sure play better than that!" I "locked up" in a rehearsal studio and reacquainted myself with the keyboard for three solid months, playing eight to ten hours per day, seven days per week. Thinking back, I'm amazed at my tenacity. When I set my mind to something, I can get lost in it.

My twelve years in the Big Apple ended in 1987 when

I moved to Boston and was hired by one of Boston's top original music bands, The Lines. We had a number-five hit music video on Music Box, Europe's MTV, and were voted the best club band in Boston.

A friend of mine and his wife moved to the Baca Grande in 1987, and I remembered the San Luis Valley, thinking this was quite coincidental. "You'll move here eventually," he said, always speaking of the place in whispered, almost reverential tones. He insisted that I should "get off the coast and move out here" and offered me a place to stay.

Hunting for gem-quality dinosaur fossils (one of several hobbies) in April 1989 in south-central Utah, I naturally placed Crestone and the Baca on the route of my return trip to Beantown. Afterwards, I blanked out what happened that first night in Utah until my brother reminded me— three years later.

We were camped in the middle of nowhere at the base of Battleship Mesa, the nearest house over twenty miles away from our remote campsite in the middle of an otherworldly Utah desert landscape. Around 1:30 A.M., both my professional empath girlfriend and a fellow fossil hunter suddenly became extremely nervous. They both swore something was lurking outside our four-man tent. I too, felt the peculiar sensation of a presence outside.

Not feeling threatened like the others, I grabbed a flashlight and volunteered to stand guard in the car. After scanning the entire area with a powerful flashlight and finding nothing unusual, I kicked back in the front seat, listening to tunes and marveling at the magnificent Utah sky.

After about five or ten minutes, strange shapes began darting around behind the back of the car. They seemed to play with me, jumping from one rearview mirror to the other as my eyes raced to follow. Turning off the tape deck, I rolled down the window to shine my flashlight toward the rear of the car and listened. Nothing. I turned to face the front, blinked and . . . it was morning!

The sun was already five degrees above the horizon! My

flashlight was still in my hand and I had absolutely no sense of ever falling asleep. I am normally a very restless sleeper and wake up numerous times each night. This night felt like it had lasted only a matter of mere seconds! I can't say why but I put the the incident out of my mind. It would not be the last time I would witness these shadowy shapes.

CRESTONE

Two days later I was finally driving down the twelve-mile access road toward the Sangre de Cristo Mountains towering over the tiny village of Crestone. I remember warning myself out loud, "This place is carnivorous. It'll eat you up and spit you out if you're not careful."

The proud, independent residents of Crestone and the Baca reflected an unhurried rural lifestyle. Everyone I met was open, friendly, and relaxed. I quickly fell in love with the high, dry climate and the pristine mountain splendor of this forgotten region of southern Colorado. While having lunch at the Bistro, the only restaurant in town, I met Robert Troutman, a master cabinetmaker. We talked at length about Crestone and the Baca, and I mentioned to him that I was tired of the East Coast. His response was simple and direct: "Follow your bliss." The next day while gliding along those lonely stretches of Kansas, with Boston on the distant horizon, it dawned on me that I would soon be hitchin' up the oxen and movin' west. Perhaps to Santa Fe.

Three months later, I arrived in Santa Fe, all my earthly possessions following in a U-Haul trailer. Two days turned out to be plenty. I witnessed the aftermath of three fatal car accidents and decided that the historic capital of New Mexico was actually a smaller, western version of New York City. This didn't appeal to my newfound sense of adventure, so I decided to call my friends (one hundred fifty miles north in the Baca) and they extended their offer of hospitality again.

Mysteries attract me like a moth to light so I was curious why there were over a dozen of the world's great religious and spiritual traditions represented in this wee mountain town and nearby development. It was also intriguing that many of the residents I met felt that everyone who moved here and stayed was "called." Was I being called? By whom, or more accurately, by what?

"This is where the teachers are taught," a resident told me shortly after my move. "You'll know very soon if it's your destiny to be here. The mountains will let you know." Now, I consider myself a pretty open-minded individual with more than a few experiences in my life that defied rational explanation but I still had to swallow a rather NYC response when I heard this. As I soon discovered, living way out here can be tough. *Real* tough.

This valley is one of the poorest regions in the United States, with an average per capita income of under nine thousand dollars per year. It was immediately clear to me that if I wished to stay in this mountain paradise I would have to be clever enough to pay for it.

Miraculously, I was immediately able to land a job on a construction crew, which enabled me to gain a foothold in the small mountain community. I hadn't worked for only six dollars per hour since high school but I was reminded how extremely lucky I was to find a job at all. Coming from sea level, I quickly discovered how hard physical labor is at eight thousand feet (it takes six weeks to acclimate).

One of the first things I did upon arriving in the Baca that first hot, dusty week in July 1989 was spend some casual time after work in "Olde Town." This simple cluster of buildings, owned by Frank and Katie Snider, could be called the Crestone Business District. A turn-of-the-century building, in the town's heyday it had housed a bank, then the assayer's office, then had evolved into a small boutique and liquor store. The Sniders are a hardy, down-to-earth family. Frank and Katie, both pushing sixty, were self-professed bikers in the 1950s.

My first foray into the Sniders' "Twenty-first Amend-

ment Liquors'' was revealing. A hitching post still adorned
the porch and a sign on the door summed up life in a small
mountain town.

> Open most days we open about 9 or 10, occasionally
> as early as 7, but SOME DAYS as late as 12 or 1.
> We close about 5:30–6, occasionally about 4, or 5,
> but sometimes as late as 11 or 12. SOME DAYS, or
> afternoons, we aren't here at all and lately I've been
> here just about all the time, except when I'm some-
> place else, but I should be here then too.

After three or so minutes of being seriously sniffed by
the Sniders' several friendly dogs, Katie appeared at the
door. ''Howdy,'' she said, unlatching the rickety screen
door that had managed to capture a couple of feeble mountain mosquitoes inside. I introduced myself, telling her as
I entered the dimly lit store of my wish to move here. I
took everything in, all the antique mementos of a bygone
era: a huge safe, shovels, picks, scales, ancient bottles, old
calenders, and numerous elk, deer, and pronghorn trophies.
I scanned the cooler, which featured beers from Europe,
Australia, Asia, Mexico, South America, and some of the
top ''microbreweries'' in America. I was looking at one of
the most impressive beer selections I'd ever seen in any
city, let alone a remote mountain town of 155 people.
  ''I'm impressed!'' I admitted.
  ''If I can find out who carries it, I'll get it for you. . . .''
Katie promised, adding, ''If you're really moving here.''
  Katie was coy, yet very informative. In a scant twenty
minutes, I was taken on a crash course into the recent social
history of Crestone. ''See that guy in the old beat-up truck,
we used to be best friends. We don't talk now!'' I squashed
the urge to ask why. An old mule was standing on the
porch outside, its long tail impatiently swishing flies in the
lazy, dry mountain air. For some reason, I felt right at
home.
  Our conversation went on for a spell, with Katie answering my queries about the town with apparent honesty

and humor. Out of nowhere I suddenly blurted out, "I've heard there's a lot of UFO sightings around here."

Katie's eyes flashed and she quickly responded, "Oh that's a lot of nonsense. Don't believe those old stories!" I noticed she seemed nervous as she hurriedly bagged my selection. I was disappointed that she didn't confirm my casual suspicion that the area I had just moved to did have the occasional UFO sighting but I didn't press her.

It had been a hard, short-of-breath day on my new job carrying one-hundred-pound bundles of asphalt roofing tiles up three floors in the still unfamiliar thin mountain air and I was bushed. I went home with an excellent six-pack of Negro Modelo.

CHEAP FIREWORKS

August 13, 1989, 10 pm, The Baca:

I was sitting on the front porch of the house where I stayed with my friends Roland and Laura Yartzoff. The star-studded Colorado sky shimmered above me as I watched the heavens. We had just experienced a spell of unusual heat during the end of July and early August and the A-frame house still baked from the ninety-five-degree day. I sat blissfully enjoying a cool breeze flowing off the fourteen-thousand-foot peaks glowing in the moonlight.

Suddenly something above me moved. A bright point of light was headed across the valley from the west. "Wow, you guys, come here . . . *quick!*" I called to Roland and Laura. They rushed out on the porch just in time to see the bright light silently explode over town, two miles north of my vantage point. A definite faint trail of smoke behind the object was momentarily illuminated by the flash.

"What in the world was that?" Roland asked as the flash faded.

"That was no shooting star," his wife replied.

"It almost looked like a giant bottle rocket!" I said.

"Like a giant cheap firework." It had appeared to be less than two miles away when it exploded right over town, and knowing a bit about meteors, I knew that if I saw smoke, it had to have been extremely close to my vantage point. Yet, the object was completely silent! The duration of the object's flight was at least seven to eight seconds, time enough for the Yartzoffs to run outside from the kitchen two rooms away and witness the object explode. We talked about it for a while and agreed that whatever it was, it was unusual.

This was the first sighting of what I have dubbed as "cheap fireworks." Dozens more of these puzzling objects have appeared to me since moving here—some as close as twenty-five feet away! They are not meteors or identifiable celestial objects, and their close proximity prompted one witness to describe a very small sighting as "watching Tinkerbell crashing."

JANUARY 1991, 3:30 AM, ROAD T, SAGUACHE COUNTY:

My new band, Expedition, had just ended a weekend in Salida at the venerable Lamplighter lounge. I played keyboards and kept the audience entertained with my own brand of questionable humor. The band was a far cry from the "pros" with whom I'd played in New York and Boston. Playing for a bunch of hard-drinking locals yelling for "country" was not my idea of the big time, but folks around the valley loved the band's unpretentious mix of old rock and country and, hey, we did get paid!

I was proceeding east toward Crestone on that moonless night, my ears still ringing from that night's performance, when I noticed a loud crackling sound in my ears. I slowed the truck. The strange electrical sound reminded me of white noise between AM radio stations. Movement over the Sangres drew my attention and, gliding from the southeast, I beheld a huge, brilliant green glittering ball of light!

Behind it streamed a tail as it remained at a constant altitude parallel to the mountaintops. The distance it traveled, from the moment I first spotted it until it disappeared from view to the north, must have been seventy-five to eighty miles. It covered the distance in under five seconds! As it faded away from me, the crackling sound in my ears stopped. I was so tired from playing and driving the eighty miles home that the sight didn't really register fully in my mind until the next morning, when I told a couple of friends about the unusual object. This was my second sighting of something out of the ordinary in the night sky over the San Luis Valley. It was far from the last.

During my first four years here, I began hearing occasional offhand comments concerning animal "mutilations" and sightings of strange lights and ships and casually began to gather tidbits from the colorful history of the area. These comments piqued my curiosity, having now seen a couple of pretty strange things myself. If even a newcomer like myself had seen something, I was willing to bet other locals had seen unusual things in the sky as well.

As time went on, my sightings of the two unexplained objects took a definite backseat to the task of making a living and trying to put together a band featuring the best rock and roll players the area had to offer.

I uncovered a curious account from the *American Museum of Natural History (AMNH) Magazine* in 1941, noting an event that occurred here in 1893:

> An outstanding event was the discovery of what is believed to be a meteorite crater—the first within the boundaries of our state [Colorado]. The find was the culmination of a search which began in 1931 and has continued through ten years. After hearing from former residents of the San Luis Valley of a great [meteorite] fall which occurred in the year 1893, Dr. [AMNH Department of Meteorites, curator] and Mrs. Nininger devoted a portion of the summer of 1937 to search for meteorites in that part of the state. . . .
>
> The immediate result was the discovery of a new stone known as the Alamosa aereolite (weight four pounds). . . . During the sojourn in the valley that

summer, Dr. Nininger called at the ranch home of C. M. King of Blanca (CO) to hear the account of the great fall of 1893. Mr. King had seen the phenomenon from a distance of only a few miles, for he declared that it had reached the earth between where he stood and the nearby range of the high Sangre de Cristo Mountains. . . .

The article reveals that the crater was on the western slope of the Sangre de Cristo Range, about six miles northwest of the Great Sand Dunes National Monument. The center measured 350 by 250 feet from rim to rim.

The lowest part lies twenty-nine feet below the highest point on the rim, which rises conspicuously above the surrounding terrain. A magnetic survey was made of the crater by Harry Aurand of Denver. His results indicated two magnetic masses which seemed to warrant investigation. A well driller was employed and both these locations were drilled. At depths of sixtynine feet and seventy-eight and a half feet respectively, objects were encountered through which it was impossible to drill. Six other exploratory holes were placed to ascertain the internal structure of the crater. These clearly revealed a disturbed condition in the boulder deposit under the sand. Plans have been made for further investigation of the masses encountered.

Although plans were made by the AMNH to come back to the site, no evidence exists that they ever returned. The original dig still adorns the western rim of the crater and the old gray boards left behind by the drillers, half covered in sand, are the only visible indication of man's casual interest in the site, fifty years ago. The two large magnetic masses still lie undisturbed, seventy feet below the shifting sands of the Baca Ranch. Incidentally, C. M. King, the only witness to the event, was the husband of Agnes and father of Nellie, owner of the notorious ''Snippy'' the horse! The Kings will figure prominently in our story.

LIGHT ON THE MOUNTAIN

JULY 18, 1992, 4:30 AM, SAND DUNES ROAD, ALAMOSA COUNTY:

Brendan O'Brien, my younger brother, and former UAD investigator Bill McIntyre had taken a trip to Cuchara, CO. While there on business, they were introduced to an alleged ''abductee'' being shielded from publicity by the towns-people. They also met an individual who, along with three other families, recently had witnessed a large diamond-shaped object extending a telescoping shaft into an abandoned mine, in broad daylight. Several of the witnesses had studied the strange object through binoculars. Brendan and Bill found that no one they interviewed would go on the record concerning the event, but all insisted that it really happened. The two took care of their business and started back toward Crestone late that night.

Brendan was driving while Bill snoozed in the passenger seat of the small Ford Ranger truck. In the predawn, eight miles southeast of the Dunes, a brilliant white explosion lit up the entire mountainside. McIntyre was awakened by the impact. ''Whoa, stop. There's no moon out. You can see the trees.''

''That's way above tree line, there's no road anywhere near there! Pull over!'' McIntyre cried. They stopped one hundred feet up a dirt road and parked with the light framed in the truck's windshield.

Brendan switched off the headlights but left on the large orange parking lights. The distant light changed to orange. ''Wow!'' Brendan exclaimed. ''Did you see that?!'' McIntyre sat quietly, staring at the light that he estimated was three to four miles up Pioneer Canyon, at about 11,500 feet.

Brendan turned his headlights back on and the light instantly changed back to white and appeared to start revolving in place. The two sat dumbfounded until Bill finally stammered, "Should I get the camera?" They had an S-VHS camera in the back of the truck but someone would have to get out and walk behind the truck to grab it.

"I don't know if it would be a good idea to tape it yet; let's get closer," Brendan suggested. Experimenting, he flipped his headlights back off, leaving his parking lights on. The object again matched the color. "What the hell *is* that?" Headlights on, he put the truck in gear and started up the mountain.

"Wait a minute, wait a minute," Bill yelled as the light mirrored their actions, and hurtled down the mountainside directly at them! The tops of the trees became illuminated as it fell below tree line. Brendan panicked, making a quick U-turn and racing back toward the pavement. Reaching the Sand Dunes Road, he hit the brakes for a quick right turn. McIntyre, never taking his eyes off the light, watched it turn red. "Hold it!" he yelled to Brendan. "It stopped."

The two shaken travelers sat silently for an undetermined amount of time as the light gradually grew smaller and more intense, reminding them of a "ruby red laser light." It then "floated across the valley" to the south, shot straight up and out at a forty-five-degree angle, and according to both witnesses, "turned into a star."

The next morning they told me of their experience, and I remembered my own strange sightings.

LANDING SITE

JULY 20, 1992, MINERAL HOT SPRINGS, SAGUACHE COUNTY:

Seventy miles north of Blanca, the black cloudless sky is punctured by a flash. Miles away, a coyote wails a mournful tribute to the moon setting in the west. A chorus of crickets are silenced as a heavy stillness envelops the dim moonlit terrain.

A vivid orange glow pulses behind a series of low hills that surround a natural hot spring four hundred yards east of a cluster of small dwellings.

Sally Sloban stirs in her sleep as her two small dogs bark furiously in the lush greenhouse that faces the main hot spring. As she wakes, she notices an orange glow reflecting off the wall in her room. Slipping on sandals, she wraps a cloak around her lithe dancer's frame and peers out through the steamy greenhouse glass at the dark terrain, now intermittently punctuated by the eerie pulsing light. Then, a sudden bright flash extinguishes the orange light source.

Sally climbs back into bed and falls into a fitful sleep. The following morning, two visiting friends walk with her out to the area from which the glowing light appeared to be emanating the night before.

Behind a low hill, one of her friends kneels beside a strange circular mark in the ground. A thirty-foot-diameter impression is clearly visible. Crushed Chico bushes and prairie grass are whirled flat around a three-foot-deep hole at the center of the depression. The hole is a foot and a half across and appears to have been caused by intense heat from a powerful, concentrated, downward blast. After looking around, they wander back to the buildings for breakfast, enthralled by the obvious landing site so close to the house.

Word of the landing circle quietly circulates for several days through Crestone. Brendan O'Brien and Bill McIntyre hear the story and, because of their unexplained sighting of the strange light the week before, drive the thirty miles north from Crestone to visit Sally at the hot springs.

Sally leads them out to the location, relating her experience the night the mark appeared. Several other curious locals have already come out to see it. They walk closer and Brendan looks down the "blast hole."

"Bill, look at this!" Standing perfectly straight "on the last three inches of its tail" at the bottom of the hole, is a two-and-a-half-foot bullsnake, its tongue occasionally flicking out to sniff the air.

"No!" exclaims McIntyre, as he quickly unpacks his video camera. "Get back, don't scare it. I want to videotape it."

He shoots several minutes of tape as they wonder aloud what the heck a bullsnake is doing standing on its tail in an apparent landing circle blast hole. The circular impression remained visible until the following summer.

THE TAR BABY

DECEMBER 31, 1992, CRESTONE-BACA GRANDE, SAGUACHE COUNTY:

My significant other, Isadora Storey, and I were in the midst of hosting a New Year's Eve party at our home. As the party wound down and folks eased toward the door, I overheard a friend recalling UFO sightings she had experienced recently with her boyfriend. She stood telling a small, captivated group about unusual lights and "glowing" objects. I, also captivated, listened to every detail.

The speaker appeared calm, yet excited, as she described the experience almost poetically. I started asking questions, trying to find out as much as I could about these occurrences. She named other witnesses who had apparently seen the unknown lights the next three nights. Some of these witnesses, including her boyfriend, were at the party. As the conversation progressed, first one then another "witness" walked in from the other room and joined the animated conversation describing sightings over the Baca Ranch on November 25 and December 9–12, 1992. I found it disconcerting to hear people talking so casually about glowing orbs and dancing lights.

Then came the clincher. Charlotte Hier, a local closet UFO buff, mentioned she had seen a short article in the regional newspaper, Alamosa's *Valley Courier*, reporting a "mutilation" on a small ranch in Costilla County. The event took place the same night that many Baca area witnesses had seen those unexplained lights. Unbeknownst to me, I was grabbing firmly hold of a tar baby!

My full-time investigation literally began that night and I can't help but look back at that pivotal evening and view my naive excitement with a smile. If I had known what I was getting into, my excitement would have undoubtedly been tempered with the realization that years of frustrating and unrewarding hard work lay ahead with no promise of any firm answers. I never actually dreamed I would solve these riddles. But I felt compelled to investigate the extent of these elusive events.

Reality-shattering phenomena are touchy subjects. I quickly found that I would receive ridicule from some people and respect from others.

RULE #1
Controversial subjects generate polarized responses.

I was oblivious to the implications of starting a murky investigation into the bizarre. Crestone is a small town in a region literally decades behind the times. I would need to tread carefully if I wanted to maintain any respect from skeptics.

My natural reporter's instinct took hold and the next day I made my first phone call to find out more about the UAD that had allegedly occurred in Costilla County. Local resident and *Crestone Eagle* publisher Kizzen Dennett, not a person to shy away from controversy, suggested I do some research, conduct a couple of interviews, and write an article for her eclectic monthly. She laughed when I asked her how much she'd pay me for writing an article for her paper. It was apparent that I wasn't going to make any money writing for the *Eagle* or, as I later learned, any "fringe subject" publication.

Luckily, Kizzen still had a copy of the *Courier* article concerning the Costilla UAD. She found the potential story compelling and urged me to contact reporter Ruth Heide to obtain rancher Manuel Sanchez's phone number. "Give him a call, let me know what he says and, please, don't make the article too long."

Ruth Heide still had her interview notes. I called the ranch and asked Mrs. Sanchez if I might speak with her husband. She put him on but he sounded scared, possibly angry. I then called Billy Maestas, the Costilla County sheriff who had investigated the report, and found neighboring Los Animas County had logged a UAD report the same day! I was getting somewhere.

I called Los Animas Sheriff Lou Girodo's Trinidad office. "They're back!" he exclaimed when I related descriptions of the lights that had been seen over the Baca Ranch by over a dozen witnesses the night the cattle surgeons resumed their work. Back? Who was back?

The apparent synchronicity between the Baca lights and the unusual cattle deaths intrigued me. What was going on? I was going to try, at the very least, to find out.

As most people with a minimal knowledge of unusual animal death phenomena, I was under the false impression that these animal deaths had ceased. I hadn't seen a single reference to cattle "mutilations" in the media for years and now that I thought about it, it seemed strange that I never saw a single reference to them in the news during my first four years in the valley.

The San Luis Valley's supposed role in the phenomenon is well documented in UFOlogy. Snippy the horse, the acknowledged granddaddy of them all, occurred here, and I wondered if Snippy's owners were still around. Perhaps they could shed some light on these recent events.

NELLIE'S DIARY

One of my neighbors, Pam LaBorde, had mentioned a diary that her husband Roger and a group of friends had found while cleaning a cabin in the foothills of the Blanca Peaks. Pam mentioned that the cabin sat on the old King Ranch and that the diary had belonged to Nellie Lewis, Snippy's owner. I called Roger to inquire. The "diary" turned out to be a handful of looseleaf pages that Roger insisted had contained descriptions and drawings of UFO-type craft, dates and accounts of visitations, even sketches of "strange beings in robes." There was a "drawing of a triangle and snake emblem the beings had on their robes."

Snake? I thought. As in bullsnake?

Roger was sure that the pages belonged to Nellie Lewis. "It had her name right on it." Then Roger told me his fascinating account.

He had been on a work party in 1988, with ten members of the Universal Education Foundation (UEF) who had just bought the old King Ranch from Mr. Berle Lewis, Nellie Lewis's husband. They were cleaning up the yard and out-buildings when he found the curious pages in some garbage. He called the rest of the work party over to see them. Hosca Harrison, who had organized the cleanup, put them inside on the kitchen counter and everyone went back to work.

"A few minutes later, two men in the work party that I didn't know left. I thought they were friends of someone else and didn't think much of it," Roger said. "Later we discovered that the pages were gone, somebody had taken them!" The UEF work crew had a real mystery on their hands. "Everyone there swore they hadn't taken the notes, and no one seemed to know who the two men were. I remember thinking they looked out of place; one of them was dressed in an undershirt and had on dress shoes and slacks. Neither of them were dressed in work clothes."

Roger LaBorde is a world-famous coma specialist. He has been instrumental in healing some very high-profile coma cases and is a spiritual, down-to-earth individual. Even so, this particular story was hard to swallow. Later, I checked with four others who were in the work party that day. All four told me the exact same story.

What would two strangers want with a handful of pages describing UFO sightings and alien visitations? I asked Roger if Berle Lewis was still alive. Yes. Nellie had died mysteriously in 1976 but Berle still lived near his old cabin at the Great Sand Dunes Country Club.

Feeling as if I had become a private detective, I called Berle Lewis. The raspy voice on the line related the strange events surrounding Snippy the horse's death so colorfully, I knew I had to arrange a full video interview with him.

I asked him whom I should call to learn more about the strange animal deaths I thought had ceased. "Call them Paris, Texas, boys," he suggested.

"Who?" I asked.

"Tom Adams and Gary Massey. They know more about these things than anyone, 'cept maybe that TV lady." (He meant UAD investigator, author, and film producer Linda Moulton Howe.)

TOM ADAMS

This was getting fun. I immediately left a message for Adams, not really expecting him to call back. But that evening, January 3, 1993, he did. At first, he was understandably suspicious and it took a little convincing that I wasn't just another time-waster, or debunker.

Adams gave me an hour of his time. What an incredible fountain of information, I thought to myself during our first conversation. Feeling a little more comfortable with me, he provided names, dates, and phone numbers of witnesses from the past thirty years, plus dates and descriptions of many bizarre, little-known accounts of sightings and UAD reports here in the San Luis Valley. With no notes, he pulled dates, names, and facts right off the top of his head. I was impressed, to say the least.

I scribbled four pages of notes, realizing that he was saving me months of hard work and research. The information I obtained from Adams during our first conversation was, and still is, invaluable. The first package he sent me contained nearly every *Valley Courier* article he had so fortuitously collected pertaining to the valley UFOs and UADs.

During the first two weeks of January 1993, I interviewed over a dozen witnesses in Saguache County who had seen the anomalous lights in November and December. Most of them didn't know that others had shared their sighting experience. I was intrigued by the exact descriptions (three of the witnesses used the words "bouncing over the Baca Ranch"). This spurred me on to find out as much as possible about this apparent upsurge in unexplained activity.

All of the incredible stories and reports of sightings from the 1960s suddenly seemed immediate. Could these recent sightings be connected? What about these reports of UADs? Was there a connection between the sightings and the unusual animal deaths then and now? I followed a hunch that more activity had been witnessed recently than reported and spent the first two weeks of January following every lead I could find.

Slowly establishing and cultivating dialogues with law enforcement officials, witnesses, historians, ranchers, and farmers, the pieces of a perplexing puzzle slowly began to fall into place. Fortunately, because I live here, I have been able to research specifics and follow up leads pertaining to an amazing collection of events that have happened and are currently happening here. The locals won't talk to nonresidents about such controversial subjects, and I had a feeling that I would be lucky to get any of these reluctant witnesses to talk with me.

RULE #2
Record or write everything down as soon as possible, no
matter how inconsequential or insignificant it might seem at
the time.

WAITING FOR THE ECLIPSE

DECEMBER 9, 1992, 8:45 PM, DENVER, COLORADO:

Astronomer Michael Robertson and a friend were scanning the heavens before the lunar eclipse when they spotted an orange object approaching from the northeast. As it reached eighty degrees above the horizon, a second object approached from the northwest. Both trained observers agreed, ''The objects did not appear to have lights and were flying just under thirty thousand feet, reflecting the setting sun.'' The two objects crossed paths over downtown Denver and headed toward southern Colorado.

Robertson stated to Colorado Mutual UFO Network (MUFON) investigators, ''In thirty years of watching the skies, I have never observed anything like those objects.''

SAME DAY, 9:15 PM, CRESTONE-BACA GRANDE, SAGUACHE COUNTY:

Kristi (not her real name) recently had moved to the Baca where her parents and grandparents lived. The single, thirty-something Chicago native was watching television in her rented chalet home. A college graduate and gifted singer with a razor wit, Kristi, like her parents, had little time for ''new age knuckleheads and flying saucers.'' She was, however, an avid skywatcher who was anticipating that night's lunar eclipse.

As she left the couch to turn off the television, she saw two unusual golden-white orbs of light flash overhead. The sixteen-foot-high A-frame window afforded her a spectacular view of the objects as they streaked over the house heading southwest down Spanish Creek, one of the many creeks that flow year-round out of the Sangres, into the valley floor. Running out onto her porch, Kristi watched the objects follow the tree-lined path of the creek as they shot out across the valley at "fantastic" speed.

SAME DAY, 9:15 PM, BACA GRANDE DEVELOPMENT, SAGUACHE COUNTY:

Luna Bontempe and Lucas Price were outside enjoying the crisp December night. They were housesitting for a friend whose home sits beside Spanish Creek in the Baca Grants and anxiously awaited the coming eclipse.

Luna was the first to notice the unusual lights, low to the ground and south of their location. The small glimmering lights appeared to be over the southern end of the Baca Ranch and were "bouncing around, creating geometric shapes." First they formed a square and hung motionless like stars in the late fall sky. "Check that out!" she exclaimed, drawing Lucas's attention as the lights formed a triangle.

Lucas suddenly spotted two brilliant orbs of light streaking down the western slope of the Sangres to their left. The two lights followed Spanish Creek at treetop level out over the valley, then turned toward them silently at incredible speed. The "large laserlike ovals" zipped directly over their heads, continued past them and hovered behind a grove of cottonwood trees, about two hundred yards due south of the house. The objects started "shooting off milky beams of light," so bright the two of them could see owl nests lit up in the tops of the trees! As they watched in amazement, the bright beams simultaneously vanished. They completely forgot about the eclipse.

The small glimmering lights reappeared and danced like clockwork over the Baca Ranch on the following three nights. Luke and Luna brought their three kids and a couple of neighborhood children up to the old Independence Gold Mine, situated high above the valley south of Crestone, for a better view. The unidentified lights "bounced around" between 9 and 9:30 P.M. while the group watched and munched popcorn.

HOLIDAY VISITORS

I learned of the following event when John Browning called a National Public Radio (NPR) program as I was being interviewed.

NOVEMBER 1, 1992, 3 AM, SAGUACHE COUNTY:

John Browning, his son, and two friends were camped about twenty miles north of Saguache during a Halloween hunting trip. The four Denver residents were dog tired after spending all day in the mountains tracking an elusive elk herd. After making camp and cooking dinner, the weary group bundled up to ward off the cold mountain air and quickly fell asleep.

At 3 A.M., Browning was awakened with a start. A strange stillness permeated the forest campsite and an unusual glow bathed his camper. He was so intrigued by the lights directly overhead that he left his warm sleeping bag and ventured out into the cold to investigate. As his eyes grew accustomed to the lights traveling slowly above, headed south toward the western side of the SLV, he could make out the outline of an enormous triangular-shaped craft that blocked out the night sky.

"There must have been fifteen or sixteen lights in a semicircle with four of them flashing around the center," he told me. "There wasn't a sound!" Browning said he felt "mesmerized" by the lighting array that flashed hypnotically overhead. "I'm telling you, this thing was huge! It must have been at least a quarter mile long!"

He hurried to wake his son to witness the incredible sight before it disappeared, but was too late. "Whatever that thing was, it wasn't from this world," he concluded.

I wasn't so sure. The immense craft certainly sounded impressive but as an investigator, I had to remain skeptical. Going with the sincere-sounding veracity of John Browning, I was sure he had seen something, but was it truly extraterrestrial? I had heard rumors of secret government craft and wondered if the fantastic sighting could have actually been top secret, and very terrestrial.

That same night, ninety miles southeast of Browning and his party, forty miles west of Trinidad, CO, rancher John Torres's herd of cattle had a deadly Halloween visitor. The following morning Torres discovered a three-year-old dead cow in a remote area of his ranch. The animal's tongue, genitalia, and eyes were missing. Torres had "never seen anything like it" in his years as a cattle rancher. "That was no predator. They were real, real sharp cuts with no ridges. There were no tracks, no blood, no nothin'!"

Later, when Greg Barman, NPR reporter, asked him who he thought was responsible for the "mutilation" of his cow, Torres answered with a nervous laugh, "Well, as far as I'm concerned, it was aliens. Seriously, I really think it was something from out of this world, to do something like that without leaving any evidence whatsoever."

NOVEMBER 25, 1992, 8:30 PM, BACA GRANDE, SAGUACHE COUNTY:

Michael and Andrea Nisbit enjoyed a quiet evening at home. The Nisbits, expert mineral and crystal wholesalers, relaxed after preparing for a trip to South America to finalize the transfer of two lucrative amber mines to their wholesale business.

He and his wife had seen strange lights and "ships" near their house (at the extreme southwestern end of the Baca Grants) on several occasions but not up close.

At 9 P.M. a powerful beam of light blasted down from outside and above the house, turning night into day. They scrambled off the couch, running to a window that faced the Baca Ranch. A bright reflection hit their cars parked outside. Above them an orange-white light traveled silently across their yard toward the end of Camino Real, a street that dead-ends less than a half mile away. Around the bright beam they could faintly make out pulsing lights.

Suddenly, as if a switch had been flipped, the lights disappeared. The Nisbits held each other in the eerie darkness while the moonless sky pulled slowly back into focus. But on this particular night, they were the lucky ones.

Barbara Benara (not her real name), forty-year-old mother of four, suddenly realized she was behind the wheel of her truck, seven miles from her home and her children. A strange force compelled her forward. That "something" was in complete control of her free will and she couldn't fight the fact that she was driving out into the Grants. Barbara was pulled as if by a magnet to the remote southwestern corner of the Baca development that borders the Baca Ranch. She parked less than a half mile from the Nisbits' home.

"What am I doing here?" she remembers asking herself as she sat numbly in her small truck at the end of Camino Real, overlooking the ranch two hundred yards away. In a sweat, she loosened her coat and turned off the heater. "What's gotten into me? Who's looking after my children?" Her watch read 8:30 P.M. The silence roared in her ears.

Barbara, now shivering, pulled her light coat around her, wiping her nose with the back of her hand. It was now freezing inside her truck. She looked at her hand. It was streaked with blood. "Oh my God!" Her nosebleed could only mean one thing. Her watch revealed it was 10:30 P.M. She shuddered. "They" had taken her again.

It had been five years since the last time Barbara awoke with a nosebleed and "that peculiar feeling." "They" had come to her many times in the preceding twenty-eight years. They always came at night. She knew because of the bloody nose. At first, when she was seven, their visits frightened her. She could never quite remember the details of what happened when they came but she remembered a voice. The voice comforted her and kept her from being afraid. As she grew older, she learned to trust the voice.

* * *

"My children!" At 10:30 P.M. on November 25, 1992, she wiped her face clean, turned the ignition, jammed the truck into gear, and rushed back to her house. Her children slept undisturbed.

The next morning, Barbara felt exhausted but elated, reminding her of another morning after an unbelievable night in 1978 when the visitors actually revealed themselves to her. It was her first, fully conscious encounter with the beings she now calls "the little brothers." A week before she had been diagnosed with ovarian cancer.

She had felt their presence that night in 1978 and had been unable to sleep. A tremendous lightning storm had swept through the area. They often arrived during lightning storms. She didn't remember falling asleep but evidently she did. Upon waking:

"I was lying on a soft table in a white, circular room. I could only move my head. I don't recall how long I lay there but I felt peaceful. Then I heard the voice. It told me that I needed their help. I asked the voice if I could see them." They appeared in front of her, around the foot of the table. "There were four of them, all identical. They were three to four feet tall, ivory white, and had large, almond-shaped eyes." A fifth being appeared in front of the four. This one was a little taller. "Its eyes were intense! I couldn't stop staring into them!" The taller being communicated directly with her mind and told her to not be afraid. She recognized the familiar voice.

"I don't remember how I got there but somehow I found myself immersed in an L-shaped tank. A long, segmented arm came out of a console next to the tank and inserted itself into me. It wasn't painful but it didn't feel comfortable. I had to relax and trust the voice that kept telling me not to be afraid." The next thing she knew it was morning and she felt extremely tired and didn't have a nosebleed.

Four days after this alleged encounter, Barbara says she returned to her doctor who, at her insistence, performed the same tests he'd used to determine the status of her cancer. The tests came up negative. "They cured me of ovarian cancer," Barbara says proudly. She is puzzled why they had her drive so far from her home that Thanksgiving Eve after not visiting for five years.

"I don't remember anything during almost two hours in my truck but I know it was the little brothers," she assured me.

RULE #3
Always credit your sources and respect requests for anonymity.

That same Thanksgiving morning, a double-propped military helicopter thundered less than fifty feet over the Nisbits' house, heading south toward the Great Sand Dunes National Monument. Michael and Andrea agree. "Every time we see lights or ships or something we can't explain here in the Baca, the next morning we see helicopters headed in the same direction."

Initially, it appeared that certain people were more prone to sighting experiences than others. But wanting the experience didn't necessarily mean an individual would have one. Some of the most ardent believers in UFOs and ETs have never had a sighting experience.

NOVEMBER 27, 1992, 2:30 AM, EIGHTY MILES SOUTH IN COSTILLA COUNTY:

Manuel Sanchez (the Costilla rancher from the *Courier* article) couldn't sleep. He peered out the window of his modest ranch house across the pitch-black pasture, seeing and hearing nothing unusual. He finally fell into a fitful sleep until just before dawn. As he left the house the following Thanksgiving morning to check on his herd, he stopped. Not fifty feet away from the house, one of his prize breeding cows lay motionless on her side, obviously dead. Her rear end, udder, and tongue had been cleanly removed, the animal's mandible bleached a ghostly white. One of the twentieth century's most enigmatic phenomenon had returned to the place of its publicized birth.

He ran toward the animal. "No! Not her!" he said to

himself. He had seen it before. The sight of the carcass filled him with the same dread he'd felt after losing a cow in identical fashion eighteen years before.

An angry, worried Sanchez immediately called Costilla County Sheriff Billy Maestas, who investigated the scene with Deputy Roger Benson. "No predator could have done that," Maestas agreed. "I've seen a lot of dead livestock in my time and this really concerns me." Maestas immediately called Los Animas Sheriff Lou Girodo to ask the UAD expert for assistance and found out John Torres had lost a cow in the same manner.

Sanchez also called the *Valley Courier* and spoke with reporter Ruth Heide. "I called the paper to warn everybody to keep their eyes open for lights or anything. I mean, if they could do this to my cow, maybe they could do it to humans. A lot of people disappear in the mountains around here and are never seen again!"

Girodo, a longtime law enforcement official, had puzzled over unusual animal deaths for almost twenty years. He had been interviewed in Linda Moulton Howe's book, *Alien Harvest*, and in her Emmy award–winning documentary, *A Strange Harvest*, about the UAD problem. He was convinced that the phenomenon was a true mystery, worthy of investigation.

THE YELLOW WHIRLYBIRD

During those first couple of weeks in January 1993, I was so intent on digging up as much as I could about the unexplained activity reported during the preceding three months and researching the colorful history of unexplained occurrences in the San Luis Valley that it never occurred to me that we were in the midst of an ongoing flap—something more involved and complicated than I, at the time, could ever imagine. I was right in the middle of it and never realized that I was actually becoming part of the story. I thought I was just researching an article for a small-

town newspaper, not attempting to investigate and antici-
pate where these elusive phenomena would occur.

As the process of painting an accurate picture of the
history of UAD reports and UFO sightings unfolded, it became obvious that more cows had been killed mysteriously
than the media had reported. Initially, it appeared that Saguache County, where I lived, had no documentation of
UADs. Several ranchers told me that cases had been reported in the 1970s, but I could find no reference to them.
Even the acknowledged top researcher in the field, Tom
Adams, was unaware of any official Saguache County
cases, or even reports.

It turned out that the local Saguache *Crescent* had never
published a single article pertaining to the many UADs that
probably occurred here. The editor explained, "Oh, they
happened but we only write about good news." I called
Sheriff Dan Pacheco and he claimed there were no records
of any "mutilations" or sightings in his office. He sheepishly told me that most of the previous sheriffs had not
kept accurate files. "We don't even have files on murders
that took place in Saguache County back in the sixties and
seventies."

Two days after my talk with Sheriff Pacheco, he called
to tell me he had been searching through old boxes in the
basement and found a packet of pictures. I picked them up
the next day. The packet contained twenty-four color photographs of eight cows and one horse that reportedly had
been "mutilated." Only two of the photographs had any
writing on the back explaining who owned the animal and
when the report was filed. But now I had proof in my hand
that Saguache County had experienced reports of unusual
animal deaths.

The photos haunted me. What could have done this to
these poor animals? The horse appeared to have been cut
with a laser. A strange tarlike substance ringed the incision
areas. The rear end appeared burned off and it looked like
the animal had been lying there for days before the photo
was taken, but I found out later from the owner of the once-
beautiful palomino show horse that the photo had been

taken just a few hours after the horse's death.

I figured that if the "top" expert in the field was unaware that reports had been filed in Saguache County, maybe this whole phenomenon was more pervasive than I had imagined. Official reports may not reflect the full extent of the mystery.

Looking through the photos, I noticed that one picture showed a Hereford bull. It took me a couple of days of sleuthing and phoning to establish that the bull had belonged to the Sutherland family, who had a large spread several miles west of Moffat, less than twenty miles from my house.

I spoke with Mrs. Virginia Sutherland and she said, "Yes, we had a bull killed in June 1980." She described the incident in detail over the phone and invited me out to the ranch the following day to interview her family.

I couldn't help but be impressed by the hardy ranching family. They remembered the incident with clarity. I interviewed them to cross-reference their accounts and found all accounts were identical.

The 1,700-pound bull had been in a separate pasture about five hundred yards south of the ranch house. At dusk, June 5, 1980, the family was sitting down to dinner when they heard a helicopter fly slowly over the house, heading south. They had seen utility company choppers checking the power lines three miles west of the house many times and found it unusual that a helicopter should be flying so low over the ranch, at dusk, so far from the power lines. Fifteen to twenty minutes later, they heard the sound of the chopper again but this time it seemed to be hovering close by.

They went outside to see. The chopper, "an old-fashioned, two-man, whirlybird type of helicopter, mustard yellow in color," was rising from the pasture where their bull was located. "It didn't seem to have any markings whatsoever. I thought that strange," commented Mrs. Sutherland. "I also thought it was peculiar that it had evidently landed in our field." The chopper flew back to the north, right over their house. "We all got a real good look at it.

It was one of those, like you see on *M*A*S*H* type helicopters. It was only thirty or forty feet over our heads."

The next morning, they discovered the dead bull, its penis and eyes gone, its rear end "deeply cored out," and a "one-inch plug missing from the brisket."

The Sutherlands, understandably angry at the loss of their prize seed bull, immediately called all around southern and central Colorado and northern New Mexico, trying to determine where the old-fashioned helicopter was based. They came up empty. No airport had ever seen a mustard yellow, whirlybird type helicopter and they were told that this type of craft was extremely rare and astronomically expensive to keep in the air because of its age. It had very limited range, due to its fuel consumption.

"It was the strangest thing. That (dead) bull was never touched by scavengers. Flies wouldn't land on one side of it and it took years for the carcass to melt into the field!" Virginia remembered.

I thanked them for their time and a graciously loaned second photo of the bull. I promised I would give them a call if I unearthed anything that might shed some light on the untimely demise of their animal. I would make that call the very next day!

The following morning as I sat over a cup of coffee in our dining room, reviewing the Sutherland interview notes, I heard the faint sound of a helicopter coming down the Sangre de Cristo Range from the north. I glanced out the window to see a mustard yellow, old-fashioned, "like you see on *M*A*S*H* type" helicopter! As it approached our house less than two hundred feet above the ground, it wheeled sideways and I saw the glint of what may have been a camera lens pointing out the passenger's side. Isadora, her eight-year-old daughter Brisa, and several neighbors also saw the chopper. I was floored that, almost thirteen years after the fact, the antique helicopter had returned, flying over the house of the investigator—me. I wondered what anyone would want with footage of my flabbergasted open-mouthed face in the dining room window. I had been so startled, I forgot to grab my camera.

RULE #4
Always be ready for anything, anytime. Look for coincidences when investigating claims of the unusual. Often, there may be a synchronistic element at work.

I remember commenting on the phone to Paris, Texas, researcher, Tom Adams, during that last week in January 1993, "It just can't get any weirder than this!" He quickly assured me that it could.

Y'AIN'T GONNA PRINT MA NAME, ARE YA?

My first *Crestone Eagle* article hit the newsstands February 1, 1993. *Eagle* publisher, Kizzen Dennett (usually claiming space limitations in her monthly paper against running extended articles) dedicated an entire page to the unusual events of the previous two months. This was the first of twenty *Eagle* articles over the course of the next three years in which I attempted to fully cover the San Luis Valley reports of unexplained activity.

Baca area residents, upon reading the first article, expressed either support or skepticism to me and each other about my investigation. It appeared to immediately polarize readers into two categories, that of either scoffers or knowing believers. There were only a few who seemed quite indifferent. I noticed a subtle current of unease in several people who talked with me concerning the implications of what I'd written, mainly about the never-stated but inferred alien involvement in the cattle death phenomenon. I realized during these conversations that it was imperative to maintain as objective a view on what I was reporting as possible. I was treading on volatile terrain and it was obvious that I needed to choose my steps and words carefully.

RULE #5
It is impossible to be too objective when investigating claims of the unusual.

The remainder of the valley at this point was largely unaware that anything peculiar was going on due to the absence of any reports to local law enforcement and the media concerning UADs and UFOs. The initial Sanchez cattle death story passed like a whisper and no follow-up story was published by the *Valley Courier*.

My first *Eagle* article did, however, have the effect of making folks around Saguache County more aware of the night sky. It encouraged area residents to keep their eyes open and report any anomalous objects to me or to the *Eagle*.

Much to my surprise, reports immediately came out of the woodwork. Presently, during sighting periods, I've received as many as four calls per day from witnesses. Many are from complete strangers who hear about me through my articles or through friends. They describe their sightings in great detail, offering names and phone numbers of additional witnesses and they always ask if anyone else has reported what they claimed to have seen.

Since the mid 1970s there hasn't been a local paper or investigator encouraging valley residents to call and report these mysterious events. As a direct result of my public request for any witnesses of unusual events to call, residents with sighting experiences now have someone locally with whom they can talk about their experiences.

During the first week of February 1993 a rancher called me and described three years of unidentified light activity on his remote Saguache County ranch. After over an hour of descriptions, dates, and observations pertaining to unknown occurrences in his area, he asked me just as we were ending our conversation, "Ya ain't gonna print ma name, are ya?" The understandable reluctance of many witnesses to "go on the record" suggested to me that this would be a major factor in the creation of confusion and mystery around these inexplicable events. The anonymity factor would be a major obstacle with which I would have to contend.

I realized that one proper course of action would be to set up a network of vigilant skywatchers around the valley.

Multiple pairs of eyes around an entire region would undoubtedly observe more than my single pair of eyes, no matter how much time I spent surveying the sky. As the reports continued, I naturally found myself spending increasing amounts of time outdoors at night.

It became apparent to me that I needed to refamiliarize myself with the night sky. As a child, I was fascinated with the heavens. I had studied star maps and learned the basics of astronomy but later, after living in midtown Manhattan for so many years, with its gross air and light pollution, I lost the opportunity to view an uncluttered sky. Fortunately, Isadora had a Planesphere star map that became instrumental in reacquainting me with the glorious high-altitude night sky.

The telltale vapor trails of mundane commercial jet traffic gave me an accurate map of the various commercial flight routes in constant use over the valley. I noticed at once that these pathways were divided into north-south/south-north, east-west/west-east, with a few planes flying diagonally. Commercial flights are at predictable altitudes and speeds over defined lanes of travel. I acquired pilot maps for the Denver and Albuquerque flight control areas.

MILITARY OPERATIONS AREA

An informative brochure from Open Space Alliance—Huerfano Valley Citizen's Alliance states:

Huerfano County (and the northeast side of the SLV) has already served as an aerial playground for the military since the late 1970s, when the La Veta Military Operations Area (MOA) was approved. According to Air National Guard figures, the current utilization of the La Veta MOA is 2,929 sorties, or individual jet missions, per year.

What the Air Force and National Guard have in mind for Huerfano, Custer, Saguache, and Alamosa counties is to create a permanent "simulated war zone" in the skies above our region. Under the new Colorado Airspace Initiative (CAI), not only will the number of sorties be increased to at least 3,120 per year, but the majority of the missions will be authorized to fly as low as one hundred feet above the ground. The National Guard's rationalization for the proposed change is that modern warfare techniques require pilots to be skilled in low-altitude, radar-evasive techniques. (The Guard also plans to release ten thousand flares per year on these maneuvers.)

Another little-known provision is Project Shining Mountain, in which, it is alleged, the government is flying prototype and secret military aircraft around the SLV region. The press was never told about this secret provision. The brochure continues:

If the National Guard's proposed plan is allowed to be implemented, the way of life that we have all worked so hard to create and sustain will be destroyed. We can either move elsewhere or spend the remainder of our days in the living nightmare of a simulated war zone.

A nightmare indeed! In 1989, I had managed to land a job on a construction crew and found myself working thirty feet above the ground on a two-by-twelve plank, painting the peak of the new two-story house from the top of a three-stage construction scaffolding. I had moved here only two months earlier and was in awe of the surroundings. A ripping sound and *whoosh*, an F-16 fighter hurtled past less than forty feet from me! I saw the pilot look back at me in that fraction of a second before I dove, belly-flopping to the plank. The sound wave hit with an ear-shattering explosion, rattling the entire scaffolding.

I jumped up, cursing the hotshot fly-boy, but the SOB returned eight minutes later for another pass! It was episodes like this, and jets buzzing the Moffat school, that sparked many here to support the Open Space Alliance's efforts to stop the harassment.

Could there be a parallel between the ebbing and flowing of military planes in the La Veta MOA and reports of unexplained aerial activity on the periphery of this low-level training area on the eastern side of the valley? If so, could this military usage also explain sightings on the western side of the valley, fifty miles from the edge of the MOA?

In January and February 1993, during my initial enthusiasm for investigating witnesses' claims of UFO sightings in the valley, my natural inclination was to jump toward the fantastic. Several pointed comments by area skeptics, whom I respected, helped temper this response. Without this skepticism, it was apparent that I could very easily have fallen into a trap, a trap of thinking that, if a witness thought it sounded, looked, and/or felt unusual, it must have been unusual.

> **RULE #6**
> **Always assume there is a mundane explanation until proven extraordinary.**

CONTACT

Some of my first inquiries were made to local sheriffs and deputies. On February 12, 1993, I spoke with Saguache County Deputy Lynn Bogle. I asked him if the sheriff's office had fielded any recent "mutilation" reports. He told me no, but that he had been on a ranch just north of Center in May 1978 when they found a "mutilated" three-year-old cow. "The rear end was gone, the eyes were gone, there was no blood, and the heart was gone!" He thought it was the military. "Our government does a lot of things they don't want us to know about."

Deputy Bogle told me that a highly visible clear-cut area on the western slopes of the Blanca Massif was supposed to be used as an artillery range but that the locals had stopped it. He had also heard of an Aryan base near Mosca Pass. His fascinating accounts included a summer-long chase of "turbo Hughes and Bell choppers" in 1991, seen in the Bonanza and Hayden Pass areas. Choppers were reported regularly and sheriff's deputies raced around in an attempt to find out where they were going. "We saw them May to frost. The Denver Center FAA (who monitor SLV airspace) had no radar reports." (Eighteen thousand feet is the lowest ceiling for radar detection.)

Then the former marine surprised me with an interesting story from his teens. "Years ago in the sixties, my parents would take summer trips with the family up to the Platoro Reservoir. There was an old miner, a hermit who lived in the Summitville area year-round. He was like the caretaker; he'd take the tourists on informal tours, that sort of thing. He told us several times that during the late fall and winter, the aliens visited him. They would land right outside. He said he even talked with them, said they were just like you and me!"

"When was that, do you remember what year?" I inquired.

"The early to mid sixties. One time we went up and he told us the military had run the aliens off. He said helicopters landed and some guy told him never to talk to them again." I asked Bogle what had happened to the old miner. He had died a few years before and Bogle couldn't remember his name, though he thought it was maybe Carter. I made a note to call around to try and find out more about this colorful character.

Bogle then mentioned a man named Glenn Anderson. I remembered some vague stories I had heard already about the man. He attracted a group of young people in the late 1960s and "channeled" all kinds of interesting information. According to Bogle, "Frank Scott has tapes and transcripts." Scott was a local schoolteacher, so I called him about the transcripts and tapes.

Frank Scott didn't have them anymore but told me some

interesting things Anderson had said. "He told us, 'The whole universe is interested in us,' and that 'there would be a lot of ET activity.' " Scott told me of other friends' experiences, including a light from high up on Blanca chasing a man in his car, reminiscent of Brendan and Bill's experience. Scott also mentioned Bigfoot sightings north of Mosca Pass near the Marble Canyon–Marble Mine area.

He eventually asked me if I'd like to visit the Alamosa aereolite meteor crater, on the Baca Ranch, with his class the following week. You bet I did. The public is usually denied access to the ranch. The crater was unmistakable and I imagined those two magnetic masses deep in the sand below us. The kids dragged magnets on strings and collected impressive amounts of iron from the sand in the stony meteor site.

A Moffat, Colorado, cowboy named Mike, a descendent of nineteenth-century naturalist John Muir, stopped by our house unexpectedly one afternoon the third week of February. He had sold a mare to Isadora a year earlier and occasionally dropped by to say hello. We spent some time with small talk but I sensed that he wanted to tell me something. Finally, after a cup of coffee, he nonchalantly told us of a peculiar experience he claimed he'd had several days before.

FEBRUARY 14, 1993, 9:30 PM, NORTH CRESTONE CAMPGROUND ENTRANCE:

Mike had been parked at the closed gate of the North Crestone Campground, two miles from Crestone. The former air force officer enjoyed driving up to the campground to view the valley from an impressive vantage point.

He parked at the closed gate and prepared to leave his car to walk the one hundred yards to the overlook. Without warning, his "headlights turned on by themselves" and then off. Before the surprised cowboy could react, a beam of intense light from overhead lit up his car. Smaller lights began sequencing in tight spots on the ground around the car and "something was trying to get me out of the car!" He struggled with all his strength to resist the pull. The lights clicked off. He looked up but saw nothing. The entire episode only lasted four or five seconds and the mystified cowboy never heard a sound. He drove slowly down the hill toward town trying to spot whatever had just "almost given me a heart attack."

He told me, "I've seen some pretty strange lights before but nothing like that." I asked as many questions as I could think of, while taking notes of his experiences. I finished my questioning and before he left he promised he'd let me know if he saw or experienced anything else out of the ordinary.

Bright white lights were seen by four Crestone residents descending through the clouds and "zipping up the (Sangre) Range" on the following two nights. They were described as oval-shaped and silent. The tar baby got stickier.

FEBRUARY 23, 1993, 8:30 AM, THE BACA:

Isadora and I were enjoying the bright cheery morning over a cup of coffee when Brisa bounded down the stairs. I was a little surprised, since it usually took her a while to wake up. She seemed excited.

"I had a really neat dream last night," she announced.

"What did you dream about?" her mother asked.

"There were these little men and they had a ship right outside. They came into my room play to with me. They were really cute! They had these funny hands that sort of looked like cactus." (She was referring to the prickly-pear cactus that dot the landscape around here.) Something about her matter-of-fact demeanor made me sit up and pay attention.

"So what happened?" I asked.

"I don't remember but I know I had fun!"

Paddle-shaped hands? Her dream was intriguing. "Brisa, could you draw me a picture of the little men and their ship?" I asked.

"Sure." I gave her a convenient manila envelope and a pen and set her up at the dining room table. She drew a hamburger-shaped ship and several tiny figures with strange little Ping-Pong-paddle–shaped hands with little spikes protruding like fingers. Isadora and I asked several more questions but didn't make a big deal or put too much emphasis on her dream.

That afternoon when I picked up our mail at the post office, there was a sizable package from Tom Adams in Paris, Texas. He already had sent along several invaluable sets of articles, reports, and accounts of the mysterious from the San Luis Valley, and I had been eagerly awaiting this next installment. Since I was catching up to speed on SLV history, I appreciated his packages more than anyone else's.

I opened the thickly stuffed envelope and started perusing the various articles and reports from a variety of sources Adams had tapped. Here was a guy in Texas sending me volumes of documented information on the place where I live.

One thirteen-page account caught my attention, entitled, "Another Unidentified Flying Object Story." In this report, a man named Bud Hooper recalls seeing two humanlike creatures with three-inch disks for hands.

Three-inch disks for hands? Here was another one of those absolutely bizarre examples of synchronicity. Brisa had gone into great detail describing "little men with cactus-shaped hands," and here I was, less than an hour later, reading an account from over thirty-five years before, describing beings with three-inch curved discs for hands. I showed Bud Hooper's account to Isadora and we both tingled at the uncanny timing of its arrival.

Adams's latest package of information contained other accounts from the 1950s in the SLV. In November 1956, then Alamosa resident John DeHerrera and his brother were delivering newspapers eastbound on State Highway 160. As the DeHerrera brothers approached town, a sudden glint of light caught their eyes.

"We observed a strange object ahead on the left side of

the highway. This object came toward us, moving slowly, approximately forty miles per hour and about five feet above the ground. . . . As the object turned and headed skyward, a long, colorful flame shot out the back. Then it turned and crossed the highway directly overhead, accelerated rapidly, and vanished in the distance.''

This daytime encounter, observed under ideal conditions, proved to be a pivotal one in John DeHerrera's life. So impressed with the unusual experience and the unmistakable reality of the object, he went on to become an eminent UFO researcher. He currently lives in southern California.

THE SILVER DERBY

During the first part of January 1993, as I chased leads and researched accounts of the many valley UFO sightings, I quickly noticed that a vast majority of these reports were of anomalous lights at night. There had been some daytime sightings of craft (or objects) but no documented cases from the last several years. Then I discovered the following accounts.

In April 1992, a Monte Vista emergency medical technician and mother of three had seen a ''bell-shaped object as big as a school bus'' hovering over her neighbor's house in the late afternoon. ''It was unbelievable! I've seen weird lights at night around here, but this was unmistakable. It looked like a big hat.'' She quickly called her neighbor who also saw the object out her kitchen window. ''I don't want to talk about it,'' the neighbor told me after I obtained her phone number from the E.M.T. ''My kids say 'it chased them' when they went outside to look at it, and I'd rather not talk about it.''

FEBRUARY 24, 1993, 10:30 AM, HIGHWAY 17, BETWEEN THE TOWNS OF MOSCA AND HOOPER:

A thirty-seven-year-old baker, Judy DeBon, and her artist mother were driving south toward Alamosa on this cold

February morning to do some shopping. As they approached Mosca, they noted a flash above them and to the east. A silent bell-shaped object, the color of brushed aluminum, flew over their car, headed toward the Blanca Massif. It was clear and still that day and they "got a real good look at it."

"My mother wouldn't let me stop to watch it," Judy told me later that afternoon. "My mother was pretty scared and thought it wasn't a good idea to stop. I'm sure the people in the car behind us saw it because they did stop. It flew over us about one hundred feet above the road. Since I was driving, I couldn't watch where it went but it was heading toward Blanca."

This was not the first time Judy and her mother had seen a "bell-shaped object." She had related this previous sighting a couple of weeks after it happened, before giving the above description. On December 21, 1992, at 2:40 P.M., they were driving north from Alamosa, again on Highway 17, between Hooper and Moffat, when they observed "the same object" hovering against the mountains. "We drove along and watched it for a couple of minutes. It was in the vale over by San Isabelle Creek. I couldn't believe how fast it shot to the north when it disappeared!"

Strange lights seen at night are one thing but close-proximity daylight sightings are pretty convincing. Because of an unexplained experience that I and others witnessed the previous September 17, 1992, at 1:30 P.M., I was in no position to argue with their stories.

Isadora was driving us southward on Highway 69, seven miles north of Gardner. I was riding in the front passenger seat and Brisa had the backseat to herself. To our right, the backside of the Blanca Massif and the Sangres loomed twenty miles away to the west across the Wet Mountain Valley. I was watching a series of steep piñon-covered hills to our left when something silver flashed between two of these low hills. "What was that?" I asked Isadora.

"It looked like a model plane," she guessed. The craft emerged from behind the hill to our left and zipped directly across the windshield from left to right. It was about seventy to eighty feet off the ground and between one hundred and one-hundred-fifty yards away.

"That's no model plane!" I exclaimed.

Isadora now suggested it might be some sort of remote-piloted drone. We were right in the middle of the La Veta low-level MOA and the craft we were watching certainly did look military. However, I could have sworn I saw a pilot. I grabbed my binoculars and watched it speed across the valley toward Medano Pass.

The craft appeared to be about twelve feet long with tiny, stubby wings and I thought I might have seen a small clear cupola and a dark headrest and helmet. I'm not sure of this but that was my initial impression. That thing was really scooting along. In a matter of seconds, it had traveled far enough across the valley for me to lose sight of it against the mountain background.

I thought it strange the way it appeared to move through the sky. It seemed to be pulled rather than propelled, as if it was on a string and was being quickly reeled in. I rolled my window down but didn't hear anything over the rumble of the Buick's engine.

Since our sighting of the miniature craft, I have seen pictures of Remote Piloted Vehicles (RPVs) that our government publicly acknowledges using but the craft we saw didn't remotely resemble any of them. I thought at the time that there was something weird about the craft but who knows what the military is secretly flying around the country's Military Operations Areas (MOAs).

My second *Crestone Eagle* article was released the first week of March 1993. Kizzen again devoted an entire page to my investigation and research. The article attempted to give a quick overview of many of the more celebrated San Luis Valley cases that had been reported through the years. Even with a full page, I only had a fraction of the space needed to scratch the surface of my findings.

After two solid months of investigative work, to be truthful, I was more confused than ever. The more data I accumulated concerning the history of reported—and unreported—unexplained activity in this mysterious valley, the more jumbled the overall picture appeared. There seemed to be a complex, multilayered scenario at work. Many of these events were filled with inconsistencies and some of the information made no sense at all. It was obvious that the sheer variety, number, and scope of these events was not fully known, even to knowledgeable local residents, local law enforcement, and outside investigators.

Then there were prehistoric traditions, even murkier than the historic record, that may provide us with some pointed insight into the nature of this remote area of the continent. I could find very little published information concerning these indigenous traditions, although Baca residents shared portions of these belief systems. I doubled my efforts to corroborate what some locals already had accepted as ''fact.''

ROCK CRYSTAL KIDS

In familiarizing myself with the valley and its traditions, I can not overlook the Native Americans, many of whom view the valley and its mountains with much reverence. The Crestone-Navajo custodian of Sisnaajini (or the Black Sash Medicine Belt Mountains), told me that the portion of the Sangre de Cristo Range that extends from the Blanca Massif north to Crestone plays an important role in the mythic tradition of many southwestern, Great Basin, and Plains Indian traditions. The Dine, or Navajo tradition, attaches particular significance to the valley in its creation myth. The following was excerpted from Peter Gold's 1990 book, *The Circle of the Spirit*:

> Let's first consider the most important of the four sacred mountains, Blanca Peak (Sisnaajini), or East Mountain. East Mountain is a distinctive, snow-capped, pine- and fir-clothed peak in the Southern Rockies of Colorado. It is considered the ''leader

mountain," because it stands as the holy mountain of the east, the place of beginnings, the dawn. It is associated with the guiding light of the day and the qualities that dawn universally signifies.

As with all significant Navajo mountains, East Mountain was created and fastened firmly to the earth by the first people to emerge into the fifth world . . . by a bolt of lightning—a "thunderbolt"—whose intense light and quality of energy is most appropriate to that of the dawn. Existing within the four sacred mountains are their indwelling forms. The large size of the indwelling divinities of East Mountain—Rock Crystal Boy and Rock Crystal Girl—indicates their relative importance. . . . Their bodies are constituted of rock crystal. This is only natural, since the mind is considered clear as crystal, and east is the direction of "thought itself. . . ."

Some indigenous peoples have a sacred tradition relating to the location of the the Sipapu, the place of emergence into the current world through a hole in the San Luis Valley. The exact location of the place of emergence may never be known but Dollar Lake and Head Lake are considered to be two of several possibilities.

PATTERNS OF DISSEMINATION— THE CREATION OF MYTHOS

After a scant two months collecting everything I could find concerning the events allegedly happening here, I found myself being recognized as some sort of "expert" on the obscure aspects of SLV history. This still makes me laugh. I feel I'm simply an interested resident taking it upon myself to document the many strange events and historical traditions. I still tell people who refer to me in this manner, "Well . . . if how confused you are about these events is relative to your level of expertise, I'm really confused, so I guess I'm a really an expert."

One thing was becoming certain. It seemed likely that a vast majority of SLV residents have some knowledge about strange goings-on, but most have no idea that this continuous activity is being reported, nor do they realize the full extent of the area's mythic tradition and the history of such goings-on. Maybe it didn't seem particularly strange or unusual to the locals on the surface—but just an odd occasional part of their everyday reality.

I naturally began to ponder the myriad patterns of response and subsequent interpretation, spin, or simple communication of these alleged events to others by the eyewitnesses. I theorized that the very realization, or understanding, and then the belief that "something was going on by the experiencers" might be an influence to others who hadn't shared their experience.

Several important questions came to mind concerning the process of communicating or disseminating a particular perception of unusual occurrences. How accurate is this process? Are the disseminating groups, either inadvertently or by design, altering third-, fourth-, fifth-hand accounts? Do they simply report the facts, or do they try to whitewash and hide them? Do they get all the facts straight, or just a portion of them? Does the media, for example, only concentrate on certain aspects of the phenomena but downplay others? I even began to wonder if the symbolic and emotional effect of the wording, "mutilation" for instance, has any impact on our culture's perception of the actual phenomenon. I found myself having to question everything, and believing nothing.

One thing was, and still is, firmly etched in my mind. Even if the events that had allegedly occurred, and still occur, were merely misinterpreted mundane phenomena, the very fact that a belief system existed, possibly for thousands of years, might add an extraordinary explanation for these events. It was worth studying.

In our age of suspicion, certain inevitable questions were

bound to arise. Are there attempts by government, law enforcement, or even publishers, to whitewash and/or obscure these perplexing events? There was just too much unexplained activity for the whole scenario to be simply due to mass hysteria, sensationalism, or wishful thinking. And yet, I was constantly reminded that for the most part, locals apparently did not know the full scope of our mysterious phenomena, past and present.

Because the whole picture appears so convoluted and complex, I began to suspect that multiple groups, or players, were behind it. If this was so, how many subtle or perhaps even blatant agendas were at work? Regardless of the implications of various "players with an agenda," I sensed that something even larger lurked behind this complex scenario, possibly something ancient and extremely elusive. I realized I had to remain open to the question, Could a separate scenario exist alongside all the various mundane and even possibly sinister agendas?

The reports themselves seemed to be subjugated by the perceptions of human culture, the inevitable creation of mythos, or folklore. Like the party game "Telephone," I had a hunch that even the truth behind the appearance of these unusual experiences was somehow, through dissemination, blurred, as accurate details of the experiences become altered with the telling and retelling of "the stories." I wondered, How can the truth behind the nature of unexplained events be found, when even the appearance of the events may be misleading? The probability that the phenomena may not reflect its true nature, possibly intentionally, is a major, almost insurmountable obstacle to anyone investigating these events.

This intuitive heaven can be a rational hell.

RULE #7
Appearances can be deceiving. There is always a possibility of more happening than meets the eye.

This realization was pretty overwhelming and I wondered at the time if, as someone investigating these phenomena, I could ever hope to identify the "players," let alone discover the essential core of facts behind these events. By now, however, any faint hope of this was firmly dashed from my realistic self. I even began to wonder if it was possible for witnesses of bizarre events in the San Luis Valley, and elsewhere for that matter, to actually differentiate effectively between reality and imagination!

Interviewing multiple witnesses of a single event, I noted subtle personal shading and slight differences of impression from one witness to the next. Most of the individuals' general impressions of a shared event were quite similar in most cases, but there was always a slight variation or, perhaps, bias. Knowing a little bit about chaos theory and the significance of even the most minute casual variations at the beginning of any unfolding sequence of events, I wondered if these slight variations in perception of an extraordinary experience may be incredibly magnified at the other end of the dissemination process, say, in a newspaper article on the floor of the proverbial chaos-theory train in Paris, or on that iceberg in the Arctic.

Yes, even more questions came to mind. Could the simple act of experiencing something new and phenomenal be altered, or shaded, by the witness's preconceived ideas concerning the nature of the never-before-experienced phenomenon? In other words, could the observer's previous knowledge of others' perceptions affect their personal, first-time perception of a hypothetically "true" phenomenal experience?

Pondering this aspect of mythologic speculation is pretty heady stuff. It probably makes some UFO-phenomenologist's philosophic head hurt. Even though I knew I was on a seemingly impossible quest, I was, and still am, intrigued about these many questions concerning the very nature of human perception. I began to suspect that this process of publicizing current and past events held some sort of key pertaining to possible first and second level players and agendas.

I didn't realize how much of an integral factor I myself was becoming in the actual dissemination process concerning these SLV mysteries. Initially, I thought I was simply reporting unexplained events that were happening virtually in my front yard for the benefit of interested Crestone-Baca and Saguache County residents. Was I wrong! Not only was I right in the middle of these occurrences, but by publicizing these unexplained events and mythic traditions, I became an influential factor in the formulation process behind some people's perception of UADs, UFOs, and the other strange, unexplained phenomena that occur here. I began to realize that I might even be contributing to the creation of "mythos." Even though at this point in time I hadn't fully realized the ramifications of my potential role in this process, I remembered the need to be extremely careful, to keep my facts straight and I tried to not add a "spin" to these reported events. I began to choose my spoken and written words very carefully.

RULE #8
If you publicize claims of the unusual, choose your words wisely, for your "spin" may have tremendous influence.

A glimmering glow called truth seemed to emanate just below the distant horizon but no matter how hard I tried, no matter how impressive my steps, I hardly seemed to get any closer. Like chasing a rainbow that skirts away playfully, I plodded forward while countless questions with questionable answers loomed like roadblocks before me. I thank God that I'm tenacious for, if I weren't, I would have given up this quixotic quest long ago.

PART TWO

"Mystery creates wonder, and wonder is the basis for man's desire to understand. Who knows what mysteries will be solved in our lifetime, and what new riddles will become the challenge of the new generations?"

—John Keel, *Why UFOs?*

SNIPPY THE HORSE

By far the most celebrated incident to ever come out of the San Luis Valley was the Snippy the horse controversy. The Snippy case is considered to be the first publicized UAD case, and has become the thing of legend. Peripheral to the case were the dozens of UFO sightings that occurred during that eventful fall and the entire next year, which inexorably linked the mysterious death with UFOs. This link, whether accurate or not, has existed ever since.

Texas researcher Tom Adams graciously sent me many *Valley Courier* articles he had saved reporting the Snippy case, and Wyoming UFO researcher Tom Rouse added dozens of additional articles from the *Denver Post, Rocky Mountain News*, and *Valley Courier*. The colorful cast of characters were perfect media fodder, and the press had a field day with the story. I decided I needed to examine not only the alleged events but the process of dissemination that unfolded that fall of 1967 to see if there were any parallels to the activity our area is currently experiencing.

First a little history and some background:

The Urraca pioneers settled the western slope of the Blanca Massif in the late 1870s and one of those hardy families was the Kings, who owned a two-thousand-acre cattle ranch that extended from the foot of the mountains out onto the valley floor. The upper ranch had a small cabin on the original homestead and the main ranch house was located five miles away in the valley, ten miles southeast of the Great Sand Dunes. A windswept area, the King Ranch sat on some of the earliest meadows visited by man in North America.

The Kings were a hard-working cattle family, putting in long hours sunup to sundown in one of the valley's most picturesque areas. Eighty-five-year-old widow Agnes King was the King family matriarch and she lived with her two sons, Harry and Ben, and one of her two daughters named Nellie. Ben King was a self-styled mountain man who could identify every animal and plant in the San Luis Valley and name every creek that flowed down the western slope of the Sangres. Harry was the King Ranch boss, running cattle and tending to the ranch's daily affairs. Nellie, married to Iowa native Berle Lewis, lived with her husband in the cabin on the upper ranch. The Kings and Lewises were truly salt-of-the-earth ranchers with a documented family history of witnessing unusual celestial events, such as the sighting by C. M. King, Agnes's now deceased husband, of the Alamosa Aereolite in the fall of 1898 on the Baca Ranch.

This much was previously known about the demise of the mare named Lady, since dubbed by the press Snippy the horse. It was a blustery morning, September 8, 1967, and Harry noticed that only two of their three horses were outside waiting for grain and water. Thinking this unusual, he headed out into the morning glow to feed them. He immediately sensed something was wrong. Lady, Nellie's filly, was nowhere to be found.

After waiting until the following morning for her to show up, Harry went searching for the missing horse. After an hour, he spotted something lying in a meadow a quarter mile north of the main ranch house that raised the hair on his neck. Lady's corpse was missing all the tissue from her shoulders to the tip of her nose, the exposed bones glistening, bleached white, like they had "been in the sun for thirty years."

The animal lay on its left side, facing east in a damp meadow. It had rained several days before and the ground was still soft and muddy in places. Harry determined that the three horses had been running full speed and Lady had been "cut from the herd" then veered away from the other two, who continued on toward the house. Lady's tracks continued for several hundred yards, by King's estimate, where they inexplicably stopped in full gallop.

I was surprised to learn that the "official" story diverges at this point into two distinct versions. Version one is supported by several newspaper articles, Coral Lorenzen's *Fate* magazine article, and Berle Lewis's account. It says the carcass was found over one hundred feet farther along the meadow. Version two, supported by several articles and Don Richmond's original Aerial Phenomenon Research Organization's (APRO) investigation, stated that the tracks went in several tight circles, like something was circling around the horse, and that the corpse was found only twenty feet away from Lady's circling tracks.

A careful examination of the area a week later, September 16, 1967, by Nellie, Harry, Berle, and friends found what appeared to be four "burned areas" in the ground at four, nine, thirteen, and twenty-one feet away from the carcass to the northwest. Like an upside-down question mark, eight burned areas in the ground were found to the southeast ranging forty to fifty feet from the body. Five eighteen-inch-wide, eight-inch-deep "giant horse tracks" were found in the Chico bushes near the body.

A University of Colorado investigation was included in the now famous "Condon Report," undertaken for the air force's Project Blue Book in October 1967. It claimed the burn areas were probably a black fungus called black alkali that is found in highly alkaline areas such as the San Luis Valley and that the "giant horse tracks" were more than likely old horse tracks made in the mud, which had hardened.

Nellie called Alamosa County Sheriff Ben Phillips to report the strange demise of her three-year-old horse. Phillips branded the horse's death a "lightning strike" and didn't bother to drive out to the scene to investigate. He later admitted that it was odd that the horse had no evidence of burn marks usually associated with a lightning strike.

Nellie, however, was convinced that something highly irregular had happened to her horse. She was aware of the several UFO sightings in the weeks prior to her horse's demise and she and Berle, and their close friends, had experienced sightings that previous spring. She was convinced there was a connection.

On September 23, 1967, two weeks after the horse was discovered, Nellie was aided by U.S. Forest Service employee Duane Martin. Martin borrowed a Geiger counter from a local civil-defense unit and checked the area for increased levels of radiation. He received, in his determination, heightened radiation readings near the flattened Chico bushes and burn marks. The readings decreased as he approached the carcass. Increased levels of radiation were also detected on Berle's boots.

Later, questions were raised about Martin's proficiency with the Geiger counter and he admitted that he had operated the equipment in an indoor training session but never in the field. I have never found reference, in any of the numerous articles about the Snippy incident, to Martin taking any control readings at the site.

(I have personally taken radiation readings in the San Luis Valley and found the increased levels of ultraviolet radiation at this altitude make a Geiger counter "click" on average of once every two or three seconds—considerably more than is observed at sea level. Without a control reading, determining true radiation levels is impossible.)

The Lewises were initially reluctant to go public with the story. Inevitably, during the first three weeks after discovery, word spread locally about the truly mysterious and unusual animal death. Curious locals began showing up at the site and, initially, Harry tried to confine the visitors to a small area near the body to maintain the integrity of the scene.

Nellie was positive the strange lights and objects she and others had seen, and reported, were involved. At the end of the first week of October, Nellie's longtime friend Pearl Mellon Nicholas, society editor for the *Valley Courier*, let the strange death of the horse out of the barn.

During the next four weeks, the Snippy the horse story emerged from the local to the regional, national, and international newspaper press. A curious element of the modern UFOlogical mythos was created (or miscreated) as the facts twisted subtly in the wind of dissemination. The Snippy case and the San Luis Valley's apparent corresponding UFO activity provided a "guilt by association" scenario which led to the inexorable linking of UADs with UFOs that October 1967. As a result of this questionable process of dissemination, this link has endured ever since. The press, by its very nature, can be careless. Even Coral Lorenzen of the well-respected Aerial Phenomenon Research Organization (APRO) got several important facts mixed up in her May 1968 *Fate* article.

Crucial elements like the horse's gender and name got mixed up, jumbled, and turned around. I wondered how basic facts could become so screwed up. The process of discerning reality from any subtle form of chaos is daunting. I had to continually check and cross-check each article against the others. As the discrepancies piled up, I wondered if anyone could weed out the misinformation in any controversy.

The facts were so irregular, I hypothesized that maybe they were altered by design. It appeared to me that a blatant process of creating misinformation may have been at work that October, which continues today, twenty-eight years later. Snippy, whether we like it or not, is now a part of our cultural mythos and I wondered if the case could provide us with an insight into this process. Maybe strange events that occur through time, and subsequently become a part of the mythic tradition, are somehow sparked by a veil of unconscious cultural uncertainty. A particular process of mythologic creation could become more dramatic with the intentional, or inadvertent, addition of disinformation.

I wanted to verify as many facts as I could about the incident. Newspaper accounts proved unreliable but the primary data, i.e., interviews with the principles, Nellie and

Berle; and notes by the original investigator, Don Richmond and Nellie's friend, *Valley Courier* editor Pearl Nicholas might fill in the blanks. By comparing the primary data against the press accounts, I hoped to reveal the true story behind the demise of Snippy the horse.

RULE #9
Media coverage of the unusual, because of its sensational nature, is often inaccurate and cannot be accepted as totally accurate by the investigator.

FLYING SAUCERS KILLED MY HORSE

On October 18, 1967, East Texas State University sociology teacher Ross Henderson and student Lonnie Furbay conducted a phone interview with Nellie Lewis, five weeks after the discovery of Snippy. Here are some pertinent excerpts.

After some initial confusion as to who was calling, Furbay asked Nellie, "The horse that was involved in the incident is named Snippy, is that correct?"

"That is correct," she replied. (This wasn't correct, according to Berle, as we will see later.)

Furbay asked Nellie to describe the scene.

"We were in the mountains. We came by the ranch on September 10 and my mother told us about it and we went out and it was just as my brother described it. All the meat was gone from the neck and head. The bones were white, as if it had been sun bleached a long time. There was no muscle, no meat, no ears, no mane, not one hair of the mane stuck in the mud, and this was a real muddy meadow. There were no tracks except my brother's and he'd sunk down two to two and a half inches in the mud. He had been stuck about a block from the horse and he said it took him two hours to get out. And his tracks still remained, even though it was suggested that there could've been tracks and they were rained out. Now, I checked with the weather bureau. There was no rain between September 7 and September 9."

Nellie described a strange smell around the corpse, "a strong medicine odor. And I have a feeling it might be embalming fluid. I've been going to try to find time to smell some. Why there would be embalming fluid, I don't know. But it was a very strong odor."

Nellie called Alamosa County Sheriff Ben Phillips.

"What was his reaction?" asked Furbay.

"I explained the condition of the horse and I said that my brother thought it was lightning but it was impossible because of the odor. There was no burn on the horse, no singed hair. The meat was just as fresh and pretty as you'd fry."

Sheriff Phillips decided the horse's death must have been caused by lightning and did not immediately pursue an investigation. Nellie then called numerous farmers, a game warden, and a health department officer, Dr. Leary, a veterinarian. "And to each one I explained the condition of the horse, and most all the farmers said they didn't believe lightning could do something like this."

"Okay. Would you describe exactly what the horse looked like as he lay on the ground," Furbay continued.

"His back body, up to his shoulders, was perfect, not a scratch or not a mark on him whatsoever. He [sic] had not struggled in the mud. He [sic] had fallen and never made a move because this is real muddy and you could have told. There was no blood whatsoever. Cuts absolutely smooth, all the way around, like you would mount a deer head, for instance, straight into the bone. And the meat was not running blood, there was no blood on the ground. And there were no tracks."

"What else was strange about the general area where Snippy was found?"

"Well, all that week, I refused to believe my husband [who said], 'Well, it has to be lightning. How could it be anything else?' So, Ernest Wellington, who died a week later, incidentally, and his wife Leona and their daughter, and a teacher from Creede, Wayne Trapouski, came out and after they looked the horse over and Ernest said, 'No, this couldn't have been lightning.'

"So, he started searching the area. He called us over, he was a block and a half to the north. And there was a bush busted down close to the ground. Most of the top of the bush was gone, and it was in an open spot all by itself, and here the ground was all riled up. Now the rest of the ground, it was rain pebbled and, you know, but this was freshly riled, and in this I found a globlike sac of substance which I didn't touch with my hands; but there was some mane stuck to this sac, and it was the color of the inside of a chicken gizzard, and tough like that. But it was shaped sort of like a chicken liver, with pyramidish points on it. I jerked this mane [hair] loose from it, and took two sticks and busted it open, and a green paste oozed out of it.''

Nellie wanted to take the sample for testing but Berle said, ''You're not putting any of the horse in the car or I'll walk home.'' He did reluctantly allow Nellie to take some of the strange black sootlike material, as long as it was placed in the trunk.

Furbay asked if Nellie had touched any of the material.

"I did touch that mane [hair] which I jerked loose. Now, there was no mane around the horse, not even stuck in the mud. And my hand started burning. It turned bright red with streaks across it, and it burned until, oh, about thirty minutes later. We got up to the cabin and I washed and washed and within an hour it had quit burning. But I knew then that something definitely had been done to the horse.''

And what became of the material?

"The NICAP [National Investigations Committee for Aerial Phenomena] team was hired by Dr. Edward Condon, who heads our government office that's financed by the air force for the investigation of flying saucers; and they hired them to come down. . . . One of the gentlemen from there did find it in the top of a bush and they took it back with them for testing.''

"I see, and have you had any other ill effects other than the burning of your hand from this piece of material?''

"No, not that I know of. The night we found the horse

I was sick all night and went to the doctor the next day for a prescription, and I hadn't been in his office for eight months, and I was dizzy and sick, and I feel it had something to do with the horse."

"Has anything, or had anything unusual happened around Alamosa before Snippy was found?"

"Well, there's saucer sightings which have been quite frequent the last six weeks. Other than that, there was another horse found dead three miles southeast of my horse Snippy. It was a good pinto stud and it belonged to Walter Alsbaugh, who takes rodeo stock around, and it had a big gash on its head about four inches in diameter; but what they decided about it, I don't know."

"According to a newspaper article, ma'am, we also understand your husband made the statement that you-all see something almost every night, or now and then. Is this true?"

"I haven't looked for ten days because I don't want to see anything. But there are a number of my friends and relatives and people here in town that have been out looking since the incident and a number of them have seen things. There's called a 'flap' going on here now. They're just getting all kinds of sightings, and it certainly isn't us. I mean, many highly respected people are seeing them and they know they exist.

"But maybe our government knows what this is, you see, and they came in to discredit this and call us liars because they do know what it is. I don't know the answer but I'm highly disgusted and I will take a lie detector test, and so will my husband, on the condition of the horse, and they ignore it. I said, 'There was no blood on him.' He said, 'Oh, your untrained eye didn't see it.' This was a rain-soaked meadow. People squished down three inches, at the time, walking in it. And there was no stain there, or anything, sir."

"Have any pictures been taken of these UFOs?"

"There was one on the front page of the *Pueblo Chieftain* today and it's taken of this ship or vehicle or whatever, airborne right near the horse's body, and it was taken last

Friday night. I don't know the boys. They go to college. But the story and the pictures are in the *Pueblo Chieftain* today. Mark Conrad, who has a program in Colorado Springs, was here. He was making some television pictures, and an object that's littler than a Piper Cub and has little short stubby wings dived right over the top of the ground by him. Now, this is the same thing that has been seen here in the daytime by quite a number of people. [Including me, twenty-six years later!] And as yet, we haven't found out what it is but we assume it's a jet, something of our government's, but we don't know what it is."

It took air force investigators three weeks to respond to these unusual reports. Nellie recalled another incident which took place the day before the horse vanished. "Something flew over the ranch house. It was airborne but my mother doesn't have very good eyesight; she's eighty-seven years old but very alert, and she went to the door, she has arthritis and walks very slowly. It was still right at the house. It couldn't have been a jet or a plane or anything; it was right at treetop level. It was bright aluminum; she could not see wings on it but she says she's not sure of the shape because of her eyesight. I'm sure this has some connection with the horse."

"How did the NICAP people treat you personally with their questions?"

"They were personally very nice but I could not get an official opinion from them, but each one gave me their personal opinion that it was 'very strange and very unexplainable.' "

"Has any organization or authority tried to censor you in any way?"

Nellie said a Dr. Adams, from Colorado State University, and Dr. Fred Ayers, who assisted with the Condon investigation, visited her ranch. They claimed the horse must have been killed by passing hunters, perhaps a mercy killing. Nellie vehemently disagreed. "A mercy killing doesn't make any sense at all because you would cut under the throat. This animal was cut all the way around, absolutely smooth, in a manner which you could not have done with a knife because I was raised on a farm and I know what it looks like when you butcher. You gotta make a jag when you pull that knife back. And who would carry this type of equipment anyway? And who would not go to the ranch house and say, 'You have a sick horse.' They can see it's got spots, it's a good horse. They wouldn't be about to cut its throat.

"I was going to tell you, when this veterinarian came in that night with Dr. Fred Ayers, to give me his report, my older sister was there. . . . I heard him on a TV program where they were interviewing him, and they asked him, 'What was the smell?' He said, 'They smelled thistle and didn't know the difference.' Well, this is a distinct lie. There was a definite, strong odor. The government, I read in last night's *Courier*, our local paper, they said there were no black spots. That is a damn lie. They are all out there for anybody to see and hundreds of people have seen them. Now, why is our government lying?"

Furbay ignores her and says, "Yes, ma'am. Would you answer this question, please? Has Snippy been moved from where he was?"

"No sir, he lays right where he was. They slit his stomach all down the middle next to the ground, and his head's been cut off when they were doing the autopsy but he is still there and I don't want to bury the horse because the government will say there was no horse. Now, why is our government . . . I thought they came in to investigate. Instead, they came in to discredit and call people liars when they were giving them the truth."

"We understand that a pathologist examined Snippy. This probably is the one who cut into the horse. What did he find?"

"There were twenty witnesses, highly respected people who were witnesses. They just happened to be spectators at the time. He told us he found the brain cavity empty. He said that's very unusual. He said it should have had water in it, and there were no brains or nothing in there. He opened the abdomen with a knife and he said, 'They're [the organs] all gone.' Now we had twenty adult witnesses

there to this but I understand they put [pressure?] on him
and he retracted, but we have all the witnesses here who
know the horse, that this was the condition of the horse.
Will you tell me why, why does the government come in
and try to make liars out of us when we in good faith gave
them our evidence and our proof and then they ignored it
and pretended we were lying? Will you tell me, sir? You
should know. Why is the government doing this? Why are
they calling us liars when they were true facts, ignoring
them?''

"Well, this is what . . . very precisely the point we're
trying to make by talking to you, Mrs. Lewis. We're kind
of upset at the fact that they would do this.''

"Well, I am not going to let the government intimidate
me. I am going to tell the truth. I told the truth in the
beginning and I will continue to tell the truth no matter
how much they try to intimidate.''

A local paper quoted Nellie as saying, "Flying saucers
killed my horse!'' The publicity generated by the horse's
death brought the UFO watchers and the generally curious
into the San Luis Valley in droves. A group of Adams State
College students even repainted a billboard outside of Alamosa to read, "The Flying Saucer Capital of the World.''

Nocturnal lights proved extremely elusive but photographs were captured during the fall of '67. In October,
two college students from Pueblo, Colorado, Bill Mc-
Phedries and a friend, with the help of APRO investigator
Don Richmond, photographed mysterious lights over the
Great Sand Dunes as they stood on the porch of the Lewis
cabin, high above the valley floor. They had first noticed
them in the Dry Lakes area, five miles due west of their
vantage point. They seemed to hover close to the ground
before flying off toward the dunes. Brilliant white and red,
they seemed to the three observers to be under intelligent
control. The photographs appeared in the *Pueblo Chieftain*
along with a story by Pearl Nicholas.

THE HORSE'S MOUTH

MARCH 12, 1993, GREAT SAND DUNES COUNTRY CLUB:

I was finally able to pin down Berle Lewis, Nellie's husband, for a videotape interview, when he agreed to meet with me at the Great Sand Dunes Country Club maintenance shop where he worked. Berle emerged from the building. The short, white-haired, stocky man in his late sixties reflected a hard life of work with his slow but sure movements. He invited me inside his shop. The place had the comfortable, busy look of projects-in-the-works. Shop tools, wood, and workbenches provided the backdrop for an hour-and-a-half video interview.

Berle asked if I'd spoken to Tom Adams yet. I noted Berle's high-pitched Coloradan drawl, a dead ringer for the real McCoy, Walter Brennen. I was struck by his colorful, humorous demeanor, which was offset by the honest and matter-of-fact way he described many unusual and some downright unbelievable stories from the late 1960s. I found Berle to be a very credible and convincing man, certain to shed some light on this controversial episode.

"Berle, when did you first start hearing about UFOs and strange lights being seen around here?" I began.

"After '67, in August."

"So all the sightings started just before the whole Snippy episode?"

"It all started right there. I never paid no attention to it till after the horse was killed."

"Until it happened right in your backyard?"

"You might say the backyard; it happened right out back of the house." Berle laughed.

"Ok, let's get in a little bit and talk about Snippy, or Lady, I mean. The press changed the horse's name, I guess Snippy was a more colorful name?"

"I never corrected them when it came out. I kinda smiled and said hell, Snippy's all right with me, Snippy was the horse I rode on, Lady was her colt, so it's kinda funny the way it turned out. They called the colt Snippy and the horse I had Lady, so I never corrected them."

"What did you, Nellie, and Harry think when you found the horse?"

"We had no idea what caused it because I know nobody with a knife could cut that meat so smooth and nobody could ever take the meat off the bones where it was as white as that piece of paper over there. Now I don't give a darn who you are, there's not a butcher of any kind that can make that bone look like it's sat there for years! The eyeballs were gone, the tongue was gone, the esophagus was gone, and the windpipe was gone, All the hair, the mane hair and hide on the neck, clear down to where the collar fit. But that cut, completely around, was smooth! It's just impossible to cut it that way!"

I inquired about the smell.

"Well, it just hung over the horse really, it seemed to be floating in the area."

"Nellie was quoted as saying it smelled like embalming fluid."

"Naw, I wouldn't say it was embalming fluid, I've smelled plenty of that. It was like medicine. That's the way I'd put it but I don't know what kind of medicine."

"Do you have any idea how they removed the brain out of the skull?"

"Hell, I know how the skull got cut open, I was there and I held the light for the guy that cut it open."

"And there was no brain in there?"

"It was dry!"

"So there was no opening in the cranial cavity?"

"The was no opening of any kind."

"How about the green glob that looked like a chicken liver that Nellie found?"

"Well, I don't know what that was, I'll be darned if I do. It was like an acid burn, but there was no smell of acid or burnt hair."

"When you look back at the Snippy incident, and understand that Snippy was the first [publicized] mutilation from all over the world, what do you think about that?"

"Well, I never thought nothing about it." Berle lifted his hat and scratched his head quizzically. "I guess, with the whole deal, I thought sooner or later I would learn what happened but hell, it's been thirty years."

"I read somewhere that Harry found a bull and calf he owned blinded right around the time of Snippy."

"He had a bull that was blind all right, it happened about a month or so before."

"A month before Snippy?"

"Yes, it just went blind. It was never tied to anything . . . but this one calf, his head looked like a basketball. His nose, off the end of a basketball, if you can figure out what that looked like. His hooves were about that long [he extended his hands about a foot apart] and they looked like sled runners. He had an awful time walking. The ears looked like they'd been frosted off, and his body didn't look like it had developed like it should have. We never tied the calf in with anything else."

"Did he ever have a vet look at it?"

"I don't think he ever did."

"Was it born that way?"

"Well, not really, I don't think so, nobody ever said anything about it. But as he got older, why he just got worse. So, that one time, he just shot the thing and I drug it off into the bushes."

I asked Berle to describe some of the various lights he'd seen.

"One time we saw, from the cabin porch down to the corner of mile eight, in that field back that way, it just looked like a switchboard! The old-time switchboard, you know, with the lights flipping on and off? Well that's what that whole field looked like. If it had been back in Missouri or Iowa, I would've swore it was fireflies. Ain't no lightning bugs around here, though."

"Did the lights move?"

"It was just like that"—he jabbed all over in the air

with his finger—"the whole field was lit up!"

They chose to watch the lights from the porch through field glasses rather than go down to investigate. The phenomenon lasted around three hours. Berle related another sighting soon after.

"I come out of a town meeting in Blanca. They were getting ready to put water in the town of Blanca and they had a town meeting. Nellie covered it for the *Chieftain* and I went with her. So when we come out and walked across the street, where the cafe is now, and over on the mountainside, we saw this light. I knew it couldn't be a house, and it was stationary. So I went back to tell them, and they all came out—I interrupted the meeting—and this one guy said he'd seen it there just before."

"How far away was it?"

"Oh, it looked like probably two or three miles. This one light, we left the meeting after they went back inside, we started back to Alamosa, and when we pulled in on [the Sand Dunes road] 150. . . . We parked there, and this light we had been watching back at Blanca, sitting on the hillside; it moved across and went clear back over to the Creede or Del Norte area. It went over the mountain, clear out of sight. We were sitting there talking, wondering what it could be and here it come! It got about eleven o'clock, and then it exploded! One light went into five, or three, then it closed and went into five, then went into six and seven, then it floated down over the Brown [San Luis] Hills."

Berle contacted an air force investigator staying at the Alamosa Sands Motel to report the incident. "He never did go down to the Brown Hills to look, he just sat there in the bar a-drinkin'. He wasn't even interested. I can't remember his name, I wished I could."

"How about the sounds everybody was hearing around here for awhile?"

"Motors, deep motors, it seemed like a big diesel engine running an air compressor and sounded like they was drillin'." This mirrors numerous contemporary reports from the Taos, New Mexico, area, a hundred miles south, which have been dubbed "The Taos Hum."

Berle remembered one night when he and friends heard the sound. "Ken Wilson and Genevee, and Pearl Nicholas and Nellie and I, we sat down there, Ken had the car. And Ken always smoked a little cigar, about that long"—he measured three inches with his thumb and forefinger— "like a torpedo, small at both ends. Ya never seen him without it. He was always chewing on that, and he had it in his mouth all the time, with only that much sticking out of his mouth. Odd way of smoking a cigar but that's the way he done it.

"So anyhow, we were sitting there looking and that motor started up on the hillside, about two miles or three miles away, and boy, I mean it was loud." Ken became excited dashed around the car and, Berle continued, "All at once, he couldn't find his cigar." [We both break into laughter.] "So, we sat there and I had a flashlight and I looked around that whole area, I mean I really looked for it. We never did find that cigar."

"He swallowed it?" I guessed.

"That's right."

Berle mentioned that he, Nellie, and a friend had sky-watched almost every night for six to eight months after the horse was killed. I asked who the friends were.

"That was Pearl Nicholas. And Father [Robert] Whiting used to come up. He had an experience through Del Norte and Monte Vista. He used to come up to the cabin quite often, he's the one that Leo Sprinkle, he hypnotized Father Whiting up there one night.

"One time, a mile west of the intersection [of the Mosca and Sand Dunes roads]. There's a dirt road there and a gate. I looked out in the field and there was a pinpoint of light. Hell, it wasn't even as big as a lightbulb. It was just a pinpoint about two blocks off the highway." They knew there were no houses, nor even roads, in that area. "Then all at once, why, I could see an outline of what I call a Quonset hut. Probably thirty-five feet high, one hundred feet long. I was standing there looking at it, and all at once it come to me that something was moving toward us. Black.

I described it as about six feet wide and about eight or nine feet high. It was coming and, of course, Nellie got to feeling bad and got hysterical, so I came around and got in the car and we left. We got over to Harmony Lane and went north about a mile and a half and with a pair of field glasses, I could see this metallic building setting off the road in the pitch-black dark! You could still see that object!''

Just before dawn Berle took a coworker back out to the site. ''We walked that over and we didn't find nothin'! Not one mark, nothin' had sat down, but I know that building had to have been there!''

I had heard from Tom Adams that Berle and Nellie were missing a few hours that night, so I asked Berle about it.

''We don't know where we spent two hours and a half. We just drove back and it was three [A.M.] when we got in the house.''

''And that's, what, about a twenty-minute drive to your trailer?''

''It couldn't have been over twenty minutes,'' he assured me.

I was impressed by Berle's amazing recall of the events which had taken place over twenty-five years before. I asked him why Nellie told reporters she was convinced that flying saucers had killed her horse.

''I don't think she was convinced it was UFOs or anything like that, but she knew it was something that we don't know about killed the horse. Now, I know it was something we, I don't know about, killed the horse. I figured after all these years I'd have the answers to it, but I don't have any answers. As far as I'm concerned, an unidentified object killed the horse! It wasn't anything natural. Couldn't be natural.''

''Do you know Ron Jousma?''

''Yeah.'' [Jousma worked at the Great Sand Dunes for many years and lives just southeast of the Great Sand Dunes Oasis, which he built in the late seventies.]

''Ron said that when he was working down at the dunes with Ben [King, Nellie's brother], he said that a government agent investigating the area's sightings interviewed Ben. Ron wasn't sure what agency he was from."

"I don't know who it was either. I never did know."

I had previously talked to Ron Jousma who had told me, 'Ben was on his knees in front of the agent, with tears streaming down his face,' and the agent was telling Ben, 'Too bad we weren't here, we have a special weapon that can bring them [UFOS] down.' Ben was begging the agent not to shoot at the craft because they would come and hurt him.

Berle shook his head. "I never heard that part of it. Ben King knew every creek, every bird, every flower, every type of grass from Poncha Pass to La Veta Pass. I mean that guy was about as good a naturalist I believe I've ever seen. And he only had an eighth-grade education. They asked him to name all the creeks from Poncha Pass to Blanca, and he only missed one."

"Do you know anybody that has photographs of some of the lights that were seen back then, or any accounts, anything written down?"

"Ken Wilson, over there in South Fork, he probably does. I don't have any."

"Did you ever have any photographs?"

"I had one picture that was taken on the sidewalk in Alamosa about the same time. I took the picture myself and it was of Nellie and her mother. They were on the sidewalk in front of her candy store. That picture turned out funnier than I ever saw! I can't find that picture, unless it's in that one box that I haven't looked in. Over the top of the head of each one of them was an object about that long [six inches] and that wide [two inches], torpedo-shaped with a little propeller turning in front of it, over both the top of them."

I tried to ask the next questions delicately. This was personal. "How about the day you buried Agnes, and Nellie didn't come down from the cemetery. That must have seemed kind of strange."

"We went to the funeral, everybody left and went back down. Don and Alice Richmond's car was in town [Alamosa] so they rode back with me. Nellie, she didn't want to go to town. She said she'd be all right at home. So I took them to town and come back. The other car we had was gone and that's when I found her up at the cemetery. She committed suicide.''

"Do you have any theories, why she did that?''

"I had no idea, no indication. When I left she said she'd be all right. She went down to Harry's and when I got back from town Harry said she just went up to the cemetery, so I beat it up to the cemetery but it was too late. That was the day they buried Agnes.''

"Did you ever suspect foul play or anything unusual about that?''

"I never thought about there being foul play.''

"Well it would seem to me that if I was in your shoes and Nellie said she was going to be all right, and that she'd see you, and then you go up there to the cemetery and find her . . . she didn't give any hint?''

"No indication at all. She put the hose in the exhaust pipe and plugged up the windows.''

"Did Nellie ever think that the things she witnessed in her life, the lights, the various things, had some kind of significance to her life? Did she have any feeling that she was special because she was getting to view these things?''

"No, not at all. She was just like anybody else. Just like we're sitting here talking now. She never had no misgivings about anything. I can't say that she had any other feelings. If she did, she never told me about them.''

"How would you describe your feelings? You must have been very surprised when this happened.''

"When I got up to that cemetery, I was damned surprised! I don't know why she done it.'' Berle stared at the floor. I noticed he was visibly shivering, probably a combination of the cold room and the intensity of the questions. We wound down and I thanked Berle for his cooperation, leaving him to the memories of his beloved wife.

*   *   *

Several rumors were heard by researchers concerning statements the mother and daughter had made to friends about passing on to the other side together. Nellie's friends claimed, "Beings would come for her and her mother on the same day."

Ken and Ginny Wilson remembered changes in her behavior after Snippy died. "Nellie became obsessed with the occult. She started using a Ouija board and reading all kinds of books about UFOs." The Wilsons also recalled that Nellie was "particularly impressed with the first widely publicized abduction of Betty and Barney Hill, and the [John Fuller's] book about the incident, *Interrupted Journey*."

So many nuances surrounded 3LV events during the late 1960s. I often wonder about the timing. Was the death of Snippy on September 7, 1967, significant? One curious element surrounding the period concerns the turmoil in our culture during the late summer of 1967. Hundreds of thousands of "flower children" across the United States were becoming psychotropically aware through the use of mind-altering substances. I have wondered if this immense wave of expanding awareness could somehow be linked to the incredible upsurge of unexplained UFO activity, and the birth of the publicized phase of the UAD, during the end of the "summer of love." Could some sort of psychic door have been opened with a "key" called psychedelics? Did something slip through this door? The timing of the Snippy case, culturally, intrigued me.

One thing is certain. The extent of the "flap" of 1967 through 1969 in the valley has become unalterably blurred through time. The true nature of the many strange events has become lost in the inevitable dissemination process, effectively beyond reach, in dusty newspaper articles and word-of-mouth tales. Facts have been mixed up, added, deleted, forgotten, and altered. Even the eyewitnesses, who should be able to clarify effectively the events they witnessed, may be contributing to creation of mythos, or folklore, by their perceptions of unusual events. The fodder of new legend. Without question, Nellie Lewis's Appaloosa Snippy has joined the ranks of notable horses in history: Pegasus, Traveler, Comanche, Man O'War, even the Trojan Horse.

DID YOU SEE IT?

MARCH 16, 1993, CRESTONE-BACA GRANDE, 9 PM:

Isadora, Brisa, and I had spent several hectic hours running errands in Alamosa and were on our way back to the Baca on Highway 17. Just south of Moffat, Brisa asked from the backseat, "Did you see it?" Isadora and I looked east across the pitch-black landscape toward the Baca Ranch where she was gesturing. We didn't see anything. She described a light that had appeared and vanished. The three of us kept a watchful eye the rest of the way home but didn't see anything out of the ordinary.

After unloading groceries from the car, I listened to my messages blinking on the answering machine. Andrea Nisbit had called just after 9 P.M. to tell me that she and Michael saw some "strange lights over the ranch and lights on the western horizon."

Remembering Brisa's comment, I grabbed my binoculars and climbed up on our second-story roof which has a ninety-degree, one-hundred-mile view of the entire northern and western side of the valley. After less than two minutes, I caught movement above the valley floor, twenty to thirty miles due west, over what appeared to be the eastern side of the town of Saguache.

A glittering orange ball of light was shooting down the western side of the valley. It covered the one-hundred-mile-plus distance in under three minutes. (For those of you without a calculator, that's around two thousand miles per hour!) It appeared to be around twenty miles away and about the size of a small house. The color reminded me of the much smaller, orange-colored, sodium-vapor farm lights that sporadically dot the valley at night. After viewing the ball of light make a dog-legged turn and disappear over Greenie Mountain, I scrambled down off the roof to the second-story deck and called to Isadora. I again scanned the area over Saguache and, surprise, here came a second orange light.

Isadora, who had heard me call her, ran upstairs to the deck and I handed her the binoculars. She located the second object, with me anxiously pointing. It was silent and could not have been the afterburner of an unlit jet, for we observed it coming and going. You can usually hear jets flying low over the valley; we didn't hear a thing.

There were four aircraft in the air over the valley during the time period when the two objects sped down south. The aircraft exhibited the standard anticollision lights required by the Federal Aeronautics Administration (FAA). The orange objects never flashed.

After the second object disappeared, Isadora and I quickly compared observations. Both orbs appeared to be well under the horizon, thus placing them in the valley proper, under three thousand feet in altitude and had identical flight paths. Isadora had hurried out without a coat and headed in. But my investigator-blood was pumping and I continued to scan the night sky.

Less than eight minutes went by before three military jets screamed over the house, thirty-foot afterburner exhaust flames, a mode usually reserved for emergencies, trailing behind. At the valley's midpoint the two lead jets swept to the left and headed south after the orbs while the third jet continued directly southwest.

Saguache County Undersheriff Lynn Bogle told me the next day that he heard a jet "roar over his house at an unusually low altitude, around 10 P.M." He had been working on his computer and ran outside to see it but was unable to spot the plane. "It rattled my windows real good," he said. I told him of the silent orbs which preceded the jets.

That same night, a couple traveling east into the Baca on County Road T observed "small dancing lights" over the Baca Ranch. As a direct result of his sighting experience, one of the witnesses, a medical doctor and avowed skeptic, changed his views concerning UFOs.

Two families also reported strange lights illuminating their houses late that night. One witness described the lights "like moonlight but much brighter," while a second witness at a different location described the lights as red.

No reports were logged by Saguache or Alamosa county law enforcement that night and none were published until my April *Crestone Eagle* article.

PERSPECTIVE

MARCH 24, 1993, THE BACA:

What is perspective? I asked myself this question during a gathering of friends celebrating my birthday. I told them I'd need to delve into valley history before completely losing my perspective concerning our current activity.

"I'm gonna write the book!" I announced to Isadora after our guests had left. All doubts dissolved and I felt ready to face the seemingly endless task of collecting historical accounts of paranormal occurrences and the patterns of response to these occurrences.

The number of sightings and unusual reports were mounting. There seemed to be an underlying order at work, a script, if you will. I asked Isadora, "Doesn't it feel like we're living inside a Hollywood screenplay? But I want to know who is writing the script and who's directing the movie?"

I wanted to "vacuum" every available bit of information concerning the colorful history of the mysterious valley, to get it all down, to write the book. I didn't realize the importance or the effect, on a personal level, of the very process I was pondering. I didn't quite get it . . . yet.

April Fool's Eve, March 31, 1993, 6:35 pm, Moffat:

Guitarist and former U.S. Olympic wrestler Chris Medina and his cousin Roy Cisneros were traveling north on Highway 17 toward Moffat, where The Business, our five-man rock-and-roll band, was to rehearse. As they approached Moffat, Roy, who was just tagging along, nudged Chris. A large, bright light was pulsing high up in the mountains, above timberline, just south of the Baca to his right.

They both watched in silence for a couple of minutes before the light, way above tree line, disappeared. They casually mentioned their sighting as they arrived at rehearsal and I made note of it at home.

Same Day, 10:30 pm, the Baca Ranch:

The cowboy finished checking on the herd bedded down on a rented Baca Ranch pasture. Driving back toward ranch headquarters, he noticed a glow toward Deadman Creek, several miles to the south. After driving to the top of a rise for a better view, he observed pulsing orange lights hovering low. The ground seemed to be lit up by a white spotlight. The lights blinked off.

Not feeling particularly brave, the cowboy made a U-turn and headed back to ranch headquarters where he told ranch hand Alfredo Rascon and Rascon's brother, ranch manager Benito, of his sighting.

The next morning, the Rascon brothers drove down to the area where the hand had seen the lights. A dead cow awaited them. According to Alfredo, the animal's "entire rear end, tongue, and udder were cut out better than a surgeon. The jaw bone was bleached white. . . . I don't care what Buddy [Whitlock, Baca Ranch manager] or Bob [Lamb, foreman of the Speartex Ranch] says, that cow was mutilated! I grew up in Costilla County, and I have seen this before."

I asked Alfredo if he'd go on record. "Hell, yeah, I will.

I know what I saw, I've seen a lot of dead cows in my time, that was a mutilation.''

After four unannounced visits and over a dozen phone calls, I got the hint that neither Buddy nor Bob, wanted to talk to me about the incident. I had worked part time for both of them, and their avoidance raised my curiosity. According to their wives, who did talk to me, they denied the whole thing, claiming it was "predators," and were very annoyed at my insistence to get a statement. I never did obtain a statement.

The evening of April 1, the day of discovery, I again called to speak with Buddy. At 9:30 P.M. I tried one more time. His wife told me he was "out on the backhoe." Really? At 9:30 P.M., in the dark, on a backhoe? Evidently they quietly buried the cow and even barred Sheriff Dan Pacheco from investigating the case.

"I thought there was something really strange about the way those two acted about the whole thing," Pacheco told me later. "They actually told me to stay off the ranch!" I called ex–Costilla County Sheriff Ernest Sandoval, who might have known the Rascon brothers [they both grew up in Costilla County], from his days as sheriff in the 1970s.

"I know the Rascon brothers well," he assured me. "They're both honest men. I have a lot of confidence in them. Benito used to work for a deputy of mine." I thanked Sandoval and arranged time later that month to head down to Costilla County and interview him about his years as sheriff.

I later learned that a rumor had circulated the community that the Baca Ranch cowhands had invented a "mutilation" hoax as an April Fool's joke on me. So why wouldn't the ranch management speak to me and why was Buddy Whitlock out on a backhoe after dark? This is a perfect illustration of the difficulty in investigating reports of this type.

April's Fool's Day 1993, The Baca:

My third *Crestone Eagle* article came out. ''Current UFO Sightings Puzzle Saguache County Residents,'' read the headline. It should have read "Puzzle Saguache County Investigator." The unusual events of that March were covered and many Crestone locals began to realize the possible scope of this activity. Since I had investigated many of the events, it was assumed that I knew what was going on, that I was an "expert." As teenagers say, "Not!"

Word of my efforts spread and calls began to come in from regional media. The *Rocky Mountain News* stringer for our area called me to say he'd heard I was investigating some "strange goings-on." He asked if he could come down and do a full-length interview and feature story on me. My investigative ego, being rather young and fragile at this point, was wooed and I agreed. He then slyly asked for names and phone numbers of the ranchers involved in the November UAD cases, and I complied.

I was pretty miffed when his article was published on April 7, with no mention whatsoever of my efforts. This *Rocky Mountain News* episode gave me the opportunity to look closely at my ego attachment and my motivations for investigation and research. It also reminded me why "the press" has such a bad reputation. I vowed I would always make an effort to credit all my sources, unless they wished for anonymity.

As a direct result of this initial experience with the press, I have never contacted any media for the purpose of promoting my efforts as an investigator of the unusual. Then again, I never needed to. Requests for information started pouring in from all over the world. At first, I naively dropped my work to answer all calls and letters. But I soon woke up to the fact that thousands of people are as intrigued by the unexplainable aspects of the SLV as myself and I needed time to become the "expert" they were seeking.

APRIL 8, 1993, 10:30 AM, THE BACA:

Someone urgently knocks on my door. It's Pam La Borde and her daughter, Angela. Pam excitedly asks me if I've seen "the helicopter with the torpedo hanging underneath.'' A torpedo underneath? Not this morning. I grab my camera and dash outside to hear the faint sound of an approaching chopper. Up to the roof I scramble. The craft approaches from the north. It's a Bell jet ranger, and slung below it on a thick, free-swinging cable, is a long skinny tube with stabilizing fins on the back. Above the longer torpedo-shaped object is a smaller torpedo. The craft appears to be headed in a direct line with my vantage point on the roof. I snap pictures and, as the pilot sees me, he veers west, practically skimming the treetops with the strange device. I climb down off the roof.

I call Lynn Pacheco, the Saguache County sheriff's dispatcher who reveals that the helicopter is being flown by Challenger Gold, conducting gold exploration of the Baca Ranch and neighboring development. The official line regarding the strange object beneath the chopper is that it is a ''magnetometer,'' used to detect iron deposits, sometimes found in conjunction with gold ore. I manage to get some fairly good photographs before it veers away.

A BENEFACTOR

Later that afternoon, I got a call from an independent UFO investigator from Denver named Rocky. I've elected not to use his last name. He had obtained my name and number from Jim Nelson, state director for Colorado Mutual UFO Network (MUFON). He'd asked Nelson where he could go in Colorado to skywatch for UFOs. Nelson told him about me, and the activity that was going on in the San Luis Valley.

I agreed to meet Rocky and his brother-in-law, Sterling, to direct them to a good skywatching location. But I had to warn them of a kid's birthday party which would be underway when they arrived at the house. It was Brisa's ninth birthday and Isadora and I were planning to ride herd over an energetic passel of neighborhood kids later that afternoon.

The investigators drove up in the late afternoon in a brand new Ford Explorer. Rocky, a huge hulking man, six foot ten, 280 pounds, in his late thirties, practically had to duck to enter the house. He introduced himself and surprised us with a small gift he had so thoughtfully brought for Brisa. We talked about the activity I had been documenting during the previous several months. I was impressed by his gracious, easy manner and found him to be a knowledgeable and articulate man, fascinated, almost obsessed, with the subject of UFOs. Around us echoed the squeals and laughter of a dozen kids in the midst of the party.

Rocky, Sterling, and I sought quiet outside to study topographical maps of the valley. I wanted to select a centralized place for them to park and skywatch that night. I suggested an area between the San Luis Lakes and the Great Sand Dunes National Monument, near the Medano Ranch.

Rocky mentioned that he had "brought some toys down." My jaw dropped with the Explorer tailgate. This guy was serious! He produced two top-of-the-line video cameras with every conceivable lens; an automatic panning tripod; three SLR cameras; a stereo camera; numerous first, second, and third generation night-vision devices; an electromagnetic-field detection device; a motion detector; several lasers; pen-holder flares; walkie-talkies; a Geiger counter; tri-field meter, and three pairs of binoculars. A pop-up trailer with a portable heater trailed behind.

"Wow, you're loaded for bear," I told him, shaking my head in disbelief.

He sheepishly admitted, "I got all this stuff, but haven't really been able to use it yet. There's no place to go near Denver that has had any sightings lately."

"Well, son," I joked, "you've come to the right place. I can't promise anything, of course, but I think I can set you up." But I knew how elusive UFOs can be, especially with cameras around.

They were just happy I agreed to meet with them. Sharing information on likely sites was more than they had hoped. After a necessary birthday cake stop, I sent the adventurers on their way.

With Brisa tucked safely into bed, Isadora and I had just flipped off the light when the phone rang at 11:30 P.M. It was Rocky on his cellular phone. He sounded very excited. "Something is chasing us down the road to Mosca!" Another voice was shouting in the background.

"What?" I asked. "What's chasing you?"

I could hear Sterling yelling descriptions in the background. "It's getting closer! Now it's going up behind some trees! Come on, let's get out of here!"

"Rocky, what's going on?"

"I just turned onto Highway 17. We're heading into Alamosa. Enough of this," he said cryptically, his voice wavering. "What's it doing now?" Rocky asked Sterling.

I could hear his brother-in-law in the background. "Now it's just sitting at the top of the trees."

I asked Rocky, again, what was happening, trying to keep him talking. He calmed down a bit and started filling in the details. "We were sitting right where you told us to go, freezing. It's really cold out. We watched for about three hours and didn't see a thing, so we tried to get the trailer and the heater set up. But we couldn't get the heater going. So, we decided to pack up the gear and head to a motel in Alamosa.

"We had just finished putting everything in the truck when Sterling saw a bright white light over by the south edge of the Dunes. We started driving to the main road that goes out to Mosca, watching this thing. When I got to the intersection, we noticed the light seemed to be rushing across the prairie right at us. Sterling freaked out. I turned onto the road and he told me to 'step on it.' I watched it in the mirror and talked Sterling into stopping and checking it out with the night vision. We stopped and I grabbed the night vision. It looked like a train headlight. That's the only way I can describe it. It didn't look anything like car headlights, it was way bigger! I could have sworn it stopped right when we did. Then all of a sudden, it seemed to start flying right at us.''

"Could you tell how far off the ground it was?"

"Well, it seemed to be about ten to fifteen feet off the ground," he reported. "Until it went up to the tops of the trees; then it was thirty or forty feet off the ground."

I started looking for a mundane explanation. I knew ground-level lights can appear deceiving when viewed at night in the valley. Temperature inversions can make a light appear to dance up in the air, or appear to shoot on the ground toward an observer, and I'd seen this effect many times, especially during the colder months. "How close to you was it at its closest point?" I asked.

"Between a mile and a mile and a half. When we got to Mosca, and it went up behind the trees, they were about a mile and a half behind us." This didn't sound like a temperature inversion to me. Rocky, who, on the surface, seemed rational and not prone to panic attacks, was now answering my questions calmly. Was he pulling my leg? Hard to tell from a phone call, although both seemed very excited and in the middle of some sort of unusual experience. I told him to stop by in the morning.

They were sure the light was unusual. They had no idea what it could have been. Of course, neither did I. Evidently they had taken a good look at it with the night-vision devices and were convinced that, whatever it was, it was extraordinary.

As time went on, Rocky would become one of the biggest and most generous supporters of my investigative efforts. He would also provide an interesting religious context upon which to examine the data. Perhaps most importantly, he provided me with state-of-the-art night-vision equipment and the computer on which I'm writing this book. I've often wondered if his first experience that cold SLV night was the moment when he grabbed the proverbial tar baby.

*   *   *

The following day, April 9, three "military-type helicopters" were spotted heading south, down the center of the valley. I remember thinking as I photographed them in the distance, "The constant appearance of choppers right on the heels of reports of unusual sightings in the SLV is just too coincidental."

WHO ARE YOU?

By the middle of April 1993, I was receiving phone call after phone call, letter after letter, from everywhere. It seemed the vast worldwide UFO network had discovered that "something was going on in southern Colorado" and somebody was on the case. Everybody wanted to know the details. Researchers, investigators, abductees, talk-radio personalities, radio and TV producers, freelance writers, occasional kooks, and the just plain curious—all managed to find me. I have an unlisted phone number and I'm constantly amazed at the ingenuity employed in finding me.

The "driven" even started showing up at my house, at gigs, and on job sites, trying to get the inside scoop about the area's activity. I found myself accommodating requests for article reprints and resource materials concerning the valley.

One of the pluses of this efficient networking process was the resulting flood of data which started flowing my way. Articles, files, letters, leads, case histories, and other potential resource materials started pouring in to PO Box #223, Crestone, Colorado 81131 (yes, now you have it too), from all over the world, sent by researchers and investigators. My response to their requests for "more info" prompted them to respond in kind. Reams of material arrived, relating mostly to UFOs, but also to the other various unexplained mysteries: UADs, visitations, secret government, Native American prophecies, conspiracy scenarios, alternative energies, new technologies, covert military operations, the new world order, New Age channeled material, mind-control research, alternative medicine, nonlethal weapons technologies, and—whew, you get the drift. I still receive and welcome this material. I have compiled boxes and boxes of these types of unsolicited resource materials, a data gold mine.

Trips to the post office have become guaranteed adventures. The next piece of the puzzle may arrive in the next package. I am constantly amazed at the wondrous synchronicity of opening a package of data and inadvertently finding an answer to a question or problem I'd been pondering, even that very day!

As soon as I go on-line (if I dare) I'm sure this potential information-highway networking resource will be instrumental in the the process of gathering even more good ol' data.

QUIET STORM

APRIL 14, 1993. 6:50 PM, ALAMOSA:

I am invited and participate in my first full-length live radio interview on the Adams State College "Quiet Storm" weekly program. The deejay, named EJ, had returned from the Gulf War with much skepticism of government secrets and cover-ups. After fielding numerous questions from listeners and giving an overview of our recent activity, I invited listeners to contact me in the event that they should experience anything out of the ordinary.

"It's really important for these events, no matter how insignificant they might appear when they're happening, to be documented. I would urge everyone to keep an accurate calender, or log, of anything you might see that you can't explain. Try to be accurate about what time that you saw it, how long the experience lasted, color, types of movement, anything that you can remember to describe what it is that you saw. I would appreciate it, and so would a lot of other researchers."

This radio interview generated several excellent sighting reports.

APRIL 28, 1993, 9 AM, SAN LUIS, COSTILLA COUNTY:

I had made several calls on April 26, and confirmed interviews with ex–Costilla County Sheriff Ernest Sandoval and rancher Emilio Lobato, Jr. These two men may hold the dubious distinction of being the hardest hit sheriff and rancher in the publicized history of the UAD phenomenon. Sandoval and his deputies were run ragged from 1975 through 1978 chasing the mysterious cattle surgeons through the dark pastures of Costilla County. Lobato lost a whopping forty-nine head of cattle during a frenzied two-week period in October 1975. Ten of the animals were reported as "mutilated;" the rest were either "shot or stolen." It had taken Lobato many years to recover from his financial loss.

Before embarking on my journey to San Luis, I brushed up on the decades-long dispute over the Taylor Ranch properties. The one-million-acre Sangre de Cristo Land Grant was originally granted to Narciso Beaubien and Stephen Luis Lee by the Republic of Mexico in the 1840s. Both men were killed in the Taos Uprising of 1847 and Beaubien's father, Carlos, picked up the property for a hundred dollars. He granted tracts of land to various individuals and families in an effort to settle the territory, also putting aside common areas for local usage.

One 77,000-acre mountainous commons, known by the locals as La Sierra, remained in public use for firewood, hunting, fishing, and other essential uses after the Mexican-American War under the 1848 Treaty of Guadalupe Hidalgo. The first governor of the Colorado Territory, William Gilpin, bought the grant (at the same time he bought the Baca Grande) under the stipulation that it would remain common land.

North Carolinian John T. Taylor bought the property in 1960 for less than seven dollars per acre, setting off one of the great land debates of the West. Alan Prendergast wrote in Denver's *Westword* magazine in July 1994:

"Taylor barricaded the access roads to the ranch and someone promptly shot up his bulldozer. . . . On the night of October 15, 1975, he was shot in the left ankle. . . . He offered locals twenty-five thousand dollars to testify in court, but no one would."

Wanting to hone my interviewing skills, I enlisted the help of former *Valley Courier* editor John Hill, who graciously agreed to accompany me to Costilla County. I asked a photographer to tag along and take still photographs. I had heard disturbing stories about racial problems in Costilla County and was glad I would not be going alone.

The three of us found ourselves in a very spartan-looking coffee shop in San Luis planning that day's activities. A woman who was sipping a cup of coffee came over and said, "I couldn't help but overhear you talking about 'mutilations.' When I was on my way into town this morning, I spotted two dead cows and a dead horse out in the middle of nowhere, east of Mesita, where I live." We thanked her for the tip and got detailed directions to find the location. Wow, another of those coincidences. There was not enough time to investigate immediately, so we agreed to go there later in the afternoon, after our scheduled interviews.

We wound our way out of San Luis toward San Acasio, a small hamlet several miles south, where Ernest Sandoval and his wife Marie live. A picturesque stream gurgled happily in the spring sunshine as we drove over a bridge. Cows grazed quietly in pastures where adobe shacks, some hundreds of years old, dotted the countryside. This was historic country, the earliest settled in Colorado.

I was anxious to ask Sandoval about specific cases I had found in Adams's material, especially a nineteen-hundred-pound bull that was found inside an abandoned adobe shack, on a wooden table!

THEY KEPT ON COMING

We arrived at Sandoval's humble little ranch, where a long metal gate barred our entrance to the property. Sandoval emerged from the house with a friendly wave. He had a slight limp and looked like a kindly grandfather in his early seventies. A small dog scampered friskily around him in the front yard.

I introduced the group and we were invited in. Sandoval sat us around the kitchen table while he rummaged through some boxes to locate files pertaining to "mutilation cases" he had investigated in the 1970s. He had taken the reports with him upon retiring as the Costilla County sheriff. With the video equipment running, Ernest began his story.

"When it first started [the first UADs], you know, we figured it was somebody pulling a stunt, doing the thing for the hell of it. But a couple of days after that we got another one and they kept on coming."

"Did the early reports have helicopter sightings associated with them, or was it just people finding their cows?" I asked.

"No, the early reports, what they sighted were lights. It was happening right around midnight, according to people who heard noises, or seen lights. But soon after that, when it started to get kind of heavy, the choppers would come in kind of early. They would come across the Rio Grande. It's isolated out there, nothing but prairie."

He gave us directions to the area where the initial chopper sightings [in the fall of 1975] occurred. This was the exact area where the woman at the coffee shop had seen the dead animals that very morning!

"People would come down and report what they described as choppers. As soon as they would see the cars, *zoom*, they'd take off. But, they never seen the chopper involved in the actual mutilation until later, when I happened to go out one time, right around three o'clock [A.M.]

when I saw these choppers land right around the Wild Horse Mesa, just west of here. They were landing at the Wild Horse Mesa, and they were landing at the Taylor Ranch.''

''You witnessed these helicopters yourself?''

''Oh, yes, I did see them quite a few times; we used to go out on patrol and we'd see them land. They would disappear right around Wild Horse Mesa. I would have a patrol car on this side of the mesa, and another one on the other side, on Highway 159 that goes into New Mexico. We would keep in touch using the radios in both patrol cars and we would spot one and he'd go across the valley to the mesa, then it would disappear. It wouldn't come out either side. So, the only explanation is that they were landing at the Wild Horse Mesa. Right around that time there was a man that moved up on Wild Horse Mesa, and he was a former army officer and he was an aircraft mechanic. Maybe that was the explanation.''

''He was a resident up on the mesa?''

''Yeah, for a while. But after this happened, he took off and I never saw him again. I can't recall his name.''

''Did you ever find any physical evidence like tracks or footprints around a mutilation site?''

''The Manzanares bull.''

''That's the one they found inside the abandoned shack?'' Aha, he had brought it up himself.

''Right, that's the only place we found where you could tell that they used a wheelbarrow, I think it was like a wheelbarrow, you could see one track, a single tire, going in one door where they killed the bull, and out the other one. This is the only case where we found where a chopper had landed. They took the testicles, they took the rectum. I think what they did was kill the bull inside the house, then they took whatever machine they used . . . they did away with their tracks. That's the only explanation, we didn't find any tracks.''

''Other than the wheelbarrow track.''

''The grass was real tall around the spot where the chopper landed. Another time these people from Mesita came in and made a report. These people came in and told me they had seen this helicopter that had a cow hanging from an apparatus, they described a harness. They were taking it from one place to another.

"Then there was another time right there at Emilio's [Lobato] place. These two loggers were coming down from La Valley [Colorado]. They seen the chopper, they seen the lights, and the helicopter was sitting by a cow in the center of the highway. There was a man on top of the cow, and they really got excited and went straight to the sheriff's office and when they came back, the cow was gone. They did find where the cow had urinated."

"Right there in the road?"

"Right in front of Emilio's place. That was right after he moved his cows from Chama Canyon to his residence."

"Chama Canyon is next to the Taylor spread?"

"Right."

Emilio had mentioned to me that he had leased some grazing land out there. "Now, to your knowledge, did Taylor ever lose any cows?"

"They never reported any that I know of. You know"— he laughs—"Mr. Taylor singled me out as the 'godfather' of Costilla County in some paper back east. He passed away a few years back, five or six years ago."

"Did you ever wonder if, or have reason to believe that anybody else might have been involved in all this, or was he the main guy?"

"He was the main guy at the time. But he had his foreman out here who was a very tough old man. See, people used to go on the ranch looking for stray cattle, maybe go in and fish, or poach, or whatever. For whatever reason, people would go in there, if he'd find them there, he'd scare them away. If he could apprehend them, he'd take the law into his own hands and beat them up, even juveniles. There were so many incidents prior to me taking office involving the Taylor Ranch; it was kind of bad, you know. By the time I took it over, it simmered down a little bit. But it still went on."

I asked when the Taylors had moved to the county.

"I don't think they ever moved here, they bought the place [in 1960] and built the headquarters. He used to have a guest house there and he used to have his own house, he used to come and go. He had tenants, people taking care of the place. They had over fifty or sixty cows and he never lost any."

"Yet Lobato was losing cows left and right during that time period. Who was the previous foreman?"

"His name was Barber."

"What part did Taylor have in all this?"

"Money can buy anything! I had to go before the grand jury on Taylor's word alone. The governor [Lamm] went along with it. The county commissioners, myself, and all the county officials went up there [to Denver] and I remember, I talked to the U.S. attorney, by the name of Smith, before I went in and he said, 'The only person who'll probably get indicted is you, because you're the chief law enforcement officer in Costilla County.'"

"Just what you wanted to hear."

"Thing is, I took with me a lot of reports as to what Taylor was doing. His foreman was beating up people. Believe me, I was prepared, notarized statements, signed. I presented them to the grand jury and they asked me about three questions and I was out of there! It didn't take ten minutes."

"Do you have any reason to believe that Taylor, or his foreman, were directly involved in the mutilations?"

"Well, I have reasons to believe the choppers were landing there on the Taylor Ranch. The hippies were going up to the Taylor Ranch. Believe me, I know all the people around here. They all tried to help me. Nobody liked what was going on. Nobody! A lot of them were losing, they probably had four or five head of cattle and you lose one, you lose five hundred dollars, right? So, that's a lot of money in this part of the county. So, everybody was trying to help me. It was happening!"

"It's kind of hard to argue with all these photographs," I commented, viewing the dozen photos he could find. "When did you notice that these animal deaths were not just a series of isolated events? When did it start picking up in intensity?"

"I believed that after the second or third one, naturally, there had to be something wrong. But it was happening and the things they were doing to these poor animals, each one was a little different. In some instances they would take the skin off the jawbone, or the eye. I had so many pictures. I don't have them. I wish I knew what happened to them."

I asked about the helicopters.

"At first they used to come in late at night. Later on, when it was happening here, and in Alamosa County, Conejos County, adjacent counties, even Trinidad and in Huerfano County. They were hitting everybody right around the same time."

"The helicopters?"

"Right, but I think there were other people involved besides the government. But the government is the only one that has vehicles such as this. They were pretty fast, you know."

My photographer was looking at the mutilation reports Sandoval had managed to save. "I noticed in some of the reports here that at various times the mutilations were sloppy," he said.

"Yeah, I had reports where people had found a dead cow. They come back the next day and it was mutilated. They didn't know if it was natural causes, it was probably done with a dart. They came down and killed the cow and came back the next day and mutilated it. In Blanca we found evidence that somebody tried to imitate the mutilators, you know."

"Copycats?"

"Yeah, copycats, but they went in with a very sharp knife, and there was blood all over the place."

I cringed as he began a series of rather leading questions. An investigator should refrain from supplying the answers.

"And in the 'classic mutilations' that you investigated there was no blood?"

"Right."

"Ever?"

"That's it."

"And the incisions were made with high heat?"

"Exactly."

"And there was no evidence that there was any blood left in the body of the cow?"

"Right."

"And there were no tracks of any kind, to or from the cow?"

"No."

I quickly took over the questioning. "Do you have any theories about this? This has gone on all around the country and not one person has ever been brought up on charges."

"These are the reports that I was hoping I would find." Again he searched unsuccessfully through his paperwork. "These guys had an altercation with these hippies that were living over in La Valley and, according to them, these hippies were involved. They used to follow them going to the Taylor Ranch. The theory was that these guys were helping with the mutilations. When one of these guys moved out, they found a big diagram on a piece of plywood at his new place. It described the full moon. The testicles, the liver, the heart, the whole thing was on that [diagram]."

"You mean actual, physical cow parts, right there?"

"No, it was a painting. I used to have pictures of that too. That thing stayed in the office, that drawing was in the sheriff's office for a long time. I don't know what Pete [Espinoza] did with it, I doubt it's still there but I left it there. Emilio was the one who found it after this guy left. I think his relatives [Lobato's] own that property, so when he went out there and found it, he brought it to me."

"So you tie that in with these hippie types?"

"Devil worshipers, or whatever, Satanic. I think that's the proper wording. We started to bring these guys in, investigating these guys, asking them if they have any part of this, where they were at certain hours of the day. I used to keep a twenty-four-hour patrol on that [Chama Canyon] road every day. We suspected that these guys were helping.

Gradually the hippies started taking off, and the mutilations stopped. According to a lot of the hippies that were here, their families had all kinds of money. A lot of them were richer than hell! It's weird, they were living a very miserable life. I guess they were living like that by choice.''

"Do you have any theories?" I asked. "I mean, you don't have the hippies around here anymore; you've had some mutilations.''

"Funny thing, they'd find an empty house and they'd move in without the owner's permission. I had quite a few incidents like that.''

"Squatters.''

"Yes. The fact is, they were doing it at night. We could never catch anybody doing it in the daytime. I think it was happening after midnight.''

"Did anybody attempt to try and find where these helicopters were taking off from and landing?''

Sandoval started nervously rummaging through his paperwork. "Um, one of these guys that wanted information on this, he told me . . . it's not in writing, but he told me that he had heard a report from somebody that one of those choppers barely made it back to base, which was Fort Carson [in Colorado Springs]. Later on, I found that my deputies could have fired at one of those. They never reported that to me [but] they used to do it [fire at choppers] all over the [six county] Twelfth Judicial District.''

"Were ranchers shooting at the helicopters? As well as law enforcement personnel?''

"I think so. I never did shoot at them and I used to tell my deputies not to shoot at the choppers unless they would catch them in the act, or defending themselves.''

Glancing at my watch, I realized we were supposed to meet Emilio soon. We thanked Ernest and his wife, got directions, and headed south two miles toward the Lobatos' house. I was reluctant to accept all the information that Sandoval gave me at face value. I felt that there was definitely some misidentified scavenger at work in at least some of the cases he had investigated. But it did appear that there was a connection between the chopper and UAD reports.

WE WERE THREATENED

Emilio Lobato, Jr., a shy, short swarthy man in his late forties or early fifties, answered my knock. The former high school teacher invited us in and I set up the video equipment. I had spoken several times with Emilio and was anxious to get his firsthand account of that two-week period in October 1975.

Emilio needed no prompting. "You know, a lot of people here, when something like this [UADs] happens to them, they don't say anything. And this is what people told me, 'You shouldn't have said anything.'"

"Who told you that?"

"Different people. Because when this happened, a lot of people came to see me to offer their help, and they'd say, 'I lost one.'"

"Do you think people are being threatened?" John Hill asked.

"At that time we were being threatened. They said they were going to drive us out of here. This is one of the fears a minority always has. You know what's going on in Bosnia. A minority is always afraid that there's going to be something like ethnic cleansing. There's always that fear, you know. You can't really do a lot, you've got to hold things down and not complain too much."

We talked for a while about the social implications of the UAD wave in Costilla County and Lobato recalled the "mutilations" he had experienced in October 1975.

"The first mutilation we had was the one that puzzled me the most. I had been there [to his Chama Canyon ranch, next to the Taylor Ranch] late one evening. The cows seemed to be very calm. The first one they did in a ditch. They cut out the rectum, and the sexual organs. There was no blood at all! Not one drop of blood. They would cut the left lip, half of a hoof on one side. On a cow, they would cut out a portion of the udder, the tongue, and one eye."

"Which one?"

"I don't remember. I've tried to forget so many things," he said, shaking his head. "But then we noticed a lot of activity on the Taylor Ranch. We noticed that so-called hippies were going over there and pretty soon I started getting [threatening] calls. We called CBI [Colorado Bureau of Investigation]. I don't know if the sheriff called the FBI at that time, or not. They told me, 'Whenever they call you, try to hold these people [on the line] to see if it's a local call, to see if they have any regional accents.' They were telling me they wanted to see me over there. It was me they were after. They wanted me to go to my ranch. I had my cattle right next to the Taylor Ranch."

"So they actually threatened your livestock?"

"They threatened me! They told me if they caught me by myself, they'd kill me. They would liquidate me. Taylor, I had had many problems with him and he had also threatened to kill me. I had never owned a gun, so I had to go and buy one, and I started shooting. Although I had been a member of the national guard for a number of years, I wasn't that acquainted with pistols. I was a medic and I wasn't too interested in guns, so I had to get one to protect myself. I told them I was going to come to my property, whether you like it or not and if you try to stop me, you'll have to kill me. John T. Taylor bought the mountain over here. We are still fighting for that land. See, I was one of the leaders in the fight for that land because that land, according to the Treaty of Hidalgo, that land was given to the people as a common. It was sold several times illegally and we're still fighting for it."

"Why do you think he threatened your life?"

"He just wanted to scare me, I think."

"Because you own property adjacent to his?"

"Yes, and he said, 'I want your property.' I told him my property was not for sale. He said, 'Everything is for sale, it's just a matter of price.' I said, 'I never will sell my place for anything.' "

"Was he actually offering you a great deal of money?"

"I told him, 'I wouldn't sell it for a million dollars.' [Taylor said] 'Just say so, and we'll pay it. Just say how much you want, and we'll pay for it.' "

"How many acres?"

"I just have a little over a hundred acres and I said, 'How come you want this place?'' He said, 'As soon as I get rid of you, I'll get rid of everybody else.' He wanted the whole valley. He had already threatened a lot of my neighbors. Here's what happened.

"When one of the first mutilations happened to my neighbors, he sold out. In order to hurt people very badly, you hurt the pocket. I made the decision, I'm not going to sell, I told my family, my wife, and my children, 'If something happens to me, don't sell, just keep up the payments, just pay the taxes.' He threatened me, and why he didn't shoot me, I don't know because I was there all the time.''

Lobato lost an incredible forty-nine head in two weeks. "Seventeen we found dead at the ranch, ten were mutilated and at that time we already had people there twenty-four hours a day, and all they [the perpetrators] were doing was shooting them [cows]. Prior to that time, they had already taken the rest. The reason why we found out they were taking them somewhere else because they'd call the sheriff, Sandoval, and they told him that they had found some cows over at the Rio Grande that were 'mutilated.' They called in the brand inspector and they found that they had my brand on them.'' [The Rio Grande River is over thirty miles west of his Chama Canyon ranch.]

"So who do you feel is doing the mutilations?"

"I feel that the first mutilation, I can't give you an explanation for it, because it wasn't the same people. But I think that Taylor had a lot of push with the government . . .When we started seeing all this activity over at the Taylor Ranch, the hippies going over there, he had brought in, uh, I don't know how many people, I talked with one person who said about five hundred people, to hunt in the area at the time. This was during hunting season.

"There was a lot of activity on the Taylor Ranch. A lot of the people who were watching and helping me watch noticed that a lot of helicopters were landing on the Taylor Ranch. They were going from the Taylor Ranch to somewhere on the [Wild Horse] Mesa over here. They knew about my comings and goings. The hippies were informing him of my whereabouts, and I think that Taylor was involved in letting whoever was doing the mutilations to come in."

[This may be the first time anyone has been named publicly as aiding and abetting or conducting UAD activity.]

"When Jack Taylor was shot, this fella told me, 'I shot at a helicopter,' he said, 'and I'm quite sure that I . . . because he was hit on the heel.' "

"Taylor was?"

"Yes, and he said, 'I think that I hit him, because we were shooting at a helicopter.' It stopped right there and turned right back. It went back to the Taylor Ranch and he said, shortly thereafter, 'they came down because Taylor had been shot.' He said, 'I think I was the one that shot him.' "

"Who was this person?"

"He was in jail, he had just been let off jail and he went with the deputies over there and he said, 'We shot at that helicopter.' "

"They said, 'We shot at 'em. I think I hit 'em.' "

"But as soon as he was shot, the mutilations stopped dead?"

"The mutilations stopped, yeah. I hadn't realized this until at a meeting in Alamosa, one time, this man told me, 'Did you know that when Jack Taylor was shot, that was the end of the mutilations?' We always figured that it was Taylor and the hippies."

I asked him who he thought was responsible for the UADs in neighboring Costilla County.

"One of my conclusions was that there was not one group involved. I think there was more than one group involved."

We again started talking about the mystery helicopters

that had been reported almost nightly during the fall of 1975. Emilio shook his head. "Some people told me that they had seen those helicopters here and that they went extremely fast. Faster than a usual helicopter or even a plane!" At first he had thought it was the motion of his own car which caused the appearance of such velocity. "But then, when they went overhead, they were going extremely fast. Stopping very rapidly! That's what threw off a lot of people.

"We see jets flying through here every day. They saw lights that were going back and forth [across the valley] so fast it seemed just like a flash of light. Very few people said this light seemed to be like a helicopter. A lot of people were telling me these were UFOs, I don't know what to believe anymore."

I was curious about the locals' response to the cattle deaths. "How about the local government, at the time, in '75. Did you ever get the impression that there was a real, legitimate desire by the local government to get to the bottom of why cows were being mutilated? I mean you lost close to fifty!"

"They got people to watch my place twenty-four hours a day. They were constantly calling me to make sure things were okay. They, CBI, they called the FBI, and they came to talk to me."

"The FBI did?"

"I told them, if the government can't protect me, I have to protect myself."

Emilio's phone rang. It was his nephew, Dale Vigil. Vigil had called Ernest Sandoval to tell him he had just discovered a mutilated cow that very morning, at his Chama Canyon ranch, two ranches from Emilio's ranch! Sandoval told him about our investigation. Dale agreed to take us to his ranch to investigate the downed cow.

Synchronicity crackled. I couldn't believe it. This trip was, without question, right out of a movie. We continued our conversation with Lobato as we waited for his nephew to show up and found out that there had been attempts on

Lobato's life back in 1975! He claimed that on three different occasions, there had been shots fired at him on his Chama Canyon ranch.

I couldn't help but exclaim, "This is too weird, this is *too* weird!"

THE MOURNFUL MOO-OO

Vigil arrived in a pickup and we followed him at breakneck speed over the windy back country roads to his small ranch. We drove around the back of the ranch house to see a knot of men standing over a dead cow less than a hundred fifty feet from the Vigil ranch house. My first "fresh one." We hopped out and, as we walked over toward the cow, I hoped feverishly that I had enough juice left in the video battery to document the scene.

Emilio introduced us to the seven or eight local ranchers and I set up the camera. The animal lay on its right side underneath a grove of scrub willow. The rear-end was missing, the udder had been removed, the upside eye looked like it had been sucked out, and a patch of hide, just above the left knee, was missing.

Vigil said the cow had given birth at "around three-thirty A.M., last night," and when he and his brother, Clarence, went out "at five-thirty A.M., they found the calf bawling over its mother, who was dead." He immediately called Sheriff Billy Maestas, who came out with Undersheriff Roger Benson to investigate the scene a couple of hours before we arrived.

They found a small amount of oily, clear, yellowish matter on the animal's side, which they collected to have tested. We also found a small amount of this strange material, which we collected into a sealed film container. We carefully cut off tissue samples from the incision areas and collected about twenty ccs. of uncoagulated blood from the body cavity. These samples would be sent overnight air to Denver hematologist Dr. John Altshuler for testing.

I asked Dale to show me where the calf had been born, and he took me one hundred yards to the east by the small creek that flows through his ranch. "She was born right there," he said, pointing to a fairly large spot of dried blood. By this time, my battery had died, and I carried the now-useless camera in my hand. As we started back to the dead cow, I noticed that a large red Limousine bull had been slowly edging over toward the carcass. The rest of the small herd was grazing obliviously three hundred yards away, at the other end of the pasture. The bull cautiously walked up to the carcass, sniffed it, and let out the most heart-wrenching, mournful *"Mooo-o-o-o-ol"*

Instantly, the other thirty to forty head of cattle came thundering across the pasture to the dead cow. They gathered around, snorting and pawing at the carcass and the whole herd started slowly circling around it in a clockwise motion. Damn, I sure wished I had some battery power left so I could have videotaped this unusual spectacle. If only I could have panned the cow ritual, then zoomed in on the line of ten ranchers, watching with their mouths dropped open in amazement, I'd have captured a classic movie shot.

I asked the ranchers if they had ever seen cattle do this before. Several couldn't even answer, they just shook their heads no. Lobato said, "In all the years I've been a rancher, I've never seen cows do that before!" Although I felt blessed to have been an eyewitness to the day's activities, I might have [almost] "kissed" the tar baby that day in Chama Canyon.

We left the Vigil Ranch and headed south toward Mesita to check on the three animals we'd heard of that morning. I spotted the faint outline of a dirt road exactly where the woman in the coffee shop had described it. I noted fresh tire tracks heading off to the south. Sure enough, there were three large carcasses about two hundred yards down the road. We hurried toward the site.

Through our open windows came the powerful smell of

cadaverine molecules. There are a lot of elements that are unsavory in UAD cases, and this is the worst of them. We were downwind and it really stunk, bad! I am often asked how I can stand it. My trick is to put Vicks VapoRub under my nose and hold my breath when I'm downwind. Unfortunately, I had not brought any this trip but vowed I would never leave home without my trusty jar of Vicks again.

I took a deep breath, and ran to the upwind side of the animals. A bull and a cow lay back-to-back in the dirt road. Twenty yards away to the east was a horse skeleton. The horse carcass had apparently been devoured by scavengers but the cattle remained intact. The bull was missing its rear-end, genitalia, and an upside eye, and upon closer examination, [holding my breath, I might add] I found that several downside ribs and the downside horn had been snapped off! It looked as if the animal had been dropped from a great height.

We noted the location of the animals in the environment. We were standing in a remote, unfenced area of sparse prairie that obviously was not used as grazing land. There were no signs at all of any other grazing animals for miles. Could the carcasses have been dropped there by a passing rancher? How about the snapped-off ribs and horn? Something didn't make sense but I hesitated jumping to conclusions. We took some pictures and we started back toward home.

When Altshuler opened the film container we sent, there was no trace of the strange yellow material! Tests on the container revealed only plastic and the traces of the film that had been in the container. Tests on the blood revealed that the animal may have been hit with a dose of carbon monoxide.

"It seems enigmatic to even perceive in the wildest imaginations that animal mutilations, that are so pervasive and so common everywhere, continue to defy witnesses," mused Dr. Altshuler.

HE WAS REAL SPOOKED

Thankfully, the following two weeks were pretty quiet in the SLV. I needed some time to digest that first trip to Costilla County. I also used this time to rehearse with my band, The Business, for a series of shows we would do throughout the region that spring. I worked feverishly on a financing proposal for a ninety-minute documentary concerning my amateur investigation.

I had approached several friends concerning leads on possible investors for the project and John Hill mentioned Hisa Ota, a well-to-do Japanese architect who owned the Zapata and Medano Ranches. Ota had recently put in a championship eighteen-hole golf course at the Great Sand Dunes Country Club. The two ranches he owns make up the western border of the Great Sand Dunes National Monument and contain some of the earliest sites of human occupation in North America.

This rich archeological locale is important to its owner. He had been financing an on-going Smithsonian dig on the Medano and I thought if anyone might be interested in the project, it would be him. After a couple of cancellations, we finally made plans to meet for dinner at his four-star Great Sand Dunes Country Club restaurant, May 3, 1993.

Coincidentally, I had spoken with Ota's Medano Ranch foreman on March 9. He had been ''chasing lights'' at night around sections of the ranch the previous summer. He told me of several fascinating encounters with what I have dubbed ''the Bigfoot truck'' lights. Evidently, he and his ranch hands, and even Great Sand Dunes' personnel, had witnessed peculiar lights that seemed to travel mainly on the dirt roads, didn't open and close locked gates and left no tracks. The foreman, a ''professional tracker for ten years,'' was understandably bewildered, and a little hesitant to talk to me. ''Ya ain't gonna put me in the paper, are ya?'' was his initial response to my call. I told him I wouldn't use his name in my articles and he proceeded to tell me about his sometimes nightly experiences.

"They come out at night around nine to nine-thirty in the late summer and in the fall. I've seen 'em, four and five nights in a row, and they coincide with helicopter activity. I've even chased 'em around on my motorcycle. The headlight doesn't work, and I try to sneak up on them to see who they are."

"What do the lights look like?" I asked.

"Well, there's two large white lights like headlights, about ten feet apart and about eight to ten feet off the ground. When they seem to turn around, there's two smaller red lights in back, like a big truck, or something. They're completely silent and don't leave any tracks. The last time we saw 'em, me and a ranch hand scoured the whole area for a whole day, all the way to the Baca Headquarters [almost ten miles] and didn't find a trace of them. No tracks, footprints, cigarette butts, anything! Last summer, we saw 'em a half a dozen times or so. The first couple a times it was kinda fun chasing them around. But then I hit a barbwire fence doin' thirty [miles per hour] and messed myself up. It ain't no fun no more."

"How close have you been able to get to them?"

He thought for a second. "Oh, maybe three hundred yards, or so. One time, one of them let me get real close, and then it blinked off. About four, or five minutes later, it flashed on just for a second, right behind me. Scared the hell outta me! It's almost like they're playin' with me!"

I asked him who or what he thought was prowling around Ota's ranch. "Well, the guys at the [Great Sand Dunes] Monument have seen 'em come right out of the dunes. I dunno, maybe they're military hovercraft, or something. They gotta be using night vision plus they don't open any gates, and don't leave tracks. I know that if there had been any tracks, I would have found 'em."

"Where do you you usually see them?"

"We usually see 'em north on the Baca border, and east between the Medano-Monument border. We've seen 'em over just northeast of the [San Luis] Lakes, near Head Lake.''

I remembered that this lake could be the actual location of the Pueblo Indians' place of emergence. ''When did you see them there?'' I asked.

''Last summer. We've seen 'em over there a few times.''

As I left the foreman I was sure that his boss, Hisa Ota, would be interested in the strange activity that had been reported historically on his ranches in the mysterious valley. As the crow flies, the distance between the Baca and the Great Sand Dunes is less than 20 miles. The only paved route is fifty miles around the Baca Ranch, a trip of almost an hour.

I found Hisa to be gracious, curious, and talented. He designed the Disney corporate headquarters in Florida and is a well-known and successful architect. The history of the Zapata Ranch and Urraca areas interest him a great deal, and having hired Berle Lewis as a handyman [who lives at the country club], Ota was aware of some of the unusual occurrences that had been documented on his property. He had already marveled at some of Lewis's colorful stories and was acquainted with my articles. He seemed eager to hear more about my investigation.

For the next two hours, over an excellent quinoa and trout dinner, I talked extensively with Ota about the area. He declined my proposal, explaining that the reason he doesn't live in the Baca is because ''so many people would be asking me for money.'' Oh, well. After thanking him and saying good-bye, I started my journey back home.

At 10:30 P.M., halfway between Hooper and Moffat, I noticed a strange, refracted glow behind me in my rearview mirror. It appeared to be a mile or so behind. I ignored it. Then, off to the right, thirty feet from the road, I saw the outline of a car. I strained to see if the driver needed help but I saw no one.

The rest of the trip was uneventful but, two hours later, my brother Brendan called. He was out of breath. It was his car I had passed. He had just arrived home after being given a ride from a Saguache County deputy.

Brendan had recognized my truck, with its homemade camper shell, and tried to flag me down. "As I ran up to the road and watched your taillights, I heard a car coming right after you with its lights off! It was a brand new, white sedan with two men in the front seat. They must have been wearing night vision, it was really dark out. It was scary. They were about a half a mile behind you and really flying, they must have been doing a hundred miles an hour."

Brendan had watched me make the turn onto Road T and head east toward Crestone. The brake lights of the mystery sedan came on as the driver made a U-turn and started back on 17 toward him, its lights still off. "I was real spooked," he admitted. "I crouched down off the road behind a bush out of sight, thinking they might have seen me. I heard the car turn off 17 about two miles or so up the road. I ran up to the road and saw that the car had turned [east] on a dirt road."

Still shaken, Brendan observed, "It's really weird the way my throttle cable had broken. It's almost like something wanted me to see that car following you."

On five different occasions the following week, military-style trucks were seen coming and going on the same road the sedan had taken the night of May 3rd.

My mind whirled with supposition. Had I became a player in a potentially dangerous game? Was I getting close to something I wasn't supposed to see? Was someone monitoring me? I refused to allow fear to dictate my state of mind. However, I did go through my paces for a couple of days. Coming on the heels of my first trip to Costilla, this latest possible example of interest in my activities was a bit disconcerting.

During the first week of May, I had set up a meeting with then Alamosa County Sheriff Jim Drury. Drury was midway through his fourth term as sheriff and I was surprised at his eagerness to talk with me. He suggested I come down to the sheriff's office the following day.

I was impressed by the brand-spanking-new sheriff's office and county jail. If he could swing the money to have this built, in the dirt-poor SLV, this guy was on the ball. I was buzzed in the reception area and directed to his office.

Drury, with a warm smile, extended his hand and told me to have a seat. An impeccably dressed, relaxed man, he surprised me with his candor and open mind. He told me that after I called, he went into his archives to find reports pertaining to UADs and UFOs that had occurred in the county. He also checked for any paperwork on the Snippy case.

"You know, it's funny, I couldn't find a single file on animal mutilations or UFO sightings," he said, scratching his Irish-red hair.

"Hmmm, that's strange, I have a lot of *Courier* clippings that mention cases in Alamosa County in the seventies." I began looking through my files for exact dates.

Drury talked a bit about the UADs and he seemed genuinely interested in the phenomenon.

"When I moved down here and became sheriff, I had no idea this kind of thing went on here. I remember reading about some of the Front Range reports from the seventies, but I had no idea that it happened here."

"I think a lot more occurred here than is officially on the record," I said, showing him my documentation of unpublicized cases from Saguache County.

He asked me if I had any theories concerning who, or what, was behind these animal deaths, and we talked at length about the various attempts to explain the mystery. It turned out that Drury had a professional fascination with "nontraditional social, political, and religious groups," better known in the media as cults. Not only did he have an interest, he was considered an expert. He'd taught college-level courses and trained law enforcement officials all across the county—a perfect person to help interpret the nontraditional phenomena I was stalking.

Drury seemed genuinely interested in helping with my investigation. I asked him about known cult activity in the valley and he told me about some investigations he'd conducted attempting to unmask a ritual magic group. I ca-

sually mentioned that I was planning to go down to Costilla
County to conduct some more interviews and he warned
me to "tread lightly down there." I didn't quite know what
to think of this. What was he intimating? I told him I'd
welcome his company and we confirmed the trip for May
6. Unfortunately, duty called, and Drury couldn't make it.
I wish now he had.

RETURN TO SAN LUIS

MAY 7, 1993, HIGHWAY 159, COSTILLA COUNTY

My initial video interviews with Berle Lewis, Ernest
Sandoval, and Emilio Lobato had gone well, and with confidence, I lined up interviews with current Costilla County
Undersheriff Roger Benson and former Costilla County
Sheriff Pete Espinoza, who had served during the height
of the UAD wave in the mid to late 1970s. My many unanswered phone calls attested to the fact that current Costilla County Sheriff Billy Maestas was not interested in
talking to me.

I also scheduled an interview with former Alamosa Sheriff Jim Cockrum. He had reported UADs in the 1970s, on
his ranch outside of Fort Garland after his tenure as sheriff.
He was now foreman of the controversial Taylor Ranch.

As John Hill and I drove toward San Luis, I was disappointed that Sheriff Drury wasn't with us. "I've heard
Costilla County is a pretty tough place for whites." I was
trying to ignore the fact that, for some unknown reason, I
was nervous.

"You'd be amazed at some of the things that go on
down here," he replied.

"After that first trip, no I wouldn't." We sat in silence,
watching the scenery sail by. "What can you tell me about
Pete Espinoza?" I asked after a minute.

"Well, he was pretty controversial during his term as
sheriff. They firebombed his house and his squad car."

It was becoming very clear to me that Costilla County can be a rough-and-tumble place.

We arrived at the sheriff's office. Three Hispanic men, clad in orange inmate jumpsuits, busily polished a brand-new, black, unmarked sedan parked out front. A loud voice that I recognized as Deputy Roger Benson's was in a conversation with the dispatcher. We nonchalantly listened in.

It would seem that Maestas and Benson were responding to a fire up at the Taylor Ranch, our second scheduled destination. From the sound of the call, it was pretty serious. Evidently a ranch outbuilding had been burned down the night before. We could simply drive up to the Taylor Ranch and talk with both Benson and Cockrum. Two cops with one mic.

We buzzed, noticing a video camera gleaming down from the corner. As the dispatcher finished her call with Benson, I asked her to tell him that I was there for our scheduled appointment.

Benson told us to come up to the ranch. One of the ranch hands would meet us at the gate and bring us up. A fire, huh? Perfect timing. We obtained directions and made tracks. We headed southeast, across the lush pasture land of an ancient floodplain, excitedly hypothesizing about what could be going on up at the Taylor Ranch.

The Chama Canyon entrance of the mammoth Taylor Ranch was located about ten miles southeast of San Luis, across the valley at the base of fourteen-thousand-foot Culebra Peak. The surrounding countryside looked innocent enough. Cows grazed undisturbed in pastures. Ancient adobe houses appeared melted into the ground next to modern, ranch-style houses.

It was difficult for me to imagine this area as one of the hardest-hit locales in the history of UADs. But I knew from talking to Sandoval and Lobato that this surface appearance was misleading. My instinctual unease didn't make sense and it made me even more nervous, like an itch I couldn't scratch.

We wound our way through the small hamlets of San

Acasio and Chama and I smiled at several old broken-down adobe shacks with high-tech satellite dishes outside. "Imagine living here!" I said to John. We started winding up Chama Canyon, crossing a rickety bridge.

As we headed higher toward the majestic mountains, I noticed that the surrounding foothills effectively hid the canyon from the outside world. A perfect little valley, lost in time. We turned onto the dirt road that led to the Taylor Ranch.

As we approached the gate, I spotted our escorts, two ranch hands repairing a section of fence next to the gate. It appeared to have been cut. We slowed down and one of the ranch hands, who was on a CB radio, motioned us to stop. He told us Jim Cockrum, the ranch foreman, was heading down to meet us. John stuck his head out the window and asked him how far the headquarters was. "Not too far, about half a mile. But I told you, you can't go up! He should be down in a minute."

A brand-new, dark purple Cadillac sedan raced down the dirt road toward us. The license plate read YA#1. The driver cranked the wheel to the left and skidded sideways, spraying gravel, stopping thirty feet away, blocking our way up the hill. A thin, craggy man emerged from the car. Cockrum strode toward us, kicking up dust clouds, taking off his sunglasses. In his mid sixties, he wore western clothing and cowboy boots.

"Sorry boys, ya just can't come up," he said, leaning on the car.

"Everything all right?" I extended my hand and introduced myself.

"I've got the D.A. and the sheriff up here investigating an arson fire," he told us nervously. "With the burning, and the investigation, we have to put the lid down tight."

"Can we meet with you later in town?" I asked hopefully.

"Well, maybe in a couple of hours. But I can't talk about the fire. I'll talk about the mutilations, like I said; but I won't talk about the fire!" Three dour, sunglass-clad, male passengers peered out the Caddy's windows at us.

We thanked Cockrum and started back down the hill. "Boy, he was sure acting strange," John said. "Did you see the way he swerved the car in front of us to block the road?" You bet I had. My second trip to Costilla County was turning out to be another mystery. Why had Cockrum acted so nervous? Was it because we were the "press," or was it something else?

We reached the bottom of the hill where we were supposed to turn, and I told John to stop. "Let's park up on the hill there and see what happens. Let's shoot some video," I suggested. We started filming.

"Look who's here!" John said. The Caddy was parked at the intersection where we should have turned to head back toward town. We puttered around for a few minutes and decided to head back into town and give Pete Espinoza a call. The Caddy followed us. We stopped twice to tape, and each time, they halted a few hundred yards back, following us all the way to town.

"There's definitely something weird going on," John mused aloud. "Let's go over to the fire department and see what they know."

Several firemen were cleaning a big pumper truck. "You guys hear anything about a fire last night up at the Taylor Ranch?" I asked.

One of the firemen looked up. "Nope." He went back to washing the fire truck.

"None of you guys heard anything about a fire?" I asked again.

"I didn't hear nothing. Any of you guys hear anything about a fire?" None of the other firemen answered.

I switched tactics. "If there was a fire up at the ranch, would they call the fire department here in town?"

"Depends. Depends on how big it was."

"We heard that at least one building was damaged."

"Hmmm. Yeah, you'd think they'd call us, we're the only fire department around." Maybe we did have another mystery on our hands.

"They try to keep everything quiet up there," the fireman said, feeling a little more comfortable with these two questioning strangers. "Who are you guys?"

"We're researching a story," John quickly interjected.

"Oh, reporters, huh." He turned away from us and resumed his scrubbing.

"Well, thanks for your help." We headed toward the phone at a nearby gas station to call Pete Espinoza.

"What's with this place anyway?" I asked John. "You can sure tell they don't like outsiders."

"Hey, there's Cockrum," John said. "It looks like they're going into Emma's restaurant."

I was tired of the runaround. "Let's mess with them a little." I suggested that we follow them inside. We ordered lunch, sitting three tables away from Cockrum, hoping to overhear something. All four ignored us, and made a show of laughing and joking, appearing not to have a care in the world.

Halfway through the meal, an imposing muscular Hispanic man in his late twenties who had been sitting with a buddy, stood. The slick-haired scowling guy, with golden chains dangling over his sleeveless T-shirt, gave a quick glance in our direction before leaving.

We had a scrumptious Mexican lunch and headed toward the pay phone to call Espinoza. The bruiser from the restaurant and his buddy followed us. They climbed into a late-model blue van and rolled in our direction.

"John, remember those two muscle-bound guys with the gold chains?" He nodded. "Well, here they come!"

They drove slowly by, watching us through wraparound sunglasses, making a U-turn at the next block, and parking.

The phone was broken and we headed three blocks north to another phone booth. I adjusted my passenger-side mirror to watch the van follow us. Again, they drove by slowly, checking us out. They turned at the next block, drove by us again, and parked across the street. The driver adjusted his mirror to keep an eye on us. "Do you have a feeling, like you're being watched?" I asked, to break the tension. The watchers certainly wanted us to know they were watching. The whole scene reminded me of a Ludlum novel. (However, the next day the fire was confirmed when the *Valley Courier* wrote an article about it.)

Pete Espinoza invited us out to his ranch. At that moment we would have accepted an invitation from almost anyone and we were grateful to have a friendly destination. Espinoza's two dogs met us, barking furiously. The blue van continued on by. Espinoza came outside and called off his dogs. He was a burly, no-nonsense Vietnam vet in his early forties who obviously kept in good shape. He spoke with a rapid-fire Spanish accent.

EVEN A CHOPPER CAN'T DO THAT

John was familiar with Pete Espinoza after writing a couple of *Courier* articles while Espinoza was sheriff. Pete seemed almost eager to talk to us, even on camera.

"Sure, I'd be happy to answer a few questions if I can," he said, extending his hand for me to shake. His grip was firm. A tasteful array of plush furniture and art adorned his house. John and I sat down on a sofa, while Espinoza took a seat at his desk across the room. Rays of sunlight knifed through a second-story window, illuminating his face. We related our aborted meeting at the Taylor Ranch and described the late-model Cadillac. Just then, the Caddy drove by.

"So, Emilio told me you talked with him and Ernest," Espinoza said, as we watched the car pass, turn around, and head back the other way.

"Yes, some of the things Sandoval told us were pretty amazing," I responded, as I unpacked the video camera. "You guys sure have a lot of weird things going on down here."

Espinoza asked what we wanted to talk about. I told him that a couple of the stranger cases might be a good place to start, and I rolled tape.

He got right into it. "When I left the office of deputy sheriff, the whole [UAD] thing just died out. But, I had a few encounters that were very close. There was a thirteen-thousand-dollar reward [to catch a mutilator] at the time and, boy, I was after it bad! I'm not after any publicity but I'm the one who came the closest, and I know I am. I was pretty into it at the time.

"There were two or three cases that were unexplainable. Like the one time I found that bull the sheriff told you about. It was a humongous bull. It was on this wooden table in an old abandoned adobe shack. The most amazing thing to me was, how in the hell did anybody, or even ten guys for that matter, put a nineteen-hundred-pound bull on top of a table? It was there! And, hey, I'm not just telling you this! That's where we found it. For some people to go into a small shack, put a bull on top of a table, and mutilate it—that was amazing to me. To this day, I can't put that together. It was my case and I couldn't come up with anything solid. We had to just close the case."

Espinoza went right into the next case, in which he and other officers staked out Emilo Lobato's unfortunate herd one moonlit night. "We walked in [to the surveillance point] and I told my deputies, 'I'm not trying to brag about what I'm going to do, but we're gonna use some Vietnam tactics here, buddy. If we have to go crawl on our bellies for fifty feet, hey, we're gonna have to do that.' "

By this time Lobato's herd had dwindled to fifty or sixty head. "So we ended up in this little shack, out there on the hill, and we stayed there from, I would say, maybe eight-thirty [P.M.]. We were like whispering because I figured if it was anybody that might have real high-tech equipment, I didn't want nobody hearing us. I didn't let 'em smoke, or nothing. At one time, the cows would kind of stray, you know, ten would go this way and I would have one of the guys watching them. I'd watch the main body, and I'd have one of the other guys watch the other side and then once in a while, we'd move over to where each other was at and we'd say 'Hey, can you still see okay?' 'Yeah, we can see. There's nothing coming down or nothing.' "

Around 1:30 A.M., they witnessed flashing lights appear to land at the Taylor Ranch. "They were like a reddish gold. Not a real dark gold but like a lightbulb, bright yellowish and red. They went down at the Taylor Ranch, and nothing came out of it, we never saw them leave, or nothing. So we just sat there. We sat there and then it was about five o'clock in the morning and behind the mountains I could already see the glow of the coming day.

Not wanting to be seen, Espinoza led his team down the road before dawn and called for a deputy to pick them up. "During this time span, maybe twenty-five to thirty minutes, Mr. Lobato got up early and went up there to check and right in front of the shack that we had been in, watching all night, there's a downed cow, and it's mutilated. So we missed it by twenty-five minutes!

"That's the closest anybody's ever got. It's amazing! This happened man, it actually happened! When we got to the office, Mr. Lobato came in and said, 'Hey guys, there's a cow and it's mutilated.' Where? 'Right in front of the shack.' No, bullshit! It can't be. He said, 'There is!' So we rushed back up there to check and, sure enough, forty to fifty yards in front of my face, exactly where I was, there's a downed cow, and it's mutilated."

He shrugged. "Some people said it was the government, and some people were talking about the aliens. Other people were talking about the government paying people to scare the Mexican people into running out, so they could buy the land for the minerals here, oil and gold, what have you, okay? I was pretty sick of it already. I was very sick of it because I couldn't reach a single conclusion.

"One night, Monica Sanchez had a bunch of teenagers in the car. They had gone to a movie that night, and they were coming back up to San Francisco [Colorado] to drop off some of the kids who lived up here. They were on Road 242, and right about fifty yards from Mr. Lobato's residence, where he had all his cattle at the time, according to them, there was a cow in the middle of the highway, blocking the road, and it had something silver sticking out from its side. They saw a helicopter right next to the cow and some of the kids said it had a cable. They went to tell me right away, and I rushed over there. I didn't find nothing except for some kind of a . . . it wasn't oil, it wasn't blood, it was some kind of liquid. A little puddle, eight inches in diameter, of some kind of fluid.''

"Ernie thought it was where the cow had urinated," I interjected. "That was his guess."

"Naw, it wasn't urine. I got down to smell it. It wasn't urine."

"Did you touch it?"

"Yes, it was oily. But it wasn't like motor oil. It sure wasn't nothing like what a normal person would touch. There wasn't enough to have tested. It was right where they said the cow was at. To this day, you know, there's something else that always bugged me. I never got the help that I wanted. You can quote me on that. I never got the help that I really wanted! Maybe a search team that really knew what they were doing, infrared scopes, whatever, I never got it. No government help, state or otherwise."

Espinoza had tried to tie this case to the Manzanares bull case, but to no avail. "How do you bring a chopper down by an adobe shack, and take a nineteen-hundred-pound bull through a small opening that's supposed to be the door, take it from there, and put it on top of a table? Even a chopper can't help you do that! Ten guys couldn't do that! As far as the other mutilations, there were a bunch that I investigated; some, I can't even remember what I did. There were so many."

I pointed out that the sheriffs in Costilla, Alamosa, and Saguache counties had no documentation pertaining to unusual animal deaths.

"Really?" He shook his head. "I sure wished I'd kept my pictures."

"Did you have the feeling, while you were doing your investigations, that the same people were doing it?"

"Oh yeah, definitely. Some people tried to tell me it was a cult. But, every cult comes to an end. For whatever reason, all cults come to an end. These [UADs] never came to an end. That's why nobody can convince me it was a cult. Call me crazy. I was after that thirteen-thousand-dollar reward. Back in '75 and '76, $13,000 dollars was like a hundred thousand dollars today. I thought it was a case that anyone could solve. Then it got hard. It got really hard! Impossible. That's the word, it got impossible.''

"Kind of hard to solve a case if they don't leave any clues,'' I said with mock sarcasm. "You know, the skeptics say, 'Oh, it's just scavengers.' ''

"In every mutilation, I ruled that out. I had a heck of an argument one day with another deputy. He said, 'Man, it has to be coyotes, it has to be a mountain lion.' I said, 'Fine, okay, fine. Let a mountain lion come and chew on a two-thousand-pound bull but that mountain lion ain't gonna put him up on a table.''

"What role did the Taylor Ranch play? We've been hearing a lot of opinions that the Taylor Ranch was somehow aiding and abetting whatever kind of craft that was flying around out here doing this.''

"If you've got the time, buddy? I'll talk to you some more.''

"That's why I'm here!''

"Understand, we claim this [Taylor] ranch is a Mexican land grant. How Jack Taylor acquired the mountains is beyond us. To this day. It's still being fought over in court. One day this man [Taylor] walks in, starts fencing, starts bulldozing the roads and we can't go up for a picnic, we cannot go up for firewood, we can't go hunting. Nothing. Zero! They started a land war. Shots were fired at him, shots were fired back. He used to take some of the locals, who were on horseback up there, beat 'em up almost to death with his ranch hands, take off their shoes, and take them high up into the mountains and make 'em walk! He did this to my cousin. I mean, this guy was brutal! But generations started growing older and older, and finally somebody shot him up real good.''

He backtracked. "You know, at first, when Taylor arrived, people here were saying, 'Wait a minute. Maybe if we talk to him in a nice decent way, we can get a different attitude out of the man.' Now we heard later on that this man was a lumber man from North Carolina, and that he had shot some, as he put it, 'niggers.'

"This man came up here with a hell of a prejudiced

attitude, and at first, our fathers and grandfathers were intimidated. But believe me, buddy, this is not a place where you come in and do that. This place is ninety-nine percent Hispanic and people here are known to kick butt. We're not going to roll over for anybody, we stick together," he said proudly.

"I myself did not hate the man. I think if he had been a little bit more cooperative, had different relations with the local people, they would have even helped him take care of the place. One man can't take care of seventy-seven thousand acres. The only way we can survive here is with our land and our cattle. This is a motive. This is how they're trying to run us out. If they hit our cattle, we got to move out.

"A lot of people would come up to me and say, 'Mr. Espinoza, there ain't another place in the whole of Costilla County that we see so many lights landing, and taking off, as we do the Taylor Ranch.' That's when I started doing a side investigation. Why all of a sudden? The Taylor Ranch is not selling lumber. They aren't renting out pasture. Why are so many lights being seen at the Taylor Ranch? Lights, always lights." No sounds were associated with these reports.

"So we started hitting the Taylor Ranch. Me, and deputy Bernie Sanchez, who owns a ranch just north of the Taylors. Every time we saw lights coming over and landing at the Taylor Ranch, we take the back roads, as far as their gate, to see where they were landing. We never, never once got permission from Jack Taylor to go in and do any surveillance. When I tried to talk to him in a decent way and ask him if I could do surveillance, he never let me. As a matter of fact, he even got a restraining order against the sheriff [Sandoval]. The only county in the United States where the sheriff of the county had a restraining order, and he can't go in! Can you imagine that? They shot him [Taylor] in 1977 and he died a few years later. Now, the family doesn't want anything to do with this place."

"This is Costilla County. Only in Costilla County, buddy. I'll tell you, when I left the office of sheriff, I got a lot of publicity. Like I said, I'm not one to look for publicity but I do like to talk about what goes on down here. People even came and fire-bombed my home. They burned my garage, they burned my firewood, they fire-bombed my cars. I made *A Current Affair* on television. They even want to make a movie about what happened to me. A modern-day, Hispanic, *Walking Tall*. People found out about me and came, just like you did today. There's a lot going on here."

I asked if he was aware that the largest untapped gold deposit in Colorado is rumored to lie underneath the Taylor Ranch.

"Yes. That's what I've heard. And not only that, but we're supposed to have oil here, and we're supposed to have geothermal water here, too. They've been talking about that for years and years. We're ninety-nine percent Spanish owners of the land around here, and that's why they can't get to it. People would rather will it, and deed it over to the next generation, than give it up."

"Have you ever had occasion to draw your gun and shoot at anything you suspected that might have something to do with the mutilations?"

"I haven't, no. I hope it doesn't get to that, because I will, believe me. Something's got to give. If something's real close to my corral, shining lights, or spinning lights, whatever, I'm going to shoot, believe me. Then, if I have to face the government, whoever the hell . . . because I shot a UFO, I shot a plane, I shot a cult member, or something, I don't give a damn. I'm going to do it. This is my way of supporting my wife and kids. I've got an arsenal right here I'm pretty good with."

"Pete, we really do appreciate you sitting down talking with us. This place, I can't believe what's going on down here and nobody knows. You go up to Alamosa and they have no idea what's going on here!"

"Like I told you, only in Costilla County, buddy!"

We watched the *A Current Affair* segment about Espinoza's experiences as Costilla County sheriff. Reporter

Steve Dunlevy interviewed an Anglo witness about some of the criminal activity in the county and Espinoza chimed in, "For a long time, he was the only white guy living here, and a couple of weeks after they interviewed him, somebody murdered him!"

John and I looked at each other, aghast. Oh great, just what we wanted to hear. I think we were both stunned by the potential magnitude of this complex hidden story. This information, and the blue van, did nothing to assuage our nervousness. It still felt like we were in a Hollywood movie that was rapidly evolving into an action thriller. Perhaps central casting had sent the wrong color guys—us.

We headed north. No one followed but I didn't breathe any easier until we hit Fort Garland, sixteen miles north. What a day! I thanked John profusely for his help with the interviews. Without him, I would have been down there alone.

John and I both agreed that this amazing valley, Costilla County in particular, was a universe unto itself. My head reeled from the complicated scenario in which I was quickly becoming embroiled. What really happened down in Costilla and Conejos Counties in the mid- to late 1970s?

I realized I needed to look into the publicized history. I wanted to see how the information from these credible witnesses I had interviewed had been covered by the media. It was during the long drive home that I realized the need to put together a time line listing of the hundreds of reports that had been separately filed in this mysterious valley. I had a veritable wealth of resource material from which to accomplish this, thanks to investigators like Tom Adams.

Initially, it was quite a daunting task but I slogged away, compiling my comprehensive listing of reported occurrences of the unexplained.

THE SLV FLAP: 1975-1978

Sandoval, Espinoza, and Lobato's incredible experiences from the seventies set me in high gear. I needed corroboration. Did the press (local, regional or national) fully cover these events? Was their coverage accurate? I suspected that aspects of the media coverage may have influenced perceptions of these events by the public.

Several elements of the local coverage stood out. Most importantly, only one person wrote the *Valley Courier* articles during the height of the "flap" period, a reporter named Miles Porter IV. Porter's descriptions of the carcasses in his many articles all had a similar tone. Descriptions attributed to ranchers and law enforcement officials all shared a similar quality. Case upon case revealed identical descriptions of the UADs and the surrounding "crime scene." There were even identical verbatim quotes from one article to the next! Hmmm.

I had heard identical descriptions of unknown anomalous lights during the New Year's Eve party that previous January. I couldn't resist diving into the hypothetical realm of the Jungian "archetype." My gut told me it was no accident that these witnesses apparently perceived these unexplained UAD-and UFO-type events in very similar ways from witness to witness, case to case.

Rule #10
The human mind, when faced with the unknown, reverts to basic primal symbols, to rationalize its experience

Premier UFOlogist and self-proclaimed metalogician Dr. Jacques Valleé has long insisted that UFOs appear to be a conditioning or control mechanism in culture. I had read every Valleé book I could find and his theoretical concepts rang true for me. I could see his rationale applied to UADs as well.

One of my hunches concerning an outbreak of UAD reports in a given area suggests that the initial cases might be the most revealing. I had a feeling that these first UADs might have symbolic impact thus effecting, even dictating, the way the general populous views the ensuing flap.

An important companion to the many UAD reports from the fall of 1975, were the mystery helicopters. Reports of choppers sighted around UAD sites poured into local sheriffs' offices all over Colorado and the western United States. Tom Adams had compiled an impressive listing of activity in his book, *The Choppers and The Choppers*, which documented almost two hundred sightings around UAD sites, many of which were reported here in the San Luis Valley.

I have utilized Adams's research to help compile the following activity. I include some pertinent regional and national UAD information for perspective. In 1975, in the valley, there was no perspective when it came to reports of what were perceived as "cattle mutilations." They became relentless.

INITIAL REPORTS—AUGUST 1975

The initial UADs of the SLV flap period of 1975 through 1978 appear to have begun in northwestern Saguache County, at the foot of Cochetopa Pass, at the western edge of Saguache Park. To my knowledge, there had been no publicized UAD reports since 1970 in the SLV, and these early unpublicized reports in August 1975 occurred during a two-week period when several others were filed from over the Continental Divide in Gunnison County.

Several Saguache and Gunnison county ranchers reported UADs during the first week of August and investigating Saguache County Deputy Gene Gray was convinced there was "something unnatural" about the condition of the cows and steers reported as "mutilated." He took photographs and interviewed the owners but no one had noticed anything else unusual. There was talk of unknown helicopters sighted but, initially, they weren't directly tied to the Cochetopa outbreak. Gray doesn't recall the exact dates of those initial reports but he remembers they were during the first week of August.

To my knowledge, SLV residents were never informed about these initial reports from the local press, although mutilation and mystery helicopter reports may have leaked out from the Gunnison and the Front Range areas through regional media. Here are some of those incidents that never made the papers:

The Loman family has a secluded ranch just west of the town of La Garita, on the western side of the north-central portion of the SLV. The night of August 7, Mr. Loman remembered hearing his dogs barking around three A.M. The following morning he went out early to feed his horses and noticed his daughter's palomino show horse lying in the pasture several hundred yards from the house. The rear-end appeared to have been "burned off," the horse's lips and eyes had been removed, and a thick, black, tarlike substance ringed the upper body incision areas.

Photographs of the horse, twenty years later, appear to show a horse dead for many days, although Loman had seen it alive the night before. Gray investigated and took photographs that morning. "I knew after that one that something really weird was going on," Gray recalls. "There's just no way that animal should have looked like that."

The following week, helicopters were spotted and reported near mutilation sites in Gunnison County. A rancher saw an unmarked helicopter hovering over a hog in Gunnison County, that he "chased off." A hog allegedly turned up missing from a neighboring ranch.

On August 21, 1975, Tom Adams (who happened to be visiting the San Luis Valley with research associate Gary Massey) wrote of the following experience:

Leaving the [Gunnison County] sheriff's office after discussing mutilation investigations with Deputy David Ellis, Project Stigma investigators Tom Adams and Gary Massey drove south toward Saguache County [Not knowing that between six or seven cases had been reported two weeks before on this exact stretch of] State Highway 114. Nearing the county line, they observed a small helicopter—of the Hughes Cayuse type—flying west-southwest across the highway toward the Powderhorn-Los Pinos area, where a cattle mutilation had occurred earlier in the week. The helicopter was filmed on Super-8 movie film as it passed out of sight over a ridge. The distance was too great to discern details.

I couldn't help but wonder if rumors of mutilations in neighboring counties contributed to perceptions of ensuing SLV activity. The *Saguache Crescent* editor's earlier assertion rang in my ears: "We only write about good news."

With much fanfare, during the last week of August 1975 all hell appeared to have broken loose in the valley. Or so the headlines read. The Friday, August 29, 1975, *Courier* screamed "Five More (SLV) Cattle Are Mutilated." I could find no reference to earlier cases but this much is known: Two cows were discovered mutilated in the mountains west of Antonito; and an additional three animals were discovered near Fox Creek. All five animals were discovered on August 26.

A bull belonging to Max Brady from Manassa had been shot, the tail and an ear had been removed. Another bull owned by rancher Farron Layton had been shot and the tongue reportedly removed with a "sharp instrument." The third animal "had been shot but was not mutilated."

According to the *Courier,* "vandals" were blamed. For me, this was the first instance of a mutilation involving a firearm!

The fourth and fifth were discovered west of La Jara. A steer owned by Jim Braiden was "missing the tail, tongue, penis, and right ear," and the animal reportedly had been drained of blood before being "mutilated with a sharp instrument." These first reports during August were confined to the western side of the valley. I noted the words *sharp instrument* constantly appearing in Miles Porter's UAD articles of 1975.

Several days later, a calf was reported mutilated to Conejos County officials. They concluded that it occurred Tuesday night, September 2. A white-faced four-hundred-pound calf owned by Ed Shawcroft was found missing its "tongue, ear, genitals, and tail."

To the east, in Costilla County, Deputy John Lobato and Sheriff Sandoval both told Miles Porter IV of seeing helicopters flying in the area where a mutilated cow was later found. Dr. Joseph Vigil reported a UAD on his ranch south of San Luis on September 3.

Helicopters were seen by Costilla County officers the next thee nights. Sandoval said that early Thursday morning he saw what he believed to be a "helicopter with a red light fly south into New Mexico."

On September 5, rancher John Catalano reported to the Alamosa County sheriff the discovery of a dead calf on his ranch south of Alamosa. News sleuth Miles Porter was dispatched to the scene. To his untrained eye, "The black heifer calf had definitely been cut in the removal of its left ear, and some internal sexual organs. The calf had been dead about two weeks." He couldn't have surmised that the rotting animal "had definitely been cut," with no veterinarian pathology training, two weeks after the animal's death.

Later that same Friday, Ted Carpenter, foreman of the Medano Ranch, found a yearling steer lying on its left side, missing its downside ear and tongue. A suspicious heel print was found near the carcass. The first thing I check is if any downside organs have been removed. Unlike many of reports from the fall of 1975 that noted only upside organs being removed, this report differed. These were the first known UAD reports in Alamosa County since the 1968 mutilations of two steers on the Zapata Ranch.

Saturday, September 6, unknown helicopters were reported near three UADs in Park County, forty-five miles north of the SLV.

*   *   *

During the next three weeks, the valley got a break as UAD reports suddenly hopped to the extreme northeast corner of Colorado, in Logan County. Reports were also filed in Texas and Wyoming during the second week of September. Apparently the cattle surgeons can cover an immense amount of geographic territory in a short amount of time.

On the night of Monday, September 22, helicopters were reported in Pueblo County by ranchers and a state patrol officer. One interesting incident is from The Choppers:

> A man in a pickup truck was run off the road by a helicopter. He called for help on his CB radio and two auxiliary policemen responded to find the victim "frantic." One policeman fired a shot from a 30–30 rifle at the still-hovering helicopter and heard a ricochet. Deputies from three counties, guards from the Pueblo army depot, and Colorado state patrolmen chased the helicopter west to the Pueblo airport before it turned to the north and disappeared. The chopper made a noise "like the whistling of air coming from a tire." Other area residents reported being chased by helicopters during this time period.

That same afternoon, a two-year-old heifer was found mutilated on rented pasture several hundred yards from a house on the Taylor Ranch. "No tracks or blood was found around the calf," Undersheriff Levi Gallegos told Miles Porter. "The heart, right eye, and sexual organs had been removed through skillful incisions. The eye was removed in a 'two-inch-diameter hole around the eye, clean to the bone, and then they pulled the eye out.' "

Porter states a continually valid point: "The number of the cattle mutilations here in the valley is not known, due to the lack of reports and also the lack of any central clearinghouse recording of the incidents." I wondered how many of these "reports" were actually true UADs, with extraordinary explanations.

Three days later, a six-month-old calf belonging to Virl

Holmes was discovered six miles north of Alamosa, missing its tongue and all the hide off its right mandible. Holmes said that he had seen the animal alive late Wednesday night. He was alerted to the dead calf by his herd of cows pressed against the opposite fence line "bawlin'." According to the *Courier* subheadline, "Predators were ruled out by authorities." CBI was sent tissue samples that later revealed some evidence of toothmarks attributed to "kangaroo rats."

Another fresh carcass was found Thursday, near Hoehn, Colorado, in Los Animas County. An autopsy determined that "a toxic substance was present in the spleen, liver, and kidneys, all were badly decomposed. Other organs including the heart appeared to be healthy," the article concluded.

Six more reports were filed in Costilla County on Sunday, September 28, by area ranchers. Sheriff Sandoval stated, "It is getting out of hand. There are no clues. This is what's really bugging me!" A bright light had been seen by locals Thursday night, near the Sanchez Reservoir, but officers were unable to get close enough to identify the craft before it vanished. Five of the reports came from Chama Canyon on the Ernest Maes Ranch. All were missing sexual organs and various other parts. A sixth was discovered six miles west.

The following day the "Manzanares bull" was discovered on the table in the abandoned adobe shack. Porter does not mention the table, and the picture in the *Valley Courier* showed the bull on the ground. I wondered why. Wouldn't this crucial fact prove, without any doubt, that this animal could not have died of attrition? Why was this fact left out?

Another animal, "a large black Angus steer" owned by rancher Bonnie Lobato was found three-quarters of a mile away from the five Chama Canyon UADs the following day. It was tied to the other reports by law enforcement.

The following week was quiet, except for several mystery helicopter sightings, including one report of a landing "on the mountain, southeast of San Luis." (The Taylor

Ranch?) Locals were alerted to keep a vigilant eye sky-ward.

On October 7, Emilio Lobato lost his first animals. It could not be determined if the initial animal had been mutilated because predators already had begun eating the carcass. Two other calves were discovered by Sandoval and his deputies while investigating the first report. Lobato had told me "Sandoval said the one calf had probably been dead only one-half hour and the other for about an hour." I wondered how this time was estimated.

Helicopters were seen nightly that entire week in Alamosa and Costilla counties. On October 10, San Luis rancher Pat Sanchez reported to the sheriff's office two UADs at his ranch two miles west of San Luis.

During the next two weeks there were no reports of UADs or mystery choppers covered in the local press. According to Espinoza, Sandoval, and Lobato, it was during this two-week period that Lobato lost forty-nine head. Why was this amazing crime spree not publicized? This was probably the ranching story of the decade in the entire country, let alone the San Luis Valley, and I can find no evidence that the press ever caught wind of the alleged fury. I believe Lobato, Sandoval, and Espinoza were telling me the truth but I wonder how this could have been kept quiet? The press had shown a willingness to cover UADs. Why was this story not covered?

During this two-week period, reports of mutilation activity appear to have moved out of the SLV, east into Baca and Routt counties in Colorado, and to areas in Oklahoma, Wyoming, Montana, and New Mexico.

On October 27, Pat Sanchez again discovered a mutilated cow west of San Luis. Later that afternoon, he found yet another one. Josephine Maestas of San Pablo also reported a UAD on October 27. Then, if the press coverage is accurate, the San Luis Valley flap temporarily ended for over fifteen months.

Debunkers have propounded the theory of "misidentification of scavenger action" to explain UADs. If these skeptics are right, and UADs are simply "media-induced hysteria," then why did the reports stop cold, following a flurry of activity? The sudden, complete cessation of reports seems to overrule them. Did predators decide to stop eating for a year?

Those who examined the bodies refused to believe a predator was involved. Did the surgeons simply move on to greener pastures? Or could the ranchers have stopped reporting UADs to officials?

NOT REPORTED

After examining the publicized UAD reports from the fall of 1975, I continued my investigation of the unpublicized accounts. Counting only the unpublicized Cochetopa cases from August and the additional Lobato animals, the actual figure of twenty-three mutilations doubles. Adding the Lobato animals shot or stolen, the amount is almost tripled. I knew the number was much higher than the publicized thirty-nine.

Granted, UADs are a strange area of investigation, and they certainly smell bad. I often times have questioned my motivations. It seems others have also. One night after returning from a gig at 3:30 A.M., I quietly sneaked into the house and noticed a message blinking urgently on the answering machine. Trying not to wake Isadora and Brisa, I listened at the lowest possible volume to the following:

" 'Ello, I'm a screenwriter from South Africa," said the cultured British voice. "And I've read several of your articles. And I'm intrigued with your fascination with the removal of cattle penis. . . ." I missed the rest of the message because it was drowned under my howls of laughter as I rolled helplessly on the floor. Isadora pounded down the stairs to investigate. After several minutes of tears streaming down my muted face, I played the message back for the unamused Isadora and we caught the ending. "Can we meet for lunch? And, oh, by the way, I am heterosexual!"

During the entire month of December 1975, mystery helicopters were reported almost nightly to Alamosa and Costilla authorities while the mystery cattle surgeons apparently turned their attention to northern New Mexico, Kansas, Texas, Wyoming, and Montana. Government officials claimed no knowledge of nocturnal chopper flights in the valley during this time period.

Another potentially important aspect of the fall flap of 1975 was the abundance of unpublicized UFO sightings. The only aerial craft reported in Miles Porter's *Valley Courier* articles were described as "helicopters" but other objects were evidently flitting through the skies over the San Luis Valley that fall. According to Lobato and Sandoval, there were sightings of objects that appeared to defy the laws of physics. In addition, I uncovered several claims of "classic" UFO sightings during September and October and none of these accounts ever made the papers.

These claims were perfect media fodder so, again, why did these sightings by Costilla County locals and law enforcement go unpublicized? Was it possible that the press had a reason for not reporting the full extent of our aerial activity? My best efforts to locate the reporter have proved to be in vain.

Five months had passed in the San Luis Valley since the last (publicized) UAD on the Pat Sanchez ranch in Costilla County. After an exhaustive search, I found no articles reporting suspected UADs during this apparently quiet six-month period, but several interesting cases did make the papers concerning the killing of livestock by "vandals."

On April 12, 1976, a single "mutilation" was reported to the Costilla County sheriff's office. Investigating deputy Levi Gallegos was at a predictable loss trying to explain the UAD.

A strange calm appears to have descended on the valley through the rest of the year. To my knowledge, no known UAD, UFO, or mystery helicopter reports were filed or publicized. Reporter Miles Porter IV left the *Courier* and attempts have failed to locate him.

The ensuing coverage of UADs during 1977 and 1978 was relegated to small, nonsensational articles in several local papers. If the local press coverage alone determined the extent of the flap, I would be led to believe the "problem" had subsided or ceased altogether. Some reports were still being filed to local authorities but were not covered in depth. I continued to ponder how Porter's style of coverage during the fall of 1975 dictated the public's perception of the UAD claims. After his departure, the tone and substance of the coverage dramatically changed, but had the local perception of UADs changed?

Ernest Sandoval brought home numerous UAD reports and files after leaving as sheriff. All his reports are from the 1976 through 1978 period, leaving him confused because much of the material he thought he had is now "missing." He was able to provide me with twelve complete reports and accompanying photographs but Sandoval claims these are a mere portion of the overall official documentation he actually brought home. Fortunately, these surviving reports cover the period between 1976 and 1978 when press coverage was scant.

As I documented more cases of UADs, both historical and contemporary, my personal life took a few zigs and zags. Even the way people viewed me, running this way and that with cameras and night-vision devices, investigating missing organs and helicopters, changed. I began to receive birthday presents such as a plastic cow with the rear-end missing. Longtime area investigator and writer David Perkins sent numerous postcards and birthday cards featuring a cow with punched out eyes and rear-ends.

THE FLAP RETURNS: 1977

According to a small three-paragraph article in the *Valley Courier*, May 27, 1977, a fourteen-month-old bull belonging to San Pablo rancher Alfonso Manzanares was reported to Costilla County authorities as mutilated. The article stated, "The bull had been cut in a manner similar to mutilations in the area two years ago."

Even law enforcement officials' cattle had been targeted by our fatal surgeons. On June 17, 1977, former Alamosa Sheriff Jim Cockrum (yes, the same foreman who prevented our entry to the Taylor Ranch) reported to the Costilla sheriff's office he found a six-hundred-pound, white-face steer "mutilated" on rented pasture at the "Lobato property at Ventero." He estimated the the time of death as being three or four days earlier. Ernest Sandoval's official report stated:

> Jim Cockrum reported to the sheriff that one of his white-faced steers was mutilated in the same fashion as prior mutilations done before. Tail was cut off, testicles were cut off. The right ear and tongue. Went to area described and verified the fact that this job was done by the same professionals as before. No tracks, no blood and no nothing.

My observation? Steers don't have testicles, they are steers. And how in the world could Sandoval tell that the animal was killed by the same professionals responsible for prior cases?

Here is a perfect illustration of how potential explanations of mysterious animal deaths can be misinterpreted by law enforcement and the public in general. Without the services of a qualified veterinarian pathologist, no one could accurately ascertain tantogenesis (cause of death) or establish the cause of damage to the carcass. It may look like a mutilated duck, it may smell like a mutilated duck, but that doesn't necessarily make it a mutilated duck.

RULE #11
When investigating claims of the unusual, one cannot reach conclusions based on intuition alone.

My skepticism grew immeasurably concerning the pervasiveness and validity of many (if not most) UAD claims. All claims need to be backed up with irrefutable, substantiating data, obtained by trained professionals. Otherwise these mutilations are just claims based solely on appearance. Specific cases might be mysterious to the untrained eye but it might be commonplace to a veterinarian pathologist or diagnostic crime lab.

This realization, that it was impossible to accurately study the historical UAD phenomenon in the San Luis Valley based only on research and hindsight, was a bit disheartening. I did not, however, let this important fact dampen my enthusiasm. That people viewed these animal deaths as a "mystery" was compelling enough. The "garbage in, garbage out" scenario is hard to avoid (when utilizing pure hindsight), and impossible to overcome.

The following reports of UADs in 1977 and 1978 were centered around three ranches, just east of the town of San Luis. The Pat Sanchez, Mike Maldanado, and Eben Smith ranches appear to have been singled out and hit repeatedly throughout this next year-and-a-half period. Emilio Lobato, Jr., and these three ranchers may be the hardest hit in the entire documented UAD phenomenon. The four together claim to have lost around eighty cattle. I looked for some common link between Maldanado, Sanchez, and Lobato.

I called Mike Maldanado and asked him about a possible connection between himself and the other ranchers. "Do you belong to the same organizations? Do you go to the same church? Are you politically active in the same party or—"

He interrupted me. "Now that you mention it, we do share something in common—we're all teachers."

COSTILLA SHERIFF'S REPORTS

The following seven official reports are from the files of Ernest Sandoval.

After an apparent three-week lull, a report was filed with sheriff's deputy John Marquez by Mike Maldanado on October 8, 1977. Maldanado claimed a 900 lb. cow had been mutilated on his ranch three miles east of San Luis, near the Sanchez ranch site of several previous recent cases.

Pat Sanchez called the sheriff on November 19 to report finding two of his cows mutilated. Deputy Marquez investigated and wrote, "I noticed the cut around the rectal area was *not so perfect* as was determined in other mutilations. . . . The cutting area around the area of the place the udders were removed was a *sloppy job* according to the owner of the cows. . . . The man [Pat Sanchez] has stated that he has seen a cow dead and then *returned to find it had been mutilated* on one occasion" [my italics].

I have italicized indications of misidentified unusual scavenger action in the above report. Ragged incision areas are often an indication of a mundane explanation or, as Marquez observed, perpetration by hoaxers, or pranksters. Although, as I've previously established, "appearances are misleading," Marquez's sense of unprofessional "mutilators" at work could have merit. The possibility of predators, or even peculiarly motivated humans, is obviously valid. Two years before, Emilio Lobato, Jr., had suffered through a similar scenario that suggests at least some of the UADs and missing animals resulted from very terrestrial human agendas. The day before, on November 18, 1977, neighboring rancher Mike Maldanado called the sheriff's office to report another UAD case on his ranch. To my knowledge almost none of these official Costilla County cases in 1977 and 1978 were covered in the local papers. The rest of the valley, strangely enough, had no official reports of UADs in 1977 through 1978, and I wondered if the lack of press coverage had anything to do with the lack of perceived and/or real UADs.

The last local article pertaining to the UAD flap of 1975 through 1978 appeared in the *Valley Courier* on Tuesday, December 6, 1977. It stated that Sheriff Sandoval was investigating "three cattle mutilations in the San Luis area." A possible helicopter sighting the night of December 1 was also mentioned.

The next local newspaper article I can find regarding SLV claims of UADs was written by the *Valley Courier*'s Ruth Heide, reporting the Manuel Sanchez case, thirteen years later!

No other reports were filed by ranchers after December 1977 until the third week of August 1978. A rather routine report was written by investigating deputy Arnold Valdez:

On Thursday, August 17, 1978, at 1:58 P.M., a Mr. Mike Maldanado called the sheriff's office to report that some of his cows had been mutilated *or so it appeared* like they were. On August 19, 1978, at 12:00 P.M., deputies Steve Benavidez and Arnold Valdez went out to the incident scene. This incident was the same as all the rest of the possible mutilations that have happened in this area. No evidence was found in the immediate area. Pending further investigation (my emphasis).

This report shows a change in perception. For the first time, we see indications that the rancher and investigating officers view these latest UADs as "mutilations, or so they appeared to be." The two animals, a cow and a bull, were not found for over a week and the photographs show bird droppings on the carcasses and the uneven incisions.

On August 28, 1978, Eben Smith again called to report a "mutilation" of a cow the previous night on his ranch. Deputy Valdez was again dispatched to the crime scene and noted at the end of his report, "My opinion is that it was unprofessional due to the fact that it was very sloppy compared to some of the previous mutilations."

Again there is evidence of doubt. Was it a true mutilation? The last official Costilla report from the decade of the 1970s stated:

> September 16, 1978, at 9:30 A.M. the sheriff's office received a call from Mike Maldanado from San Luis reporting that another one of his cows had been mutilated. . . . Mr. Maldanado said that he would not be there today because he was going to take them [his cows] to the auction because he could not afford to lose any more.

So ended the official UAD wave of the 1970s. We will never know how many animals were truly mutilated and how many had mundane explanations for their demise. It is impossible to ascertain the true extent or quality of any anomalous event based on perception of the principle witness[es], or with simple research and hindsight [or wishful thinking].

Sinister hands were hard at work during the 1970s in the pastures of Costilla County, and in countless other pastures around the world. The guilty part[ies] may never even be identified, let alone be brought to justice. In my estimation, unusual scavenger action can be assumed as the causal factor in many of the San Luis Valley cases, but not all. There were, and still are, numerous cases that defy rational explanation and warrant scientific attention and cultural scrutiny.

Another mystery is why so many UFO sightings during the mid 1970s were not reported. I have uncovered accounts from the time period, but unfortunately, only a handful can be corroborated. Witnesses have come forward regarding an incident in the fall of 1975 when a large cordoned-off area was set up by "troops," just north of the Taylor Ranch, while rumors circulated of a possible crash retrieval operation. One account mentions a "UFO dogfight'' with one combatant ship evidently shot down by another.

There seems to have been a press blackout regarding this alleged event and many other anomalous aerial craft and light sightings. The late fall of 1975, in particular, had many sightings of unexplained, nonballistic craft but they were downplayed as being "helicopters."

THE FEATHER BUNDLE

UADs and UFOs were not the only mysteries striking the San Luis Valley in the seventies. The following eye-witness report comes from Daniel S. Johnson, currently re-siding in Crestone.

"After graduating from college in 1976, I was invited to house-sit for a couple who lived north of the town of Blanca, by the Arrowhead Ranch. It was during the big flap and my buddy, Tom Nugent, and I used to get a good-sized campfire going and hitchhike."

"Along the highway?" I asked.

"No, we'd dance around and invite UFOs to come down and give us a ride. Here we were at the base of Blanca, where people told us there was a secret city and an inter-dimensional passage used by space travelers to bend space, and we never caught a ride.

"The strangest thing happened to a good friend of ours I'll call Robert. He was a huge man, powerful but kind to everyone. He lived toward San Luis and was one of the few whites in the area. His wife was a lovely Hispanic woman and they had two beautiful kids.

"Anyway, Robert was suddenly struck by a malady which he described as 'being overwhelmed by heat.' He'd feel this weakness come over him and he'd hit the floor and pass out. Doctors ran hundreds of tests but the only thing they could determine was that his blood sugar would drop, just before he would."

"Weren't you into herbs?" I remembered.

"That's right, I was picking American Indian medicines and drying them to make my own mixtures but this one was too puzzling, until one day . . . Robert's wife was cleaning and she found something behind the books, a feather bundle. She and I had both been in a class at Adams State College which studied folklore and she recognized it as a Navajo witchcraft bundle. She pulled out one of her textbooks and there was similar bundle, right on the cover."

"Did they think the bundle was responsible for his ailment?"

"Robert didn't know what to think. He wasn't a superstitious guy but there was something happening to him which no one could explain. They contacted an old Indian woman in Blanca who gave them the name of a priest who was considered an expert on witchcraft. The priest sent three blessed candles and instructions for taking the feather bundle apart."

"And you participated in the ritual?"

Johnson nodded. "Robert asked Tom Nugent and I to help. We were told only to handle the components with our right hands, because the left hand supposedly allows things to enter. We just did as we were told. The bundle had one eagle feather, three crow feathers, five grouse, and so on, all wrapped up in a deer tail. We placed the feathers on panes of glass and dripped the wax over them, sealing them to the glass. The panes were then sunk into a cold stream."

"Did Robert get better?"

"He never had another attack."

"Did you ever find out who did it?"

"He did. It was a woman in town who was jealous of him. He was a well-loved man, even by her own family. Robert eventually had to move because the same woman convinced some of the cops that Robert was dealing drugs to kids. It was a complete lie but he had a family to protect. He left the valley for good."

PROBABLES

"Everything you believe is wrong . . . but I like your enthusiasm," stated David Perkins with over twenty years of firsthand experience investigating UADs. Perkins spoke with me during a visit to his mountaintop home during the third week of June 1994. "We're dealing with a reflective phenomenon that has no answers, we won't ever figure it out!"

When analyzing any series of events, one looks for patterns. Often the patterns indicate trends, as we have seen in our "microcosmic" analysis of the San Luis Valley birthplace of the UAD phenomenon. But, even though researchers invariably encounter patterns that help to confirm various UAD theories, the phenomenon seems to counter all attempts to analyze it, supplying data to both affirm and negate all possible explanations. In other words, one theory works as well as another theory, which works as well as another, and so on. Is it possible for a measurable, physical manifestation not to have a "cause" to account for the "effect"?

Some probables in the UAD phenomenon:

- A true UAD is a real, measurable, blood-based phenomenon.
- There are true UAD cases that defy all known laws of science and are, by definition, impossible.
- True UADs are occurring with the aid of high technology such as a high heat.
- Soft-tissue body parts are excised.
- The number of UAD reports increase in areas where the media has publicized other UAD reports.
- A sizable percentage of these subsequent UAD reports are misidentified scavenger action or other mundane phenomena.
- The government, or a faction thereof, has not dis-

closed the full extent of its knowledge concerning the UAD phenomenon and may be actively engaged in undisclosed aspects of the phenomena.

- There are very few additional clues ever present at a UAD site and as a result, no one has ever been charged with a UAD.
- Helicopters or UFOs are often seen around UAD sites.
- Certain (rural) areas are more prone to be hit than others.
- Certain ranches are hit repeatedly.
- There appear to be multiple groups or agendas involved.

There are several historic elements that need to be addressed. Paranormal phenomena have always existed alongside humankind. Angels, demons, ghosts, spirits, jinn, fairies, and trolls have always been with us, couched in the technology of the times, as pointed out insightfully by research investigator and astrophysicist Jacques Vallee in his book *Dimensions*. (Vallee was the real-life model for the French scientist ''Lacome'' in Steven Spielberg's film *Close Encounters of the Third Kind.*)

The UAD phenomenon is a new face (high technology) on an age-old mystery that could be, in part, responsible for man's ancient practice of animal sacrifice. It stands to reason that an ancient rancher would rather sacrifice an old or sick animal than wake up in the morning to find his prized breeding stock or seed bull dead.

The UFO phenomenon historically could be likened to Ezekiel's Wheel, the descent of the Blessed Virgin Mary at Lourdes, and countless other reported historical examples of the descent of superior beings. If this is so, various groups appear to be currently capitalizing on this perception of what may be ancient anomalies and pursuing their own current agendas. They are masters of deception.

Even assuming that a majority of UAD reports have natural explanations, i.e., predators and lightning, we are still left with a sizable percentage which are unexplained.

There is a small percentage of true UADs and true UFO sightings that I describe as The Real Thing. They are the UADs and sightings that are by definition, physically unsolvable, and may tie in to the ancient history of the paranormal. The majority of real UADs, however, seem to be perpetrated for different sociological, political and scientific reasons by human groups who I believe became directly involved in fostering deception in 1947, with the advent of the modern UFO era, and in 1973, with the advent of the cattle mutilation as part of our cultural mythos.

Probable human involvement in perpetrating these mysteries has deflected serious investigation and disclosure of the phenomenon by dedicated investigators. It's probable that the very belief that "the government knows more than it's admitting" is being manipulated cleverly by the mix toro of deception.

There is evidence to support the conclusion that our government, or a faction thereof, may be actively involved in a program reflecting a multilevel process of societal, political, scientific, and/or mythologic manipulation of an unsuspecting public. It is conceivable that the government is capitalizing on the true nature of "the Real Thing" while pursuing its own agenda. It is also highly probable that this group or groups within the government is simultaneously hiding "the Real Thing" by imitating it.

A BLOOD-BASED MYSTERY

The ultimate truth behind the UAD phenomenon may be ancient and elusive. In our scrutiny of "the Real Thing" I suspect that a shadowy "presence" started the modern, publicized era of the UAD phenomenon on the King Ranch in 1967. Could this "presence" have existed alongside humankind for thousands of years, mocking our attempts at proving its very existence and agenda by hiding its true nature and purpose behind a veil of religion, magic, superstition, and man's perception and manipulation of this veil?

Modern-day blood-based belief systems can be found in many primitive cultures that still exist in remote areas of the earth. Sorcerers in South Africa create a powerful *muti* out of animal blood and glandular tissue as a ritualistic receptacle of will, that is used negatively against perceived enemies.

The United States Supreme Court overturned a Hialeah, Florida, ban on animal sacrifice, which allows the legal sacrificing of animals for religious purposes by the estimated seven million people who have been involved in doing so illegally in the United States alone.

In the U.S. there are an estimated eight hundred thousand followers of Santeria, a Christianized form of pantheistic worship with its roots in the West African Yoruba tribe, who use chickens and goats for ritual sacrifice. Their numbers are growing. Voodoo and macumba are other ritualistic belief systems attracting more and more followers here and in South America.

Santeria has a curious feature during some rituals that involves the drawing down of various deities (through rhythmic drumming and blood sacrifice) to "mount" special participants. The god (one of twelve different Orishas) then controls the motor functions of a specific person who has abandoned him or herself to the deity in ecstatic frenzy.

The roots of this occult form of belief system are ancient and primitive but what happens when you bring high technology into the equation? A researcher passed along this "what if" speculation to researcher Tom Adams in 1978.

What if there existed an organization which dabbled in the headier realms of "Black Magic?" What if they succeeded in creating a "thought form," a very powerful entity brought into being by sheer force of will, couched in ritual and agreement among these occultists, who were impressively powerful and proficient themselves. Perhaps things got a little out of hand when the "thought form" became too powerful to control and began demanding "blood sacrifice" and, again, life essence. Both magic and technology, a powerful combination, might be employed to obtain the life force of animal victims to be fed to an increasingly powerful "thought form." Undoubtedly the hope would be that this "thought form" would remain satisfied with the life force of lower animals, without developing a "taste" for its creators.

The western esoteric tradition contains elements and several belief systems that still use blood in an occult manner. The transformation of wine into the "Blood of Christ" in the Catholic mass could have deeper hidden significance, if looked at in a slightly different "occult" context. The Hebraic tradition of Passover, with the story of "the Angel of Death" passing over houses of the Jews who put lamb's blood over their doors, sparing the families' firstborn, also has a curious "blood-based" tradition.

It appears that this theoretical "thought form" has attempted to manifest itself into culture as an "alien" presence. As we have seen, "the Real Thing" appears to have its own peculiar, albeit unknown, objective, that it is highly selective and has an arrogant veneer of impunity. But what form does this objective take and what is the agenda?

Linda Moulton Howe, the most visible of all UAD experts, put forward an argument for the extraterrestrial hypothesis in her excellent 1988 book, *An Alien Harvest*. Many paranormal researchers share the suspicion that extraterrestrials are directly responsible for true UADs.

Theories have been suggested, some with revealed secret government documents, that "ETs" require cattle blood and glandular material for: 1. Food source, 2. Medicinal use, 3. Genetic engineering.

If the animal tissue is gathered for food, why would they usually harvest only one eye? This question also holds true for medicinal use. If ETs are conducting genetic engineering, why are they so indiscreet? Certainly animals could be more easily harvested in third-world countries with less media and ability to be spotted or caught. If, as some suspect, our government is involved in genetic experiments, why would they employ all their high-tech equipment to steal animal parts from ranchers instead of buying their own herd for privacy? Every theory gives rise to more questions.

Could there be a more complicated scenario involving "mythological engineering?" Could the mythos of cultural blood sacrifice be perpetuated by a alien presence? Can we surmise that aspects of this process, with its roots in pre-history, may involve a portion of our shared genetic memory, enacted through ritual, to a supernatural presence or being? Furthermore, could this supernatural presence be these same aliens?

Researchers close to the UAD phenomenon have come up with several theories concerning possible culpable parties and their agendas. There are several manuscripts gathering dust, completed years ago, pertaining to the UAD question that have remained unpublished. Jacques Vallee spent two years investigating UADs yet is unwilling to release his findings. He states in his book *Confrontations*:

> Another domain I have explored concerns cattle mutilations. Over a two-year period I interviewed ranchers, veterinarians, and law enforcement officials in Arkansas, Missouri, and Kansas. Today a number of the episodes I investigated are still unexplained. They may have a direct relationship to the UFO phenomenon. Because I cannot yet prove this relationship, I have decided not to burden the reader with what may be irrelevant data. But the entire subject remains very much open in my own mind, even if the UFO research community, except for a few courageous investigators, prefers to sweep it under the rug and keep it there.

Perhaps the evidence connecting the government, or a faction thereof, to some of these animal deaths is discouraging investigators from disclosing the connection. Vallee goes on to state his suspicions concerning the potential for abuse in the UFO controversy:

Like many of my colleagues in the field, I have become convinced that the U.S. Government, as well as other governments, are very involved in the UFO business. . . . The belief in extraterrestrials, like any other strong belief, is an attractive vehicle for some sort of mind control and psychological warfare activities.

A sobering thought. Is it too fantastic to suggest the possibility of the government's role going even further into the realm of societal or military control mechanisms to be engineered and administered through beef, a primary food source?

I am convinced that the UAD and UFO phenomena represent two distinct aspects that merge in the valley and may have far-reaching ramifications. UADs and UFOs at the core of the phenomena are "real," physical manifestations. But it is important to remember that these phenomena, even in the modern age, also exist within the framework of cultural symbolism, or shared psyche. In our culture, the very perception of the San Luis Valley as the "birthplace" of the UAD phenomenon is important.

Here is a typical scenario:

When a UAD occurs and is subsequently discovered by its owner, the first phone call is usually placed by the distraught rancher to his local sheriff, who is, and always has been, rendered impotent by the parameters of the phenomenon. The sheriff then calls a government agency that claims no knowledge of, and offers no answers or solutions to, the unexplained physical event and further solidifies the local law enforcement official's feeling of impotence. This effectively negates his symbolic protector role in the rural community. He can do nothing but downplay it.

Often, mystery helicopters are seen in and around UAD sites, further frustrating law officers and ranchers and reinforcing the belief that "the government" must be involved. The rancher then calls friends, neighbors, and relatives, starting a chain reaction of disclosure and response by dozens of people: second, third, fourth-hand, etc.

The local media only hears of and reports a portion of these animal deaths. The regional media reports a series or outbreak of deaths. The national media only carries ongoing waves of UAD reports.

We are witnessing what appears to be a systematic mythologic program with the lid of disclosure, media coverage, bouncing on and off the phenomenon. This program is conditioning our law enforcement system (and our perception of it) to feel helpless in the face of "the unknown." The phenomenon and the agenda behind it toys with our protective defensive systems, leaving a feeling of total vulnerability, which many refuse to face. Why does an aspect of our government appear to be helping perpetuate this perception?

One could easily envision some frightening scenarios as to why someone or something is programming perception of impotence into our cultural awareness of the protection structure, staging the phenomena in select rural areas, and letting the subliminal impact filter into mainstream consciousness through the vehicle of the media.

But why in rural areas? The SLV can be described as the perfect remote laboratory, one of the only pristine areas left in the continental United States. This valley is the perfect location for a "control group."

Another possible explanation could be that the inhabitants of remote areas and the inherent isolation that it implies might be more susceptible to mythologic and/or psychotronic programming. Is this isolation, even today, by ranchers a sufficient rationale for them to be targeted? Taking into account the subtle undercurrent of fear experienced by mostly poor, subsistence ranchers and their families, it's no wonder a sizable percentage of sightings and UADs may go unreported.

Here in the valley we find the case of truck driver Henry Ozawa who saw strange lights around 1945, two years before the term "flying saucer" was coined. "The lights were floating around. It looked like an automobile, they were blue, you know, like headlights. They were floating all over the place. You'd think it was a car coming and, before you knew it, it floats away."

Ozawa said he was not frightened by the spectacle and returned to the site, five miles north of Antonito, with many of his friends. "I wasn't married, I was single back then, so I'd take a girlfriend out there. I and another guy, we'd go out there in pairs." He even took one of his sons out to see the lights.

Years later, the same son who had viewed the lights with his father returned to the site with his high school buddies. They were not disappointed, although some found the strange phenomenon disturbing.

The modern era of the "classic cattle mutilation" began when the media discovered the phenomena and begun dis seminating awareness of it to the public in 1967. But there are documented cases from the Midwest that have been uncovered by researchers that lend credence to the proposition that the programmers have been at work for far longer.

A case in point:

Oklahoma City, OK, Leon J. Sale in a 1978 letter to *Stigma* (magazine) reports on a 1934 or 1935 incident.

We found a hog slaughtered in a mysterious way in a pasture after we had seen a shiny object flying over the farm at about treetop level, and we thought it went down in the pasture across the creek from the house. By the time my grandfather and I walked over there it was gone, but there was a ring about twenty-five feet in radius burned in the grass and the hog was laying in the middle of it. At that time we had never heard of UFOs and I don't think my grandfather ever said anything to anyone about it.

This is but one of many incidents that has been uncovered by researchers looking for clues in the historical record, hoping to uncover the definitive case that will enable us to finally solve this enduring mystery. How many other residents of remote regions of the world have had similar experiences?

There are literally thousands of stories from rural areas of the world that attest to strange beings, objects, lights and other unexplained phenomena. If the complete history and tradition of the San Luis Valley's original part-time inhabitants is taken into account, we discover a very important clue. The ancient legends of many Indian tribes who used the valley are rife with alienlike references and the valley is one of several holy, revered locations in the Southwest with unusual electromagnetic and gravitational anomalies.

George C. Andrews, in his book *Extraterrestrials, Friends and Foes*, excerpted in *The Leading Edge*, writes:

> After purchasing maps from the United States Geological Survey, it became evident that there was indeed a valid connection between these areas and UFOs to Mr. Lew Tery, who gave a public lecture about this relationship in Arizona. He was subsequently harassed by the FBI and ceased to give public lectures on this subject.
>
> Both the Aeromagnetic and Gravitational (Bougier Gravity) maps indicate basic field strength, as well as areas of high and low field strength. Interestingly enough, the areas of maximum and minimum field strength have the following:
>
> • All have frequent UFO sightings.
> • All are on Indian reservations (sacred sites), government land, or land the government is trying to buy (or restrict usage).
> • Many of them, especially where several are clustered together, are suspected base areas and/or where mutilations and abductions have taken place.

The SLV contains all the elements stated above. The aeromagnetic and gravitational qualities mentioned above are readings of basic field strength, gravitational or magnetic fluctuations attributed to various areas on the earth's surface. The valley contains both minimum and maximum intensity zones in close proximity to each other (a very unusual occurrence). The interaction between these zones, the Dunes area, for example, is often the location of our unusual activity.

The field of UFOlogy has several systems of classification including the Hynek "Close Encounter I through IV" and the Vallée addition of the effects of "Anomaly, Fly-By, and Maneuver" classes of UFO sightings and encounters. As the number of UAD reports continues to climb, it is about time that a system for classifying these on-going mysterious deaths and the potpourri of other unexplained mysteries be devised. Standardization and education of the public is essential. These are no longer "closet" subjects, there is something going on in the world around and above us. It seems there always has been.

PART THREE

"I have data upon data upon data of new lands that are not far away. I hold expectations and the materials of new hopes and new despairs and new triumphs and new tragedies. I hold out my hands to point to the sky. . . ."

—Charles Fort, *New Lands*, 1923

OLD SCRATCH

MAY 8, 1993, THE BACA:

I was tracking the mystery rancher who had reported a UAD to Costilla authorities on the morning of the mournful moo-o-o. He lived south of Questa, New Mexico, and had (I assumed) called Sheriff Billy Maestas, to report that a helicopter that had flown out of his pasture where his bull was "mutilated" the night before. According to Maestas, he (the rancher) watched the helicopter head north into Colorado. The New Mexico State Police had investigated the report but I could locate no one at State Police Headquarters who would comment on it.

I called the Questa police chief to find out the status of his investigation of the matter. He said his deputies chased red and white lights flying from the huge molybdenum mines that sprawl to the east along Red River Canyon. They flew over town and headed out into the SLV. "My guys were chasing the lights all over. I guess they were helicopters. What else could they have been?"

I asked about other reports of the unusual. He hesitated, then told me this peculiar tale. A close relative, an uncle, had been driving home late at night, north of Questa on Highway 522, in early April 1993. He was heading south when he spotted a "woman hitchhiker dressed up in red," walking along the side of the road. He naturally stopped to see if she needed help or a ride into town. Without a word, she climbed into the pickup next to him, silently looking straight ahead. As he turned to ask her why she was walking along the road alone so late at night, he noticed she had "goat's legs and cloven hooves." Before the startled man could react to the sight, she dematerialized!

Huh? I scratched my head. Here was a police chief sincerely telling me a story that sounded like a *Twilight Zone* rerun.

"My uncle is a church-going man whom I and everyone respect, and if it had been any other witness, I would have told him to stop drinking!" According to his police chief nephew he was extremely "honest and stable" and that he wouldn't "make up such an outrageous story for any reason. We tried to talk him out of making a report, but he insisted!"

I'd heard other stories at various times about mystery hitchhikers and "shape-shifters" occasionally reported in the Four Corners area but this incident was alleged to have happened right here in the valley. I couldn't help but shake my head in wonder. I was surprised he had confided such a story to a reporter, and after thinking about it, the account sounded somehow familiar. Then I remembered.

Two *Rio Grande Sun* articles recently had arrived in a package from Tom Adams just prior to the Questa incident. I remembered dismissing them as another case of creative journalism. They had mentioned appearances of a "devil," so I dug them out.

Written by Gail Olson, excerpts from the first article suggest, tongue-firmly-planted-in-cheek, there were 1984 reports of the devil:

The story began when a dark, handsome stranger, a young man dressed in white, entered Red's Steak House in Ranchitos [New Mexico] and began buying drinks for a covey of besmitten smiling maidens. One source said the stranger ordered a Red Margarita.

The devil focused his attention on the table at which the four most attractive young ladies were seated, charming them with his urbane airs, compelling smile, and dancing eyes. The young man attending the maidens glowered at the intruder, but left.

The devil, as yet unrecognized, danced with three of the maidens, saving his last dance for the youngest and prettiest of all, the Rose of Espanola. She blushed with delight, but felt a chill as he took her hand, an inexplicable shiver of fear. He smiled, removed his glove, and she screamed. His hand was a claw.

The alarmed intruder made a hasty retreat, but his boot fell off as he ran, revealing a cloven hoof, according to reports. As he rushed through the door, a spiked tail trailed behind his impeccable tailored white sports coat.

The maiden, in a dead faint, was rushed by ambulance to the hospital in a deep state of shock, the story goes. A photo taken at the bar that night of the mysterious gentleman showed no image of him when the film was developed, though the table and the girls were clearly visible in the photos.

The owner disagreed with the alleged encounter. Tales like this could be bad for business.

Red Roybal, owner of Red's Steak House, where the devil was supposed to have appeared, called from Red River [just up the road from Questa] Tuesday to declare the story a fabrication, a tale spun by a competitor he would not name, but whom he claims is envious of the business a new country and western band is drawing to his establishment. . . .

"The story is all over, even in Sante Fe," he said, saying it is purely a bit of folklore, an oft-told tale that in the past has focused on other businesses. "It started with the Line Camp," he said, "Then it was Mr. G's, and now it is my place."

"There is a lot of black magic in the Valley," Dennis Salazar, owner of Saints and Sinners Lounge, said Tuesday. . . .

He said though his establishment seems a likely one for the Devil to visit because of its name, no such visit has happened.

Meanwhile, reports of dogs barking for no apparent reason on the streets of Espanola persist, and an anonymous man called the [Rio Grande] Sun after deadline Tuesday night, asking to place a Lost and Found classified ad. He said he had lost his pitchfork.

A week later, on April 19, 1984, the second Olson article ran. The *Rio Grande Sun* headline read: "Sightings of Valley Visitor Increase." Her follow-up article had a slightly more serious tone.

Since his [the devil's] alleged initial appearance at Red's Steak House April 11, [1984] he's been spotted a number of times. He has visited Saints and Sinners, where he went into the men's room and "just disappeared"; Emilio's Restaurant; Foster's in Chama [NM]; and Club West in Sante Fe.

Most reports, though, have placed him in the Pojoaque-Nambé [New Mexico] area. . . . One man had an encounter with the intruder last Friday, April 13, on Nambé Road as he returned to Chimayo [New Mexico] after an evening of merrymaking in Santa Fe, his cousin said.

At his favorite night club, the Forge in Santa Fe, his cousin said, he noticed a man in a white suit. He thought he recognized the man, but couldn't quite place him. The man sent drinks to his table, then left, looking at him significantly as he walked out the door. "I'll be seeing *you* later," the stranger told him.

Shortly after he turned off U.S. 285 at Pojoaque, on the road to Nambé, his car sputtered to a stop. The car was dead.

He jumped out and lifted the hood. Then, out of nowhere, the man in white just appeared, but he still couldn't recall his name. "This is Juan," he said, introducing the familiar-looking stranger to his friend. The stranger looked shocked, then just disappeared. . . .

Max, a musician from the Chama Valley area, still bears the scars from his encounter with the devil, storytellers say. He is a pious man now, but it wasn't always so. He was a carefree musician in his youth, a fiddler popular at dances in all the northern villages. Instead of using his musical talents to praise God, however, he was led astray, and began playing dances at Lent, despite warnings from his mother of the danger.

It was on Good Friday that the devil appeared at one of the dance halls he was playing, and he came up to the stage to claim Max's soul. A tremendous struggle followed, but Max was young and strong and managed to escape the devil's clutches. His face is still scarred from the scratches he received the Friday from the devil's claws, but his soul now belongs to God.

Could this be how the devil received the name "Old Scratch"?

I find it very intriguing that the devil's alleged initial appearance (at Red's Steak House) probably never happened. The so-called visit may have been a fabrication or an outright hoax. The story circulated around the area like wildfire for two weeks, creating quite a stir in communities where this apparition traditionally has been said to have appeared in the past.

SUBCULTURAL MANIFESTATIONS?

Several points spring to mind concerning Olson's first article: The owner of Red's insisted he could prove the story untrue. We're never told exactly what night during that first week of April the event was supposed to have occurred. Nor are we told the identity of the "Rose of Espanola." We are told a photo was taken but we aren't told the identity of the photographer, nor do we see the picture. The hospital where "Rose" was taken couldn't confirm her admission. The police claimed no knowledge of the event. There is no evidence whatsoever to document "Old Scratch's" initial appearance at Red's Steak House. Olson never names her source(s) for the story.

Within a week of Gail Olson's first article reporting the pervasive rumor, five more appearances were said to have occurred in the north-central New Mexico area. This time, we even have two witnesses that went on the record, "Friday the 13th."

If the initial appearance at Red's never happened, how can we account for this perceived flurry of activity the following week? Could widespread knowledge of an event, in culture (or subculture), manifest the very phenomenon itself? In this instance, does "energy" truly follow "thought?"

> **RULE #12**
> **There is a possibility that the (sub)culture itself may cocreate manifestations of unexplained, individually perceived phenomena.**

This realization, if valid, may have important ramifications in our scrutiny of the mysterious as it's perceived in the San Luis Valley. If a devil could be manifested by some aspect of the (sub)culture, why not UFOs, UADs, or for that matter, religious apparitions and miraculous healings?

Is there a link, or connection, between "cultural" manifestation, and the perceived, true phenomenal experience itself?

Edgar Cayce, America's Sleeping Prophet (and medical diagnostician), claimed to have had an encounter with an angelic being with wings while reading the Bible one 1880s afternoon in May, when he was thirteen. After being told by the being, "His prayers had been heard," the being then asked Cayce to "tell me what you would like most of all," so that it could be given to him. Cayce responded, "Most of all I would like to be helpful to others, especially little children when they are sick." Then, "suddenly, the being was gone."

Immediately running to his house to relate the experience to his mother, according to biographer Thomas Sugrue, he asked her, "Do you think I've been reading the Bible too much? It makes some people go crazy, doesn't it?"

If angelic beings can allegedly impart extraordinary medical diagnostic powers to a poor farm boy in Kentucky, can devils shock sinners into observing the forty days of Lent? Or dissuade pious men from picking up lady hitchhikers late at night on a dark country roads?

Stories of apparitions, like a vanishing devil, can't help but stretch one's rational view to the breaking point. Granted, this particular phenomenon may not be unique to this particular subculture, or bio-region. Stories of a "devil" abound in other rural, fundamentalist Catholic regions as well. Regardless of the true nature of the phenomena perceived, stories of this ilk do tend to grow, through the dissemination process, into something more than they actually are, solidifying perception of the myth in the (sub)culture.

Perception and dissemination of these manifestations really got me thinking. Was there a (sub)cultural trigger, at the core of the initial (false?) Red's Steak House story? If the subsequent experiences were indeed real, were these individuals experiencing phenomena that had been triggered for them by the (sub)culture itself? Why them in particular? Just because they were merrymaking during

Lent? Would the subsequent five additional events have occurred (or been created?) if the initial Gail Olson article had not been published?

What about the personal experiences themselves? The police chief's uncle, according to his nephew, was convinced of the appearance and disappearance of the hitch-hiker. It is important to remember that he sought no publicity and insisted on filing an official police report. This indicates to me that the man had what he perceived as a real experience, the true nature of which is impossible for us to accurately determine, solely through anecdote.

There are too many reports, credible and otherwise, of too many alleged encounters, with a type of entity that is, as yet, undefined, for this phenomenon to not have some basis in fact. In hindsight, all one can do is compile the data, try and locate witnesses and keep asking questions.

Armed with Gail Olson's intriguing articles from 1984, and the "Woman in Red" account, I asked around the southern portion of the SLV, that spring, about other alleged appearances of what has been interpreted here as a devil, or demon. Most of these supposed encounters, I noticed, tend to be clustered just over the southwestern edge of the valley, in the Espanola Valley, which is our neighbor to the south.

In the early to mid 1970s, rumors of appearances of a shadowy urbane devil circulated through the southern valley towns of La Jara, Capulin, and San Luis. One account had the devil making an appearance at a community dance, in front of dozens of witnesses, in La Jara or Manassa. I couldn't find a bona fide eyewitness to the devil's alleged antics. Several locals heard the story, which varies little from account to account, and two even had friends supposedly in attendance. However, after checking these leads, none of these witnesses panned out. Not one was actually in attendance when the encounter occurred, although one apparently left a dance just before the incident was said to have happened.

*   *   *

Eppy Archuleta, world famous weaver, and one of our country's national artistic treasures, has lived in the area for over seventy years. She is a veritable encyclopedia of local folklore and traditional phenomena that are said to occur here. She has related several intriguing stories of manifestations from her own personal family history.

One account has Eppy's eldest son, Fernando, in the late 1970s, walking briskly toward home at dusk, near Capulin. He spotted a "very old man" walking stiffly in the same direction. The young Archuleta caught up with the man, and as he passed him, the old man, without a word, picked up his pace and stayed right behind, shadowing him.

Archuleta nervously walked faster but the old man effortlessly kept pace. This scared him, and he began running. But the old man stayed right behind, close enough for the terrified Fernando to hear him breathing. No matter how fast he ran, the old man stayed with him. As he turned the corner to his house, he looked back, and the old man had inexplicably vanished.

Eppy also relates many accounts, some personally experienced, of hearing the plaintive wail of La Llorona. This apparition is said, by locals, to be the ghost of a pioneer woman, or Mexican mother, who lost her children. The distraught woman was said to be so overcome by grief, that she drowned herself. (Other versions say she drowned her children and went crazy with guilt.) According to the legend, her wails can sometimes be heard on dark nights, around the new moon, echoing eerily through the gloom.

The story of La Llorona, locally, often has been attributed to mothers and grandmothers simply trying to scare young children, like tales of the bogeyman. The source of the legend may be found in the dim regions of this bioregion's mythic tradition. There is a possibility that the legend arrived in the SLV area with the conquistadors, and the early Spanish settlers, hundreds of years ago. The story is very similar to folklore accounts from rural Spain and may have been imported with the eighteenth-century Spanish influx into the region. With a slight geographical difference, our local story strikingly parallels the old-world version.

Hispanic locals have reported seeing La Llorona for as long as the legend has been passed from one generation to the next. In the seventies she was spotted numerous times in the southern valley near San Antonio Peak. More than one driver reported a woman in a long flowing nightgown, suddenly standing directly in front of his or her car. The drivers all swerved or locked up the brakes before passing right through the apparition. None of the witnesses made reports to official sources, but my neighbor Daniel S. Johnson recalls hearing numerous versions of the La Llorona story related during a Folk Medicine college course in 1975.

The question arises, Can an ancient Spanish folktale create the physical sound associated with La Llorona? Is the wailing sound countless people have reported a real, measurable sound? Can their perceptions simply be attributed to overactive imaginations or preconceived notions about La Llorona? It's primarily local Hispanic people, not tourists, who experience this particular phenomenon. They should be familiar with the mundane nocturnal sounds of the region that could be misidentified, i.e., cougar screams, coyotes, birdcalls, the wind, etc., and insist this sound is different.

To remain objective, I have to consider mind conditioning as a possible explanation for paranormal experiences. For instance, young Hispanics who have heard the story of La Llorona all their lives seem to be the ones who later have experiences involving her apparition. I have never heard of a Buddhist meditator seeing Jesus Christ appear, nor has a single Hindu been visited by Mohammed.

It seems to be part of the individual ego that its religion, political structure, country, and ways of comprehending the surrounding world are the right ways. The mind appears capable of projecting desires outwardly, such as the longing to meet God or discover a meaning to life.

Fasting, psychotropic plants, and methods of self-torture have long been used as catalysts to receiving visions, such as employed by many Plains Indian tribes. Perhaps, in fasting, the life energy usually used in digestion is freed for the mind to project its desires, fears, and repressions, much the way drugs can induce trancelike states.

In relation to the UAD, UFO, and even the devil sightings, it appears that the initial reportings set into motion a flurry of similar sightings, experiences and interpretations.

RULE #13
We must be extremely careful not to perpetrate our own beliefs, suspicions or actual experiences into the minds of those who want desperately to have a "special" event happen in their lives.

This theory is in no way meant to discredit the UAD, UFO, or other paranormal phenomena, but it may explain some misinterpretations of mundane events as extraordinary. It also, as I've said, may influence the way we perceive an event which in turn influences the way we report it.

Modern physics teaches a theory in which the mere presence of an observer may influence the outcome of an experiment or even create a particle. Employing this theory to unexplained phenomena, it is conceivable that the expectations of the observer may actually be a causative factor in the way the event occurs. As a result of these new revelations concerning the unexplained and truly bizarre in the southern portion of the valley, I realized I needed to expand my investigative efforts to fully encompass the greater SLV region. Is there a mundane or an extraordinary explanation for the unearthly wailing ghosts, devils, mystery hitchhikers, etc., solemnly said to roam the remote valleys of the Southern Rocky Mountains? I was convinced that more data was out there to help answer this question.

The further my investigation went, the more I realized these subject matters are mysteries wound around a riddle, locked inside a puzzle that's effectively obscured by haze, behind a veil. . . .

MANHUNT

Spring had finally returned to the valley, and the shrill, buzzing sound of the newly arrived broadtailed hummingbirds filled the still mountain air. Things seemed to have blissfully quieted and I was looking forward to our six months of warm weather. It had been a fairly mild winter and it sure felt good to be outside in the warm spring sunshine.

My new band, The Business, was getting down to business as we prepared for back-to-back weekends at a local Alamosa biker bar called the Eastside. The gigs went well but I found out in the paper the following Monday, April 24, 1993, that quite a drama had occurred right next door to the bar that previous Saturday night, as we rocked.

Evidently, two illegal Mexican immigrants had been stopped for a defective taillight. A cooler on their front seat contained a couple of ounces of marijuana. The cop handcuffed one of them, leaving the other man uncuffed because he was missing one of his arms below the elbow.

According to the article, the officer was then hit in the face with the top of the cooler, and both men escaped across the bar's parking lot, disappearing into the new moon night.

I was returning from Alamosa, up 17, with my brother Brendan. As we approached Road T, we noticed bright lights and a knot of cars parked at the intersection. I made the turn with bright spotlights shining in my face and a police officer motioned me to stop. I rolled down my window. "What's going on?" I asked.

"Do you both live here?" the cop inquired.

"Yes, officer . . . what's all the commotion?"

"We're looking for two escapees that may be up here," he answered with a frown, jotting something down on a clipboard.

"You mean those two guys in Alamosa I read about in the paper?"

"That's them," he said, backing away from the car. He waved me through. As I drove slowly by all the official looking cars, I noticed the monograms of several federal agencies. Brendan asked, "Did you see that guy with the FBI hat on? There's a guy with a DEA jacket." Why were almost every law enforcement arm of the federal government, Colorado State Police, and local county sheriffs manning a roadblock for two unarmed Mexicans, one cuffed, the other with one arm? For a couple of ounces of pot? And I saw bluish-white flashes when they had the spotlights in my eyes. Were we photographed?

As we approached the Baptist church just outside of Crestone, we noticed the parking lot filled with squad cars, four-wheel drives, and unmarked sedans. There must have been twenty to twenty-five of them. Many of these vehicles stayed around town for nearly a week, presumably searching for the two scared men, even when it was announced that one of the fugitives had been captured. The thought ran through my mind that this activity could be hiding other objectives.

Two weeks before military trucks had been seen coming and going from the Baca Ranch. And this was just after it appeared I'd been followed by a car with no lights. My level of paranoia rose another notch. I had to take a deep breath and remind myself that all this activity was just circumstantial, it's just a coincidence! Right?

ALTSHULER AND GOOD

I had received a letter from English UFOlogist Timothy Good. His new book had just been released and he was coming to the United States to see Dr. John Altshuler. They planned to fly down and visit with me in Altshuler's plane.

In September 1967, Dr. Altshuler, straight out of his residency, had come to the San Luis Valley for a camping trip in the Great Sand Dunes. While in the dune field, Altshuler observed four unusual lights approaching from the north. "They came down, stopped, and then they turned ninety degrees or one hundred degrees and came toward me. There were four of them. One of them came right in front of me. You know, maybe fifty feet away. It was big."

Years later, Altshuler underwent hypnosis to recall the following. "I saw two things in front of me. . . . They were not the typical gray kind of creatures. They were different. I don't know if that's simply a figment of my imagination or not. I don't know. They have huge heads. Huge, with a very small body. The head had four definite wrinkles on the forehead. The eyes were wide open, literally."

Early the following morning, after stumbling out of the dunes, he met a ranger who, upon hearing he was a doctor, asked him to accompany him to the Snippy site. He anonymously conducted the now famous examination "within three or four days" of the horse's death. As a result of this sighting and visitation experience twenty-five years ago, Altshuler has not gone camping since.

COMMUNICATION BREAKDOWN

Pilot Altshuler, Good, my brother Brendan, and myself were winding up our flight around the San Luis Valley. As we flew over the old King Ranch and headed toward the Alamosa Airport, I casually asked John to fly over the Dry Lakes. "It's where compasses have been known to spin for no apparent reason." He banked the plane and we flew directly over the glittering ponds that mirror the San Luis Lakes to the north.

Altshuler called the Alamosa tower to obtain clearance for landing. There was no response on any of his three radios. He called again, still nothing. Someone joked, "He must be in the bathroom." After a third call, he continued south, lining up his final approach.

We touched down and taxied toward the terminal and I

noticed someone running toward us waving his hand. It was the furious tower operator. "Why didn't you answer me?" he shouted. "What's the matter with you? I had cleared another plane for a landing, they had to break off!"

The four of us looked at each other as the other plane landed and taxied toward the terminal. John explained, "I called three times, and there was no answer." The three of us backed him up, we had heard him but no response. John radioed the plane that had just landed and received an immediate reply. We were lucky the other pilot was able to spot us in time. We could have easily collided in midair!

Altshuler was shaken by the episode. "Nothing like this has ever happened to me in over five thousand hours of flying!"

Tim Good interviewed me about our recent reports over lunch. I was surprised to learn that this was Altshuler's first trip back to the SLV since his "abduction," as he called it, in the sand dunes and his subsequent examination of Snippy the following day.

Altshuler remained quiet during the rest of our visit. Good promised to send me some photographs he had taken during the flight and Brendan and I drove them back to the airport.

Another unusual aerial episode over Alamosa was brought to my attention. I received an interesting letter from pilot F. X. Rozinsky and copilot Mark Calkins (holder of the round-the-world speed record of 49 hours, 21 minutes) who were referred to me by psychologist Dr. Leo Sprinkle:

I had an experience that might be related to a UFO. I am a retired marine corps pilot and, after I retired in 1965, I started to fly corporate aircraft . . . After forty-two years of flying for a living I decided to be a free spirit and get away from structured life.

I have about 15,750 hours of flight time and this experience was the only time an unusual thing happened to me. . . . I was captain on a Learjet 24 and we were flying our boss and his wife from Palm Springs to Denver [on February 24, 1989] where we

were based. We were at 41,000 feet near Alamosa, it
was between 2200 and 2300 [hours] or very close to
that time, according to my log book. The cockpit
lights were out, instrument lights were on and we
were not talking. As well as I can remember, it was
a clear night.

All of a sudden the cockpit and outside the aircraft
turned to daylight for about one second, maybe one
and a half seconds. . . . We looked at each other and
one of us said, "What the hell was that?" We were
really perplexed because it was such a strange event.
I called Denver Center and explained what we experienced and asked if they had any reports of a similar event. There was a pause, I assumed he asked
other controllers, and then came back and said,
"Negative on any reports."

A moment after this, a United pilot came on the
frequency and said, "Where was that aircraft that
saw the light?" The controller said, "He is about
twenty miles ahead of you." The United pilot said,
"We saw that light." The controller said, "Do you
know what it was?"

The United pilot said, "Negative" or "No I
don't." That was it. To this day I regret that I didn't
try to contact the United pilot and ask him to describe
what he saw . . . I wish I knew what I saw.

BOOMERANG

MAY 31, 1993, 7:20 PM, ROAD T, SAGUACHE COUNTY:

Isadora and I are returning from a soak at Cottonwood
Hot Springs and approaching the last S turn, eight miles
east of the Baca. "What's that, over there?" Isadora slows
the car and points straight ahead.

A wedge-shaped, boomerang-looking object skims north
toward San Isabelle Creek and we catch a clear view of it.

It is about thirty to forty feet across and appears to be about five miles away. As I watch, for about three or four seconds, it suddenly slows and performs a rapid-falling leaf descent toward the ground. I see the orange glow of the setting sun glint off the bottom, then the top, then the bottom, before it rocks downward out of sight. "Wow, it landed! Quick, let's drive over to Camper Village and see if we can spot it!" I excitedly say to Isadora, who, because she's driving, has not seen it descend.

We race the five miles to the RV park and try to find a dirt road to the location where the object has landed. We can't find access. It went down in a depression that was invisible from the dirt roads, crisscrossing the area of open prairie.

"It may have been even further away than I thought," I say. "If that's the case, that thing could have been pretty big." Darkness ends our search.

The following afternoon, I am talking with a woman rancher who lives several miles west of Moffat about a construction project at their ranch. I mention my sighting the day before and she counters with this story.

"I was approaching 17, on Saturday and I saw an army truck heading south on the highway with a small, old-looking yellow helicopter flying above it. Then, awhile later, I saw them again, going back north."

Whoa! I ask her to describe the chopper. It fits the description of the Sutherland chopper, and the chopper I'd seen, perfectly. She also tells me her husband and his partner had seen a whole formation of Apaches on May 28, headed south from Bonanza.

JUNE 29, 6 AM, THE BACA:

A loud boom echoes through the mountains. Startled piñon jays take flight in a raucous chorus as the last remnants of the sound dies away. "Honey, what was that?" I ask Isadora, rubbing the sleep from my eyes. I sit up and listen. I hear no sound of jet engines, just the laughterlike cries of the jays. Isadora, who had been up for a while, also had

not heard any plane go over. The boom came out of nowhere. Oh, no, not this morning. There'd been a late rehearsal the night before. I yawn, roll over, and go back to
sleep for another hour.

Later that day, I ask a few people if they heard the early
morning boom. About half had. The boom seemed localized. I quickly forget about it, and continue my day. The
following morning, three Huey helicopters are reported flying down the Sangres toward the dunes at 10:30 A.M., and
I watch two smaller choppers head the same way at 2:30
P.M.

IZZY'S EVOLUTIONARY IMPERATIVE

JUNE 19, 1993, LIBRE 25TH ANNIVERSARY PARTY, FARISITA:

Tom Adams, who had been quietly assisting me over the
phone for six months, bringing me up to speed concerning
this region's shadowy past, had mentioned several times
that there's someone in my area I've got to meet, "as soon
as he gets back from the South Pacific."

David Perkins, "Izzy Zane" to his friends, had been
fascinated with the UFO and UAD questions since 1975,
when he investigated an UAD near his home. Perkins, a
Yale graduate, had arrived in Colorado in 1969 to study
nontraditional communities. He was so fascinated by the
people and the idyllic setting of the Libre commune that
he moved to the alternative community. Twenty-five years
later, he still calls Libre, in the Huerfano Valley, his home.

During the first week in June, Adams informed me that
Perkins finally had returned from his trip to Indonesia, so
I gave him a call. I found that he hadn't spent much time
actively investigating (UADs) recently due to the illness
and death of his wife, Carrie.

My investigation and enthusiasm was well received and
he told me several interesting Huerfano/Wet Mountain accounts. We had something else in common—we were both

musicians. Perkins and his band, The Roids, had played the Colorado/New Mexico circuit for years. He mentioned a twenty-fifth anniversary party Libre was having on June 19 and 20, and suggested The Business come over and rock!

What a day! Several hundred people converged on the commune and enjoyed good music, sunshine and each other. Adams had told me he couldn't make it but his research associate, Gary Massey, was headed up from Texas. I stayed for three days, much of it spent around a campfire, engaged in philosophical debate with Perkins and Massey and going over (and over) the more salient points surrounding UFOs and UADs. I learned that these many subsequent get-togethers would be fun, with good-natured razor-sharp, deadly earnest, repartee. These two guys obviously had been arguing for years.

Some of Perkins's early investigative UAD work in the 1970s centered on the phenomenon as a form of environmental monitoring program. Perkins is the acknowledged formulator of this theory. He noticed that areas of high incidence were downstream and downwind of nuclear plants, weapons labs, uranium mines, and nuclear test sites. He noticed that someone was monitoring the environmental contamination of cattle in these areas of high incidence.

Perkins has been working on a unified theory which attempts to explain all paranormal phenomena and has developed a "big picture" theory he calls the Evolutionary Imperative. He defines it for me:

"Virtually everything that happens to humans can be viewed through a new science called 'evolutionary psychology,' which is trying to examine human behavior and all human action in light of where we came from as hunter-gatherers. It boils down to a few basic ingredients. Food, sex. Survival. As humans we have reached the point where it has become evident that we cannot last here as a species forever. Something will do us in. Anyway you look at it, our sun is going to burn out and the earth will die, if we don't get hit by a comet first. So, if we know, as a species with an incredible survival instinct, that in even the best-case scenario this is going to be a cold, floating cinder in four to five billion years, maybe much sooner, then we're going to have to start thinking of ways to get off the planet if we're going to survive.''

Perkins suggests that UFOs, UADs, and many paranormal phenomena are somehow being created by us as a species to stimulate our innate human curiosity as a collective imperative to pull us ''off-planet.'' He feels we are seeing the formation of a belief system that accepts the existence of extraterrestrials as part of this process.

''UFO mythology, something that's pulling us into the future, is somehow geared into an evolutionary perspective of what we rationally and intuitively feel we need to do and to mobilize ourselves to get it done. If you look at the whole theme of science fiction, this hugely powerful mythology has many of the elements of classical religion. It has that much power. Just as the bleeding wounds of human stigmata are spontaneous manifestations of faith [miracles] for traditional Christianity, the animal mutilations could be the stigmata of a space-age religion. Both phenomena give their respective belief systems the transformative power needed to perpetuate themselves.''

I'VE BEEN CHASING THEM FOR YEARS

Traditionally, during extended flap periods, UFO and UAD reports in the valley take a nosedive during the June-July summer months. At the start of August 1993, I looked carefully through my sighting log and found only a handful of publicized reports during the summer months. The steady trickle of calls reporting helicopter activity, and my intuition, told me something was afoot.

AUGUST 1, 1993, 10 PM, FIVE MILES SOUTHEAST OF THE GREAT SAND DUNES:

Rocky arrives from Denver and we find ourselves traveling north toward the Sand Dunes Road intersection. I see a flare just below the horizon. Rocky slows. A single, bright white light appears at the western edge of the dunes at the eastern border of the Medano Ranch. There are no roads in this sand-swept area.

"Let me roll some tape!" I call, as I quickly power up the camera and shoot eight or nine seconds before we pull over at the intersection. I scramble out of the truck and begin to set up the camera and tripod in the middle of the road. The light fizzles out.

"Damn, I was ready to start shooting again," I say. We both stand there to see if the light returns. A loud humming sound punctuates the still August night. We walk toward the side of the road in the direction of the sound. The corner utility pole, on the line that stretches to the dunes, is vibrating so loudly, we can hear it thirty-five to forty feet away. I carefully approach the barely visible pole. It is definitely vibrating. A loose insulator covering at the top of the pole rattles randomly but there is no transformer on it.

I put my ear against the pole and hear a complex mixture of hums, rattles, clicks, whooshings, and a deep rumbling. I ask Rocky to grab a flashlight which reveals nothing out of the ordinary, just a visibly vibrating utility pole. I crouch near the base and listen. The sound seems louder the closer I get to the ground.

The next day I get a call from the Medano-Zapata Ranch foreman. "They were back last night!"

"What time?" I ask.

"Between nine thirty [P.M.] and ten [P.M.]."

"You're kidding," I say. "We saw a weird light around ten, right out on the edge of the Medano!"

"The dogs started barking pretty good around nine thirty. My ranch hand called me and said they surrounded his house and lit it up real good. I could see the lights from here."

"How many were there?"

"Five of six, at least," he says, adding, "I've been chasing them for years but that's the most I've ever seen at once."

The timing of our sighting was perfect, the right place at the right time. There was a good chance that we had witnessed and partially videotaped one of the mystery bigfoot truck lights the ranch foreman had been chasing at night on his motorcycle over the past two years.

Gary Hart, an investigator from Illinois, previously had managed to record an SLV vibrating utility pole with sophisticated recording equipment. The electric company suggested that it was simply the wind vibrating the wires but, as in my own experiences, Gary's recording suggests a much more complex phenomenon.

AUGUST 5, 8:30 AM, THE BACA:

Brisa slithers down the stairs and I say, "Good morning," although I hardly look up from my work.

"Did you see the helicopters outside last night?" she asks.

"What helicopters?" She has my full attention.

"The quiet ones that were outside my window."

"What are you talking about, sweetie?" Isadora asks.

"I got up to go to the bathroom, around two or three o'clock, and on my way back to bed, I noticed a beam of light outside. It was going from one helicopter to the other. They were right over the tree, right outside. I never would have seen them if I hadn't noticed the red light. I pinched myself to make sure I was awake even!"

We ask her what else she noticed, and she tells us that the tree underneath the craft was swirling around. She didn't remember going back to sleep. Brisa, is a bright, well-adjusted child, not at all prone to flights of fantasy. I carefully observe her earnest account of the experience.

Later on that day, David Perkins phones. He has just got off the phone with a rancher who had evidently found a "mutilated" bull under a power line on the other side of Medano Pass the day before. The rancher had noticed a dark, military-style chopper making low-level passes over the rented pasture and discovered the slain animal.

My hunch is right. There appears to be a surge of rare, midsummer activity underway.

August 14, 1993, The Baca:

The second week of August was quiet, with no reported activity. Then Sherry Adamiak, head of the Center for the Study of Extraterrestrial Intelligence's (CSETI) Rapid Mobilization Team (RMIT) calls to introduce herself. She has heard about our ongoing activity from Jim Nelson, head of Colorado Mutual UFO Network (MUFON), who suggested to "give Christopher a call."

Sherry, a paralegal, is interested in driving down to the valley with three other CSETI members to do some "vectoring" (the CSETI system for calling in crafts using an elaborate attraction system utilizing powerful spotlights, coherent group thought sequencing, and amplified sounds that had been recorded in an English crop-circle formation). She speaks about attempting to attract a UFO, climbing aboard, and establishing "contact." Sure, I have nothing better going on.

Each CSETI team member has a specific role in their "protocols." They have step-by-step instructions of what to do in case a ship lands and they interact with an extraterrestrial intelligence. I tell them I'll be happy to meet with them and take them to a good skywatching location.

They arrive and we set off toward the switchbacking Radio Tower Road, and ascend the side of the Blanca Massif. The weather is perfect for a skywatching exercise. I show them the basic airline routes and bid them good hunting.

The following day, they arrive back at the Baca. Sherry is pretty nonchalant about their sighting. "We saw an amber light appear right over town [Crestone] at about three thirty or four [A.M.]. Then two smaller white lights came on, one just to the east and one to the west. They didn't stay on very long. We all watched the larger amber light hover for quite a while before it finally went out." CSETI would make several trips back to the valley, organize a local CSETI group, conduct trainings, and "vector" out into the infinite sky.

FROM SHADOWS

August 19, 1993, 11 pm, Baca Grande Development:

Isadora and I had just climbed into bed. The cool breeze of of the late August night oozed under the slightly open window. Fall arrives early in the mountains. I reached up and turned out the light. Instantly I sensed something out of the ordinary. I noticed faint movements streaming into the room through the wall from the outside. I blinked several times to see if I was somehow seeing things. I wasn't. Whatever it was, it had entered our bedroom and stopped at the foot of our bed. My eyes grew accustomed to the dark. I blurted out, "Honey, do you see this."

"What?"

"I swear something just came in the room, and now it's standing at the foot of the bed!" The only way I can describe it is like reflections bouncing off shadows, like a faint, localized shimmering, or rippling of energy hanging in the dark. "It's moving . . . it's coming around to your side."

"I don't see a thing," Isadora answered, sitting up in bed.

"It's really faint, but it's definitely there!" I said slowly, watching the faint shimmer in the dark. I had never observed this phenomenon before. I looked around to see if an external light source was somehow reflecting into the room. I couldn't locate any light that could account for this effect I perceived in the room.

"I don't feel anything from it," I said. "It feels kind of . . . neutral."

I lay there for several minutes just observing, running through my mind various possible mundane explanations to rationalize the visual oddity I was sure I was perceiving. Finally, I fell into a deep sleep.

AUGUST 19, 1993, 1 AM, BACA CHALETS:

Two hours later the widow of a famous author fluffed her pillow and settled into bed. She hadn't been able to sleep and had watched some late-night TV. As she turned out the light, she heard a noise coming from the kitchen. Several residents had reported bears rummaging through garbage cans lately, and she was concerned that a bear had gotten in. She got up, called out, "Who's there." Not hearing anything, she got up to go see who, or what it was. Nothing, no sign of anything. She felt a little "spooked."

Puzzled, she climbed back into bed, reached up, shut off the light. A "few seconds later," just as her eyes were getting accustomed to the dark, "through the wall, ten or twelve creatures, about three and a half to four feet tall" glided into the room in a "tight group," less than three feet from where she lay. She sat up in amazement, looking at them.

"When they were coming in, I could see right through them. They looked like the color of water. As they got into the room, they became solid and I couldn't see through them." They clustered around the foot of her bed, looking at her. "At first, I wasn't afraid." She described her impressions.

"They were cold. They seemed completely indifferent, well, maybe a little curious. It was hard to tell . . . they were small and slight and had huge almond eyes."

Sleeping right next to her bed was her five-year-old son. He is a special boy. He had been waking up occasionally over the past year, telling his mother about the "earth shaking." She made notes, and was surprised to find out that he was "predicting earthquakes." She hadn't told many people about her son's apparent abilities, she wanted to make sure she wasn't just reading something into her small boy's curious statements. Several more times his "predictions" came true. Each time he would mention these dreams, she said, "sure enough, I'd read about an earthquake somewhere."

She suddenly thought of her boy and became afraid. She

remembers thinking, They're here because of him! She forcefully "banished them," telling them, "If you're not of the light, leave, and don't come back." They silently glided out the wall, the way they came in.

The woman didn't know what to make of her experience. She never had any interest in UFOs; she'd never read any books or saw movies about them. She fought the urge to tell anyone for a couple of days, but finally confided in a friend, who immediately urged her to contact me. She did three weeks later, and I found out that she had written down the night and time of her perceived experience.

The suggestive timing of her and my perceived experiences sent a shiver up my spine when I looked at my calender. Her friend Jean told me of her experience, and that same night, a scant two hours earlier, I could have sworn something came through the wall into our bedroom. I was now completely convinced that something very strange was going on, even around me.

September arrived. I figured we were in for some unusually heavy activity. Nothing. No activity was reported to me for almost six weeks. I used the time whipping the band into shape and fielding the dozens of requests from around the country for information about our activity. These requests slowly began to overwhelm my time and my energy. I found myself writing a generic form letter, listing the various reports, then just typing in the person's name.

This helped, but it didn't provide a very viable format. I began to kick around the idea of a time line, a formatted newsletter, documenting my ongoing investigations. I figured, if I could write down all the information in one place, I could publish it, charge folks a nominal fee to cover printing and postage, and send it out bimonthly. The *Mysterious Valley Report*, for over two years, has reached investigators the world over.

October 14, 10:40 pm, The Baca Chalets:

As is my usual custom after the late local news, I usually step outside to take a few minutes to look around. This night found me preparing for the next day's trip to Boulder, where I was to conduct a short seminar for the Colorado MUFON organization pertaining to my investigations.

As I stood outside the door, marveling at the still, partly cloudy sky, a large white, oblong blob of light slowly curved silently overhead, headed south. As it disappeared behind the trees, it left a ghost image behind that slowly faded. I estimated its visible duration at about three or four seconds. The blob of light looked like a giant glowing kidney bean. The curved shape mirrored the curve of its flight through the air. I had just seen another "cheap firework." It looked like it was less than a half a mile away.

These puzzling orbs of light still baffle me to this day. Some have a liquid appearance as they undulate like a blob of water flying through the air in slow motion. At various times I've seen them under complete cloud cover, light up the tops of trees, make right-angle turns, and hover. They give me the impression of plasma, in all variety of sizes and colors.

THE QUICKENING

AUGUST 15, 1993, BOULDER:

I was looking forward to meeting State Director Jim Nelson, second-in-command Ken Spencer, and several other MUFON members to whom I'd spoken over the past few months. They seemed genuinely excited to have me address one of their monthly MUFON meetings, and we finally were able to work out a good afternoon for me to travel up to Boulder.

My first out-of-town talk was underway. The video camera across the room did nothing to alleviate my nervousness. I calmly introduced myself and gave the thirty or so attendees a brief personal background. Then I asked the audience:

''Why are we all in this room right now? There's something going on. I think everybody who has an interest in this subject matter has a gut feeling that there's something going on in the world. There probably always has been. We seem to be witnessing a quickening. We have more and more activity worldwide, and researchers, who really keep their fingers on the pulse of 'what's going on' in the paranormal, I think, would all agree that we're seeing a flowering of activity right now, and we have been for the past year.'' The rest of the hour and a half was spent relating the results of my investigation and research.

I was pleased with the ease in which I accessed my data. I had a feeling that this would not be the last public lecture I would give concerning my investigation into the mysterious valley.

The following three nights, lights were reported over the Baca Ranch by multiple witnesses. These lights were described as ''rapidly blinking dots of white light,'' similar to reports that surfaced the previous December. No one I interviewed was able to positively identify them and two sighting reports awaited us on the answering machine when we returned from Boulder.

The same three nights, strange glowing lights were reported one hundred miles east, just south of La Junta, Colorado, out on the front range. Jacob Magdelano, Brisa's father, had heard about these La Junta sightings from his sister, who had witnessed the unexplained lights. The timing and description of the concurrent reports, as usual, were too coincidental.

OCTOBER 31, HALLOWEEN, 6 PM, THE BACA:

Dusk was gathering over the valley and Arnette Cookerly was talking long distance with her daughter. Arnette and her husband Jack had moved to the Baca the previous summer and bought a house way out in the Grants with a breathtaking view of the Sangres. Arnette had sold her advertising company, and Jack, a world-class composer and inventor, had moved his sound recording studio to their new house.

Jack played on many of the golden age of television series including: *The Twilight Zone*, *The Untouchables*, (the original) *Star Trek*, and *The Fugitive*. His list of television and movie soundtrack credits is endless, over six hundred in all.

Arnette claims her daughter's voice on the line slowly faded, as Poet, their dog began barking furiously at the sky. A half mile away, their neighbor's two dogs also barked and whined at the sky. Jack stepped outside to see what all the ruckus was about but saw nothing.

The next day, Poet fell "sick and lethargic." Jack called his neighbor to see if they had seen or heard anything that previous evening, but they hadn't. He mentioned Poet's unusual behavior and found his neighbor's dogs suffered the same symptoms after barking madly "around dusk." He called me to report the the incident later that afternoon.

NOVEMBER 3, 1993, LIBRE, HUERFANO COUNTY:

Tom Adams, Gary Massey, and David Perkins had organized a meeting of UFOlogists and investigators in 1987 and dubbed it "Crestone I." Adams had wanted to conduct "Crestone II" for several years. Notables like Linda Moulton Howe, John Lear, and screenwriter Tracy Tormé had attended the first three-day confab, and all in attendance agreed that future meetings should be organized. Several years went by, then lo and behold! They heard that someone at the Baca was investigating strange activity, the perfect impetus for a second Crestone conference.

Tom had kicked around the idea with me that previous summer and had suggested the first week of November. His hope was that our activity would provide the attendees with a well-timed fury.

Two days before "Crestone II," Brendan and I drove around the Sangres to meet Adams and Massey at Perkins's house at Libre in the Wet Mountains. Both of us were anxious to meet Tom before the conference. I had talked with Tom for hours on the phone but now we would meet in person. I had already met Gary and David that previous June during Gary's trip to the Libre anniversary party.

Over the course of the next night and the following day we tossed around many questions concerning UADs and UFOs. The lively arguments rose and fell in intensity, as Perkins baited Massey with triggers well honed over the many years of repartee between the two. Adams, a usually quiet man with dark hair and medium build, occupied a strategic corner and provided detailed information upon request to bolster everyone's arguments. His computerlike memory never ceases to amaze me. Very few people, incidents, or details escape his steel-trap mind and recall ability. The evening ended with a rousing dice game named "Farkle." I was cajoled into participating, much to their misfortune.

NOVEMBER 4 THROUGH 7, THE BACA:

"Crestone II" was on. What had started out to be an "invitation-only" affair had blossomed into a full-blown conference. Tom had asked all invites to keep word of the conference "low key." Of course, word of an event like this has a way of leaking, and the week before the conference I received several inquiries.

A whole contingent from New Mexico MUFON attended, including Gail Staehlin and Debbie Stark. They arrived early and eager. The Denver contingent of John and Barbara Altshuler, Kalani and Katuiska Hanohano, and Candice Powers arrived shortly after. Hollywood screenwriter and producer Tracy Tormé and a friend, Marc Friedlander, flew in, arrived at the conference, and tossed a football outside. Steven Greer and Sherry Adamiak brought a no-nonsense contingent of CSETI members. Other attendees included, from Dallas, *The Eclectic Viewpoint*'s (magazine) Cheyenne Turner, researcher Bill LaParl from Hopkington, Massachusetts.

Linda Moulton Howe had been invited but unfortunately was unable to attend. Author and abductee Travis Walton had also wanted to attend but at the last minute had to cancel. He sent along a friend to attend in his stead.

Pointed debate was to be expected from this assortment of investigators and researchers with such divergent views. I recorded an exchange between Greer and Tormé concerning Greer's enthusiastic claim that official disclosure of the existence of extraterrestrials to the public was imminent. "Ninety Days!"

NOVEMBER 7, 1:45 AM, ROAD T:

Three members of CSETI were leaving Crestone to head back to Denver. As they approached the first set of S turns, six miles west of town, someone in the backseat saw something pacing the car, off to their left.

Next to them, about "thirty-five feet from the road," zipped a "twelve-foot craft." They all got a glimpse before it disappeared into the gloomy night. As if on cue, a smaller reddish globe also was seen for an instant as they entered the S turn.

They called me the next morning with a good description of their sighting.

NOVEMBER 17, 9:30 PM, MOFFAT-BACA RANCH:

I'm traveling home from Alamosa after the first rehearsal with our new guitar player, George Oringdulph. I scan the horizon and surrounding terrain for any unusual lights, as is my usual custom driving on the twenty-five-mile straight-as-an-arrow Highway 17. As I get to the halfway mark between Hooper and Moffat, I notice an orange-amber light out in the middle of the Baca Ranch, in an area that has no roads. I pull over to have a look with my night-vision binoculars. It appears to be moving toward me. I estimate its distance at about five miles away. I watch for several minutes before I see the light move straight up in the air, maybe one hundred feet, simultaneously as it appears to extinguish.

Six miles up the road, Al, Donna, and Alta Koon are

outside with two friends for their nightly skywatch. It's a foggy night with intermittent cloud cover scudding by at low altitude. Al notices an orange light flare, low to the ground, directly east. They watch for several minutes before the light appears to go out. A scant five minutes later, I'm passing and notice the Koons standing outside in the cold, looking toward the Baca Ranch. They have seen the same light I had observed just minutes before.

No matter how often it happens, I love it when others see the same puzzling sights I see.

THEY'RE WATCHING HER

NOVEMBER 18, 1 AM, THE BACA CHALET II:

Healer Kimmy Martin awoke with a start. She looked into the gloomy night outside her window and wondered why she felt like someone was watching. Something moved on the porch outside. A "large group of grays" peered in the window at her. She was not sure if they were physically manifest, or just on the other side in "the etheric" but she had no doubt that they were definitely out there, watching her. Not the least bit threatened or frightened, she watched them "for almost an hour" while they watched her. Finally, wanting to go to bed and not too crazy about her "twenty to twenty-five visitors," she told them to "go away, and let me sleep." They trooped away obediently and a nonplussed Kimmy rolled over and fell asleep.

NOVEMBER 23, FIVE MILES SOUTH OF EAGLE:

It's early. The morning chill permeates the air and rancher Lloyd Girard rubs his hands briskly together to warm up his cold fingers. He walks over from his truck and opens the door of his potato barn, enters, and stops in his tracks. Lying several feet inside the door is a dead cow, the entire left side of its head and neck laid open, the exposed bones gleaming. He kneels down and carefully looks at the dead animal. The tongue, windpipe, and all the tissue are gone.

He searches the barn for clues. There is no visible indication of a struggle, footprints, or blood. He angrily heads back to the house to call the sheriff, muttering to himself.

That same morning, neighboring rancher Bill Bradford is outside when he notices one of his cows missing from his herd, which is milling around, agitated. Bradford scans the pasture and there, several hundred feet away, he spots it. It's lying on its side motionless, upside legs stretching straight out. The animal's mandible is exposed, all the hide on the jaw and the tongue are gone, one eye is missing.

The local newspaper, the *Eagle Valley Enterprise* noted in its article:

> Bradford says the animal was found after a fresh snowfall, and there was no sign of blood on the carcass or the new snow beneath it. The only nearby tracks were those of the cow.

The story also mentions a local veterinarian who, when asked by the reporter about hypothetical extraterrestrial involvement, said:

> [The veterinarian] waves aside the idea that scalpel-wielding visitors from outer space might beam to planet earth so they could nab beef parts, noting that a good, sharp hunting knife in the hands of an experienced skinner—or prankster—can appear to be quite surgical.

FIREBALLS

NOVEMBER 30, 1993, 6:07 PM, THE BACA GRANTS:

Composer Jack Cookerly, also an ex–naval aviation navigator, arrived home in the Grants and had just stepped out of his Blazer when he realized that he was casting a shadow. Something bright was above him.

"It was bright white as it streaked for three or so seconds directly over my head, and I instantly thought it was a meteor. But as it approached the horizon, it flared up about ten times its original size, turned into an oval shape, and stopped. It was *huge!*" Then to Cookerly's amazement, "It changed from its original white color to a bluish white and started to descend slowly like a parachute flare, for five or so seconds. I looked for an object like a parachute above the oval but I didn't see anything."

Unlike a parachute flare which fizzles out, Cookerly observed the object instantly disappear. "It couldn't have been a meteor because, whatever it was, it made a ninety-degree, right-angled turn, and changed its color, shape, size, and velocity."

I asked him how far away the object appeared to be. Cookerly stated, "I'm absolutely sure it came down in the valley. I thought I could run right out and find it. It seemed so close that I actually waited for an explosion to blow me off my feet!" Cookerly ran inside and called to inform me of the incredible celestial sight he had just witnessed, seconds before. He wasn't the only one who witnessed the sky-borne phenomenon.

6:07 PM, MOFFAT:

Al Koon, also a trained ex-military observer, was sitting with his family in their living room with its panoramic view to the south and west, seven miles west of Cookerly. The

Koons described what they saw.

"It was a little bigger than a full moon and visible below the horizon before it blinked out." Al, along with his wife, Donna, and daughter Alta, is convinced that what they saw was not a meteor. "It appeared to break apart into several pieces just before it blinked out."

Three other locals also reported the object's arrival into the SLV. It streaked in from the northeast "through the clouds," directly over the development, and appeared to descend on the western side of the valley. Fort Garland residents, forty miles to the southeast, also reported seeing the object, as was reported in the following day's *Pueblo Chieftain.*

After some digging, I found that SLV residents weren't the only folks who saw something strange flash through the darkening sky on November 30, 1993. Something undoubtedly flew along the border between New Mexico and Colorado. Bill Papich, of the Farmington, New Mexico, *Daily Times* wrote on Thursday, December 2:

> A bright light seen Tuesday evening in skies over San Juan County remains a mystery, although a federal agency says it probably wasn't space debris.
>
> The light was reported by numerous people who saw it streak across the sky between 6 and 6:30 P.M., traveling from east to west. Some strange stories about the light were being told Wednesday.
>
> Pilots flying over the Four Corners area Tuesday evening radioed air-traffic controllers in Farmington [New Mexico] about a bright light traveling from east to west.
>
> Sgt. John Harrison of Kirtland air force base in Albuquerque [New Mexico] said he's not aware of any air force operations that could have caused the light.
>
> Professor Mark Price of the observatory at the University of New Mexico in Albuquerque said the light could have been a meteor or space debris burning up as it entered the atmosphere. "They are very bright,"

Price said of burning space debris.

However, the North American Air Defense Command (NORAD) in Colorado Springs, CO, had no reports of satellite debris burning up in the earth's atmosphere Tuesday evening. The agency monitors objects entering the earth's atmosphere.

In a follow-up article Papich interviewed two witnesses of an unusual celestial object that traveled overhead on Monday, November 29, 1993, the night before the fireball.

Rig workers who read newspaper accounts of a strange light over San Juan County Tuesday night say they saw something in the sky Monday night that may have been even stranger. "I've never seen anything like it before," said Pete Corey of Farmington.

Corey said he and four other men were at a drilling rig four miles southwest of Aztec [New Mexico] at 8 P.M. Monday when they all saw what appeared to be a mysterious object with lights pass overhead. "What we saw was big. That thing was low enough where you could almost see the whole body of the thing," Corey said. "To me it was square looking with four lights. There seemed to be a light on each corner of this thing. There was no sound. We couldn't hear a thing."

Corey said the object drifted across the sky for fifteen to twenty seconds before it was out of sight.

Gabe Montano of Bloomfield [New Mexico] was among the five men and said the lights didn't blink like airplane lights. He said the object looked rectangular. "It was kind of gliding across the sky. It wasn't going very fast," Montano said. "It wasn't very high at all. It was right there." He said the drilling rig was 110 feet high and the object appeared to be only about four hundred feet above the top of the rig.

Several questions spring to mind when looking at the eyewitness accounts. First off, the fireball was seen over a very large area. The Crestone-Moffat sighting was about 135 miles from Farmington, New Mexico, the furthest point west. Both Koon and Cookerly were sure the object, or a piece of it, had gone down in the valley. If accounts from New Mexico are correct, the main body of the object continued on to the southwest, passing over Del Norte and Pagosa Springs, crossing the border near Arboles into New Mexico.

Koon's description of the object breaking apart may be significant. Perhaps an initial piece did fall off and descend in the SLV, while a second piece may have crashed just north of Cuba (New Mexico). This is where witnesses saw a large flare, trailing smoke, descend.

Ethel Baca, of Cuba, described it as "a big firework," that apparently landed on Cuba Mesa, just to the northeast. Could this have been a second piece? One of two, or three pieces may have separated off the main body of the unidentified object and veered south, slowing as they fell. Reports of a boom indicate the main object slowed through the sound barrier near the Bloomington-Farmington area.

NORAD claimed they observed nothing unusual in the region that night. How could they have missed it? If this had been a routine, mundane celestial object, like a meteor, wouldn't NORAD have been immediately forthcoming about its nature? They must have seen it on their scopes as it entered the atmosphere. Over a dozen ground observers, over a 135-mile corridor, apparently witnessed the arrival of something. Why the denials?

What about the sighting from the night before, on Monday, November 29, of the large rectangular craft with four unblinking lights? The strange object was spotted south of the witnesses' location which, by my estimates, would have put it directly along the flight path of the next day's fireball. Were the pilots of this strange looking, slow flying craft, somehow preparing for the object's arrival?

The ensuing two months of incredible activity would continue the following night.

DECEMBER 1, 1993, 8:45 PM, THE BACA RANCH:

Rocky had called me Tuesday night, and I related the sighting reports of the fireball earlier that evening. He immediately made plans to drive down the following day.

It was 8:30 P.M. and we were sitting in his Ford Explorer, four miles south of Road T on the Baca Ranch. Rocky brought his latest toys, a scanner which he had "tweaked" to extend its capability for receiving bandwidths and a new pair of third-generation night-vision goggles and a video camera night-vision lens.

As we listened for any activity on the scanner, we both witnessed a small flare fizzling out about five miles south of our location. The two of us clamored out of the truck into the minus-ten-degree cold. Rocky fired up the night-vision-equipped video camera, ready to capture anything we saw. I put on the goggles and looked south where the flare had vanished and immediately picked up movement.

Four bright, unblinking objects were approaching from the southwest. Right behind them came three, possibly four more.

"That's military," I said. "Film that!" Although this may not have been an accurate assessment of the grouped objects, it was my first impression.

Over the next half hour, freezing our tails off, we videotaped seven or eight lights milling around in the area where the piece may have landed the night before. Several shots are spectacular as the objects flew behind a large silo in the foreground. I took off the goggles at one point and noticed that the objects were invisible to the naked eye. We could not tell if they were helicopters, although several times two or three of them reversed course and/or hovered. Although the objects appeared to be fairly close to our vantage point, with the wind in our faces, we didn't hear a thing, no sound of engines or props. We could not tell what they were doing. There did not seem to be any particular pattern to their aerial coverage but the sky was swarming with them.

We hustled back into the warm truck and watched for

almost forty-five minutes for any additional craft or objects to appear. After an hour of excitement, we were positive there would be a finale. About 10:15 P.M., Rocky suggested that we head toward Del Norte for a closer perspective. As we were driving north to hit Road T, I put on the goggles and caught sight of a large unblinking orb that appeared from behind the mountains, just north of Villa Grove. Rocky pulled off the ranch road.

"Quick, fire up the camera," I call as we get out and start filming the large, slow-moving orb. The unidentified object skims the tops of the mountains moving west. It appears to go behind some peaks and in front others. Later, I would determine that it was forty-one miles away from us.

The object would have been invisible to anyone close enough to have observed it with their unaided vision. It was low, and just far enough into the mountains, to be invisible to a casual observer. Only with night vision, and our proximity so far to the south, were we able to see it.

Another interesting aspect of this fifteen-minute sighting were three smaller blinking lights which flew below and to the south of the larger, unblinking orb. It was as if they were riding interference between the object and any observers in the northern part of the valley. All four appeared to be traveling slowly, less than one hundred miles per hour. We filmed their entire transit until they disappeared to the west.

We gave each other a high five in the cold darkness. Yes! It's one thing to "claim" sightings of unusual aerial activity, it's another to whip out a video camera and document an event. Hours and hours spent chasing elusive aerial phantoms and we finally wound up in the right place at the right time. We had captured something on tape. Viewing the footage, I still don't know what they were but no one can claim we invented it.

DECEMBER 2, 1993, AFTER SUNSET, ANTONITO:

Ray and Lucy Jaramillo reported the following to the Conejos County sheriff's office. Apparently the Jaramillos, with some friends and relatives, were watching through binoculars what they described as a "large fire" on the hillside, west of Antonito. They gave the dispatcher directions which placed the fire near the (narrow gauge) Cumbres-Toltec train stop, halfway up the mountainside.

The witnesses said they had "such a good view" of the fire they "could see thirty-foot-high flames. The sheriff's office dispatched deputies and, together with four of the initial witnesses, they rushed toward the site.

They found absolutely no trace of a fire or explosion! After a couple of hours scouring the hillside, they found no evidence to back up the Jaramillo's report. The sheriff's party finally called the search off.

December 5, 5:30 pm, The Baca Grants:

I'm on my way to visit Jack Cookerly, the glow of sunset lighting up the western horizon, heavy clouds approaching from the east. Two lights slowly appear together, about five degrees apart, over the distant silhouetted mountains. I quickly pull over to watch. They just hang there, possibly reflecting the still-setting sun. They diverge from one another, one appearing to descend westward, the other heading directly north, toward me. As it collides with the earth's shadow, it fades into the darkening sky.

December 9, 12:08 pm, The Baca Grants:

Arnette Cookerly is working at her desk when the whole house rocks, walls shaking, shelves rattling.

My phone rings. "Did you just hear a huge boom a few seconds ago?" Arnette asks innocently. I hadn't. "I know this may sound weird but it sounded like a cow just landed on my roof!" In the background I hear Jack's voice. Arnette asks him if he just heard the boom.

He takes the phone. "I was out in the studio and I felt a huge boom, not like a sonic boom, but more like a huge fist hitting the ground. I didn't really hear it as much as I felt it. I did hear the garage door rattle from the shockwave, though.''

A half mile away, musician Barry Monroe and two housemates also feel the shockwave rattle the house around them. I call Barry several minutes later to check if anyone else near the Cookerlys had heard the localized shockwave. He described it in a similar fashion, ''like something really big hitting the ground.''

Nobody else I called in an ever-increasing circle around the apparent epicenter had heard it. Five people, in two houses, in a two-square-mile area, had experienced the mystery boom. This was the same area where the barking dogs fell ill.

DECEMBER 13, NEW MOON, 9:35 PM, THE BACA CHALETS:

Rocky calls from Denver and I fill him in about the activity that's taken place since he was last down. He sets up a time to meet me in the late morning the following day. I kid him that he's ''coming back for more punishment.'' Rocky and I, by this time, have spent at least one hundred—mostly uneventful—hours skywatching since his first trip to the San Luis Valley the previous April.

An hour, or so later, us ''boys'' are gathered for a weekly American exercise of *Monday Night Football* male bonding. Several local football fans are friends of mine, and we gather ritualistically every Monday night during football season.

Halfway through the first quarter, Brendan's girlfriend, Faye, calls and asks for me. ''What's up?'' I ask.

She tells me, ''I just now saw a dime-sized glowing white orb fall into the ground south of the Baca. It was three or so stories off the ground when I first saw it and when it disappeared it was like it went underground this side of Hooper.''

I cover the phone and tell the guys about Faye's sighting. Dr. John Short chimes in, ''Earlier, right around sunset while I was on the phone, I saw a streak outside and the phone faded out for a couple of seconds. . . ."

Bob McClaren blurts out, "You saw that? I saw something weird like that around sunset too!"

I thank Faye for the report and we start talking about these "cheap fireworks." We only forget the game momentarily.

MORE MUTES

December 14, 1993, 6:30 am, The Bradford Ranch, Gypsum:

Bill Bradford was up early. He quickly set about his daily morning tasks on this cold, frigid morning. Around 7:30 A.M., he headed out into the pasture to find another mutilated cow. He called the sheriff to report the UAD.

"This is getting too weird," he told me later. "When I dragged the second cow up to my bone pile, the first one I lost last month in November was laying there missing a perfect ten by ten by ten [inch] triangle of hide off its side. Someone had to have cut that triangle out but who would go up there and do that? I put that bone pile where it's pretty remote; no one goes there."

Bradford described the condition of the second carcass. "She was missing an eight-inch plug out of the brisket. I didn't look but I'm pretty sure they took her heart. . . . Do you know what in the heck's going on?"

I assured him I really didn't.

7 am, The Vigil Ranch, Costilla County:

It had been a bitterly cold night. A sharp wind cut through Chama Canyon, gusting down from the tall mountains just a mile east of Clarence and Dale Vigil's secluded ranch. A snowstorm had dumped two inches two days earlier.

According to both brothers their prize Limousine seed

bull had appeared healthy and normal the day before. As Dale went out for his routine check of the herd, he felt uneasy. He drove around the frozen pasture, looking for the bull where they had last seen him, off by himself. Nothing. Vigil climbed into his pickup and drove back to the house to get help to locate the bull. Clarence and his young son accompanied Dale back out to the snow-covered pasture to look.

"There he is," Clarence's son called out. They looked toward a row of scrub willow, and sure enough, there was their bull. The red-colored animal lay on his left side and they could see a faint trace of steam rising from the carcass in the frigid air. They climbed out of the truck to check him. He had been mutilated. The animal's rear-end had been cut out and his genitalia was removed. Both brothers were angry as they carefully examined the area around the animal, looking for signs of predators. This was getting out of hand. They couldn't find a single track.

"Over here," Dale, who was examining the scrub willow bushes twenty feet to the east of the animal, called out to his brother. They looked at the branches carefully. Small clumps of red hair adorned the tips of branches that looked like they'd been bent over and snapped off. One clump of hair even had a small drop of blood on it.

I received a worried call from Dale that morning. "I had another one," he told me. "I can't take this! I'm going to sell my herd, I can't afford this!" He asked me to make the long trip down to his Costilla ranch to help investigate the animal death.

Ironically, Rocky was due to arrive momentarily, so I gathered my field equipment for the trip. Rocky arrived and quickly agreed that we would go. We were both quiet, lost in our thoughts as we headed south.

We arrived by early afternoon and headed out into the frozen pasture. The Vigils were gathered around the dead bull.

"Thanks for coming down, you just missed the vet," Dale told me as we unloaded the video camera. An Alamosa veterinarian had done a necropsy on the animal and found that the bull's lungs were riddled with pneumonia. It had been laid open during the necropsy, and his examination determined that the animal had died of pneumonia and scavengers had inflicted the suspicious wounds.

The Vigil brothers were pretty confused by the vet's findings. "The vet said he died of pneumonia but I don't know about that," Dale says. "He seemed to be perfectly healthy, he didn't appear sick at all. We looked everywhere for predator tracks but there aren't any." He then led me over to the scrub willow thicket, just to the east of the animal. "Look at this." He pointed to the broken branches with bits of red hair sticking to the tips. "It looks like they crashed him into the bushes here," he concluded.

I examined the six-foot-high branches. There were clumps of red hair, the exact shade of the bull's hair. "I didn't know cattle could high jump," I said, trying to lighten up the distraught brothers who shook their heads.

We returned to the bull. I studied the immediate area. The animal lay under overhanging scrub willow branches, and about six feet above the carcass, the tips of the branches had also been broken off. I bent one downward to snap it off. Freshly broken branch tips littered the ground below it. "These branches were broken off too, and it really looks like they were broken off from above, in a downwards motion," I told the Vigils. "It looks to me as if the animal had been dropped." I suggested, "I'll bet they tried to sling him in under the branches and missed on their first try. They must have snapped off the branches when they initially tried to drop him."

We began taping. I noticed Vigil's dogs stayed twenty feet from the carcass. They seemed wary and hesitant to venture any closer.

I sent forensic samples to Dr. John Altshuler in Denver. He reported a couple of weeks later that, "Evidence of high heat was found around the incision areas." Gee, those predators are getting clever!

TOO MUCH POWER

DECEMBER 15, 1993, THE WESTERN UNITED STATES:

An extensive power outage "zaps" the western states. Providers of electricity check their systems and backups but no one can figure out why the blackout has occurred.

Later, I hear through the grapevine that the little-known High Frequency Active Aural Program (HAARP), the world's largest high-frequency radio transmitter, may have gone on-line that day, and this may have been the cause. The remote facility, housing the transmitter, is located near Gakona, in southeastern Alaska, and is a United States navy, air force, and Department of Research program run by Atlantic Richfield (ARCO) Power Technologies, Inc.

A published excerpt from contract specification order no. SS-HAARP-02, section 4.1.1, dated March 2, 1990, describes the project's aim:

> The HAARP is to ultimately have a HF [High Frequency] heater with an ERP [effective radiated power] well above 1 gigawatt [1,000,000 watts]; in short, the most powerful facility in the world for conducting ionospheric modification research.
>
> From a DOD [Department of Defense] point of view, however, the most exciting and challenging aspect of ionospheric enhancement is its potential to *control* [their emphasis] ionospheric processes in such a way as to greatly improve performance of C-3 [command, communication, and control] systems, or to deny accessibility to an adversary. This is a revolutionary concept in that, rather than accepting the limitations imposed on operational systems by the natural ionosphere, it envisions seizing control of the propagation medium and shaping it to insure that de-

sired system capability can be achieved. A key in-
gredient of the DOD program is the goal of
identifying and investigating those ionospheric processes and phenomena that can be exploited for such
purposes.

I wonder if this HAARP program, that includes stated
"ionospheric manipulation" capabilities [jet stream manip-
ulation], could be inadvertently responsible for the strange
weather patterns that have plagued the continent since
1993. Floods, hurricanes, stalled low-pressure systems,
even earthquakes might be triggered by such a powerful
transmitter. One aspect of the program is to pulse signals
for communication directly through the earth. Some investigators of the HAARP project wonder if this could somehow adversely effect the earth's core and magnetic field.
Could this even trigger earthquakes? The deepest earthquakes ever recorded occurred a short time later in Bolivia.
The Northridge quake occurred a mere month later.
    Several sources agree that when they turned the HAARP
transmitter up to full power, the resulting power surge was
responsible for the widespread outage simultaneously experienced by millions of Americans in the western United
States on December 15, 1993.

DECEMBER 17, 9:35 PM, GLENWOOD SPRINGS:

One hundred and sixty miles northwest of the San Luis
Valley, a silent, brilliant flash of light was observed by the
occupants of a car headed west on Interstate 70. Although
no activity was reported here in the valley that night, I
mention this incident because the witnesses were so struck
by the size, intensity, and location of the unexplained flash.
    One witness told me, "It couldn't have been a lightning
strike, it lasted too long and there were no thunderstorms
at all in the area—I checked. It was really strange, the
whole canyon was totally lit up for a second . . . like daylight!"
    The following day on their return through the canyon,

headed east, they witnessed ''six silent black helicopters land in a crater, a couple miles east of Eagle. We stopped and got out and they were only three hundred to four hundred yards away and we still couldn't hear them.''

DECEMBER 29, 10:10 PM, MOFFAT:

As is my usual routine, I was traveling north after rehearsal on Highway 17 during my sixty-mile commute. We had realigned the band, adding a new drummer and a new name. Laffing Buddha was now the moniker, and the addition of new blood found us writing new songs, rehearsing, and honing our stage skills.

As I approached Moffat, I noticed a bluish-green light appear directly north over the Alfred Weiss Ranch in town. I quickly grabbed the camcorder from the seat beside me and tried to focus on the light. It blinked off. I took stock of what I'd just seen. The light had appeared to be less than four miles away and hovering around one hundred feet above the ground. I slowed the truck and put the camcorder down.

Flash! There it was again. It had moved west about a mile. I fumbled with the camera and managed to get two or three seconds of footage before it went out again. I slowly made the turn onto Road T scanning the area for the evasive light. It appeared to be playing with me.

The following morning, Brendan mentioned seeing a Bell jet-ranger flying low up Burnt Gulch at around 2:30 P.M. the day before. He thought he would mention it because, ''It sounded strange, like a jet airplane.''

BIGFOOT

DECEMBER 1993, THE NEW MEXICO—COLORADO BORDER:

During a seven-day period from the last week of December into the first week of January, seven "Bigfoot" encounters were reported to local authorities. The encounters all were reported within a seven-mile area. Because of the locals' reluctance to go on record, I've not pinpointed the exact location of these events. These locals seem very protective of the occasionally seen Bigfoot, not to mention their own privacy. The following events were related to me by an undersheriff.

Several days before, a niece of the undersheriff called to tell him that "she had found some tracks that he'd better come look at." She described them as being huge, human-looking, barefoot tracks. Not taking it too seriously, he didn't immediately investigate. On the morning of December 31, he followed her to the remote location with a video camera to document the scene. He wished he had gone out the day she called, for what she showed him was incredible.

Descending for hundreds of yards down a cow trail were two sets of human-looking tracks. One measured twenty inches, the other eighteen inches long. They descended over a variety of terrain: rocks, snow, and bare ground. They were unmistakable. One of the larger prints was so pristine that "you could see toenail marks!" I have seen the footage of these tracks, and visited the site and there is no mistaking the classic Bigfoot tracks. Shaquille O'Neal would be the smaller one's baby brother. Shaq has a size twenty foot, these tracks were a size thirty-five to forty!

The undersheriff's niece also related a strange story. On the eve of discovering the tracks, she had heard her dog bark furiously outside. She went out to see why he was barking when she heard huge "footsteps go running by the house." Outside, she found her dog cowering inside the fenced yard. The dog had been locked out of the yard. She put him back outside the fence. A short time later, he started barking again, and once more she heard the huge running footsteps and "a twang of something hitting the barbwire fence." She went back outside and found her dog shaking inside the fence again!

The following morning, while stalking a herd of deer to take photos, she happened to stumble on the giant barefoot tracks. She called her uncle to report the possible encounter and the tracks.

The undersheriff related several other recent reports. One found a mother and son driving back from the mountains just after sunset. As they rounded a curve, their headlights revealed a creature covered in hair with large glowing eyes and pointed ears in the middle of the road. The mother slammed on her brakes. Not knowing what to do, since the thing was blocking their way, she put the car in reverse and backed up. This evidently scared the thing, for "it dropped down on all fours and ran away like a dog!"

They proceeded directly to the sheriff's office to report what they had seen. According to the undersheriff, "They were real upset about it." This impressed the authorities enough for them to mount a search for the creature. They combed the hills but found no sign of it.

One interesting correlation to the above, during this same two-day period, a Washington State man reported seeing a Bigfoot with large pointed ears and wings near Mount Rainier.

Two additional reports were subsequently filed by motorists who had spotted large, hairy, humanoid creatures at night, next to the highway. One report was made by a trucker who claimed the one he saw was "all white."

Yet another report was filed by a man who claimed he witnessed a pair of Bigfoot "stalking a herd of elk" on the side of a mountain. He was close enough to see them "signaling to each other" while watching them through his binoculars.

Great timing! I had heard about alleged Bigfoot sightings during my research of the SLV but could find no hard evidence in the form of names of witnesses, dates, locations, etc., so naturally I had figured that these few "legendary" sightings were nothing more than local folklore. Since these reports, I have finally learned that these creatures have been historically sighted in several valley locations.

When the Independence Mine first began operations around the turn of the century seven miles south of Crestone, large human-looking footprints were said to have been found by area miners near the entrance. A lifelong valley resident and local tracker was told by his grandfather that he had seen a Bigfoot one night in the late 1920s. According to the tracker, the locals had named the elusive creature "Boji." Sightings of this ilk have appeared to be rare in the southern Rocky Mountains but the hesitance of locals to come forward, during our recent flurry of encounters, illustrates why it may be so difficult to investigate.

A New Mexico cattle inspector who lives in Rancho de Taos, New Mexico, told me he watched with binoculars "a white Bigfoot" clamber up a rocky slope during the late fall of 1993. It ascended the seemingly impossible slope in minutes. He became impressed with the creature's agility when he tried to make the same climb the following day. It took him over two hours.

DECEMBER 30, THE *VALLEY COURIER* OFFICE, ALAMOSA:

I called the *Courier* to see if they would allow me to peruse their newspaper morgue of back issues. They said it would not be a problem. "Come on in."

I arrived and introduced myself to Ruth Heide, the reporter who had written the "mutilation" story in November 1992, concerning the Manuel Sanchez cow. I had talked to Ruth over the phone a couple of times but had never actually met her. She seemed very interested in my research and investigation and asked if she could "interview me, and take some notes." I agreed, so we spent an hour going over some of the stranger cases that had been reported in the area. She seemed fascinated with the amount of information I had managed to compile concerning these unexplained events. Most of these reports were news to her.

I whipped through back issues, looking for additional stories to bolster some of the more vaporous cases while she snapped some photographs of me.

The following day, her article appeared as the front-page story! I had an idea that she would write a story but not a front-page story. I was stopped by complete strangers who wanted to comment on what they had read. Since this article, many stories have appeared in local, regional, and state publications concerning my efforts. I have never made calls to the press to promote myself, or my investigation since my experience with the *Rocky Mountain News* stringer. Somehow, the press invariably finds me when things are popping around here.

Because of the local articles covering my investigative efforts, I've gained a weird sort of celebrity status around the valley. It's flattering but a bit cumbersome to now have to deal with strangers who stop me, call me, even show up at the house to pick my brain, or relate some unusual experience that "Grandpa told us about."

Other people avert their gaze as I approach. There is a fine line between getting enough exposure to let people know I'm here on the case, and too much coverage that clutters my investigative environment. Not to mention the inevitable perception by some, "That guy is nuts!"

PART FOUR

"Flying saucers, real or not as objects, clearly introduce a central element in an already troubled future landscape. It would be overly optimistic to predict that they will decrease its dangers. It is none-the-less interesting to ask what will happen to our civilization if the next step in the development of the phenomenon is a massive change of human attitudes toward paranormal abilities and extraterrestrial life."

—Jacques Valleé, *Dimensions*

HIGH GEAR

Two years had passed since that fateful New Year's Eve party when Saguache County witnesses described their peculiar experiences. Time had flown and I'd come a long way since that night when I began my amateur investigation. By 1994, and with a lot of help, I'd managed to compile an impressive collection of legends, reports, stories, photos, videos and my own personal experiences of the high strange, yet I was no closer to figuring out what was going on than when I began. In some respects, it felt like I was further away.

It is inconceivable to even contemplate the process a single individual would undergo to effectively analyze the proverbial mountains of data which have been patiently accumulated by investigators and researchers of the unusual the world over. My intentions have never been to solve mankind's last remaining mysteries but rather put forth simple intuitive insights based on my own experiences. In true Thoreauean style, the valley may be a envisioned as a microcosm of the macrocosm. Understand the part and you have a glimpse of the whole.

Because the UFOlogical database is not yet standardized, there are no steadfast systems of classification and the mind reels from the kaleidoscopic effect of dealing with misinformation from possibly unreliable sources. My microcosmic approach decreases, but does not eliminate, having to question everything.

I feel that the individual, and his or her perception of an unusual experience, may be as important as the actual experiences themselves. Taken as a whole, these millions of perceptions melt into a cauldron of mythos. They may retain their original character but become part of the greater, mythic whole. Data alone may not be able to solve these mysteries.

JANUARY 5, 5:30 AM, HIGHWAY 160, ALAMOSA COUNTY:

Less than eighteen hours later, another impressive fireball descended through the clouds and dazzled witnesses. The LaBordes were headed out of the valley for a day trip, headed east on 160, about ten miles outside of Alamosa, when the sleepy foursome witnessed a "large, green fireball" descend straight down into the Blanca Massif. (The Indians, viewing similar phenomena since ancient times, regarded these celestial phenomena as portents. I can identify with this attribution quality.)

So can the LaBordes. They are convinced that their sighting was not of the usual mundane variety. "It was really big," Pam told me several days later. Evidently, Roger, Pam, and their two daughters, Angela and Jennifer, all got a good look at it. I asked Angela how long the green object was visible. She estimated the duration of the sighting at "about three seconds."

Pam agreed, "We saw it for about two to three seconds."

Jennifer described it as looking like "a big green golf ball."

JANUARY 7, 6:45 PM, HIGHWAY 17, FIVE MILES SOUTH OF MOFFAT:

One of my "skeptics," a former guitar player in my former band, The Business, Scott Olson (music teacher at Moffat School), called excitedly from Hooper.

"I just had a sighting. I don't know of what but I just

saw something," he exclaimed on the phone in a rather low-key but breathless voice.

"Sighting of what?" I asked.

"It looked like a swarm of bees. They were all lit up."

"Bees? What do you mean? How many of them were there?" I asked, enjoying that one of my "skeptics" had seen something unusual.

"It was a large, tight formation. There were, oh, maybe twenty-five or thirty lights. They were all blinking rapidly . . . but at random."

"What color were they?"

"White."

"Which way were they going?"

"They were coming from the dunes. From the east and headed west, I saw them right at the sand piles [seven miles south of Moffat, on Highway 17]. Has anyone ever reported seeing something like this?" He obviously was intrigued by his experience.

I was reminded of Berle's "old-time switchboard" sighting from his porch.

"Well, I figured you'd want to know about it, so I raced down to Hooper and called you right away so maybe you could spot them. I've got to get down to Alamosa, so I've got to go. You know, I never thought I'd ever see something so out of the ordinary."

I thanked Oly for calling me right away, grabbed my night-vision binoculars, and raced up to the porch. I scanned the far side of the valley for fifteen minutes and, seeing nothing, retreated from the frigid night.

Our activity had hit high gear. Get a little publicity, people start looking, and presto! If things are truly going on, you've got more reports than you can possibly investigate. The following is a comparison between the San Luis Valley NORAD Event of January 12, 1994, and New Mexico's Gallup Incident, January 12, 1983.

One of 1994's dark-horse events occurred in the valley on January 12. Exactly eleven years before, a eerily similar sequence happened in northern New Mexico. Both unexplained series of events feature green fireballs, mysterious fires, unexplained explosions, and unusual attendant military activity. Obviously, no two UFOlogical events are exactly alike but the parallels between these two cases are striking.

The most comprehensive look at 1983's Gallup Incident can be found in the Project Stigma publication, *Pardon the Intrusion or UFOs Over, On & Under (?) The State of New Mexico*, written and compiled by Tom Adams in 1992, who immediately noticed the similarity between the two events. The following are excerpts from that publication.

THE GALLUP INCIDENT

The Farmington, New Mexico, *Daily Times* article on January 13, 1983, headlined: "Goodness Gracious—Great Ball of Fire," written by reporter Rex Graham, stated:

> What investigators believe was a meteor smashed into the side of a mountain about fifteen miles east of Gallup Wednesday night about 5:50 P.M., starting a fire and causing a deluge of calls to the McKinley County sheriff's office. The incident is believed to be part of a broad "meteor shower" that caused sonic booms in Gallup, Farmington, Aztec, Bloomfield, and north to at least Durango, Colorado.
>
> McKinley County Sheriff Benny Padilla said today that his office had received 126 calls after as many as seven "booms" were heard by area residents beginning at 5:50 P.M. and continuing until about 8 P.M.
>
> Undersheriff Jack Graham quickly drove east of Gallup to investigate a fire burning on a hillside in the Springstead area, thought to be connected with the "explosionlike noises." Padilla and Graham initially feared an airplane had crashed. Graham walked through an empty crater about twenty-five feet across and six inches deep. There was no sign of plane

wreckage. Then, about 10 P.M., Padilla and Gallup Police Chief Frank Gonzales were driving in the area when they saw a "green-object" traveling toward the ground. "It looked like a fireball," Padilla said today, "and it disintegrated before it hit the ground; it was kinda scary."

Reporter Chip Hinds wrote in an article for the *Durango Herald* on January 13, 1983:

Durango police dispatcher Ruth Mastin reported that her office was told by Federal Aviation Agency officials in Grand Junction that the noise was created by classified military aircraft and that they had been instructed not to answer any further questions. McKinley County Sheriff Benny Padilla in Gallup said that a "green object" which "slowed, struck the ground, and went out" was spotted near there. . . .

A Farmington man, Rick Wilkie, reported seeing hunks of a "meteor falling off" as the meteor came in from the western sky as he was watching from a point about twenty-five miles from Farmington. Research associate Norman Thomas of the Lowell Observatory in Flagstaff, Arizona, said authorities should be "skeptical of any meteor theory unless a full investigation is made."

The United Press International release of January 13 reported, in part:

[McKinley County Undersheriff Jack] Graham said he and other officers trying to get to the fire site Wednesday night "saw a falling star or meteorite fall, and it burned longer than it should. I saw three or four falling stars, lasting longer than usual, about fifteen or twenty seconds."

One' other report written by Rex Graham on Sunday, January 16, 1983, in the *Farmington Daily Times* stated in part:

> McKinley County Sheriff Benny Padilla said the noises around Gallup ceased about 8 P.M. At about 10 P.M., Graham, Padilla, and other law enforcement officials saw a "green fireball" swing across the sky for about fifteen seconds, then disappear. This time there was no sound as the meteor vanished. Residents in the Farmington area reported seeing a similar glowing object in the sky. To many, the booms, meteor sighting, and explosion and fire seemed part of the same phenomenon.

Reporter Lynn Bartles wrote the front-page story in the *Gallup Daily* on Friday, January 14, 1983, which contained the following:

> Continental Divide resident Cheryl Meyers said today there have been numerous military helicopters and vehicles in the area (just east of Gallup) since the investigation began Wednesday. . . .
> And Chip Hinds, a reporter with the *Durango Herald*, said today that the Federal Aviation Authority (FAA) in Grand Junction, Colorado, still denies someone from its office commented on the booms Wednesday. Hinds said a spokesman on Wednesday [January 12] said there was a classified military aircraft in the area, but not to ask any more questions as "it was over. . . ."
> On Thursday morning (January 13), FAA authorities said no one from their office issued any statements about the noises.

When Tom Adams contacted Lynn Bartles he found that Chip Hinds had unfortunately been killed in a "mountaineering accident" shortly after covering the Gallup-Farmington events for the *Herald*.

Other peripheral events and reports that accompanied the events in the Four Corners area (northern New Mexico) on January 12, 1983. These include evidence of dynamite and blasting caps at the (possibly diversionary) burn-site crater, noxious gases fifteen miles south of the burn site, and rumors of some sort of crash-retrieval operation near Chaco Canyon.

Were the rumors heard by Tom Adams during and after his immediate investigation an indication of what actually transpired that cold January evening and during the following several days? He shares some of his information from his insider sources about the Gallup Incident:

Then we began to hear rumors, from sources previously reliable. Some of the bits and pieces were said to be "the word" making the rounds among the military-intelligence-scientific community in New Mexico:

- Some of the confusion resulted from the deliberate injection of mis- or disinformation. This was necessary to obscure the highly sensitive "truth" to what actually happened
- A "top secret" operation was in progress that night, and a classified aircraft crashed or exploded.
- The aircraft was indeed a highly sensitive experimental military device or . . .
- An extraterrestrial craft crashed or crash-landed. One account says that it sort of skip crashed, bouncing into or along one site before finally coming to rest at another site.
- The primary crash site was somewhere near Chaco Canyon.
- A "retrieval" operation ensued, while attention was diverted to Gallup and Farmington and Durango. "Something" (be it terrestrial or otherwise) was removed from the side of the canyon or ravine into which it crashed. It was transported by air to Kirtland air force base. It was set down and a pro-

tective structure was built around it.

- There were reports, unconfirmed, of "silver spheres" descending and ascending somewhere in the Gallup area.
- There were also reports of independent investigators in the technical community in Albuquerque (civilian scientists and technicians working at Kirtland AFB or Sandia National Laboratory) who were threatened and/or harassed or otherwise warned to stay away from the Gallup area, after they had expressed interest in pursuing their own investigations of the event[s].

Was this entire collection of reported events more than a synchronistic array of mundane coincidences? Compare the above to the following.

The (ongoing) NORAD Event investigation was initially covered by Mark Hunter for the *Valley Courier* and in the *Crestone Eagle*.

THE NORAD EVENT

The NORAD Event was actually a series of events over a six-week period (including reports of two green, two blue, one white, and two orange fireballs, two orange orbs, two mystery fires, mysterious booms, a flurry of Bigfoot reports, a documented unusual cattle death, and many reports of accompanying military-esque activity) that began on the night of November 30, 1993, at 6:05 P.M., and continued until the early evening of January 17, 1994.

The height of these events occurred during the afternoon of January 12, when a NORAD official contacted the Rio Grande sheriff's office at 3:40 P.M., and reported "a significant explosion" logged at 2:55 P.M. in the Greenie Mountain-Rock Creek Canyon area by a NORAD satellite scope operator in Cheyenne Mountain.

Exactly two hours later, at 4:55 P.M., Florence resident Lieutenant Colonel Jimmy Lloyd (retired), a thirty-year veteran fighter pilot and self-professed UFO skeptic, reported seeing "a battleship-sized," glowing green group of "six or seven objects in close [crescent] formation" streak overhead just south of him that appeared to "go down into the San Luis Valley."

According to Lloyd, the objects were not mundane celestial objects, i.e., meteors, or any type of conventional craft, or missile, and were completely silent. This effect-first, fireball-later aspect appears to have had the same two-hour time-lag characteristic of the explosions and fireballs heard and seen in the Gallup Incident.

Going with the questionable assumption that all these objects were under intelligent control (no aspect of the newspaper accounts or witness reports from either event suggests that they were), maybe in this January 12 event, for the sake of argument, the fireballs decided to arrive together, more inconspicuously instead of separately over several hours as in 1983. Could the significant explosion which NORAD detected have been the heat signature of the tight formation of objects as they swept into the mysterious valley two hours later?

The fireball jockeys must have figured out how to silence the boom part. The NORAD Event made no apparent noise. There were several curious reports of "booms" but they did not occur as the primary focus as in the Gallup case.

At noon on December 9, 1993, five witnesses in two houses about a mile apart reported a localized sound like "something huge hitting the ground." Unsubstantiated reports of explosions were reported between January 13 and 15 in the Rock Creek Canyon area, on the northern side of the Greenie Ridge portion of Greenie Mountain. These booms did not appear to occur in conjunction with any of the other "fireballs" that were reported in the six-week period.

Portions of north-central Texas heard several loud, boomlike noises on the afternoon of January 20. Could these reports be significant, or were they just another bunch of noisy Texans?

Aerial craft or helicopter sightings and rumors about ground activity were present at both the Gallup Incident and the NORAD Event, combined with probable misdirection by the government. Major McCouch, FEMA supervisor of the NORAD scope operator, may have given Brian Norton misdirections to search a rugged area nearly twenty-five miles from the probable impact site.

Was this to allow a military search of Greenie Ridge with the B-52s and helicopters reported the following four days? Heavy-equipment and snowshoe tracks were reported by two UFO Institute members who also claim to have stumbled on huge "metal doors" in the ground a week after the NORAD story broke. The area is dotted with closed up, abandoned mine shafts.

To my knowledge, there is no verifiable evidence of a retrieval operation in either the Gallup Incident or the NORAD Events. Perhaps some other agenda was at work.

Eyewitness accounts, eleven years apart, are similar. Sheriff Padilla's description of a "green object" breaking into pieces just before it appeared to crash echoes Al Koon's description of a "green fireball" breaking apart before appearing to strike the valley floor. Both relate the unusual flights as slowing, making a forty-five-degree turn, and then descending straight down towards the ground.

Most witnesses of the NORAD fireballs mentioned the long duration of the sighting. This was repeated by Padilla and Undersheriff Jack Graham in their observation of the objects near Gallup.

As usual, more questions are raised than answers. What are these fireballs? Are these the same type of fireballs that have been seen periodically in the southwest since the 1940s? Who, i.e., what agency, or group, is conducting flights in and around the sites of these unexplained occurrences? How many unknown witnesses are there to the known events and do these known events represent the full scope of the localized phenomena? Were the preceding booms and the two-hours-later fireballs related? Were the Bigfoot sightings related?

JANUARY 15, 6:30 PM, CAPULIN:

As the glow of the setting sun faded, three Capulin residents, Jonas Archuleta, Clint Valdez, and Randall Trujillo, were walking downtown. One looked up to see, hovering above, two bright orange globes.

"They hovered for two to three minutes over Cap [Capulin] and at first they were pretty high and they looked just like two orange streetlights. Then they seemed to get closer. Man, when they took off it was like a streak! They went across the valley and disappeared over Romeo," Archuleta told me. "It was pretty freaky; one of the guys was pretty scared about it and swore he would go to church every day!"

Several minutes later, Chama rancher Dale Vigil observed "a very bright orange light" west of San Luis. According to Vigil, who was on his way to watch the local high school basketball team, the light hovered for several minutes. It was then joined by a second "bright orange light," and both lights "shot straight up and out of sight. There is no way those were planes or helicopters—they moved too fast."

Vigil claims he and a friend had observed a similar light two weeks before, "around New Year's" over the San Luis Hills, which are located in the south-central valley between San Luis and Capulin.

WHO DONE IT?

A source close to the NORAD Event told me in March 1994 that a newly promoted captain in her third trimester of pregnancy was found dead in her garage of carbon-monoxide poisoning, two weeks after the NORAD phone call to Undersheriff Norton. A note was allegedly left but no death notice was carried by local papers. I hit a brick wall trying to corroborate the source's claim.

Then in April 1995, almost a year later, an unexpected source turned up. I was asked by Timothy Green Beckley to speak at the first annual Pikes Peak UFO Conference. I was scheduled to follow the keynote address of abduction investigator, Budd Hopkins, one of UFOlogy's most eloquent speakers.

I overcame my nervousness and championed the coordinated-teamwork approach of investigation. My twenty-minute talk was very well received by the standing-room-only audience of 250 and I was included in a UFO talk show called *UFOAZ*, hosted by Ted Loman, right there at the conference.

During my workshop the next day, after fielding several questions about UADs I quipped, "The Ancient Mariner had an albatross around his neck; I guess I have a dead cow around mine!"

I was enjoying the conference when a NORAD employee introduced himself. I mentioned the NORAD captain's alleged suicide, hoping he could confirm it. "One death?" he asked. "There were three!"

He went on to tell me of two additional suspicious base suicides. He insinuated that the three deaths might be related. My initial NORAD source had also hinted that the pregnant captain's death might be related to the Event call made to the sheriff's office. What could be so secretive as to warrant death?

When Varied Directions, a film production company contracted by Ted Turner's TNT network to produce a UFO documentary, told me they were planning a trip to NORAD to cover the NORAD Event, I told the producer the rumors about the suspicious deaths. NORAD initially granted permission for the film crew to visit the secret base at Cheyenne Mountain. When it was revealed that they were interested in the NORAD Event, their visit was promptly canceled.

Varied Directions was the first film crew allowed aboard a Trident submarine to produce a documentary on the sub for the PBS program *Nova*. They had also worked with NASA on a documented history of the space race, called *Moon Shot*. This is a well-connected production company. But even with these impressive credentials, permission to film inside Cheyenne Mountain was rescinded by NORAD, without explanation.

THE WHEAT FROM THE CHAFF

Many longtime residents of the SLV profess to be able to differentiate between the usual and the unusual. Newcomers, not fully accustomed to our glorious night sky (this place is a skywatchers' paradise at eight thousand foot above sea level), sometimes report mundane celestial objects as UFOs.

On February 11 and 12, 1994, I received a total of four reports of a "light hovering over the mountains." After rushing to my roof within seconds of their calls, I realized that these earnest folks were probably viewing the star Sirius that happened to be rising above the mountains. Although spectacular, these sightings of the heaven's brightest star did not make it into my sighting log.

How many reports of stars, planets, satellites, and space debris litter UFOlogists sighting logs? Another call came within minutes and, the following night, I had two more! (At least people around here are keeping their eyes open.) These reports underscore the importance of careful separation between the wheat and the chaff.

MARCH 2, JUST AFTER 10 PM, THE BACA CHALETS:

A visitor to our area possibly experienced "the real thing." The witness, a professional photographer from Seattle, Washington, was photographing the vivid night sky four days after the full moon. After venturing outside she found herself facing the Great Sand Dunes, fifteen miles south, where she noticed a group of red lights pulsing and flashing.

She had the conscious thought to raise her camera and take pictures but was so mesmerized by the display that she felt paralyzed. Excited by her sighting, she was puzzled why she was unable to photograph the lights. I can't count the number of times I've heard a similar story. This woman was a professional photographer, the camera was loaded and set up for nighttime exposures, yet, over the course of this alleged ten-minute sighting, no pictures were taken. I've done it myself.

Four nights later around 9:15 P.M., a cheap fireworks display was observed traveling southeast to northwest over the Sangres where it flared out over Crestone. I wonder how many of these displays go unnoticed by our sparse population. (If a fireball falls in the valley with no one to see it . . .)

The rest of March was quiet, with no other logged reports until the morning of March 30 at 10:45 A.M. I was four miles south of Moffat, heading south on 17 heading to the Eureka Springs (Arkansas) Conference. A bright silver reflection directly ahead of me, forty-five degrees above the horizon, caught my attention and I watched an apparent silver sphere hover about three thousand feet above Hooper for about fifteen seconds. Denver UFO researcher Candice Powers and Baca resident Richard Copeland, who were driving in a second car directly behind me, also saw it.

As I fumbled with the 35 mm. camera on the front seat, the reflection flashed off. The object could not have been a fixed-wing airplane reflecting the sun, which was only twelve degrees east of it on the same horizontal plane. I slowed my truck and fixed my eyes on the spot where I had observed the object's reflection, not having to watch the road which continues south, straight as an arrow, for twenty miles.

After five or six seconds, the reflection was back and it had moved fifteen or so degrees to the right and away from me, directly south. It hovered for another ten or so seconds before disappearing south. Because the reflection was so bright, I could not discern structure, but it had to be round (or spherical) to be able to reflect light at the angle we observed.

I have seen many conventional aircraft reflect the sun (I grew up near McCord AFB in Washington State and currently see military and private aircraft constantly) but I have never seen this reflection effect in such close proximity to the sun, nor have I seen the hovering action we observed. The sky, that morning, was crisscrossed with contrails. The sphere left no trail.

This was near the location of the bell-shaped object sightings of December 1992, and the "swarm of lights" the night of January 7, 1994.

The night we arrived in Eureka Springs, multiple sightings of our cheap fireworks were made by area residents over the western slopes of the Sangres. Four low-altitude displays were seen sporadically over the next three nights. All were described later as being at treetop level before, as one witness described, "they flared. Like, poofed out."

During this three-day period at the Eureka Conference, a calf was discovered mutilated sixty miles south of Eureka Springs, and a cow was discovered with "classic mutilation" incisions right in Taos, New Mexico.

The day I returned from Arkansas, I met with Bob Weiss, a director for *Unsolved Mysteries*. Janet Jones, a researcher for the program, had heard about our activity and my investigation. I discussed with Weiss some of our most spectacular reports, including the NORAD Events. Weiss agreed that there were many stories here.

April and May are traditionally two of the most active months (in the greater SLV region) during these years of heightened activity and 1994 was no exception. From April 1 through May 31, there were nineteen sightings of anomalous objects and/or lights, three reported UADs (and a reliable unreported case of two, possibly three cattle deaths complete with a twelve-foot-by-twelve-foot-square burn mark nearby), and numerous sightings of helicopters and military vehicles. The usually subtle presence of the watchers became less translucent that spring. Local law enforcement officials professed to be as mystified as ever.

SLV residents were becoming more aware of our unexplained activity due to increased sightings and newspaper coverage. Specific areas (where activity continues) were buzzing with rumors. It appeared the locals were gaining the courage to report these sightings to police and reporters.

My daylight sighting of the sphere on March 30 was followed by three reports of cheap fireworks on April 1 and 2, just after 10 P.M. These displays were bluish-white and appeared to be just above treetop level. They are only reported in a ten-mile-wide corridor extending from the Blanca Massif, north to Valley View Hot Springs on the western facing slopes of the Sangre de Cristos. This eastern area where I live traditionally has had more reports of anomalous aerial objects than the remaining valley.

The pattern abruptly broke in December 1994. The western valley now has its share of sightings. The epicenter moved northward in April and May.

On Thursday, April 7, at 10 P.M., an orange light was seen by three witnesses, rising above the La Garita Mountains in the west, toward Creede. The light hovered 30 degrees above the horizon for almost ten minutes before "blinking out." It was described as brilliant and "much larger than a planet."

SATURDAY, APRIL 9, 9:30 PM, MOFFAT:

Several lights hovering "low in the western sky" were seen by (trained observers) the Koon family in Moffat. The remote unpopulated area near Creede, where they estimated these two lights were hovering, is a large, minimum-intensity aeromagnetic anomaly area that's rumored to have a possible underground facility.

APRIL 21, AROUND 6 AM, MONTE VISTA:

Two complaints of a "large jet flying low over Monte Vista" were forwarded to me. The military was still attempting to expand the La Veta Military Operations Area, and according to public relations officer Major Tom Schultz of the Colorado Air National Guard, "We have more pilots than planes." As a result, pilots are "careful to fly according to regulations to keep themselves from being grounded." Regulations include remaining subsonic and well above five hundred feet to avoid noise complaints by area residents.

According to witnesses, the "huge jet" lumbered "less than two hundred feet above the trees."

THE SPHERE RETURNS

APRIL 30, 10 PM, CRESTONE:

Lifelong Crestone resident and local historian Jack Harlan witnessed something he'd "never seen before" in his seventy-plus years. "It was large and round, like a sphere," he told me the next day. "There were red and green lights blinking [in sequence] around the underside."

Another witness, a neighbor, thinks he also saw the strange craft. "I had just stepped outside when I saw a large bright light going straight up and out [to the southeast], with sparks shooting off it!" According to this second witness, "Jack [Harlan] said it was so close he could see two raised ridges on the underside that were lit up by the bright blinking lights." Harlan told his neighbor that he felt unusually fatigued the entire following day.

Dr. Steven Greer, founder and head of CSETI conducted a Rapid Mobilization Investigation Team (RMIT) training May 5 through 9, 1994, here in the valley. Greer arrived in the late morning of May 4, after flying into Denver, and observed "two large camo'ed dropped-bellied semis" near Villa Grove. "We saw similar [military-esque] activity when we were in England," he told me.

The next morning, Greer observed "a silver sphere hovering silently over the mountains" while jogging in the Baca. The sphere did not leave any vapor trail [unlike the aerial traffic observed at the time]. According to his description, the sphere hovered silently for several minutes before heading east, out of sight. Greer was unaware at the time that a similar sphere had been reported five days before by Jack Harlan and Harlan's neighbor. He was also unaware that similar objects had been seen during the same time period near Blanca and Fort Garland, or my March 30 sighting.

RMIT-head Sherry Adamiak and Dr. Greer instructed over a dozen CSETI-ites in the system of protocols that Dr. Greer has devised to elicit contact with extraterrestrial craft and their occupants. Aspiring RMIT team members included "Bootsy" Galhbraith (wife of a United States ambassador) and George Lamb, who is a top administrator for Lawrence Rockefeller.

The CSETI agenda appears to be a strong step forward out of the morass in which UFOlogy finds itself. An investigative presence in flap areas of heightened activity makes a lot more sense to this investigator than yet another rehashing of the Roswell case (New Mexico, 1947).

CSETI has had some apparent success in attracting craft to specific locations in the United States, Mexico, and England, but no boardings have occurred. CSETI's expedition into the mysterious valley couldn't have been timed more perfectly. On May 7 and 8, the group had several additional sightings of unknown lights and objects.

Their sighting reports pointedly coincide with Blanca and Fort Garland residents reporting unknown lights in the sky on the same nights, thirty miles southeast of Crestone, and the flurry of reports forty miles to the west, near Monte Vista.

At 10:30 P.M. (as reported by Mark Hunter in the *Valley Courier*), six Monte Vista residents reported to Undersheriff Brian Norton a fast-moving, brilliant "white strobe light" low to the ground in the area of Rio Grande county roads 4N and 3W, known as "Maxiville" to the locals. Norton himself saw the light, which he said was "just above the trees and really moving! It had to have been traveling at least as fast as two hundred to two hundred fifty miles per hour." Norton added that his office had received two calls Saturday night and four calls Sunday night officially reporting the unusual low-flying strobe light.

Valley Courier editor Mark Hunter told me "cars were lined up along 285 watching it." Norton said those present "refused to go on the record" about the sighting. The undersheriff said the light seemed to mirror his actions when he and others tried to get close enough to identify it. "I would chase it north, and it would head south. I would stop, and it would stop. Then I made a U-turn and headed back south, and the light immediately headed north."

Many objects appeared to have been attracted to the entire valley that weekend of May 7 and 8. I mentioned to Greer and Adamiak that, when CSETI was vectoring in craft that weekend, maybe they gave bad directions.

Norton also mentioned seeing a "dark unmarked helicopter" the next morning (Monday, May 9) while investigating. "The chopper appeared to be buzzing the area where the light was seen" during the previous two nights.

He called me because he knew that back on January 21, I was videotaping over Greenie Ridge in a dark purple chopper, which was reported in the *Rocky Mountain News* as a "black unmarked helicopter." Evidently two Rio Grande county sheriffs had chased my craft all the way across the county. I assured him it was not me this time, and I would inform him before flying in his jurisdiction again.

Several reliable sources told me of a rumor that a Maxiville-area farmer had two, possibly three, cows mutilated on Monday night, May 9. These sources also mentioned a landing by some sort of craft on the farmer's property. The landing traces allegedly consisted of "a twelve-foot-by-twelve-foot burn mark" in the farmer's freshly irrigated field. According to his neighbors, the farmer didn't want to officially report these cattle deaths and landing because "he doesn't want to scare folks." Evidently the farmer quickly disposed of the carcasses and possibly covered the evidence of a landing. Overflights of the area by a local pilot revealed nothing.

This possible example of a witness's reluctance to acknowledge the high strange is probably the norm, not the exception. Again, it may be the fear of ridicule. And the human mind has built-in mechanisms to help to deal with that which it cannot comprehend and very often the result is denial. If they close their eyes, maybe it will go away. . . .

EAGLE TO EAGLE'S NEST

The field of "muteology" (as coined by long-time Gardener mutilation researcher David Perkins in 1979) seems to have a propensity for name-game synchronicity. The father of muteology, Tom Adams, observed that the three recent UAD cases in Eagle, Colorado, in November and December and the two new cases that occurred the following May in Eagle's Nest, New Mexico, have that tantalizing name connection.

In the fall of 1993 there were reported UAD cases in Adams and Perkins counties in North and South Dakota. Is someone (or something) sending blatantly subtle messages to Tom Adams and David Perkins? When investigating this unsolved serial crime spree of the century, one must scrutinize the evidence from as many angles as possible. Clues, dear Watson, clues.

Two cows were found by rancher Eli Hronich on May 10, 1994, next to a lake in Eagle's Nest. The UADs were found with "classic mutilation" incisions, rear-end cored out (ad nauseum!), and represent a historic first. New Mexico paranormal investigator Gail Staehlin, New Mexico cattle inspector Philip Cantu, veterinarian Tim Johnson, and hematologist Dr. John Altshuler, were all on scene together within ten hours of discovery. To my knowledge, there has never been such expertise on-site so quickly in the history of the UAD phenomenon. Initial results derived from preliminary forensic testing indicated cooked hemoglobin and cauterization of the incisions.

Doctors Altshuler and Johnson also noticed that both animals' lungs were riddled with pneumonia. Altshuler remembered the Vigil bull and the finding of pneumonia in that animal's lungs, and thinks the affliction may prove significant. Very few animals, that appear to be true UADs, are examined as carefully as the two Hronich cows.

The area just beyond the southern end of the SLV (near Taos) has quietly undergone a wave of unusual cattle deaths since the fall of 1993. By this time, Hronich had "lost [and reported] ten head since September." He is only one of several ranchers in the area that have been plagued by the mysterious cattle surgeons of late.

These cases (and the cow found last March right in Taos) were a prelude (publicity campaign?) to the Animal Mutilation Conference presented by Gail Staehlin, held on May 21, in Taos. The conference was publicized in the area for three weeks and "somebody" may have seen the ads and flyers. Proper forensic, postmortem photographic, and general investigative techniques were presented to a dozen ranchers, two state cattle inspectors, and a local veterinarian over the course of the five-hour gathering.

This type of networking with ranchers and local officials is crucial. Expediency is of paramount importance when investigating UADs. In the words of Gail Staehlin, "Somebody's got to help these folks!"

I HEARD WHAT I HEARD

As reported by Mark Hunter in the *Valley Courier* on Tuesday night, May 17, 1994, at 9:30 P.M., Monte Vista residents Stephanie Malouff and Debbie Jiron reported seeing a "huge bright light with lots of little bright lights around it." Malouff and Jiron found it far too large to be a conventional craft, flying in a northerly direction south of the town. They also observed that this larger object was being "chased by a second smaller object at high speed." As the smaller object closed in on the larger one, the larger one appeared to turn from bright white to red, as it "all of a sudden made a forty-five-degree turn to the west and disappeared over the mountains near Greenie."

Hunter reported that the two witnesses were excited about their sighting, and they said, "You couldn't miss it. It was bright and it was huge." As a strange twist to this story, Malouff told Hunter that, although the objects were silent, she heard a "pinging sound" like bullets ricocheting off metal. Was the smaller object shooting and hitting the larger one? Malouff didn't care to speculate about this but she insisted, "I heard what I heard."

Malouff said she called several relatives to see if anyone else had seen the strange objects and one woman told her she had seen a similar object the previous night at around 2 A.M. On that same Monday, 7 A.M., Colorado Springs radio station KKFM apparently broadcast a "live" UFO sighting report of a strange silver object hovering over Colorado Springs. According to a friend who told me of the broadcast, a similar object had apparently been spotted the night before over Trinidad. I have heard an official version, that the object was a "six-hundred-foot-long weather balloon flying at one hundred thousand feet."

My sources said that it was launched by the National Weather Service "out of New Mexico." Supposedly, it was launched on May 15 in "northern New Mexico" and it drifted east, towards Trinidad, then it went north towards Colorado Springs. Knowing a little about our weather patterns and factoring in our activity during the following two nights left me with some doubts. A six-hundred-foot-long weather balloon?

The following week, Undersheriff Norton received a report from a Southfork resident of a twenty-to-thirty minute sighting on May 24, from 9:30 to 10 P.M., of a large silver sphere (the one with the multicolored lights blinking around the underside) flying south down the Rio Grande between South Fork and Creede. This sphere certainly gets around. That made five sightings since March 30, of what appears to be the same (or same type) craft.

MAY 25, AT 9:35 PM, THE BACA CHALETS:

As May progressed I wondered if our activity would wane as usual in June and July. So, naturally, I immediately witnessed the most bizarre cheap firework display out of the dozens I have seen to date.

Our house sits two hundred feet above the valley floor and I was standing on our second-story deck. It was completely overcast with uniform cloud cover seven thousand feet above the entire central and northern valley floor. I was looking directly south, out over the southern part of the Baca Ranch, when I saw a bright blue light appear (thirty degrees below the horizon) that appeared to be flying in a slight arc, parallel to the ground, fifty to one hundred feet above the treetops. It was about a mile or so away, at a lower elevation than my vantage point! I was actually looking down at it as it flared for almost a mile over the piñon trees one hundred to one hundred fifty feet below me.

These objects are real, and I only have a couple of theories. We could be witnessing an as yet undefined natural phenomenon like a form of static, or plasma discharge. Or they could be an effect caused by a craft, much like a jet produces a contrail. They come in all sizes; the smaller ones tend to be bluish, the larger models are greenish and orangish. The really comical tiny ones (that are only reported as occurring very close to the observer) are especially puzzling.

MAY 30, EARLY AM, NORTH OF QUESTA:

Ranch foreman Tom Reed found a three-month-old heifer mutilated, and reported it to cattle inspector Jerry Valario. Valario drove out to the ranch to investigate the death.

Cutting the animal open, Valario was startled to find that the meat looked like it had been boiled, or cooked in a microwave. It was was gray and flaky. He probed inside the calf's mouth, inadvertently getting the animal's saliva on his hand. "My hand started getting irritated," he later told me. "It started itching and turning red. It was like an acid burn, or something." He noticed the burning sensation several minutes after examining the calf, as Nellie Lewis had twenty-seven years earlier.

11:15 PM TO 11:30 PM, MOFFAT:

At six that evening, Isadora dropped me at our rehearsal studio for our four-hour-plus rehearsal. Later, George Oringdulph, guitarist with Laffing Buddha, offered to drive me home. George and I found ourselves headed north on 17 toward Road T and the fourteen-mile jaunt east toward the Baca.

As we approached the sand piles halfway between Hooper and Moffat, I noticed a picket line of four faint blinking lights over the Sangres, near Crestone. I pointed them out to George, and we watched them hover for almost five minutes.

Three of the lights (about three or four miles apart) proceeded west, across the valley, where they stopped in a line between Highways 17 and 285, just hanging there, blinking. George pointed out a large, unblinking, orangish-white light appear just south of where the fourth light was still hovering.

George asked me as the light slowly brightened, "Is that a planet?"

"No way. There's no planet in the northern sky." The bigger fifth light began to drift west toward the first three lights. We estimated its speed at around fifty to sixty miles per hour. The larger light did not resemble airplane landing lights or any other mundane effect of a conventional craft. The smaller, fourth blinking light appeared to escort the larger light toward the three blinking lights now hovering over the center of the valley.

George stepped on the gas toward Moffat (where my night-vision binoculars were sitting on the front seat of my truck) trying to get underneath the two lights as they crossed the highway, just south of Moffat. Realizing we couldn't get there in time, I suggested we stop the car, get out, and take a good look at them.

George turned off his headlights but left on his rather large, orange Ford Tempo parking lights. We stood in front of the parking lights for better night vision. As soon as we obscured the parking lights, the large unblinking orange light slowly started going out, as if in slow motion. It took almost ten seconds for the light to totally extinguish. The smaller fourth light that had been accompanying it kept flying west at the same apparent speed, toward the other three blinking lights, still waiting. They all vanished to the west.

Around 2:30 A.M., George, back at home in Alamosa, was awakened by a large helicopter hovering "right over my house." After several minutes, he realized it wasn't passing over. As he ran outside, the chopper bolted. However, a second one hung low in the air at the end of his street for several minutes before leaving.

I received reports of unusual aerial activity on (almost) every thirtieth of each month since November 1993. Although February has no thirtieth of the month, there was a sighting on the "thirtieth" day, May 2.

The first week of June featured an increase in reports of unexplained military (-esque) activity. According to Rio Grande County Undersheriff Brian Norton, the local national guard unit was shipped out to Kansas on May 27 for two weeks of maneuvers. Then who was driving the eastbound thirteen-truck convoy on June 4 on Highway 160? The convoy consisted of ten green-camouflaged one-ton trucks, two identical unmarked white semis, and two brand new Dodge scout-type trucks at the head and tail of the two-mile-long convoy. Our national guard unit has surplus vehicles that are at least ten years old. All the vehicles in this convoy appeared to be new. Could this convoy be related to the many helicopter sightings reported between June 1 and June 8?

Or might they be related to the convoys with UN equipment on flat cars sighted on Interstate 25 during the first week of June near Fort Carson, south of Denver, and in Montana and Wyoming? Over fourteen different helicopters sightings were reported during the first week of June 1994 (June 1, 3, and 8) in central SLV. Most of this aerial activity was reportedly traveling north and south, up and down the Sangres.

One rather unusual chopper seen by several people, including myself, was a immense white, single-prop type with a flat rectangular box attached directly underneath. Two antennas appeared to be sticking out the front of the box. Just below the tail rotor were two black objects that looked like large tires but obviously weren't. It flew over the valley about seven thousand feet up and I studied it with binoculars as it traveled towards Greenie Mountain.

There had been numerous reports of a fast-moving strobe light seen north of Monte Vista during the first weekend of May. The skeptics claim everyone was just observing a strobe light on a center-pivot sprinkler and, curiously, no additional reports were noted until Sunday, June 5, at 2:30 A.M., when three Saguache residents on 285 observed a rapidly blinking strobe light pacing them a half mile west of the road, "going over the treetops."

They stopped and watched it continue northwest until it disappeared. When I told one puzzled witness that this light had been reported in May and was dismissed as a strobe on a center-pivot sprinkler, he remarked, "I've never heard of a fifty-foot-high sprinkler that can travel at sixty-five miles per hour."

10 PM, CRESTONE:

That same evening, a sizable cheap firework display was observed over Crestone, traveling west. It was brilliant white and left a glow behind.

JUNE 9, BETWEEN 10 AND 10:30 PM, RIO GRANDE COUNTY:

A large reddish light was observed by several witnesses zigzagging over the South Fork area and reported to the sheriff's office.

ALL OVER THE PLACE

JUNE 21, THE MEDANO RANCH:

Three A-10 Warthogs flew less than two hundred feet high as part of the air national guard's noise-level study for their "Air Space Initiative" (their attempt to expand the La Veta Military Operations Area into the SLV). The air force brass met with the foreman of the Medano Ranch to monitor his bison calves' reaction to the low-flying jets.

The foreman was concerned about low-flying military aircraft scaring his herds. The A-10s (quietest of the military jets used here) appeared out of the north, passed over and . . . the herd didn't even look up. As the brass patted themselves on the back for their successful demonstration, three jets screamed out of the south at less than one hundred feet, making all those present "jump out of their skins!" The embarrassed brass professed no knowledge of the identity of the mystery pilots or their planes. The bison nonchalantly looked up at the roaring jets, then returned to grazing.

It would appear the right hand doesn't know what the left one is up to! (What, in our government?) Could this innocent-sounding example of professed ignorance be an indicator that our military is genuinely unaware of other agendas at work here in the valley?

JUNE 27, 11 PM, MOFFAT:

Six witnesses were skywatching when one of them noticed a moving shadow. There were no clouds, yet something was slowly blocking out a large portion of the Milky Way. When the witness called the others' attention to it, they all claim they saw a "triangular ship with no lights" slowly fly eastward.

"It was so big it blotted out the stars!" observed one witness. Based on their descriptions, the craft was "the length of three hand-widths [at arm's length] or, about fifteen degrees. They attempted to shine a million-candlepower spotlight up as it passed overhead but had no success illuminating it at that height. It appeared to be at least one thousand feet up.

The witnesses also reported a smaller triangular craft following the first. Sightings of triangular craft have been reported during the past four fall seasons by hunters before dawn in the mountains surrounding the SLV, but I have no other report of a summer sighting.

I was writing on my computer when the phone rang, again. Probably another inquisitor of the paranormal who'll keep me from catching up with my research, I thought. Then again, I picked up the receiver as I always do. "Christopher, Mark Vertullo, *Sightings*. We spoke last winter." I had already been contacted by *Unsolved Mysteries* and *Encounters* about my investigation but nothing had panned out. Vertullo assured me that *Sightings* would like to produce a segment on the UADs our area was experiencing. I offered to field-produce the segment. This would entail location scouting, case selection, and witness scheduling. He agreed and we set a shoot date for the third week in July.

Okay, national TV. I'd better have my "proverbials" together.

JUNE 30, 10 PM, THE BACA CHALETS:

Dan and Joanie Retuda and two visiting friends were skywatching when six small orange objects, traveling east, shot across the sky with a pulsing, zigzag motion.

"They were really high and at first, we thought they were just satellites. But I've never seen satellites jerk like that. Two of the lights even did the same moves in tandem," said Dan Retuda. "They sure weren't regular satellites." They appeared to blink out as they moved east into the earth's shadow.

That same evening, investigator Gary Hart, visiting our mysterious valley from Illinois, recorded a vibrating utility pole five miles south of the Moffat sighting location. There are several poles in our area that sporadically vibrate during sighting periods. Gary is the first investigator, to my knowledge, that has successfully recorded a vibrating utility pole. The tape indicates a complex, multisource group of sounds that together reveal a low vibration. There was no wind that night and the sound seemed to emanate from the ground. The closer to the ground, the louder it grew. The poles I had discovered near the dunes never seem to vibrate when we are not experiencing sightings.

From July 3 through July 7, there were seven sightings of anomalous craft by sixteen witnesses in the north central valley. These sightings include: more "jerky satellites" on July 4 and 5, the before-mentioned dunes area sighting on July 3, a daylight sighting of a "bell-shaped" sphere seen near Hooper by two witnesses on July 6, and a fireball that dazzled witnesses on July 7.

Four witnesses in the Baca claimed to see a "large, fluorescent orange fireball" descend through the clouds over the Baca Ranch. They called again, seventeen minutes later, to report two white, unblinking dots flying over the area where the fireball supposedly went down. The eight-to-ten-second fireball traveled from west to east. They usually have been observed going in the opposite direction.

July 13, 8:42 am, Colorado and New Mexico:

A loud boom echoed across most of central Colorado from Wyoming to New Mexico. Windows were reportedly broken in Denver. According to a FEMA spokesperson, the boom was caused by an SR-71 Blackbird on a "classified mission for NASA." This boom was heard for hundreds of miles, and I didn't believe that a conventional sonic boom could be heard over so vast an area. When the FEMA worker returned my call, trying hard to convince me, he was unable to answer any questions concerning the supposed flight. Even if the plane made a sweeping turn over the state and the atmospheric conditions were right, I have serious doubts that the resulting boom could be heard over such a large area.

Then–MUFON State Section Director Jim Nelson told me that afternoon he had read that all six NASA Blackbirds had been grounded two weeks before! The article mentioned cracks in the planes' tires.

SIGHTINGS

July 18 Through 21:

We were in the midst of three days of hectic shooting of the *Sightings* investigation team's scrutiny of the UAD phenomenon. Director Keith Fialkowitz planned a hard-hitting segment. Ernest Sandoval, Emilio Lobato, and Clarence Vigil met us in San Luis. We caught up with Eli Hronich in Eagle's Nest.

Fialkowitz jumped at my comment that the UAD phenomenon may be "the greatest unsolved serial crime spree of the twentieth century." (I repeated it for all fifteen camera takes.) The segment aired in September 1994.

A follow-up segment on UADs was filmed in August for broadcast that fall. It featured myself, Gail Staehlin, and the Eli Hronich cases.

JULY 19, AROUND 9:30 PM, LA VETA:

A red, pulsing light seen near the town of La Veta and the Spanish Peaks was reported to investigator Barbara Adkins. The next morning choppers were spotted over the same area.

JULY 24, MORENO VALLEY, NEW MEXICO:

Eagle's Nest rancher Eli Hronich found another steer mutilated. He also reported that a gray, unmarked helicopter hovered over him as he examined the animal. This happened five days after being interviewed by *Sightings*.

JULY 30:

Barbara Adkins reported that on July 30 just after midnight, witnesses saw a large orange light "with a tail" moving "real fast" from south to north, again near La Veta.

Three dark, military-type choppers were seen in formation flying south down the Sangres and a Huey was seen landing at Alamosa airport at 2:15 P.M.

There was apparently a flurry of unpublicized activity in the La Veta area, just east of the SLV, that spring and summer. Although I haven't received verifications for most, including several sightings and a possible landing during the spring of 1994, there is evidence to suggest that the La Veta area has experienced UADs in the past that have been hushed by the locals. An insurance agent claimed that three ranchers lost twenty-one head of cattle in a short time to supposed lightning strikes.

Another case features an isolated farmer who found three dead pigs, mutilated (by literal definition) in their pen. He said they had been "slashed up with a machete-type knife." There was no blood, tracks, or evidence of a struggle. After calling the sheriff, who came out with a deputy to investigate the case and bury the bodies, the farmer occupied a trailer to watch his remaining animals.

In the middle of the night, he heard digging. With shotgun in hand, he approached a dark figure who was attempting to dig up the pigs! The surprised digger apologized and swore he was retrieving the carcasses for the Colorado Bureau of Investigation for analysis. The farmer helped him dig and load the bodies into a pickup. When the farmer called CBI several days later to see what they had found, they denied someone from their office had picked up the carcasses!

FOR THE RIPLEY FILE

One Baca couple has been reporting a perplexing phenomenon to me. "Dozens of times" since October 1993 they have seen a two-to-three-foot-long creature darting around their yard. It appears to be partially translucent and tapered at both ends while opaque in the middle. It moves quickly, the couple's dog responds to it, it leaves no tracks, and it seems to disappear into thin air.

They made the decision to report it to me after an unexpected indoor sighting. Around 9:45 one evening, "it" was seen entering the living room through the closed stereo cabinet doors, scampering silently across the floor to the other side of the room, and out a spot in the wall six to eight inches above the floor, within inches of the couple's feet!

The next morning, when they let out their dog, he "immediately ran to the outside wall (where whatever-it-was had disappeared), dug up his bone," and went to bury it somewhere else. The amazed witnesses (who requested not to be named) said they both have seen the thing move through the dining room and out through the wall twice since January. To my knowledge, this was the first encounter with such a creature in the area, a notoriety they would rather have missed.

AUGUST 8, 8:55 AM, THE BACA:

I was refinishing the same couple's floors while they were away. As I walked out their front door, less than fifteen feet away, there one went! It reminded me of a two-to-three-foot-long lizard gliding quickly across the gate opening in the low picket fence that surrounds their house. I heard a trilling sound in my head as I saw it. I immediately ran to the spot. It had been visible only in the gate opening, appeared to be eight to ten inches off the ground (I didn't see any legs), and left no tracks in the treeless desert sand. This one will have to go in the Ripley file.

AUGUST 17, 1994, MORENO VALLEY:

Eli Hronich found another mutilated steer near Eagle's Nest, and the following day, three UADs were found twenty miles south, near Truchas, New Mexico, on the Max Cordova ranch. Cordova was sure the cows were pregnant but no fetuses were found. According to Albuquerque investigator Gail Staehlin, who has spent considerable time investigating New Mexico cattle death cases, "These latest ones seem to decompose abnormally fast." They may have been killed and kept for a day or two before being dumped where they were discovered.

Two members of the Cordova family reported that they received chemical-like burns after touching one of the animals and the entire family coincidentally suffered "flulike symptoms" the following day. Hronich claims his hand "burnt like hell for two weeks" after touching one of his dead cows, just as Inspector Jerry Valario had a burn-type rash on his hand after touching Tom Reed's dead calf. I've never heard this reported anywhere since Nellie Lewis burnt her hand on the piece of Snippy's mane hair.

I left to visit my parents for a week in Washington State starting on August 19, 1994. Two nights later at 9:15 P.M., witnesses driving up 17 claim they saw a "low-flying flashing light move parallel to the highway." Later, outside their house in Moffat, they also saw an orange light that moved east toward Crestone, then disappeared.

Around midnight, twenty witnesses in Del Norte saw a formation of twelve lights hovering over "D" Mountain (a painted-stone "D" signifies Del Norte). According to Mark Hunter of the *Valley Courier*, who interviewed five of the witnesses, the objects created the capital letter G, then a circle, then a triangle as they hung silently in the sky. Then one of the objects descended through the clouds and flew close enough for them to see a sphere shape and "red and blue lights" that reminded them of sequencing "Christmas lights." The show went on for almost an hour.

Other Del Norte witnesses claim lights were seen nightly the entire third week of August. More sightings were confirmed on the nights of August 24 and August 28.

AUGUST 23:

A thirteen-month-old bull was found mutilated fifty miles northwest of Colorado Springs on the Ted Hasenbalg ranch.

There were reports the afternoon of August 24, that a white, four-prop plane was making several low, illegal passes over the Great Sand Dunes.

On August 29, a second *Sightings* film crew arrived in the SLV for a segment on the previous winter's NORAD Event. I again field-produced for director Keith Fialkowitz and was interviewed extensively. As we arrived at the *Valley Courier* office to interview Mark Hunter, he was on the phone fielding a previous night's sighting report. Resident Mary Jones claimed that she and two other witnesses saw a "honeycomb-shaped object" west of "D" Mountain for an hour between 11 P.M. and midnight on August 28. (The phone call was reenacted for the camera after it was revealed to be a sighting. Jung would be proud of yet another example of synchronicity.)

This segment aired on November 10, 1995, and featured interviews with Jack Cookerly, the Koons, Brian Norton, and Mark Hunter in addition to myself.

On August 30, Eli Hronich found yet another dead steer. "I wish I knew why they're picking on me," he wondered while informing me. It was grazing on rented pasture at the T. V. Gorman ranch south of Eagle's Nest. Hronich has suffered a substantial financial loss at the hands of these mystery cattle slayers who seem to have singled out his herd of twenty-five hundred. "This whole thing just doesn't make sense," he added, "We've got to get some help from somebody." Meanwhile, Eli moved his herd down to his winter pasture and hoped for the best.

A wave of UAD cases were reported to the west, to the east, and southeast of Taos. The Raton, New Mexico, area had filed several reports and Sandoval County rancher Ray Trujillo had reported twenty of his cattle slain on his Jemez Mountain ranch since April 1993. One of the animals allegedly had its spinal cord excised. An April 1994 case in Arroyo Secco, north of Taos, said a nine-day-old-bull was found with its jaw mandible exposed.

SEPTEMBER 2, HIGHWAY 160, EAST OF DEL NORTE:

While driving between Monte Vista and Del Norte, the South Fork ambulance crew had an unusual experience. The vehicle went dead for three or four seconds. Rio Grande County Undersheriff Brian Norton was told, "Even their pac-set went dead," ruling out electrical system failure in the ambulance. The crew didn't see anything unusual and the vehicle quickly resumed power, the pac-set came on, and everything returned to normal.

WEIRD AND WEIRDER

FRIDAY, SEPTEMBER 9, 1994, HUERFANO COUNTY:

Investigator David Perkins called. "This one's real bizarre," he prefaced his account. According to search and rescue personnel and local residents, it seemed that two hunters, in a week period, ended up missing. When the first showed up a day later, the frightened man "raced away in his truck without saying a word."

The second, Mark Hays (not his real name) wandered into Libre and approached the ornate house of a local artist. Hays told the artist an incredible story of an ordeal he claimed he'd suffered over the past four days. He didn't seem hungry or thirsty, appeared to be rational, "remarkably calm," and "didn't seem traumatized." The artist told Perkins, "He looked like a cop with a four-day growth of beard."

The hunter claimed he had arrived at a rented cabin on Dry Creek on Greenhorn Mountain, high above the Libre Community, on September 2, for a weekend hunting trip.

Hays claimed that a large group of "aliens dressed in camo appeared" at his campsite and before he could react, he was gassed, captured, and tied up. They never spoke to him and never fed him. He said he survived by eating grasshoppers. The camo-clad, human-looking aliens appeared to Hays to be conducting "some sort of maneuvers." He said that at one point the group started to get aboard a small ship. Hays was astonished when the "ship expanded" to accommodate them all. The ship allegedly took off, morphed into the shape of a bear, then morphed into "a three-headed wolf," then turned into a cloud! (Could it have been Amanita mushroom season, or another flashback from the sixties?)

Perkins also didn't know what to make of Hays's claim. "This is so weird!" he said several times, with a nervous laugh. It supposedly occurred on the mountain right behind Perkins's house. When law enforcement officials went up to the cabin they found Hays's vehicle trashed, with the passenger-side door open and the remains of a campfire just outside the open door. His "half-burnt clothes" were scattered around the area.

There may have been another "abduction" in Eagle's Nest, and another case claiming a close proximity encounter near Tres Piedras, New Mexico during this same period. I heard that a woman in Eagle's Nest apparently told area residents privately that she had experienced some sort of visitation experience but I'm not going into details because I could not obtain her identity. Another woman near Tres Piedras claimed she saw "grays" standing by her baby in the bedroom. They "shuffled out of the bedroom" and left aboard "a silver disc-shaped ship."

SEPTEMBER 5, EL PASO COUNTY:

Pikes Peak Cattlemen's Association board member Clyde Chess found one of his cows missing its genitalia, tongue, lips, ear, and udder. The heart had been removed from an incision behind the leg. The cow's unborn fetus was also reported missing. The hide around the incisions was "curled, as if they was cut with something hot." Chess also noted that rigor mortis never set in, the bones were bleached clean of meat, and all the hair fell off the face within days.

SEPTEMBER 7, 8:25 PM, THE BACA CHALETS:

Six witnesses observed another one of those unexplained satellitelike lights, zigzagging and pulsing across the heavens, from west to east. "When the kids ran in to tell us to come look, I thought they were just seeing a satellite," observed Al Koon (based on the description). "But it sure wasn't any type of satellite I've ever seen. I wonder what we have up there?'' The diligent skywatcher ran out with three other witnesses and verified the kids' sighting.

September 12, El Paso County:

Rancher Mary Liss found a twelve-hundred-pound cow mutilated on her ranch, northeast of Colorado Springs. The animal's reproductive organs had been removed with what she described as ''a technology that's not readily available to just anybody. This was a cow that you don't just walk up to. We had a hard time getting her in for a vaccination.'' She had seen the cow alive the evening before. She also mentioned in an article in the *Rocky Mountain News* that a nearby rancher had found another ''mutilation'' about a month prior.

September 13, 4:30 pm, Chacon, New Mexico:

Investigator Linda Moulton Howe investigated this highly unusual case. Evidently, Larry Gardea was bear hunting on the ranch where he worked when he heard a loud humming sound. As it began, a group of cattle nearby were startled and ran from the noise. According to a Las Vegas newspaper, Gardea claimed that a cow was dragged by the sound backwards, up the hill, into the underbrush. He said it appeared to be struggling to get away but was unable to escape. Gardea said the animal sounded as if it was being tortured. Being understandably spooked, he said he fired several shots from his 30.06 towards the sound and it stopped.

Gardea headed to the sheriff's office and returned to the site with a deputy. They found that one cow had been mutilated, a second cow crippled, and the third cow, which had been dragged uphill, was missing. Gardea also mentioned the humming sound being heard by locals several times before the incident he reported. (My repeated calls to Gardea went unanswered.)

7:30 pm, Highway 160:

Three hours later, a Del Norte woman called to say she and her teenage son had just seen ''two fluorescent orange lights that looked like streamers moving in tandem.'' She said the two lights were between four and six feet in length and flew right across the front of the van she was driving. The location was the exact stretch of road where the South Fork Ambulance went dead on September 2.

They rushed home and called me. I immediately fired off a call to one of my watchers, an amateur astronomer who lives within two miles of the alleged sighting, who revealed that his satellite TV had inexplicably ceased functioning for several minutes during the approximate time when the fluorescent orange streamers were sighted.

SEPTEMBER 24, HIGHWAY 285, NORTH OF ANTONITO:

Laffing Buddha was rocking the Office, an Alamosa hot spot. As we wound up our first set, my *Sightings* segment flashed on the bar's TV. The last chord was still ringing as I dashed to the bar to watch. An attractive blonde woman was glued to the set, sipping beer between takes of dead cows. Her mouth hung open and she nodded as the Christopher O'Brien on the set intoned, ''I believe this to be the greatest unsolved serial crime spree of the twentieth century.''

I sat next to her, accidentally brushing her arm. She glanced over and let out a shriek, looking back at the TV, then at me. ''That's you! On TV,'' she squealed. I had even worn the same shirt, and simply smiled at her.

SEPTEMBER 25, 1:15 PM, DENVER:

Two witnesses reported a train (with thirty flatcars) traveling north through Denver. The last flatcar had a loosened, ''flapping tarp'' under which they viewed a ''Russian T-67 tank.'' One of the witnesses, a 'Nam vet, claimed to have been an army trainer of Soviet tactics in the U.S. military and recognized the tank. It was olive drab, ''looked brand new,'' and had a ''Russian-style camo'' pattern. Both witnesses assumed by the shape of all the covered vehicles that the rest of the flatcars had Russian tanks on them as well.

I had been receiving tapes and reading material from investigators pertaining to the "patriot" (militia) perception of the political economic situation that exists in our country. Although some of the material is rather alarmist and rings of paranoia, the majority of it seems well grounded in reality. The list of presidential executive orders waiting in the wings for a declared emergency is very sobering. So is the preponderance of military (-esque) activity the SLV is quietly experiencing.

According to my sources, shiploads of European military equipment arrived in Louisiana and was expedited to various sites around the northern tier states. I have seen numerous photographs purporting to be examples of this equipment that is supposedly being used for multinational training exercises under the auspices of the United Nations.

September 26, Clayton, New Mexico:

That same Monday night, at 9:50 P.M., I was visiting with Texas investigator Gary Massey (who declares wherever he goes, he scares the phenomena away) when we watched a sizable cheap firework display streak from west to east and descend straight down into the foothills between the Baca and the mountains. It was bluish white and had a duration of about three seconds. It appeared to descend about two to three miles east of our vantage point. It wasn't a meteor, even Massey agreed.

September 29, 10:30 PM, Great Sand Dunes Campgrounf:

A bus load of Del Norte Middle School students were bushed after a day of dune climbing and, after some good-natured rambunctiousness, settled down in their tents to sleep.

One fifth-grade student, Kodi Whitehead, felt restless. He couldn't sleep. He and his two tentmates, Michael Richardson and Justin Kerr, had stopped talking and goofing around and lay quietly looking out the tent flap at the partly cloudy sky facing the dunes a mile away. Suddenly, a "large whitish-red ball of light" sailed over the dunes headed north. Kodi shook Michael and pointed it out. They promptly roused Justin and dashed outside to watch. After ten or so seconds, it disappeared behind the trees.

About a minute later, the "oval-looking" ball of light returned. It seemed brighter as it streaked by their campsite. By now, six or seven other kids, scattered in tents around the campsite, had been alerted by the boys' shouts. They all watched in wonder as the circular light suddenly flared up many times its original size and "lit up the whole valley." And then it was gone.

Two teachers stumbled out of their tents amid the chaos of excited, pointing kids. They had missed the spectacle.

SEPTEMBER 30, AROUND 10 PM, HIGHWAY 17, SAGUACHE COUNTY:

Three Pagosa Springs residents, traveling north just outside Hooper, observed what they described as a pulsing red light, north of Center about twenty miles west of the dunes. They also noted the red airport beacon south of the larger pulsing red light. The unusual light appeared to be a floodlight, above the ground shining downward, and was estimated at less than five miles away. I heard them talking about their sighting while visiting Al and Donna Koon in Moffat. This happens a lot to me around here.

Salida rancher James Neppl reported to the Saguache County sheriff's office finding a dead cow and (forty yards away) its dead calf. The site was rented SLV pasture on the former Triple L Boy's Ranch. Neppl thinks they were both killed the night of September 30. This is the exact area where the three women claimed to have seen the red pulsing light that night.

It was the first official UAD report in Saguache County (to my knowledge) since June 1, 1980. Both animals were missing udders, rear-ends, and ears. Neppl said, "I do most of my own vet work. I've never seen anything like those two animals. The cuts were so clean and precise, there was no blood anywhere . . . the hair quickly fell off the faces." He also noticed that they were untouched by scavengers until human scent had been introduced to the crime scene. The calf had the entire left side of its skull "peeled and cleaned" of tissue, and all hoof material had been removed with the underneath foot bones bleached white. "The joints were cut as smooth as could be," he observed.

Neppl said that the animals had not been hit by lightning and the calf was cut from chin to rear-end with what can only be described as pinking shears. A front foreleg had been completely excised of tissue and hide. I obtained video footage for the *Sightings*' UAD update segment. This case was reported by Michelle Le Blanc Hynden in the *Center Post Dispatch* on October 14 and in the November issue of the *Crestone Eagle*.

As per the norm, the entire crime scene was gone over with a "fine-toothed comb" by investigating officers and no tracks, footprints, or additional physical evidence was uncovered. Saguache County asked the Colorado Bureau of Investigation for help with the case. "You hear about them [UADs], but you don't think they'll ever happen in your county. Then when they do, you really don't know what to think. There was something real strange about those cattle!" commented then–Saguache County Sheriff Dan Pacheco.

OCTOBER 7, CONEJOS COUNTY:

Rancher Mack Crowthers reported to the sheriff a mutilated steer had been found on his ranch in Sanford. The ears and testicles had been removed and a "leg had been boned out" (all the tissue and hide excised from a leg bone). The steer was found in dense scrub-willow, suggesting it may have been dropped. The boned-out leg is very similar to the Jim Neppl case from the previous week.

A neighbor, Mrs. Warren Reed, claims to have seen "weird green floodlights" in the Crowther's pasture the night this steer had apparently been killed. Investigating

Deputy Steven Gottlieb and Undersheriff Joe Taylor, Jr., found fresh tire tracks heading into the pasture near where the animal was found. These tracks stopped cold and there was no indication that the vehicle turned around nor that the tracks had been obscured. "It was like it [the vehicle] had been picked up from the air and whisked away," Gottlieb said.

Crowthers reportedly lost three more cattle the following week. Two of the animals were found dead on their stomachs with their legs splayed out to the sides. There was no evidence of bullet holes nor obvious signs of cause of death. The animals with "classic mutilation" wounds seemed to decompose unusually fast and "did not bloat," similar to the last five Hronick cows in Eagle's Nest. Complete photographic evidence was obtained.

According to Gottlieb, another Conejos County rancher had "found a bunch of dead cows" on his ranch in a similar condition. They happened during the last week of September and the first week of October.

Alamosa County, having escaped any official UAD reports for over a decade, may have had three unusual cattle deaths during October and two more in November. During a lecture I gave at Adams State College on November 4, I was approached by an Alamosa Wildlife Refuge worker named Donna Knowles who had attended my first lecture at the college two years before. Evidently she had been trying to locate me since the first week of October and learned I was going to speak again that Thursday night.

She said she'd been patrolling late in the day during the first week of October when she found three mutilated cattle in a remote part of the refuge. There were many locked gates and fence lines between the cattle and any nearby pastures.

She returned early the next morning with a 35 mm. camera and a coworker and found only one cow. The other two had vanished without a trace. She told me emphatically, "There is no way cows could get in and out of there without being dropped and then picked back up!" As she and her coworker examined the animal, according to Knowles, they both heard a "high-pitched whirring sound."

She took four pictures at the end of a roll and dropped the film later that afternoon at an Alamosa one-hour photo shop. She later picked up the pictures, slipped the negatives in her purse, put the packet of photos on the dashboard (including the four shots of the dead cow, which she looked at immediately to make sure they had come out), and went into a store.

When she returned to her vehicle, she discovered "the four pictures of the cow were gone!" Because she had separated the negatives from the prints she was able to provide me with reprints. The animal was missing the hide and tissue from the left side of its face and the rear-end appeared to be cored out. Knowles says the animal's wounds appeared to be caused by a laser-type instrument.

OCTOBER 8, PACIFIC COAST, OREGON AND CALIFORNIA:

Blue spheres were reported on the coast from southern Oregon down through northern California, all the way to San Diego. The local TV coverage was extensive. Joan Bishop, from Redding, told me the next day, "Every channel I turned to last night had a story about the sightings."

OCTOBER 9, 11:15 PM, CASITA PARK:

A massage therapist, visiting the Baca from Colorado Springs, and several Casita Park residents observed a glowing ball of bluish-white light slowly arcing over the Sangres, above Mount Adams. It made a slow seventy-degree arc over the mountains for a duration of about fifteen seconds. It appeared to two of the witnesses to be slowly moving away to the southeast.

Five hours later, at 4 A.M., eighty miles south in Questa, rancher Tom Reed observed a "a bright blue floodlight lighting up the forest in the [Sangre] mountains . . . around the [Colorado–New Mexico] border." Reed saw the light while traveling north on Highway 159 on his way to La Junta with a load of sale cattle.

Then we were blessed with a three-week lull. When I began investigating these mysterious events, I never thought that there would be times when I would actually welcome the quiet periods of no reports. There was time to catch up on my sightings log; my band, Laffing Buddha, was offered a recording contract; and I finally felt the attraction to stop at Arby's for a roast beef sandwich.

OCTOBER 18, 10 PM, HOOPER:

George Oringdulph, Chris Medina (the two guitarists in Laffing Buddha), and myself observed an orange light flying over the north central valley. The unblinking light made a slow turn to the northeast and disappeared over the Sangres. Minutes later, two smaller unblinking white lights were seen heading on the same flight path.

The cattle surgeons returned to the eastern Colorado plains that same night. But this time they were playing a different game. A mutilated bison was discovered the following morning on the Denver Buffalo Company ranch near Simla. Linda Moulton Howe was fortunately in Colorado and investigated the case. (A second bison was found in similar condition later on the same ranch, November 8.) According to Howe, the necropsy of the first bison showed two holes between the ribs, and no break in the hide. Tissue around the incision areas on the cored-out rear end was hard and the spleen was an abnormal pinkish-white. Lab results revealed no virus or bacteria and the vet said the animal had "died of illness four days before."

This was impossible, for the bison was seen inside its pen with twenty other animals at 6:30 P.M. the previous night when the rancher was medicating his herd. The genital incision area had an unusual characteristic. One side of the incised oval was hard, the other side soft. There were holes in the muscle tissue.

Linda told me, "I couldn't believe that this buffalo death

was just a few hours old." She noted that fresh liquid feces was present and that the blood present was not congealed. The lab called her back two days later with the observation that the tissue was already rotten. Could this be yet another example of the Eagle's Nest–style "advanced necrosis?"

I finally confirmed rumors of an additional UAD case south of Alamosa in October. My bass player, Lyman Bushkovski's uncle-in-law rancher, John Harr, told him of a strange occurrence. Harr and his family were awakened the night of October 20 by what Harr described as a terrible noise. It sounded like a "huge helicopter hovering right over the top of the house." Harr, also the Del Norte postmaster, said. "I went outside and all I could hear was the downdraft from the propeller, there were no engine sounds. I didn't hear anything mechanical!"

Two days later, October 22, Harr's two sons discovered two cows and two calves one half mile away from the house to the east, dead for "no apparent reason." According to the rancher, the oldest cow, who "would've died soon anyway," was discovered missing the flesh off her jaw, and the tongue and rear-end were "cut out." He also noticed that "it looked like she'd floundered around a bit before she died."

The other cow and two calves "looked like they had just died in their sleep." These three animals displayed no incisionlike marks and scavengers made short work of two of them. The second cow was untouched, even by birds. No additional clues appeared to be present at the site. No tire tracks, footprints, scavenger tracks, or any blood was discovered at the scene. No vet examined these animals, and Harr never bothered to roll the mutilated cow over to ascertain if the downside had been butchered.

Alamosa County K-9 Deputy Jim McCloskey investigated the Harr report. For some reason, he left his animal partner in the car while at the site and no animal reactions were noted.

The Alamosa River snakes through a corner of the ranch where the animals were discovered. This river is polluted with heavy metals forty miles upstream in the mountains for seventeen miles by the Summitville Mine superfund site. It is one of the only known sources of pollution in the pristine greater SLV. This appears to give more ammunition for "the UAD as environmental monitoring" theorists.

Harr "stewed for a couple of days" and then started making phone calls. He called Senator Ben Nighthorse Campbell's office about the matter and was referred to the governor's office. The governor's office told him to talk with the state's veterinarian advocate, Dr. John Maulsby. The vet spoke knowledgeably about the phenomenon. "He [Maulsby] told me he was going to put an article in our local paper requesting that ranchers provide him with fresh samples for testing," said Harr. "But if he ever put one in, I never saw it."

Dr. Maulsby has offered to help in any way he can with any future cases that are found in a timely manner.

With all the attention that's been paid the Greenie Mountain–Rock Creek Canyon area on the west side of the SLV, not many people know about the intense activity the La Veta–Spanish Peaks region has been experiencing. This area was home to several reports that summer. A multitude of interesting rumors had been circulating the area but confirmation of these stories proved difficult.

I received a call from David Perkins concerning a new series of UAD cases that had just come to his attention.

It seems that rancher Ermenio Andreatta, five miles east of La Veta, had discovered a crippled cow on Sunday, October 23, in a remote, rugged section of his ranch. Returning to the same area the following day, he found a mutilated cow. The rear-end, reproductive tract, and left-side teats were removed, and the animal was half submerged in a small creek. Nearby were several nine-foot-wide circular discolorations in the grass. "They look like giant tractor-tire marks," Andreatta later told Perkins. Two more mutilated cows were found over the next three days.

The *La Veta Signature* article on November 3 stated, "a

fist-sized dark spot was visible on the chest of each of the dead cows.'' District Wildlife Manager Lonnie Brown investigated the site, and according to the *Signature*, ''Brown just shook his head in amazement and perplexity as he examined the cattle for bullet holes or other causes of death.''

A carload of Huerfano residents told Perkins that they witnessed an unusual aerial craft hovering over the Yellowstone Road shortly after the Andreattas lost their livestock. The craft was silent and was seen shining a powerful spotlight down toward the ground. The witnesses were ''pretty freaked-out'' by their sighting.

The Andreattas experienced a fourth case later in November. Linda Moulton Howe, who had arrived in the San Luis Valley at my invitation for a sheriff's UAD training seminar, went to the Andreattas' Middle Creek Road Ranch and conducted a thorough investigation of these four cases. They were included in her Research Grant Report of UAD Cases in 1994.

Howe even obtained plant samples from the scene for analysis. She has begun carefully collecting flora from the head and rear-end of a UAD, along with a control sample some distance away from the carcass. Preliminary results from other UAD cases have shown changes in the plant's respiratory process. According to Howe, this result is similar to findings from plants affected in crop-circles.

The La Veta-Blanca-Forbes Trinchera reports continued. They were all found within the La Veta Military Operations Area, previously associated with UFO activity. Now the same areas were handing out UADs. Locals are used to seeing military flights over their area on a daily basis. Some of the UFO reports could be misidentified conventional military flights but several reports remain unexplained.

OCTOBER 26, 1 PM, BLANCA:

A Blanca resident observed what she described as a ''large silver oval'' hanging for about five minutes in the cloudless sky above Mount Lindsey, just east of Blanca

Peak. She claims she has seen the object before in the same location and a third time in 1987 over the sand dunes. It "was completely silent" when it flew out of sight and left no vapor trail.

OCTOBER 28, THE BACA CHALETS:

I received a call from Joe Taylor, Sr., who works at the Conejos County sheriff's office with his son. He told me of several recent sighting reports and then casually mentioned that there was a man there who wished to speak with me.

A man named Alan got on the phone and related several wild stories. He lives with his extended family near the New Mexican border, near the mouth of the Rio Grande Canyon. He told me rather matter-of-factly that all during the previous spring, he and his family had been watching "every kind of ship you could imagine," flying around the desolate semiarid desert near where he and his family live.

"Some are discs. Some are triangles. Big ones and small ones. Some of them even give off red and blue flashes like a laser disc." He added, "My mother found out that they would come closer if you called to them in your mind" (a self-styled, CSETI approach).

"One night, toward the end of May, a friend [who didn't believe they had been seeing the craft] and I went out a couple miles north of the ranch to watch. It was around nine to nine-thirty P.M. We were sitting in his pickup truck, out in the middle of nowhere, when a strange bank of fog rolled in and surrounded us. We saw a light straight ahead shining out of the fog and a craft appeared and hovered in front of us, about two hundred yards away. I started to call it closer and it approached and just sat there about fifty feet away. Well, my friend kind of freaked out, grabbed his rifle from the rack, and popped off a couple of shots at it. It went above us and somehow it lifted up the truck and put it in the bar ditch!"

Evidently, the family has tried to photograph the ships but the objects have other ideas, zipping away out of camera range. Alan's mother had recently seen "three blue balls of light bouncing over the prairie" near their ranch.

One investigator told me that over the border in New Mexico, somewhere in the Rio Grande Canyon, a secret underground base entrance may be located. "I watched a large door open and a concrete pad extend out from the opening. A helicopter was sitting on the pad and it flew off. The pad went back in and the doors closed."

I have not confirmed this particular claim but it is known that one, or possibly more, secret bases are located in that area. New Mexico Representative Bill Richardson, while investigating possible sources of "the Taos hum" (a seventeen-cycle humming sound that has been heard in the Sangres around Taos since 1989) was assured that the source was not coming from a secret facility on the Colorado–New Mexico border. New Mexico Senator Pete Dominici, a member of the Senate Intelligence Committee, publicly chastised Richardson for revealing the existence of the before-mentioned base.

Helicopters were reported over La Veta Pass on the next three days, October 27, 28, and 29. On Friday, October 28, around 10 P.M., a large disc-shaped craft was spotted by a Forbes Trinchera resident that appeared to be shining a spotlight at the ground. A short time later helicopters were seen "buzzing" the area where the disc was seen.

Four hours later, the Koon family was arriving at their home in Moffat (forty miles to the northwest) when they observed "three bluish balls of light" descend separately in a four or five second period with a zigzag motion, just south and west of Moffat.

On October 29, at around 10 A.M., two Crestone residents on their way to Gunnison spotted a military convoy on Highway 50, headed west. According to their description, the convoy consisted of seven humvees, and two of them were "large ones;" the other five were the standard smaller versions. What immediately impressed them was the fact that none of the vehicles had license plates or insignias. All vehicles had "desert-style camo." I was under the impression that all vehicles, private or otherwise, were required to have license plates and identifying markings.

Any relationship between this activity and the unusual aerial craft reports could be anybody's guess but my suspicion is that there is a link. These reports of government activity have a tendency to ebb and flow in concert with the reports of unusual craft.

THE MOTHER SHIPS

NOVEMBER 4, 1991, 7 PM, GREENIE MOUNTAIN:

According to Undersheriff Brian Norton, Sharon Compton reported to the Rio Grande County sheriff's office seeing "something glowing, landing near Greenie," and drew a picture of the object for sheriff's deputies. Compton and other witnesses watched the object for several minutes before it disappeared behind the mountains.

Also according to Norton, November 5, at around 1 P.M., a man was working in his front yard when he heard a roar overhead. He saw helicopters escorting a triangle-shaped craft. As he was watching the aircraft, someone pulled into his driveway and, as he turned to see who it was, the sound above him stopped. He looked up and saw nothing! He had only looked down for "a couple of seconds" before all the craft "just plain disappeared."

NOVEMBER 6, 11:15 PM, COLORADO–NEW MEXICO BORDER:

While returning from a seminar I had conducted in Madrid, New Mexico, Isadora and I saw an unusual light across the valley, just above the eastern horizon (over the La Veta area). We were traveling north on Highway 285, near Antonito.

Ten minutes later we noticed that the light began increasing in velocity, towards our location. Isadora pulled over and I grabbed my 3.5 magnification night-vision binoculars (never leave home without 'em) and viewed a tight wedge-shaped configuration of three unblinking orange lights fly directly overhead. It silently moved almost twice as fast as a conventional airliner.

It may have been an F-117 stealth fighter (which I have never seen here). The fact that it flew right over us and was silent is puzzling. It did not appear to be more than a couple thousand feet up—we should have heard something.

Several hours earlier on Sunday, November 6, at dusk, two Crestone residents had seen "two large iridescent lights over the western horizon," near La Garita. Both witnesses (independently) reported the sighting, which were on my answering machine when I arrived home that night. Each viewed the lights for several minutes before they appeared to blink out.

The following two weeks in the SLV must have constituted a UFO rush hour. Multiple reports of numerous aerial craft were reported by valley residents, with some claiming the lights were chasing each other and "in a dogfight." Two of these reports claim as many as twenty craft were observed at one time. Could these reports be of military maneuvers?

On Sunday, November 6, a hand on the Crowther ranch reported to the sheriff seeing ten or twelve jets flying in formation around Antonito. Deputy Steven Gottlieb of the sheriff's office told me that three families had called to report a "two-hundred-yard-long saucer flying over Antonito" on November 7, accompanied by as many as a dozen jets. Gottlieb hurried out and claims he saw the craft himself.

In another probable example of the fear of ridicule (and of the unknown), reliable independent sources have told me that several firemen saw as many as thirty UFOs flying over Greenie Mountain on November 7. All secondhand versions of the alleged event were similar. Law enforcement and reporters in the area have obtained off-the-record confirmation of the event from several of the firemen but cannot get anyone to go on the record about it or (heaven forbid) call me. I have received several suspicious-sounding denials concerning the alleged event, leading me to believe the incident was genuine. Sometimes all I can do is grind my teeth in frustration. Aarrgghh!

NOVEMBER 8, AT 10 PM, ALAMOSA:

I received a call from Adams State College student John Finehart, who claimed he and several friends were watching five bright lights, (four blinking white lights and one solid red light) wheeling around in the sky over Alamosa. He said they appeared to be in a dogfight with each other and that the white lights were chasing the red light, which was "outmaneuvering the other lights."

Five minutes later I received a second call reporting the aerial display. All witnesses mentioned that the white lights were chasing the red one which, to one witness, appeared to be "playing with the other [white] lights." A Rio Grande County captain also observed "a bright light" over the Greenie area that same night.

NOVEMBER 9, 11 PM, FIVE MILES NORTH OF VILLA GROVE, HIGHWAY 17:

Chris Medina, George Oringdulph, and myself were returning from a mix-down session in Salida when we observed a picket line of eight small blinking white lights in the west, stretched from Saguache to La Garita. There were approximately three to four miles between each light and they did not appear to be in motion.

As we watched the line of lights with our night-vision binoculars, we noticed a ninth light appear low on the horizon. This light was much larger and reddish-orange in color. It never blinked. The new light appeared to be moving in front of the picket line from Greenie to the northwest. It moved slowly past the other lights and disappeared toward Gunnison. George asked, "How come whenever I drive somewhere at night with you, I see something weird?"

NOVEMBER 9, DEL NORTE PEAK:

A Rio Grande County deputy and two of his hunting partners reported seeing a group of helicopters over Del Norte Peak. The following night, the same three hunters saw what they described as a "huge craft" which they thought might be a "sky crane" chopper accompanied by another group of helicopters in the same area. They could not see structure, and assumed it to be a gigantic helicopter.

On his job at the Del Norte Post Office, rancher John Harr hears a lot of local scuttlebutt concerning unreported sightings in the Greenie Mountain area. According to one account (which he verified by finding two other witnesses who claimed they were present), "Cars were parked along State Highway 160, near the Comnet tower, watching a house-sized ship" glide silently across the highway in the middle of the afternoon during the second week of November.

One of those who confirmed the details of this sighting was the son of a local astronomer. He claimed the object had a "thruster-type propulsion system." The object appeared to be under a thousand feet in altitude.

An SLV undersheriff told me he was called in to the sheriff's office to respond to a peculiar request late Thursday night, November 10. It seemed an ex-sheriff had called for an officer to "come out to his home and arrest him." The undersheriff went to the man's home and found him sober, dressed, and ready to go. He, however, could not remember why he should be arrested but was adamant that he should be. "It took a while" for his family and the officer to convince him to stay home. The undersheriff and the family had no idea why he made such a bizarre request!

That same Thursday night, the Hinsdale County sheriff was murdered near Lake City, Colorado. The resulting hunt for the man and woman suspects went on for several days before their bodies were found near where they had abandoned their truck in the snow. Their deaths were attributed to suicide.

Also, that same night, a group of investigators met between Taos and Eagle's Nest to pool data and discuss the ongoing activity in the southern Colorado–northern New Mexico region. Gail Staehlin, Carolyn Duce-Ashe, Becky Minshall, and Debbie Stark made the trip from Albuquerque. Tom Adams and Gary Massey arrived from Texas. David Perkins arrived on Friday. My brother Brendan and a friend, Richard Copeland, went with me.

At one point during the chaotic get-together, Gail brought up an alleged incident where an Eagle's Nest rancher, in broad daylight, watched his cattle form into a group out in the pasture. When the cows moved apart, there was a mutilated cow lying there. All in attendance instantly voted that the cattle mutilation phenomenon must just be "a cow thing" and we should let them work it out amongst themselves. Information was then exchanged in a more serious manner.

TRAINING

The following Monday, November 14, Linda Howe, Tom Adams, David Perkins, Gary Massey, investigator Chip Knight, and myself met with sheriffs and deputies from six Colorado counties. I had been asked by several law enforcement officials if I would consider conducting a UAD training seminar. With all the recent publicity surrounding the latest wave of animal deaths, the officers wanted some info.

Because Tom and Gary had planned to be in the valley during the first two weeks of November, I planned the session for November 14. Linda, who thought the idea was good, flew out to join us.

The turnout was less than expected. Due to the murder of the Hinsdale County sheriff, adjoining counties were involved in an extensive manhunt and could not send anyone to the training. Officials who attended included: Brian Norton (Rio Grande), Steven Gottlieb (Conejos), Martin Dominguez and John Luther from the Alamosa County sheriff's office, Bill Mistretta and Tom Davis from the El Paso County sheriff's office, and Kevin McClellan and Steve England from the New Mexico Livestock Board.

Tom Adams started the session by giving the attendees a quick overview of the history of the UAD phenomenon. He also detailed the helicopters sightings he had documented around mutilation sites. David Perkins covered some of the most prevalent theories about who is conducting these experiments and why. I covered some of our region's most recent cases. Then Linda began the training session.

Armed with videotape, Linda took the officials step by step through the UAD investigative process. The burly lawmen sat politely and listened, seemingly a little bored. A couple of them seemed to be dozing. Then, while showing video of one of the recent bison mutilations, Linda pointed at the screen showing a veterinarian excising a bison penis. Someone coughed as I took a quick glance around the room. Everyone was wide awake.

The lawmen watched, riveted, as the vet expertly removed parts of the organ with a scalpel. Several eyes grew wide, postures stiffened, and a couple pairs of legs were crossed. You could hear a pin drop as Linda, with her back to the audience, described the process in detail. David Perkins and I had to stifle chuckles. Here was an attractive woman, surrounded by burly lawmen, innocently describing most males' darkest fear, oblivious to the subtle responses in the room. You could have cut the air with that scalpel.

As a result of this training seminar, Linda has addressed the regional sheriff's organization and has made in-roads with the national organization as well.

NOVEMBER 14, 8 PM, ROAD T:

Linda, David, and I were returning from Alamosa after the training, when I observed an orange light over the south central portion of the valley. I first noticed it flying over what appeared to be the San Luis Hills, southeast of Alamosa, and I pointed out the light to Perkins. We watched it travel directly north towards our location. As we continued towards Crestone, Linda, in the car behind us, and I noticed two smaller blinking white lights headed north from Rio Grande County out of the southwest. They were about two miles apart and flying in formation. They seemed to join with the first orange light (which now appeared to be faintly pulsing) over the Sangres behind Crestone.

As we arrived in town, I mentioned the sighting and its possible importance to the others. My day was finished, although Linda was all set to drive to Greenie. We should have

According to Brian Norton, that night between 8 and 9 P.M., a group of lights were reported circling the Greenie Mountain-San Francisco Creek area. Two lights peeled off the main group and headed north. It was these two lights we saw as they headed north over the Sangres into the La Veta MOA.

At around 10 P.M., an Alamosa student named Robbie Trujillo left a message with Isadora that he and friends were watching "ten to fifteen planes chasing three or four rapidly flashing strobe lights, west of town."

November 18, 19, and 20 were intense. Multiple fires, auto accidents, fights, unusual numbers of animal kills on the roads, and the sheriff's murder were covered extensively by local and regional press during these three days.

On Friday, November 18, 9:45 P.M., seven helicopters were spotted circling Greenie. A deputy saw them himself. Two of the choppers were shining spotlights at the ground and witnesses watched them for almost forty-five minutes. I wondered at the time if the military could be pulsing microwave frequencies around the valley, similar to the covert "Woodpecker Signal," aimed at the U.S. Embassy in Moscow by the former Soviets to disrupt embassy personnel.

NOVEMBER 22, 9:09 PM, LA VETA:

A family in the La Veta Pass area called to report that a flying triangle had just flown over their house. They insisted that it was not a stealth aircraft. It was silent and much bigger. The following night, just after 10 P.M., a Conejos County deputy saw two "weird looking planes fly over." He described them as having rows of lights, and said they were "odd shaped and real quiet."

NOVEMBER 23, CONEJOS COUNTY:

Joe Taylor, Sr., father of the Conejos County undersheriff, reported seeing "two planes with lots of unusual blinking lights" flying over the northern part of the county. The craft made no apparent sound and were flying below five hundred feet. Taylor mentioned that he had never seen planes with lights like that before.

NOVEMBER 29, 12:40 PM, 1:10 PM, AND 1:39 PM, THE BACA:

A series of low-frequency rumbles were heard by workers at a job site three miles south of the Baca in the foothills. One of the three workers, Creede de Avenzar, noted that the rumbles had an eight-to-ten-second duration and sounded as if they were "coming from deep underground" and appeared to be centered "just north" of where they were working.

DECEMBER 2, AROUND MIDNIGHT, MOFFAT:

Baca musician Barry Monroe was driving north on 17, near Moffat, when he observed a large ball of light northwest of town. "It appeared and moved parallel to the ground. It had almost a tumbling effect and lasted for almost four seconds. The colors were different from something just on fire." He noted that the object was below the clouds and that it didn't look anything like a shooting star; it was "way too big."

DECEMBER 6, 6:45 PM, THE BACA CHALETS:

Two reports were logged of a reddish-orange light hovering over the Sangres, just east of the Great Sand Dunes. From 10:45 P.M. until 11 P.M., I was traveling north on 17, returning home after a rehearsal in Alamosa, and I noticed a bright reddish light hovering over the mountains to the east. The light I saw was two to three times the size and brightness of Mars. After repeated sightings over fifteen minutes, I looked up from the road and it was gone.

The following morning, two winter campers three miles east of Crestone in Burnt Gulch told friends that around 11 P.M. a large formation of jets flew over and, seconds later, a blue spotlight shone down on their site, illuminating the entire area. They claimed that they "heard eight to ten thumps" emanating out of the ground under them. There was about an eight-second interval between the extremely low-frequency sounds that they could "hear in the ground."

DECEMBER 7, 5 PM, HIGHWAY 160:

Valley Courier editor Mark Hunter reported seeing a green cheap fireworks display with a duration of around two seconds over Greenie Mountain while traveling on 160.

That evening at 10:12 P.M., an Alamosa resident standing on his front porch looking west observed "an orange light over Greenie." The light moved in fits and starts for several minutes, before it flew off to the north.

DECEMBER 27, 4 AM, OSIER PARK, CONEJOS COUNTY:

While on a holiday snowmobiling trip with his family in the mountains west of Antonito, UPS driver Dave Jaramillo shot more than just family footage. He woke in the middle of the night and looked out the south-facing window of the remote cabin. A light appeared to be hovering under a mile away. He grabbed his camcorder. Over the course of the next hour, he shot twenty minutes of video. At several points, the bright oblong light appeared to tilt backwards, revealing a large black spot on the underside. A light beam then snaked out of the bottom with a second light at the end of the beam.

The twenty minutes of footage of the unexplained object shows some possible electromagnetic interference. Jaramillo never took the tape out of the camcorder and the footage of the family's activities from the previous and next day were crystal clear. There were, fortunately, ten to twelve seconds of jitter-free footage. I watched this footage of the unknown craft on a thirteen-inch TV screen and could see details.

Later that same evening, at 5:42 P.M., a cheap firework was observed by several Crestone residents in Saguache County. It was described as a slowly falling fireball.

JANUARY 1, 1995, 4 AM, THE BACA GRANTS:

A majority of nocturnal sightings of unexplained lights or craft occur between 9 P.M., and midnight. This usually holds true for the valley as well. The first two weeks of January were the exceptions. I received a call on New Year's Day from a puzzled Baca Grants resident who saw unusual lights around four in the morning.

JANUARY 8, BETWEEN 4:03 AM AND 4:35 AM, SOUTH OF ALAMOSA:

A couple driving on 285 ten miles south of town noticed an unusually bright light just east of them. As they drove towards La Jara, the light appeared to shadow them. At first they thought it was stationary but then realized it was moving slowly south, pacing them.

After a stop in La Jara, they drove back north towards Alamosa. The light appeared to move closer and again began moving with them, appearing to get closer and bigger. They became "a little nervous" and sped up. Home in Alamosa, they watched the strange light continue to the north for several minutes before it disappeared.

"My girlfriend was pretty scared," the man told me.

"We were the only car on the road, and that thing was definitely watching us!"

JANUARY 16, 10:10 PM, SOUTH OF ALAMOSA:

On January 16, Adams State College student Amy Mascarenas had just turned onto 368 to go a quarter-mile home. She was startled by a craft resembling "the top half of a slightly oblong bubble" hovering over some trees less than a thousand feet directly northwest of her. "It was glowing a yellowish color" and had "randomly blinking yellowish-orange and bluish-green lights around the rim and underside," she said.

"It was the size of a small house, or large garage." She called me from her home. "When I first saw it, it was hovering just over some trees. It looked like it was about seventy feet up. The bottom was flat, like a pancake. I think it knew I was there, because when I stopped in our neighbor's driveway to get a better look at it, it went and hid behind the trees!"

Mascarenas reported the incident in a calm manner but was obviously excited. "I kept glancing at my watch to make sure I wasn't missing some time." She said her car never experienced any problems and that she heard or felt nothing unusual after rolling down her window and watched the craft light up the trees for several minutes.

JANUARY 17, 6:15 PM, HIGHWAY 160:

According to a report filed with Brian Norton, a man was driving west toward Del Norte on 160, just northwest of Greenie, when he noticed "a large triangle-shaped" craft hovering near the Comnet tower, east of Del Norte. He told Norton it was about two hundred feet in the air and between forty and fifty feet in length, silent, and exhibited a bright bluish-white strobe light. The amazed witness pulled over and, for about twelve minutes watched the object hover and then slowly move southeast. Then the object "suddenly disappeared at great speed."

This was the exact location of the triangular object sighting during the second week of November.

I called back to verify some details of Amy Mascarenas's sighting two days later and talked with Amy's father, Pat, to leave a message for her. The elder Mascarenas told me, "Amy is a very down-to-earth person and there's no question in my mind that she saw something all right. It's funny you should call, I just saw something pretty strange fly over the house about five minutes ago!" (9:35 P.M.).

I got a detailed description of a "line of brilliant strobe lights, flashing in exact sequence with one another, flying west toward Greenie." Mascarenas, an ex–air force officer, said, "They were flying real low, with a yawing motion, at great speed. I've never seen these types of lights on an aircraft. And it was flat cookin'!" He heard a roaring "that almost sounded like a Pratt-Whitney J-67." He has seen unusual craft in the area before. "Who knows what the government's flying around here."

Less than five minutes later, I received an excited call from Georgia Van Iwaarden, who lives less than two miles from the Mascarenas. "Something really weird just flew over, and is flying around over by Greenie. My husband is outside watching it," Georgia told me excitedly while her husband, Steve, yelled descriptions from outside in the yard.

"It's blinking, moving up and down. Now it's going sideways," Steve called. "Now it's taking off over the mountains!"

I asked Georgia to give me a description of the lights. "They are bluish-white, and blinking randomly, there is no pattern to the flashes. The lights are really bright, brighter than anything I've seen fly around here!" I asked her how big and how close it had come to them. "It was pretty big, about the size and shape of a horse pill [at arm's length]. I'm not very good at estimating distances at night but it seemed pretty close, maybe a mile or so away."

1:09 PM, ALAMOSA:

That same night, I received a call from my bass player, Lyman Bushkovski. He told me, "I thought maybe you'd like to know that six green camouflaged helicopters just landed at the Alamosa Airport." He described three of the craft as large and the other three as smaller two-man choppers. A call to the airport revealed that it was a shuttle flight, headed south into New Mexico. I never did figure out to which agency they belonged, nobody would claim them.

JANUARY 19, 10:15 AM, THE BACA:

Four witnesses saw four more helicopters flying north in the SLV executing some unusual maneuvers. The lead choppers, three Cobras, would dive to below one hundred feet and then climb to around one thousand feet, then dive again, roller-coasting up and down. The other scout chopper followed along behind.

I spent that afternoon making phone calls to every military branch and government agency that is known to fly around the valley. A call to Buckley AFB came up empty. I then left a message on the Colorado Air National Guard Hotline. A call detailing the morning's sightings was made to Fort Carson. No one could speak with me but they promised someone would call back.

Less than fifteen minutes later, Fort Carson Community Relations Officer Liz Kalish called. She seemed very accommodating and helpful. "Yes, those four you saw today were ours. I just talked with the flight commander but he denied his group made any unusual maneuvers while flying in the valley." She claimed that she had "no idea who else had been flying around the previous three days" and said that "if they came from another installation, we wouldn't necessarily know about it, we have our own fly zones."

I then called FEMA. I spoke with a man named Fletcher. "If it was a classified mission, I couldn't divulge anything

. . . but I have no knowledge of any activity, classified or otherwise, going on in your area.'' I proceeded to tell him about some of the activity that had been reported over the course of the last year. He seemed interested but didn't really comment about the sighting claims.

At the end of the conversation I made the light comment, "What am I telling you for? I'm just barking up the wrong tree."

"How do you know it's a tree?" he quipped.

The following morning, I received a call from Lieutenant Colonel Buck Buckingham. He claimed to have no knowledge of any nocturnal flights in the valley. He was very interested in the sighting reports and mentioned he had been reading my *Crestone Eagle* articles. He also said he would very much like to read my newsletter, the *Mysterious Valley Report*! He said, "If I was aware of classified flights in your area, I would tell you I knew about them."

JANUARY 23, 10 PM AND 10:15 PM, HIGHWAY 17:

While driving north on 17 near Mosca, I saw a rapidly sequencing series of strobe lights flashing around five to ten miles away, directly west. I slowed and watched the low-flying light show travel up the entire west side of the SLV and disappear near the town of Saguache. The five- or six-light strobe had a duration of less than a second. It would repeat the series every two seconds with machine-gun-like precision. It appeared to be under a thousand feet above the valley floor and traveling around 150 mph.

Fifteen minutes later, as I turned onto Road T, I saw that pesky orangish light hanging just over the mountains. About three to four times brighter than Mars, it disappeared north behind the mountains after I watched it for about four or five minutes. It wasn't a star or planet and it moved to the north.

THE CREEPS

On March 7, I received a call from Brian Norton. He had attended the UAD training seminar in November, and up until now, he had never investigated a UAD case. He told me of a report filed that morning by a rancher a mile south of Del Norte.

Bob Kernan had been driving past his pasture when he noticed his herd circling something on the ground. At the time, he thought this unusual but didn't check. Later, he noticed the herd had drifted away from the area and saw a calf laying on the ground. Thinking the animal was sick, he went out and made a grisly find.

Of the dozens of UAD cases I personally had investigated or researched, this is the one that physically gave me the creeps. When I arrived on site and viewed the unfortunate calf, the hair literally stood up on the back of my neck, and I got a severe case of goose bumps.

The month-old female was missing its spine from the hips to the skull, and the brain was gone. Also missing were the right front leg, all but two ribs, both eyes, plus a two-inch circle of hide around the upside socket, both ears, the intestines, reproductive track, lungs, and a small two-inch diameter coring out of the rectum. The heart and liver, scavenger favorites, were left intact. The spine appeared to have been savagely torn out.

The rancher's dogs had never barked, there was no blood, tracks, or signs of scavengers, and a strange cloying smell emanated from the body cavity. Kernan had put the calf in his garage on a piece of plastic and after five days there wasn't even a hint of decay. The closest description I can think of to describe the unusual odor would be "a sweet, pungent, earthy smell." Not everyone agreed. Visiting Colorado Springs investigator Ed Burke swore it smelled "just like a bathroom disinfectant."

Bob Kernan initially didn't want the animal death publicized. He told me, "I don't want to alarm people." This reaction made sense after seeing the carcass. Kernan was overwhelmed by the response to the death of his calf. "If I had it to do over again, I wouldn't even have called the sheriff." Because an official report was filed by Kernan, Sam Adams, of the SLV Publishing Company, caught wind of the case and called him. Kernan granted Adams an interview which resulted in a front-page article in the *South Fork Times*, March 16, 1995.

Another rancher, half a mile away, reported to the sheriff's office that he had watched a strange beam of light shining straight up in the air, just north of his ranch, at 3 A.M., around the night the calf was killed. A motorist driving on Highway 160, west of Del Norte, also reported a strange light coming out of the pasture, near where the calf was found.

Kernan also lost another calf during these two days. "It just plumb disappeared," he told me. "We never did find any trace of it."

The spring and early summer of 1995 was blissfully quiet. Ironically, this extended period of nonactivity seemed to prove that something weird is, and has been, going on. If these animal deaths and reports of unusual aerial craft were just mundane, misidentified phenomena, we should see a constant trickle of reports. Since reports of unusual activity and UADs ceased during the spring of 1995 (usually the time when cases are reported), I was convinced that a portion of our unexplained activity could not be attributed to simple misidentified phenomena, or mistaken impressions by honest observers.

By May, I was awaiting a suitable ending to this book. A collection of strung together UFO and UAD reports and my personal experiences were compelling but I needed a good exciting ending and felt the paranormal would provide.

EAST MEETS WEST

MAY 22, 1995, 6:30 PM, THE BACA:

While trying to track down Sherry Adamiak and Dr. Steven Greer, who were conducting a week-long advanced training seminar with a group of twelve CSETI trainees, I met Louis Jarvis. He had been in town for several months working with Hanne Strong to facilitate a second visit by the Tibetan Head of the Nyingmapa School, or ancient school of Tibetan Buddhism. The spiritual head of the "Red Hat, Red Cape" sect, Kusum Lingpa, had visited the previous month and had just left after his second visit where he had met with Hopi Fire Clan elder Martin Gashweseoma.

Gashweseoma had been the keeper of the Sacred Tablets until he was stripped by the Fire Clan for an attempted unauthorized speech at a press conference in 1990. He and Thomas Banyaka tried to warn the world about the impending strife they foresaw for the planet and gave a press conference in which he "brought the Sacred Tablets out." This did not sit well back home at the "rez." A political struggle ensued, with Gashweseoma stripped of his custody of the Sacred Tablets in early 1991.

Jarvis had driven down to Hotenkopi to pick up Martin and his interpreter, elder Emory Holmes, to bring them to the Baca for their historic meeting with the Tibetan Rimpoche. On the way down Jarvis experienced "a hailstorm that almost broke my windshield." The following day, while driving back from Denver with the Tibetans, another hailstorm almost broke the windshield of a second car.

Scholars have long known the cultural and spiritual parallels between the Tibetan, Navajo, and Hopi belief systems. Philip Snyder, Ph.D., executive director of the Center for Religion, Ethics, and Social Policy at Cornell University, wrote in his forward for Philip Gold's "bold exploration'' of the Tibetan and Navajo cultures, *Navajo and Tibetan Sacred Wisdom: The Circle of the Spirit:*

> This book reveals many correspondences at all levels between these two peoples, despite their complete isolation from one another. In their recent histories both have been shattered by imperialistic, dominating cultures—the Chinese colonization of Tibet since the 1950s, and, over the past 500 years, the Spanish and Anglo-American control over the Indian Southwest. Both peoples continue the struggle to retain their identities, their sacred cosmologies, in the face of secular forces that in obvious and subtle ways seek to dismantle their traditional lifeways. . . . For the Tibetans and the Navajos, sacred ways of knowing and living are not solely symbolic constructs existing within their heads, but are keys that connect them with the inside of the whole universe, *quite beyond the human realm alone.* [his emphasis]

Both the Hopis and Tibetans are very concerned about the planet. Gashweseoma feels he was given an important sign in December 1990. ''Purple flowers and a pear tree bloomed in the winter'' which was a sign to the elder that the ''final war fought with the gourd of ashes [H-bomb] had begun.''

Some Hopi and Navajo elders have interpreted recent world events as a signal that World War III has begun, and the end times are at hand. Bear Clan elder Thomas Banyaka had been instrumental in setting up the meeting with Lingpa but, because of a prior commitment with the Seneca Indians, was unable to attend the historic meeting at the Baca. Gashweseoma and a delegation of Hopi had recently met with the Dalai Lama concerning a ''ceremony to stop the earth from turning over.''

In their tradition, Palulukang is the water serpent, or leviathan, that encircles the earth and keeps the waters in check. The twin warrior grandchildren of Spider Woman keep the serpent in check and hold the earth in balance.

The elders feel we are at the end of an age because a breakdown of the sacred rituals is occurring, which will lead the warrior twins to abdicate their responsibilities. The balance is upset and the earth will turn over four times, utterly destroying everything.

Some Hopi elders predict that the United States will go to war abroad in the summer of 1996. Civil strife and the danger of enforced martial law is seen. Gashweseoma arrived in the Baca and showed Kusum Lingpa the Mayan-Toltec glyph showing "World War III and the new world order" that he had brought, and expressed the Hopi's concern over these impending events.

Gashweseoma had come to ask the Tibetans if they knew about the water serpent. He found that the Tibetans were also worried about serpents, the Nagas. In the Tibetan tradition, these energy forms cause earthquakes and upheaval and are the source of much immediate concern. After several deliberations, Kusum Lingpa offered to conduct the Hopi ritual himself.

Three days prior, on May 10, Gashweseoma and interpreter Holmes had accompanied Jarvis to the Blanca Massif to perform a smoke ceremony. Like the multitribal contingent in August 1991, they too had decided to drive up the zigzag radio tower road that climbs to Zapata Falls.

They performed the ceremony without incident and returned to the Baca. Later, Kusum Lingpa, in front of over fifty onlookers, conducted a Hopi ceremony to placate the Palulukang. At the "exact instant he finished chanting," bolts of horizontal lightning flashed overhead, rain fell, and spontaneous applause broke out among the onlookers. Gashweseoma solemnly agreed that these were auspicious signs.

The Hopi and the Tibetans are excited about the newly established relationship that has been forged between the two cultures. They spoke of building a joint retreat on the slopes of Blanca, for both parties to utilize.

Where else could these two diverse cultures first meet but in the mysterious San Luis Valley? I'm convinced that the Native American connection is a key element in understanding the significance of this remote valley. I had the feeling that some clue will present itself to help me better understand this connection between these original inhabitants and our unexplained activity.

INTO THE SUNSET

Brendan and I strolled into the blazing sunset, shoes in hands, across Medano Creek and into the forbidding Great Sand Dunes Wilderness. The unusually high spring runoff sent rare two-foot waves coursing down the sandy creek, challenging our footing as we struggled across. "Cut! Could you guys do that one more time?"

We had already done it three times. Varied Directions, a production company, had been hired by Turner Network Television (TNT) to produce a four-hour documentary. Entitled *UFO: The Quest*, the film would premiere in September 1996. I had been selected as a principal character.

TNT had sent a second crew, with a second director, to film the first crew filming us. For four days I was followed by an entourage of directors, producers, editors, audio technicians, camera people, and all those other names you usually see scroll by at the end of a show.

THE SKULL

JUNE 6, 1995, 1:30 PM, THE BACA CHALETS:

The phone rang. It was ex–air force member Tom Blunt, the Saguache County appraiser. It seems he had just returned from appraising a ranch and had been shown something very unusual. Dana Case (not her real name) claimed that she had found something unique the first week of February. Blunt was shown the object and agreed that it was highly unusual.

Dana had been enjoying the uncustomarily warm February day while riding her ATV along the fence line of her new ranch. She and her husband, Billy, a hard-working, salt-of-the-earth rancher couple had just closed on their spread and Dana was making the half hour trip around the perimeter of the ranch on an all-terrain vehicle. She was accompanied by the former caretaker, a teenager who had lived at the rundown ranch for several months.

Sixty yards from the highway, the young man noticed a glint of sunlight from the ground and stopped to investigate. He called for Dana to come see. She braked her ATV and turned back. He was grinning, holding a glittering object in his hand, the sunlight refracting beams of light around him.

Blunt told me, "Give her a call, and go out and see what she found. I won't tell you what it is. I want you to see it without any preconceptions, but I guarantee you won't be disappointed."

I called immediately. Dana invited me to come out to her ranch and have a look at the artifact. I honored Tom's request and didn't ask specifically what the object was. Isadora accompanied me.

We arrived at the ranch to a warm greeting and were seated in the kitchen. The house was decorated with hunting trophies, rifles, and other cowboy-style decor. It had the feel of a modern wild west. Dana returned from the back of the house carrying something wrapped in silk. She studied my face closely as she uncovered the artifact.

There in her hands was a most unusual glass skull! At first glance, it didn't look remotely human. The San Luis Valley Skull, as I've dubbed it, is six inches high and three and a half inches wide, and appears to have been created from a single piece of molten glass. It does not appear to be carved. Its unique form doesn't suggest a typical human skull, rather, it is highly stylized. Dana fondly describes it as looking like an "ant person" skull.

The three-pound skull is asymmetrical and was obviously not made to sit on a mantel, or an altar. This asymmetric nature could be significant and unique. Smooth, graceful lines flow effortlessly through the form, suggesting to one viewer a prenatal, feminine quality. One verified unique feature is the elongated jaw which twists down and to the left with what appears to be a tongue protruding from between the upper and lower teeth. The nose hole in the front actually extends over an inch into the interior of the skull, and it features an earring hole on the right side.

The skull was apparently on the surface of the ground, partially covered with blown sand, which filled the crevices. Undoubtedly, the San Luis Valley Skull is destined to generate controversy. However, regardless of its origin, there is no question that the find is an exceptional work of art.

Crystal skulls, traditionally, have been discovered only in the Yucatan region of Mexico and Central America, and if this skull is authentic, it could represent an archeologic find of historic significance. The SLV has always had its share of unexplained events but most have not left behind any trace of their fleeting presence.

I had brought a video camera with me and documented the find. The woman who found it is understandably hesitant to publicize it, and has asked that the exact location of their ranch and their identities remain confidential. They don't want people tramping around the pasture, scaring their animals.

"Some people are plumb scared of it when they first see it," the rancher told me. "A friend came to see it and now she won't step foot on our property." The skull grimaces— almost daring you to touch it, let alone attempt to explain its origin.

Other peripheral elements have come into play. The woman owner is convinced that the skull cannot leave the property unless she personally takes it. She and her family related some very interesting stories about how they claim they discovered this.

One of the first things they did was try to find someone who could appraise the artifact. Her son volunteered to take it to an art appraiser on the Front Range. The following day, the son was inadvertently hit on the right side of his head with a hammer, and her husband was hit in almost the exact spot by a truck boom. "They both have scars to prove it," she told me.

Her son added, "It damn near laid me out."

In another incident, a woman took the skull outside to look at it in the sunlight. As she approached her pickup, parked in the driveway, a spare tire in the back of the truck exploded. I went outside to see the Michelin tire. "It was a cool day, and there is just no way that tire should have blown like that," the rancher told me.

In another incident, Billy opened up the cabinet where the skull was kept and he smelled "a ladies' perfume that about knocked me over. It smelled just like a busted bottle of perfume. We couldn't locate the source of the smell and we've never smelled it since."

As I videotaped the artifact at the Cases, the camera I was using inexplicably stopped. I still don't know what was wrong with it.

Dana told me of a psychic reading she had received soon after its discovery. "I didn't tell him what I'd found, but he told me, 'It is very old. It's not man-made and not of this earth. You must be very careful with it. It can be very detrimental. . . . You must be balanced, or you will be hurt.' "

She asked the psychic if she should do anything in particular with it.

He told her, "You don't need to do anything. Someone you didn't contact about it" would appear and help do what needed to be done.

"That's you!" she said, pointing to me.

I assured her, "I'm no crystal skull expert," but I offered to help in any way I could. I suggested that we get several expert appraisals and see if it could be authenticated.

This was better than an Indiana Jones movie. I made a phone call to Timothy Green Beckley, who had put on April's Pikes Peak UFO and New Age conference. Coincidentally, Joanna Parks, the Texas-based keeper of "Max," the most famous crystal skull, had brought it out for a rare public viewing at the Colorado conference. Having just seen Max, I obtained her number from Beckley and called. Parks immediately told me to contact Nick Nocerino, considered by many to be the world's foremost crystal skull expert.

Nocerino, as I expected, was very intrigued by the find. He asked me several questions about it, including, "Does it have an earring hole?" Affirmative. My description evidently impressed him enough to offer to fly out to see it personally.

It took a couple of days for this latest mystery to sink in. My gut feeling was that the object was genuine but had been placed where it was found. But after running that whole scenario through my mind, I realized the implications of someone just leaving such a valuable thing on a fence line on the chance that it would be found by the new owners.

I was certain of one thing. Even if it was placed there by someone for the new owners to find (a fantastic, but real possibility), the object itself is worthy of scrutiny. If the San Luis Valley Skull was determined to be an ancient skull, the implications would be startling. What would it have represented to ancient man, who has visited here for almost eleven thousand years?

Dozens of crystal and glass skulls have been discovered in the Yucatan and several are quite famous. These skulls are thought to have been used as healing tools by Mayan and possibly Olmec and Toltec priests for ceremonial healing practices. Their true age is unknown and difficult to determine. Several may be well over a thousand years old.

One of the most famous of these crystal skulls is the Mitchel-Hedges Skull. This life-sized, incredibly beautiful artifact was unearthed in 1927 in Belize on an archaeology dig by F. A. Mitchel-Hedges, an English archaeologist looking for evidence of Atlantis, while excavating the Mayan ruin at Lubaantun. The Mitchel-Hedges skull is considered to be the most perfectly formed of all the twelve major crystal skulls.

Another famous skull is Joanna Parks's "Max," the life-sized crystal skull carved from a single piece of clear quartz said to be over ten thousand years old. Joanna Parks says she was given the skull by a Tibetan Rimpoche.

The British Museum Skull is a less perfect, possibly unfinished skull brought out of Mexico by a British soldier during the reign of Emperor Maximilian, shortly before the French occupation. The Mexican government has tried unsuccessfully to reacquire the skull which they consider to be Mixtec in origin.

The Aztec Skull which resides in Paris, France at the Musee de L'Homme, Pailais de Chaillot, is rather gruesome looking and probably represents Mictlantecutli, the Aztec god of death.

Crystal skulls were undoubtedly venerated in ancient Mexico. Small skulls of varying degrees of sophistication can be found in the Christy collection at the British Museum, the Metropolitan Museum of Art, the Douglas Collection and Blake Collections, and at the Trocadero Museum. Dozens of these skulls have been found, although most are crude looking and all obviously represent human skulls. The San Luis Valley Skull may be different.

Speculation concerning the actual origin and age of several of these crystal skulls centers around the lost civilization of Atlantis. Some think the Yucatan civilizations were not the actual artists who fashioned them. They may have inherited them from a much older civilization, possibly Atlantis. They point to the cruder, smaller skulls as being made by the later Yucatan peoples.

Edgar Cayce, America's Sleeping Prophet, stated in 1933, during reading number 440–5:

Initiates of Atlantis engineered and manipulated precious power crystals for the production of galvanic and spiritual energies. The crystals were so potent they were in large part responsible for the Atlanteans' advanced technology. Later, in Atlantis history when crystals were improperly used, they contributed to the final destruction of the island-empire. The crystals were housed in an oval temple, the roof of which was rolled back to admit light from the sun and stars which activated the "white fire-stones."

Other "channeled" information from additional sources mentions three crystal skulls—one red, one blue, and one clear—as being the main power source for the Atlantean civilization. A story circulated several years ago concerning a diver discovering an underwater room off Bimini that he alleged contained a crystal skull.

I wonder if the SLV skull is truly an important piece in this multifaceted puzzle or a hoax? Could it truly be a link from the past to the present? If the skull is authentic (ancient), could it represent a connection between the indigenous peoples and our present-day mysteries? Maybe only the Navajo's "Crystal Boy and Crystal Girl" know for certain.

Being a so-called expert in the field of the paranormal, as I sometimes find myself dubbed, does not mean that I know the answers. It is about informing and educating and being available to listen to and document the experiences of others. It is about becoming a clearing house for collecting these reports from a certain area, then comparing the data to other areas.

Questions still remain, in fact, more than before I began my investigation. In this book I have put forth my own questions in hopes that readers will seek the answers in their own lives.

As I look back on my past years of investigation, I see that this has not been merely a quest to explain unusual lights in the sky nor to explain the unusual deaths of hundreds of (mostly domesticated) animals. It has been a quest to learn more about humanity's perceptions, about the origins of human consciousness, about myself.

Is this glass skull, which plopped so timely into my script, a message or symbol from the unknown? Is it a device to aid in our evolution or a symbol of impending doom? Will we someday make contact as a species with visitors from faraway galaxies, who may be peaceful explorers or galactic conquerors? If, as some suspect, our government (or others) is involved, are we facing a confrontation over freedom as raised by many militia groups, whose concerns were revealed after the Oklahoma City bombing?

If these questions are ever to be answered, the stage on which many of the acts are likely be played out may well be this mysterious San Luis Valley. I, for one, am watching.

Bibliography/Suggested Reading

Adams, Thomas R.	Project Stigma Reports, Paris, TX, 1974–1978.
Adams, Thomas R.	*Crux*, 1974–1987, Paris, TX.
Adams, Thomas R.	*The Choppers and The Choppers*, Paris, TX, 1991.
Altshuler, Dr. John	"Tissue Changes in Unexplained Animal Mutilations," MUFON.
Bond, Janet	*Flying Saucer Review*, FSR Publishing, Kent, England, 1970.
Brandon, Jim	*Weird America*, Millenium Press, 1976.
Brandon, Jim	*The Rebirth of Pan*, Firebird Press, Dunlap, IL, 1983.
Bryant, Alice	*The Message of the Crystal Skull*, Llewwllyn, St. Paul, MN, 1989.
Dongo, Tom	*The Mysteries of Sedona*, Hummingbird Publishers, Sedona, AZ, 1988.
Dongo, Tom	*Unseen Beings, Unseen Worlds*, Hummingbird Publishers, Sedona, AZ, 1994.
Eker, Anne	"Shedding Some Coherent Light on Mutilations," UFOlogist, 1993.
Elliott, Mark	*The Bloodless Valley*, Gatesgarth Productions, Crestone, CO, 1988.
Fagan, Brian M.	*Journey From Eden*, Thames and Hudson, New York City, NY, 1990.
Fell, Barry	*America B. C.*, Wallaby Books, New York City, NY, 1976.
Foor, Mel	*Kansas City Star*, November, Kansas City, MO, 1967.
Fort, Charles	*New Lands*, Ace Books, New York City, NY, 1923.
Fort, Charles	*Wild Talents*, Ace Books
Fort, Charles	*The Book of the Damned*

Foster, Dick — *Rocky Mountain News*, various articles, Denver, CO, 1993–1994.

Gaddis, Vincent — *Mysterious Fires and Lights*, Dell Books, New York City, NY, 1970.

Good, Timothy — *Alien Contact*, William Morrow, New York City, NY, 1993.

Green, John — *Sasquatch*, Hancock House, Seattle, WA, 1978.

Greer, Dr. Steven — "Foundations of Interplanetary Unity," position paper, 1993.

Greer, Dr. Steven — "CE-5: A Proposal for an Important New Research Catagory," 1993.

Harlan, Jack — *Post Marks, and Places*, Golden Bell Press, Denver, CO, 1976.

Howe, Linda M. — *An Alien Harvest*, LMH Productions, Huntingdon Valley, PA, 1988.

Howe, Linda M. — *Glimpses of Other Realities*, LMH Productions, PA, 1994.

Howe, Linda M. — 1994 Animal Mutilation Research Grant, LMH Productions, PA, 1994.

Hynek, J. Allen — *The UFO Experience*, H. Regency Co., Chicago, IL, 1972.

Iler, David — "Up The Creek," *Crestone* article, Denver, CO, 1992.

Jung, Carl G. — *Flying Saucers*, Dell Books, New York City, NY, 1969.

Jung, Carl G. — *Man and His Symbols*, Dell Books, New York City, NY, 1968.

Kagan, Daniel — *Mute Evidence*, Bantam Books, New York City, NY, 1983.

Keel, John — *Operation Trojan Horse*, Putnam, New York City, NY, 1970.

Keel, John — *Why UFOs?* Manor Books, New York City, NY, 1970.

Le Pour Trench, B. — *The Sky People*, Neville Spearman, London, England, 1960.

Levesque, Tal — "The Call of the Four Corners," *Atzlan Journal*, June 1978.

Lewis, Berle — Interview with author, February 1993.

Lewis, Nellie	Interviews with East Texas State University, 1967.
Lorenzen, C. E.	*The Appaloosa*, Fate Llewellyn Pub., MN, 1967.
Lorenzen, C. E.	*Flying Saucer Occupants*, Signet, New York City, NY, 1967.
Lorenzen, C. E. & L.	*Encounters with Flying Saucer Occupants*, Berkely, New York City, NY, 1976.
Olsen, Gail	*Rio Grande Sun* articles, Sante Fe, NM, April, 1984.
O'Sullivan, J. J.	*Deep Underground Construction*, The Rand Project, 1959.
Perkins, David	*Altered Steaks*, Am Here Books, Santa Barbara, CA, 1979.
Perkins, David	*Boulder Monthly*, Fall 1979.
Perkins, David	*Spirit Magazine*, Fall/Winter 1994, Spring/Summer 1995.
Porter III, Miles	*Valley Courier* Alamosa, CO, articles from 1975–1978.
Randles, Jenny	*UFO Reality*, Robert Hale Publishing, London, England, 1983.
Simmons, Virginia	*The San Luis Valley*, Pruett Publishing, Boulder, CO, 1979.
Sitchin, Zecharia	*The Twelfth Planet*, Avon Books, New York City, NY, 1976.
Steiger, Brad	*The Rainbow Conspiracy*, Windsor, New York City, NY, 1994.
Strieber, Whitley	*Communion*, William Morrow, New York City, NY, 1987.
Sugrue, Thomas	*There Is a River*, Holt, Rinehart, Winston, New York City, NY, 1942.
Talbot, Michael	*The Holographic Universe*, HarperCollins, New York City, NY, 1991.
Temple, Robert	*The Sirius Mystery*, Destiny Books, Rochester, NY, 1976.
U.S. Dept. of Transportation	FAA Report on Mystery Helicopters, 1993.
Valarian, Val	*The Leading Edge*, various articles 1990–1995, LERG, Yelm, WA.

Vallee, Dr. Jacques   *The Invisible College*, E. P. Dutton, New York City, NY, 1975.

Vallee, Dr. Jacques   *Messengers of Deception*, Bantam Books, New York City, NY, 1979.

Vallee, Dr. Jacques   *Dimensions*, Ballantine Books, New York City, NY, 1988.

Vallee, Dr. Jacques   *Confrontations*, Ballantine Books, New York City, NY, 1990.

Vallee, Dr. Jacques   *Revelations*, Ballantine Books, New York City, NY, 1990.

Vallee, Dr. Jacques   *Forbidden Science*, Ballantine Books, New York City, NY, 1991.

Watkins, Leslie   *Alternative 3*, Sphere Books, London, England, 1978.

Wood, Ryan   Agenda, "NORAD Incident," Ryyan Wood, San Francisco, CA, 1994.